Praise for the novels of

ELIZABETH PALMER

FLOWERING JUDAS
"*Flowering Judas* is a brilliantly written satire
laughing at contemporary adult fairy tales…
Elizabeth Palmer scores big time with this comical novel
of mis-manners among the English elite."
—*The Midwest Book Review*

OLD MONEY
"A triumph of understated comedy,
an interesting examination of the fall-out of
incomplete relationships, and ultimately an enjoyable
vicarious slice of the lives of the rich and famous."
—*San Antonio Express-News*

PLUCKING THE APPLE
"With an impeccable blend of empathy and mocking wit,
Palmer delivers a novel of high-society slapstick
that is nearly impossible to put down….
A savvy and highly literate romp."
—*Publishers Weekly*

SCARLET ANGEL
"In the deliciously deadpan, confidential tone
of an avid gossip, Palmer gives us a world in which
the evil are very, very bad, and the good are often betrayed
by their own timidity."
—*Kirkus Reviews*

ELIZABETH PALMER

Flowering Judas

MIRA®

ISBN 1-55166-593-X

FLOWERING JUDAS

Copyright © 1996 by Elizabeth Palmer.

First published by St. Martin's Press Incorporated.

All rights reserved. Except for use in any review, the reproduction or
utilization of this work in whole or in part in any form by any electronic,
mechanical or other means, now known or hereafter invented, including
xerography, photocopying and recording, or in any information storage or
retrieval system, is forbidden without the written permission of the publisher,
MIRA Books, 225 Duncan Mill Road, Don Mills, Ontario, Canada M3B 3K9.

All characters in this book have no existence outside the imagination of the
author and have no relation whatsoever to anyone bearing the same name
or names. They are not even distantly inspired by any individual known or
unknown to the author, and all incidents are pure invention.

MIRA and the Star Colophon are trademarks used under license and registered
in Australia, New Zealand, Philippines, United States Patent and Trademark
Office and in other countries.

Visit us at www.mirabooks.com

Printed in U.S.A.

For David

1

By most people's standards, Charmian Sinclair led an unconventional life. It was one that was concealed not only from her immediate family but also from others who shared it on an intimate basis, or who thought they did. Charmian believed in variety, and that to experience as much as one could in every conceivable way was the sole point of earthly existence. It was with this aim in mind that she had a series of London lovers, one for every day of the week except Friday when she went off to the country to spend the weekend with Giles Hayward.

Giles, who loathed big cities and especially capitals, lived in Sussex where he eked out a small living running his own organic garden centre and arboretum, and landscaping gardens. Theirs was a bittersweet relationship, for both, in their heart of hearts, realized it to be doomed: Giles because he knew he ultimately wanted a wife and children to share his cottage, and probably a dog as well, and this would involve a degree of rural commitment foreign to Charmian's nature; and Charmian because she liked her life as it was and was aware that with the arrangement as it stood she got as much of the country as she wanted. Any more would have been surplus to requirements. Yet the country was Giles's life, and their weekend arrangement, she recognized, could not go on forever. All the same, without being in love with Giles, she probably loved him more than she knew and because he was her only unmarried lover felt in an odd way proprietorial where he was concerned. Eventually, said Charmian to herself, I will lose Giles, but whoever takes him had better be good because if she isn't good enough I won't let him go. Separately, then, they both took the decision to enjoy one another for as long as possible, and never speculated about their joint future. This tacit acknowledgement of evanescence clouded their relationship and at the same time gave it a poignant intensity which enhanced it, and Giles knew that, whoever else he might meet, he would never quite forget the lift of his heart as Charmian stepped lightly off the train and into his arms on a Friday evening.

The other lovers were different. Charmian saw each of them on a different day of the week. Always the same day, though, otherwise confusion might have set in. So Monday was Dominic Goddard night, Tuesday was Gervase Hanson night and so on. They were all hand-picked for similar qualities, namely a talent to amuse and good looks, and all four were high-flyers, though in different professions. Charmian liked the aura of power, finding it exciting. Like a fire in a winter landscape, success drew others to it, bestowing its glamorous burnish on those privileged enough to be able to draw near. And because they were all happily married (or so they said) the other lovers evinced little curiosity as to how she conducted her life when she was not with them. That suited Charmian down to the ground. So there were dinners and lunches and opera and ballet and, since all the lovers came from different disciplines, it proved possible to compartmentalize her life successfully without embarrassing anybody in the process. Discretion was all and, because everybody knew the rules, so far it had worked.

It was the second week of June and, in his garden, Giles was tending his herbaceous border, watched and occasionally unhelpfully helped by Charmian. Charmian's knowledge of horticulture was greater than it had been before she met Giles but not much. Observing her pulling up a camellia, apparently believing it to be a weed, Giles silently took it from her and heeled it back in. Unabashed, his lover smiled up at him.

'I'll never be a gardener,' said Charmian.

'No, you never will,' said Giles, kissing her on the lips. 'Why don't you leave my herbaceous borders alone and go and cut some roses for the house instead?'

Obediently she went.

For the first time ever Giles had invited a neighbour to supper while she was staying there. Whether Giles himself recognized the fact or not (and he probably did not) Charmian intuited that this heralded a change in their relationship, possibly a profound one. She found the secateurs. The day was close and dull. It was very hot, with distant thunder circling around. The massed clouds were aubergine and there was a sluggishness in the air of the sort which is only ended by a violent electrical storm. I'd better be quick, thought Charmian, before the heavens open.

The loaded atmosphere had brought out the fragrance of the flowers. Standing among the roses, a basket on one arm, Charmian experienced a sudden feeling of peace, stability even. She cut a few of the long-stemmed variety for the one vase Giles possessed and a cluster of floribundas for the table. Some drops of rain fell, heavy and straight like stones, causing the baked earth to release its own heady smell.

With a theatrical explosion of thunder the storm broke.

There was no question of getting to the house in time and Charmian did not even consider it. Instead she let one hand fall so that the basket dangled, pushed back her long, dark hair and turned her face up to the heavy blows of the rain. Its warm assault drenched her and at the same time filled her with elation.

When Giles found her she was still there, standing stock still, face uplifted, eyes closed. She looked ecstatic. Her thin cotton dress clung to her slim body and her bare feet were spattered with wet earth. Like an Indian bride she was surrounded by heaps of rose petals which had been plucked and scattered by the sheer force of the deluge. It was an image which was to remain with him until the day he died. Without a word, he unzipped the wet dress and peeled it off her, kissing her as he did so. They made love lying on the soaked aromatic earth among the drifts of rose petals.

'Oh, this is what life in the country should be about,'

murmured Charmian, enjoying herself and him, 'not weeding at all.'

Laughing and, at the same time, deeply pessimistic, he pressed her to him. 'Promise me you'll never leave me, Charmian! Please promise!'

'I'll never leave you. It is you who will leave me.'

Silencing his protest with a finger to his lips, she rose to her feet.

'You look like a bacchant,' teased Charmian.

'And you look like a nymph. The goddess of the garden!'

She slanted a smile at him. 'Would it were so!'

Separately thoughtful, they went together into the house.

Sitting opposite Karen Wyndham that evening, observing her by the light of two candles which Giles, still a student at heart and without a candlestick to his name, had pushed into the necks of a couple of defunct red wine bottles, Charmian knew without any shadow of a doubt that she was the one. Giles, of course, did not know it, and neither did Karen herself as yet, but nevertheless, there it was. Sooner than Charmian might have hoped.

Karen was not as slim as Charmian. Rather there was an elasticity about her figure and a mobility about her face which together suggested pliability without weakness. Karen would bend but she probably would not break, decided Charmian. So quite tough, in the best kind of way.

'Have you always lived in the country?' asked Charmian, refilling Karen's glass and then Giles's and lastly her own.

'Always! I wouldn't want to live anywhere else. What about you?'

Charmian imagined an AGA-ed Karen baking her own bread, wearing a long, very white apron. It was a wholesome picture.

'I'm a city girl, born and bred.' She did not elaborate, but noticed the other woman shoot a speculative glance at the back of Giles who was currently standing by the oven carving a roast chicken which was the only thing he knew how to cook. She can't work us out, thought Charmian. She feels we don't quite add up as a couple and, of course, she's right.

Into the lull which ensued, Karen said, 'We used to farm…'

'We?' queried Giles unexpectedly, who had appeared not to be listening to them while he concentrated on dismembering the bird.

That question told Charmian as nothing else could that, still without knowing it, Giles was drawn to this woman.

'My husband and I.' There was a short silence while Karen took a sip of her wine. Putting the glass down, she followed it up with, 'Until he died, that was. I was widowed two years ago. The farm went bust at around the same time. I've always wanted children and regretted that we didn't have them before his death because now I have nothing that was ours.' Symbolically she spread her empty palms. Her speech was delivered with a philosophical resignation of spirit which was impressive.

Getting up to sort out the vegetables, Charmian thought: every so often Life gets it absolutely right. Karen's attractive, likes the country, liked being married and is a widow. So there's none of the baggage that disillusioned divorcees carry around. She wants children, Giles adores children. It's all in place for Giles. All he has to do is consciously notice her, really *see* her as opposed to just looking at her. *And I think he already has.*

And what will I do? Charmian asked herself, draining sprouts.

Quite apart from heartache, there would be empty weekends. The other lovers were all married and Charmian knew full well that the hallmark of mistresses of married men was that they were generally at a loose end at Christmas, Easter and weekends. Most of all at weekends. Hitherto this had not mattered, but now it would. Turning her attention to the potatoes, she caught herself thinking, I probably can't go on like this. Eventually my looks will start to go and before they do I should perhaps think of settling down. Otherwise I will end up alone. But who would want me, given my odd ideas on independence and the fact that I don't want children?

'Is there a gravy, Giles?' (Knowing that there was not.)

Sounding fugitive Giles said, 'Sort of.'

They both stared at the greasy mess in the bottom of the roasting tin. 'If you don't mind waiting, I'll make one,' offered Charmian. 'Why don't you go and sit down?'

Gratefully he did so. Karen, one elbow on the table, her chin resting on her hand was pensively staring into her wine glass. The quality of her silence was such that nobody felt awkward. As well as everything else, she appeared to possess the inestimable gift of repose. Her hair, piled on top of her head apart from several long stray curls which delicately framed her face, gave her a Hardy-esque look. Bathsheba Everdene rather than Tess, though. Not as vulnerable as Tess, decided Charmian, in spite of her bereavement.

Giles said, 'I feel I should apologize for my lack of tact just now, I'm sorry.'

'Nothing to apologize for.' The luminosity of her candlelit smile was unexpected. 'I'm almost over it now. Or rather, I've come to terms with the loss. I loved him and he's gone. That's it.'

Before he stood up to help Charmian, Giles's blond head inclined fractionally towards Karen's, in acknowledgement of what? Her gallantry perhaps. Or her beauty. For Charmian suddenly saw that Karen was beautiful.

At the end of the meal they sat outside. The air had warmed up again, although the closeness was not as oppressive as before. One of Giles's cats materialized from a flowerbed and, having afforded Charmian only the most minimal of greetings, jumped onto Karen's lap.

Now that *does* irritate me, thought Charmian, watching it. Even though I don't like them particularly and it probably senses it, after all the disgusting little bowls I've put down for that animal one would think it could at least afford me the time of day.

Giles went into the house to put a record on his ancient player. Moving like a somnambulist towards inner knowledge, he chose Mozart, and sitting in the wet, sweet-smelling garden the three of them listened to the Trio from *Così fan tutte,* whose haunting singing reverberated in the still summer night air long after the music had come to an end.

In the middle of the following week, Charmian got home late from an evening out with Nigel Guest. Of all her answer phone messages, and there were quite a few including two from current lovers, the one which caught Charmian's attention had been left by her half-sister, Alexandra Curtis.

She checked her watch.

It was getting on for midnight. All the same the un-characteristically expressionless voice of her sister had said, 'Ring *whatever* time you get back. I have to talk.' A call at that hour of the morning was not likely to be popular with Oliver, her brother-in-law, Charmian rec-ognized. On the other hand maybe Oliver was not there. Something was plainly wrong and maybe the something was that the Curtises had split up. She en-tertained this notion only briefly before dismissing it. Although like everybody the Curtises had their rows, on the whole their marriage looked durable. She rang the number.

'Alexandra, it's Charmian. Sorry to ring so late. I've only just got back. Is there a problem?'

'Yes, there is,' said Alexandra. 'On Friday Oliver was fired.'

There was a profound silence at the other end of the line. Charmian, who ran her own PR firm and therefore mixed in more various circles than most, had not actually had any dealings with Circumference but nevertheless knew of its Chief Executive, Reg Spivey, by reputation. Oliver had run one of the company's subsidiaries.

Eventually, 'Spivey's a ruthless power freak who's not as clever as he thinks he is,' pronounced the unbiased sister. 'Word has it that the City no longer rates him. Maybe that's why he got rid of Oliver. Too successful and too close for comfort.'

'I don't know.' The catch in Alexandra's voice was audible. 'But whatever the reason, it doesn't help us.' She sounded dazed.

Charmian said, 'How's Oliver holding up?'

'Well, so far, but he's going to be very busy for the next few days sorting out the chaos into which our financial affairs have been thrown. To be honest I don't think the shock has really hit him yet. The worst thing of all will be if he doesn't land another comparable job straight away. You can imagine the prospect of Oliver without enough to occupy him.'

Listening, it was clear to Charmian that after a reversal such as this it would probably take her brother-in-law at least a year to get himself back on his feet. In the case of Dominic Goddard, who had had a similar career accident and with whom she was having dinner next week, it had taken two years, and even then he had never re-established at quite the same level. It looked as though her much-loved sister might be in for a long haul. Charmian stared into the middle distance, conscious of a feeling of outrage and of a vengeful desire not just to help but to settle this particular score. Nothing to be done now, however.

In the end, she said, 'Alexandra, I'm going to have to go to bed, I've got a breakfast meeting tomorrow with an important client. Oliver will need you to himself for the next few days but when things begin to settle down let's meet. By the way, where *is* Oliver?'

'Gleneagles.'

'*Gleneagles?* I didn't know he played golf!'

'He doesn't. Look, I'll tell you all about it when I see you. Let's have a drink together, or come over here for supper if you like.'

'No. As things stand that would be an intrusion into private grief. Oh, and Alexandra...' Charmian paused.

'Yes?'

'You're the key to it. You have to hold up. If you don't, he won't.'

'I've worked that out. I'd have gone into the garden for a therapeutic scream but I dare not give way.'

'Poor you. I'll ring you tomorrow. And, remember it isn't the end of the world.'

Monday was Dominic Goddard night and since the only play he and Charmian wanted to see was fully booked, they settled for dinner together. There was a lull as they both scrutinized the menu. Trying to decide between steak tartare and duckling, Charmian said,

'Have you been following the Circumference up-heaval?'

'Vaguely,' replied Dominic. 'It had a depressingly familiar ring to me. Odd though, because word has it that Curtis was very effective.'

'I think I might have the foie gras to start with. Have you ever met him?'

Charmian did not disclose her own connection here.

'Yes, I did. Years ago at some function or other. I couldn't claim to know him. He has a stylish wife, I seem to remember. I can't decide between the foie gras and the asparagus.'

'Have the foie gras. It makes the wine easier.'

'Okay, maybe I will. I know the aggressor, Spivey, better than Curtis.'

Well, well. Here was an unexpected piece of good luck. Seek and ye shall find. Charmian did not immediately pick up on this nugget of information, but said instead, 'What about the second course? Steak tartare for me plus a green salad, I think.' She closed the menu.

'You look far too sylphlike to be such a carnivore,' said Dominic. 'Mine's the coq au vin.'

He seized the wine list.

'What were we talking about? Oh, yes, Circumference. It's years since I last met Spivey and he wasn't very nice then. I don't suppose he's improved with age.'

'What sort of a person is he?' Charmian was carefully casual.

Dominic thought for a minute. 'Intimidatingly large, corpulent with it, and very vain, by which I mean he dyes his hair *and* his eyebrows. I suppose I could sum him up by saying he's an unpleasant bully with a predictable penchant for vast camel hair coats to match his vast bulk. You couldn't miss him in a crowd. Must be close to retirement, I should have thought. He's sixty if he's a day.'

'Is there a Mrs Spivey?'

Dominic cast his mind back. 'Yes. Or there used to be. Made no impact on me at all. Why are you so interested anyway?'

Ultra-casual by now, Charmian said, 'I'm not really. It just suddenly occurred to me to wonder what makes that sort of person tick.'

'Oh, in his case that's easy. His parents came over here from Latvia during the war. Ergo I'm willing to bet he'd kill for some sort of quintessential English honour. Lord Spivey of Chipping Ongar or wherever his rose-covered country cottage is, that sort of thing, so that he can feel a social success by throwing his considerable weight about in his local club. And if that ass Hugo Rattray-Smythe has anything to do with it, Spivey'll probably get it too. Reward for services rendered before Reg retires. Can we stop talking about him. It's spoiling my foie gras. Let's talk about us instead.'

Later, as they left the restaurant, Charmian said, 'Your place or mine?'

'Has to be yours tonight; Laura's in town.' Laura was Dominic's wife.

Charmian raised her eyebrows. *'Laura's in town?* Out of interest, where does she think *you* are?'

'At a meeting.' Dominic was sheepish. 'Well, I am, in a manner of speaking.'

'Yes, in a manner of speaking I suppose you are! You should be careful. One day your sins will find you out.'

'Not until I've made love to you, I hope!'

Later that night, when Dominic had finally gone, Charmian lay in bed considering what he had told her. I shall have to infiltrate the upper echelons of Circumference, she decided. In order to prevent the thoroughly undeserved elevation of Spivey, I shall have to ensnare Hugo Rattray-Smythe. Assuming Dominic is right, and I'll bet he is, it would be an artistic revenge and very telling. There must be someone among all the contacts I have who can get me an introduction. She briefly entertained the idea of quizzing the gossip columnist Julian Cazalet, who, although not a lover (too indiscreet, which was, after all, the name of his particular game) was close enough for Charmian to ask the occasional favour, but rejected this on the same grounds. Maybe Nigel Guest, advertising, Wednesdays, was the answer. Circumference must have an agency and although she recognized that it would be too much to hope that Nigel's own would be the one, he knew everybody who was anybody in that particular neck of the woods. He could make a connection for her, if he felt like it—and by the time I've finished with him on Wednesday night he will feel like it, predicted Charmian.

2

As was his habit, Toby Gill, Chairman and Chief Executive of the conglomerate Stellar, arrived at his office at 7 a.m. and prepared to spend the first two hours of his working day carefully reading the quality daily newspapers, beginning with the business pages. It was in this fashion that he learnt of the sudden dismissal of Oliver Curtis.

'Good God!' ejaculated Gill aloud.

'Curtis leaves Circumference,' announced one headline, continuing, 'The unexpected resignation of Oliver Curtis has taken the City by surprise.'

'Well, well!' said Gill, preparing to read on and wondering what on earth Reg Spivey had thought he was up to. Or maybe Hugo Rattray-Smythe had done the deed, as in the case of his own firing from the same company years ago. After his premature departure from the position of Chief Executive which had taken place at the beginning of Hugo's tenure as Chairman, there had been an attempt by Hugo to suggest that he should take over the Chief Executive's role as well. This had been firmly squashed by a combination of the non-execs and the shareholders. Following this setback, Hugo's brief flare of ambition guttered and died, extinguished as much as anything else by his own natural laziness.

Which was why Spivey was where he was, and very powerful as a result.

I'll bet Spivey has done to Curtis exactly what Rattray-Smythe did to me albeit for different reasons, thought Gill. He swung his chair round and stared across the park. At that early hour the pale sky was opalescent and the sun had a milky quality which would only last until another brash blue day asserted itself. This was Gill's favourite time, a breathing space which allowed him to read the papers and clear the desk before his hectic schedule commenced.

He walked to the window, a tall spare figure with a rosebud in his buttonhole in memory of Clare who had cut him one every morning when the garden roses were in bloom. On the grass of St James's empty deck chairs clustered forlornly in striped twos and threes, still damp with the dew of the night before.

As if it had happened yesterday, Gill remembered his own dismissal.

Surprise had been the predominant reaction, followed by disbelief. Later had come depression and finally fury. Even after all these years he was still angry. In his mind's eye he saw himself sitting in the anteroom of Rattray-Smythe's office, glancing through the papers he had brought with him for the scheduled meeting. Outside the early evening glittered amethyst. The lights of the city, pinpoints from this height, traced the winding course of the river, defining the outline of bridges and delineating tall office blocks, bestowing on these an ethereal cubic beauty not evident during the day. Funny, thought Gill, how that sort of irrelevant detail sticks in one's mind.

He had had no idea what was coming.

Finally, having taken a message over the intercom, the secretary said, 'Mr Rattray-Smythe will see you now, Mr Gill.'

He had entered to find Rattray-Smythe writing. The Chairman continued doing this and did not look up, a familiar ritual display of bad manners. Gill recalled the minutes ticking by, no sound except the unnerving scratching of the fountain pen. Even the roar of a capital city was inaudible up there. It was like sitting in a hermetically sealed cell, and very claustrophobic.

At last and still in silence, Rattray-Smythe stood up and walked to the window where, a pigeon-chested, faintly Napoleonic figure with one hand slotted inside the buttoned up jacket of his suit, he stood for a few seconds looking out before finally turning around. And that was it. The beginning of the end. And, ironically in Gill's case, in his end had been his real business beginning because his dismissal had pushed him into forming his own company and had therefore precipitated the great business success which was Stellar. At the time however he had had no inkling of any of this and had found himself outside on the pavement at the end of a fraught hour with no job, no car and no prospects. It had been the beginning of a very rough year, during which the first symptoms of the illness that had finally engulfed Clare had presented themselves. Illumination had set in, too, since certain people who had professed themselves friends during the high-profile days had melted away. Toby Gill, not a man to forgive or forget, had kept a list.

The phone rang. This was how his day would now continue. Call after call, meeting after meeting, decision after decision, a merciful blotting out of the emptiness of his personal life.

Gill flicked a switch.

Mildred, his secretary, said, 'Hambros on the telephone, Mr Gill. Shall I put the call through?'

'Yes,' replied Gill, 'and Mildred...'

'Yes?'

'Could you possibly find out Oliver Curtis's home number? It won't be as easy as you think because as of Friday he's no longer at Circumference.'

'I expect I'll succeed,' said Mildred, who had not been a career secretary for the last twenty years, ten of which had been spent working for the exacting Toby Gill, for nothing.

'I expect you will too,' observed Gill, 'and when you do, find a slot in the diary which suits both him and me and book an hour's meeting, would you?'

In the wake of his dismissal, and before travelling to Scotland, Oliver Curtis went to see his old friend Marcus Marchant, who was a barrister.

Scrutinizing Oliver narrowly, Marcus handed him a drink.

'What happened?'

'It was an ambush. We were scheduled to have a meeting much like any other. I had a list of things I wanted to go through with him, but never got as far as that. Spivey's opening gambit was, ''I've decided to dismiss you,'' after which he handed me a letter and said, ''Read that and when you've read it, sign it. It's a letter of resignation.'' I said, ''I've no intention of signing anything until I've consulted my lawyer,'' at which point he began to bluster and finally, stabbing the air with one finger, shouted, ''If you don't sign it *now* the offer's off the table!'''

Suddenly very attentive, Marcus leant forward. 'So what did you do?'

'Stood my ground and refused, of course. I'm not about to be browbeaten by a brute like that. On the other hand that's probably been part of the trouble all along.'

'Good man!' Marcus was visibly relieved, although Oliver had always had a cool head in a crisis. 'What is the reason being advanced for their action?' Marcus, who owned a substantial number of Circumference shares and who therefore followed the company's financial fortunes fairly closely, was intrigued to hear what the answer might be, knowing as he did that, after managing through recession, the profits of that side of the conglomerate run by Oliver were up.

'A clash of management styles.'

Marcus was unsurprised and cynical. 'That means they have no real reason to give.'

'Ironic, isn't it, when you consider what a thug Spivey is in his dealings with other people.'

Oliver put his head in his hands.

'Are you prepared to litigate?'

'Probably not, on balance,' said Oliver, 'because a mudslinging, acrimonious court case, even if I won it, would ensure that I never worked again. Besides which

I couldn't afford to take on Circumference in the courts. You know that as well as I do.'

'Are they offering a generous settlement?'

'Fairly. I may be able to bump it up. It all depends what happens in Scotland.'

'Scotland?' Marcus was startled.

'Yes, I'm flying there tonight first class courtesy of Circumference and staying in the Royal George Hotel at Perth. Hugo Rattray-Smythe is playing golf at Gleneagles and I'm going to try to persuade him to change his mind.'

Struck by such bravery in the face of disaster, Marcus stared at his friend with undisguised admiration, though unfortunately such a dramatic appeal was likely to fall on deaf ears in his opinion. It was Marcus's view that Rattray-Smythe was a virtually unemployable apparently upper-crust individual whose removal the shareholders had spasmodically attempted to effect for years without success, largely because he owned three per cent of the company. Still, nothing ventured, nothing gained. Maybe Oliver would be able to shame a famously thrifty company, one of whose founders had been a particularly careful Scot, into paying him off rather more generously than they were at present prepared to do at the end of a long and, for them anyway, profitable career there.

Deciding to keep his own counsel, Marcus observed aloud, 'For them to have done this after all the years and loyalty you've given the company, there must have been a lot of treachery. You'll find you've been comprehensively undermined.'

Oliver smiled bleakly. 'Well, it has to be said that

managing successfully through recession with all the cost-cutting that entails is not the road to popularity. On the other hand I thought forward momentum would protect my back.'

'Who gets your job?'

'No idea. But, whoever it is, he'll do all right. It looks as though we're about to move from recession to growth and it's all in place for him, courtesy of me. He'd have to be a complete moron to get it wrong and assuming he's a better diplomat than I am the air will resound with cries of, "You're right, Reg! Good idea, Reg!", which will be music to Spivey's megalomania.'

Marcus was silent and then, glancing at his watch said, 'What time is your flight?'

'I'm booked on the ten o'clock and hope to see Rattray-Smythe tomorrow morning.'

'Who's your financial adviser?'

'Amanda Jennings.'

'She's brilliant!'

'Yes, she is. I'm seeing her tomorrow afternoon.'

Marcus scribbled a name on a piece of paper. 'Here's the name of a shit-hot solicitor who knows how to play corporate hard ball. The family variety will be of no use to you with the problems you're facing. I'll ring him first thing and alert him.'

They both stood up.

'Let's have lunch and a council of war in a few days' time when you're less embattled. And, meanwhile, write out a list of anyone who could be of help. Call in all favours. You're going to need the support of your friends and you shouldn't be too proud to ask for it, although in actual fact you probably won't have to.'

After a sleepless night Oliver Curtis was sitting opposite Hugo Rattray-Smythe, who was having a mid-morning cup of coffee in the clubhouse. Rattray-Smythe was a passably good-looking man in his forties with sandy hair, sandy sideburns and a florid complexion which might possibly have been the hectic result of too much whisky. He projected a bluff air of Woosterish conviviality belied by round, pale eyes which would not have looked out of place in the head of a cod. Despite his air of belonging to the squirearchy underlined by his upperclass accent, he was not to the manner born at all but a first generation product of the English public school system whose family actually came from Australia, a fact Hugo preferred to forget.

'Nothing I can do about it, old boy,' claimed Rattray-Smythe. 'Can't interfere. I employ Reg Spivey to run Circumference, and if he wants to get rid of you, regrettable though that may be, that's his decision.'

'Are you saying that you're not in charge, he is?' Oliver was incredulous, not so much by the fact, which he had always assumed anyway, but by the open admission.

For the first time Rattray-Smythe looked uncomfortable. He ran one finger round inside the collar of his Jermyn Street shirt as if it was suddenly too tight, and shot his cuffs. 'No. Yes. In a manner of speaking.' And then, in a burst of cornered desperation, 'It depends what you're talking about.'

Doesn't everything, thought Oliver wearily. This man's even more of an ass than I thought.

Leaning forward in his chair and speaking slowly as to a bear of small brain, Oliver said, 'Look, Hugo, I've worked for Circumference in various capacities and very successfully for twelve years. Circumference has just fired me—'

'Resignation, Oliver. We're calling it resignation.' Rattray-Smythe was sorrowful.

'Circumference has just *fired* me, Hugo. This means that it will be very difficult for me to get another job. As a result of what Spivey has done I may never work again. In the circumstances, the sum which you are offering is not enough. Although of course the alternative,' said Oliver, thinking as he uttered the words, oh, what the hell, 'is to rescind the decision and reinstate me.'

The fish eyes bulged with panic. Rattray-Smythe's brow was slimy with perspiration. Indecisive even when the way forward was obvious, he now found himself between two strong characters pulling him in opposite directions, one of whom was tormenting him in the flesh and the other by remote control. The spectre of Reg shouting, 'You shouldn't have done that, Hugo,' rose before his inner eye to be overtaken by a perverse desire to demonstrate that on paper, if not in fact, he, Hugo Rattray-Smythe, was in charge.

'Reinstatement's out of the question.'

'Why?'

Why? Rattray-Smythe blinked. Normally when people were sacked, they stayed sacked. Now here was

Oliver Curtis, admittedly always an independent spirit, refusing to conform.

'As far as I can see,' continued Oliver, 'I haven't done anything wrong. Unless you call managing towards profit through the worst recession we've had for decades wrong.'

Still groping for an answer to the exacting question, Why? Rattray-Smythe came up with, 'The board wouldn't wear it.'

'You mean Spivey wouldn't wear it! After all, we both know for all intents and purposes Spivey *is* the board.'

Stung by this into trying to retake the initiative and at the same time bring what had become a very uncomfortable meeting to an end, Rattray-Smythe decided a speech was called for. '*I'm* the Chairman of Circumference and while, as I've said, reinstatement is out of the question—I think we both know that, don't we, Oliver?—in the light of the years you've been with the company and your loyalty, you have my word that we'll improve the severance settlement.'

Thinking, pompous penny-pinching prat, and further reflecting, this must be the way he condescends to staff at the Rattray-Smythe house in Gloucestershire; next thing you know he'll be giving me a carriage clock for long service, Oliver decided to give up on it. He shook the proffered hand without warmth.

'Goodbye, Hugo.'

Turning on his heel, he walked off.

Oliver caught the next plane to London and went to see Amanda Jennings, his financial adviser.

'The key to it all is the pension,' said Amanda, a small, cerebral person whose expensive competence was legendary and who ran her office solely aided by one efficient cost-effective secretary. She thought as she spoke the words: Oliver Curtis looks as though the stuffing has been knocked out of him today. All confidence gone. And because of the scale of the damage it will take him longer than it otherwise might have done to re-establish. Aloud she continued, 'I suggest that you and I see Reg Spivey at Circumference together and hammer it out face-to-face. Who's advising you on the legal side?'

'A solicitor recommended by Marcus Marchant, called Gervase Hanson. I'm going on to a meeting with him when I've finished here with you.'

'Oh, I know him. He's just what you need. Look what I think should happen is that after you've seen Gervase, soonest possible, he and I should make contact and once we know what we want to get out of them, and what is and isn't possible, all three of us should see Spivey together.'

'Fine,' replied Oliver, whose mind suddenly seemed to be elsewhere. 'Do you realize, Amanda, that I was locked out of my own office after I was fired? They literally put me out onto the street! After twelve years.'

Although she did not show it, Amanda was appalled. Of course, the whole world knew Hugo Rattray-Smythe to be a dope, but the general perception was that he was a relatively civilized dope. Clearly under Spivey's stewardship the culture of Circumference had changed, and not for the better. He must have loathed Oliver Curtis, decided Amanda. In the event being very

professional she did not voice any of this but murmured instead, 'Sadly, I'm afraid that's the way of the
world these days.' She opened the file Oliver had given
her. 'Okay. Let's go through the figures. See what we
can salvage.'

When it finally did take place, the meeting was a
classic of its kind. There was a great deal of posturing
and strutting, no other word for it, plus a ritual verbal
castigation of his secretary for some small lapse or
other, which was conducted in front of the three of
them. Has to dominate, was Oliver's view, watching
this familiar scene. Being in charge isn't enough, he's
got to be *seen* to be in charge. And that's been one of
the troubles between him and me all along. I didn't
grovel.

He forced himself to concentrate on what they were
all saying. Gervase Hanson, who was willowy and dark
and very elegant, lolled in his chair, looking decep-
tively languid. Currently Amanda was talking, trying
to sort out the complexities of the pension. Unless invited to do so, Oliver did not contribute. Finally, she
turned to Hanson.

'There's no legal reason why Circumference can't
do that, is there?'

Underestimating Gervase, as he was quite possibly
meant to, Spivey butted in with his own dismissive
opinion of what their legal position was. The Hanson
correction was swift and deadly and consummately
cutting.

Amanda lowered her eyes.

Spivey turned brick-red.

In the wake of this effective and humiliating strike, matters moved much more swiftly, Spivey appearing to have lost stomach for the spoiling exercise on which he had been bent in the beginning. It was apparent to Oliver that they were going to get almost everything they wanted. Except his job back, of course. In the absence of any move to do so on Spivey's part, Gervase wound up the meeting with a summary and a suggestion that he and the Circumference lawyers should get together as soon as was mutually convenient. They all stood up to leave.

Oliver said to Hanson and Amanda, 'I'll meet you both outside.'

When they had gone, Spivey looked at his watch. 'What is it? I have another appointment.'

'I have a request to make.'

Toad-like behind his desk, Spivey stared suspiciously. 'A request? Oh, you mean you want a leaving party.'

Oliver stared at him in disbelief. 'A *party?* Of course I don't want a party! As far as I'm concerned this is a wake, not a wedding. No, I want to remove my own belongings from my office.'

Spivey did not miss a beat. Bile which had been seething beneath the surface after the contemptuous attitude of Hanson welled up and spilled over. 'No! Out of the question! No, no and no! Everything will be sent on. And don't raise the matter again.'

Outside, waiting for Oliver to re-emerge, Hanson, who came from the same sort of meritocratic background as did Spivey, but had acquired more polish along the way, said to Amanda, 'What an odious man!

Did you see the way he treated his secretary? Curtis is well shot of him in my view.'

'In that way, certainly,' replied Amanda, 'but re-establishing at that level isn't going to be easy.'

The sound of a raised voice on the other side of the door made them both sit up, though neither could hear what was actually being said. Seconds later the door opened.

'Let's get out of here,' said Oliver, grim-faced. 'I never want to set foot in this building again.'

3

The Sinclair family history was an odd one and probably explained the way both Charmian and Alexandra led their different lives. Austin Sinclair, father of both, had inherited a certain amount of money from his own father, though he would have said not enough, and had proceeded to spend it pursuing the time-honoured though unproductive profession of Man About Town. When his own cash ran out he married Alexandra's mother who, until she had the misfortune to meet him, still had some, though not for long. Alexandra had been born two years into the marriage, by which time her father was absent more than he was present. Money worries had begun to accumulate and what had been a reasonably romantic liaison in the first place, albeit with foundations built on one side's need for hard cash, became acrimonious. It was increasingly plain to Alexandra's mother that whereas she still loved her husband, he no longer cared for her at all and that his affection had dwindled at roughly the same rate as her capital. Finally their straitened circumstances had forced Austin Sinclair to take a job, the ultimate humiliation and one that the first Mrs Sinclair was made to feel was all her fault.

Even at the age of five, it had been apparent to Alexandra that Father did not live in the real world at all. In spite of a good education and a quick though not academic brain, he had had a blind spot where reality was concerned, which no doubt made him a very tricky marital partner. For his daughter, his unevenness was disconcerting too. One minute he was showing her off to the few friends they had left, hugging her and petting her and boasting about her achievements and the next he was gloomy and introspective and totally ignoring her, his dissatisfaction with his marital lot practically tangible.

Finally the whole thing had fallen apart.

Alexandra still recalled with a shudder being woken by the noise below and creeping out of bed onto the landing where she sat quiet at the top of the stairs listening to Father's inflexible voice saying that he was leaving because he wanted to marry somebody else and Mother's escalating anguish. Alexandra felt afraid and asked herself what would happen to her and her mother when he had gone, for even at that young age she had been able to work out that Father would not be able to support two families on the moderate salary that he currently earned. Crouched in the dark and shaking, she wondered *why* he wanted to remarry. He had, after all, had plenty to say on the shortcomings of marriage as an institution and yet here he was preparing to do it all over again. What she did not know, and was not to find out for another four years, was that his mistress had been pregnant and that she, Alexandra, had a half-sister.

That, however, was all in the future. The immediate upshot had been his departure and after it her mother had succumbed to a deep depression which had lasted for months. The child Alexandra had found this hard to understand. Her parents had not, latterly anyway, been happy together so why did her mother pine so much? Perhaps, perversely, there was something about neglect which bred dependence or maybe Mother was simply a born victim. Whatever it was, for Alexandra, carefree childhood ended and coping began. There were frequent occasions when Mother took to her bed saying she simply could not face another day. Then one day the miracle had happened. Mother arrived at the breakfast table one morning clear of brow, her old self in fact. The only explanation Alexandra had been able to come up with for this extraordinary transformation was that, as with widows and their weeds, Mother, after a ritual period of mourning, had felt herself able to cast aside grief and was ready to take on life again.

And did.

There was no looking back.

With commendable resource Mother, who had always been a capable seamstress, reinvented herself as a maker of theatre costumes so that the sparsely furnished flat in which they still lived was festooned with sequins and spangles and velvets and shimmering gaudy bolts of cloth which draped themselves over hitherto drab sofas and were eventually transformed into doublets and cloaks and gowns by Mrs Sinclair with the aid of an ancient Singer treadle sewing machine.

It was as though the past had not existed.

But of course the past did exist. It existed, Alexandra recognised, in every action one took in the present. Everything was rooted in it. So, seeking security in the wake of a turbulent and unsettled beginning and rating loyalty as one of the more important virtues, Alexandra married for love but also for safety. I do not ever want to be poor again, thought Alexandra at the time, and because of the history of precariousness and financial insecurity, the firing of her husband years later affected her more profoundly than it otherwise might have done and reawakened the childhood dread of what tomorrow might bring.

After he left them, they never heard from Father again. The contact completely ceased. Sometimes, thought Alexandra, it was hard to believe he had ever existed. It was as if she had come about by virgin birth. The news therefore that she had a half-sister whom she had never seen came as a shock.

'Can't we meet the other family? Now I've learnt I've got a sister I'd like to get to know her,' she suggested to Mother.

'No, we can't.' Mother was short. 'I only know the fact, nothing more. I have no idea where they live and I don't want to find out. As far as I'm concerned what's past is past.'

It seemed unwise to push it and Alexandra did not. All the same the knowledge that somewhere there was a sister whom she had never met caused a bereft, incomplete feeling which would not leave her.

The second Mrs Sinclair trod a path very much akin to that of the first Mrs Sinclair. There was an idyllic wedding followed by a falling off of her husband's attention while she was pregnant, which finally matured into rampant womanizing during the course of which her money, now their money, was spent at an alarming rate. Feebly the second Mrs Sinclair had remonstrated, irritating her husband and provoking the tetchy command, 'For God's sake stop bleating Violet!' Her father's chronic infidelity probably explained Charmian's lifestyle too, for the sexual freebooting had been on blatant display all through her childhood and later, and more tellingly, throughout her impressionable girlhood as well. In Charmian's eyes, as she witnessed the contrast between her mother's understandable but ultimately depressing aura of martyrdom and her father's selfishly destructive but cheerful hedonism, there was no doubt as to which presented a more attractive prospect.

At a very early age Charmian had decided that she would be beholden to no one. Because her father would not allow it, the two families, who were really one family, never met and it was not until he decamped for a second time that Charmian, who had never even seen a photograph of Alexandra, decided to make it her business to seek out her half-sister. By then she was a rebellious over-sophisticated fourteen-year-old going nowhere at the local comprehensive and loathing every minute of it, and Alexandra, aged nineteen, was at art school. The search through the jumble of papers and old diaries, which Father had left behind, for a clue as to where they might be living was tedious but ultimately rewarding. Posing as a friend, she rang the number, elicited the information from the first Mrs Sinclair, who had no idea who she really was, and went in search of her sister.

Alexandra saved me, recognized Charmian. From the day I played truant and went to the college she was attending in London, I never looked back.

'Alexandra Sinclair? She's over there,' said the hirsute leather-jacketed youth whom she finally accosted, pointing her sister out. Alexandra was tall, reminiscent of a Burne-Jones painting in ankle-length crimson crushed velvet with a bandana encircling her brow and holding back the fall of thick blonde hair. Had she been anywhere else other than part of a group of art students she would have looked striking but eccentric. Anticipating a possible cold shoulder, Charmian hesitated and was precipitated into moving forward as the fellow she had been talking to shouted, 'Alexandra! Someone here to see you.' In an aside he said, 'What's your name?'

'Charmian Sinclair,' replied Charmian faintly.

'Name of Charmian Sinclair.' Abruptly, Alexandra stopped talking and slowly turned.

Transfixed, she stared at Charmian and then as though in a trance moved toward her. Charmian stood stock still. Alexandra's first impression was of a slim girl in school uniform, whose dark hair was cut boyishly short and whose grey eyes were dilated with apprehension. Wonderingly she looked the other up and down and then put her hands on Charmian's shoulders, saying as she did so, 'You're the little sister!'

'Half-sister,' Charmian said, feeling as though she might be about to burst into tears.

'No halves. All the way. You're either my sister or you aren't.'

There was a tremor in her voice and it became apparent to Charmian that Alexandra, beautiful, popular Alexandra, was as moved as she was. They fell into one another's arms, spent the rest of the day together and then stayed up all night talking. She gave me back my sense of worth, thought Charmian. It was Alexandra who focused my mind on my education and persuaded me to go to university. Without her encouragement I would not be where I am today. At the end of the day I would do anything for her and that includes organizing Reg Spivey's comeuppance.

There was only one area on which they disagreed. Charmian, it transpired, was still in touch with their errant father.

'I never want to see him again *ever*,' said Alexandra, very steely. 'I mean that!'

After that they never talked about him, and it was only latterly, now that Father was on his physical and financial uppers, that Charmian had felt able to bring the subject up again—or rather had felt that she *had* to. For, apart from herself and meals on wheels, Father was alone. It could be argued that, at the end of a hard-hearted and manipulative journey through life, Father *deserved* to be alone. On the other hand thought Charmian, if we all got our just deserts, and that includes myself, the world would be a drab place all round. The other debatable point was whether Father noticed his own isolation since he appeared to live almost entirely in the past with a magnificent disregard for the unpalatable present. When Charmian visited him, which she did without fail once a week, he was invariably to be found with one of his large morocco-bound photograph albums on his lap.

Where were the days of wine and roses now?

Gone. Transfixed like butterflies in a lepidopterist's collection between the covers of the albums whose black pages he ceaselessly turned while she was with him, but, nevertheless, gone.

Look, Charmian, this is Cannes and this, this, Charmian, is Biarritz. Those were the days. We knew how to live then. Look at her. Isn't she beautiful? What an affair that was! Christ, I loved her!

Fascinated, Charmian stared at the mistress parade as he leafed through the book. Thin, predatory, lipsticked women, usually with more money than he had, pictured at the races, on yachts and in expensive restaurants. Most of them, in her view, were not particularly beautiful, but then fashion had changed. Conspicuous by their absence were the two he actually married. There was no sign of them. Charmian noticed but never commented on this. There was no point. It was the past now, only memories were left. He remembered it all as if it was yesterday. The dull, penurious present held no attraction. When not reminiscing he became discontented and fretful.

He had gained no self-knowledge at all with old age, Charmian recognized, but remained the prisoner of an exaggerated perception of his own importance in the scheme of things. He would never understand why Alexandra did not come to see him. Sitting opposite her father, it was indescribably painful for Charmian to witness the way in which the handsome sexual buccaneer of her childhood had diminished into a shrunken old man huddled in a shabby two-room rented flat, nourished only by the dreams of past glories. The last time she had gone to see him he had suddenly dropped off in the middle of a sentence, one finger resting on a photograph of one of his shallow society beauties. Taking the album from him and quietly closing it, Charmian was poignantly reminded of Browning's lines:

Dear dead women, with such hair, too—what's become of all the gold
Used to hang and brush their bosoms? I feel chilly and grown old.

And saddest of all:

What of soul was left, I wonder, when the kissing had to stop?

For the answer in her father's case was nothing. Nothing at all.

Existence in the wake of calamity was strangely detached, Alexandra discovered. She was aware of herself performing the usual mundane tasks but it was as though her mind and her body were not engaged and everything seemed to take twice as long as usual. As she had done every morning of her adult life after her shower and before she dressed, she prepared to apply her makeup carefully and would probably have done the same even in the event of nuclear explosion. For Alexandra a lowering of that sort of standard would have been unthinkable. Which was probably the reason why the disgusting state of her daughter's bedroom, for instance, upset her as much as it did. Staring at herself in the hand mirror she said aloud, 'Christ, look at me!' Then she commenced the tedious but, in her view, essential process of damage limitation.

When Alexandra had finished, she dressed, choosing to wear black jodhpurs with ankle boots, a man's shirt and a waistcoat. She finished off the whole ensemble with a gypsyish black and red paisley neckerchief and a very large citrine and silver ring which was known in the family as Mummy's knuckleduster. The roots of this sartorial style could probably have been traced back to the theatrical costumes' incarnation. Her thirteen-year-old daughter, Alice, had once ambiguously remarked, Mummy doesn't dress like other mothers do, a remark which could have been a compliment or its opposite. Probably wisely Alexandra had decided not to pursue the matter. Standing in front of the cheval glass, she brushed her dark blonde bob and then sprayed herself with scent. It's like putting on my armour, reflected Alexandra, surveying her own reflection. I now feel capable of facing anything. Which was just as well because that afternoon she was to drive to the country to tell the three Curtis children who were all at the same co-ed boarding school, and knew the fact but not the detail, exactly what had happened. First, however, lunch with her sister was on the agenda.

'What are you going to say to them?' Charmian wanted to know.

'What can I say? I'm going to treat them like adults and tell them it's just one of those things. That everybody gets fired sooner or later in these uncertain times, it appears we're no exception and that we'll just have to get on with it. It's serious but not insurmountable in other words. Luckily the school fees are largely accounted for so there's no question about taking them away.'

'I shouldn't expect any thanks on that front!'

Charmian knew that, courtesy of her chequered childhood, Alexandra had a very tough, inflexible streak. And a very unforgiving one as well. She would expect the kids to take their father's change of fortune in their stride, just as she herself was going to have to. A Roman mother, in other words. It was the reverse side of an otherwise golden coin. Once Alexandra made her mind up about something, as with the whole situation vis-à-vis Father, it was virtually impossible to budge her. Ironically it looked as though the less lovable side of her character might be about to stand her in good stead now. There would be no turning the other cheek. And Oliver's tough as well, thought Charmian, who had not always hit it off with her brother-in-law.

He may be down at the moment but he's certainly not out.

Aloud she observed, 'It's a good thing the children are away at school perhaps. It'll give you a chance to spend some time with Oliver while you both regroup,' thinking as she said it: and because Alexandra in this sort of situation has tunnel vision and her main priority will be Oliver, and the practical, I'll bring up the rear where the children are concerned by taking them out and so on. Supportive aunt will be my role. 'What's your plan of campaign, joint plan of campaign, I should say?'

'First, sell the London house and retreat to the place in the country until the way forward becomes plainer. At least then we'll have a regular income from the bank interest on the money from the sale. After that it's all in the lap of the gods. Oliver's currently compiling a CV and preparing to put himself about. Talking about imponderables and the lap of the gods in particular, I thought I'd go and see Mrs Hemingway. What do you think? I have moments when I feel as though nothing is going to happen to us ever again and I'd like some reassurance that that's not the case.'

Mrs Hemingway was a clairvoyant whom both Alexandra and Charmian had consulted from time to time.

'I think that's a brilliant idea. If there's reassurance going, she'll give it and if there isn't you'll know where you stand and can plan accordingly. I have to say I think she's amazing. Not always comfortable but definitely amazing. It's probably time I went to see her as well.'

'Oh, really?' Alexandra gave her sister a speculative look. 'Don't tell me it's all going wrong for you too?'

'No,' said Charmian, 'it isn't, so don't panic. My preoccupation is with time passing and nothing to show for it!'

Alexandra was surprised. 'Charmian, I wouldn't say that! You're running your own highly successful business and although you don't confide in me concerning your social life you're never in when I ring in the evenings so it must be a full one.'

'As of now, yes, but I'm not getting any younger.'

Ah! So that was it.

'Well, maybe while you've still got your looks you should decide what you want and go for it.'

'My problem,' said Charmian, confronting it properly for the first time, 'is that I have no idea what I *do* want. I just know that I can't go on like this for very much longer.'

'A tall dark handsome stranger is what you want. It's obvious.'

'So obvious that I've already got quite a few of those in tow. No, what I probably want is a change of lifestyle.'

Telling the children the whole story of the loss of their father's job was nothing like as traumatic as Alexandra had feared it might be. Confident offspring of an affluent, high-achieving marriage, they seemed to take it for granted that he would find himself another highly paid job and life would go on more or less as before. In one sense this (possibly) unrealistic view of events was a relief. It would help Oliver too to know his children saw him still as infallible, Alexandra reflected, with a surge of love for them all. And, after all, she thought, digesting their attitude along with her cream tea, what's the point in spreading alarm and despondency when there might be no need? So the prepared rallying speech was put away and in the process of doing this and filling them in on all the other family news, Alexandra missed the shadow her announcement cast over Dan, always more introspective and sensitive than Alice and his twin brother, Nick.

She finally arrived back at the London house at 9.30. Oliver was still out, which was disappointing for she was keen to share the children's calm reaction with him. Feeling suddenly exhausted, Alexandra decided to go straight to bed and, tired out mentally and physically, she slipped into a deep sleep during which she dreamt that she and her husband were flying, higher and higher towards a wonderful diffusion of golden light. So close were they to its source that both were gilded by it, when suddenly, Icarus-like, Oliver fell and she, Alexandra, resisting the magnetic pull of this strange sun, turned and swooped down after him so that, by now unable to arrest their descent, they plunged together in terrifying free fall towards... What? There was no answer to that, nor was there likely to be for at least another year.

4

As she had said she would, Alexandra rang Mareka Hemingway for an appointment and was lucky enough to inherit a cancellation the following week. Mrs Hemingway, whose bookings were organized by her talkative mother, was used a great deal by businessmen, the majority of whom kept this fact very quiet. Famously accurate, she was consequently much in demand and the wait for a sitting could be a long one.

Sitting on the tube as it racketed towards Hampstead, Alexandra tried to read her book and failed. The fact that a confrontation with the occult was in the immediate offing unsurprisingly prohibited concentration. Finally arriving at her destination, she went into a newsagent and bought a ninety-minute audio tape. Further along the street en route to Mrs Hemingway's flat there was a small Italian restaurant where she could have lunch afterwards.

As she rang the bell, Alexandra experienced the familiar frisson of anxiety, for who knew what the upshot of this visit would be? On the other hand worst of all would be nothing on the cards, indicating that a life of country seclusion and good works was to be her lot for the foreseeable. She entered just as the previous sitter was leaving. As they passed in the hall, they looked curiously at one another. Alexandra was shown to the usual chair. Mrs Hemingway, who was known to her regular clients by her Christian name and who was addicted to the weed, lit up.

'You don't mind, do you?' she asked Alexandra. 'There are those who do.'

Alexandra dared say there were but would not have cared to own up to being one of them.

As requested she took the tarot pack and shuffled it. Mareka slipped the cassette into the recorder. 'Cut with your left hand and choose one of the packs.'

There was a faint hiss as the tape began to unwind, prior to recording heaven knew what. With a flutter of the heart, Alexandra thought, we're off!

'It's not your birthday coming up, is it?'

'January.'

'And is there anybody else's birthday around that time too?'

'Yes, My husband's. December.'

'What about your wedding anniversary?'

'March.'

'For some reason the first things they have come up with are birthday or anniversary dates which must mean... Have matters around you been delayed a lot recently? Or just not happening in the way one *expected* them to happen?'

'Oh, that certainly!'

'So it's quite likely they are not meant to until the birthday periods start coming in. You're coming into a clearing up period. Going back to your last birthday, did you find that things were not happening in the way one expected then?'

Alexandra cast her mind back. It was true to say that there had come a point when Neville Cruickshank, the Finance Director of Circumference, formerly ingratiating, had verged on rudeness and, round about then, others had become offhand too. Alexandra had been at a loss to account for this change at the time. Because he was habitually unpleasant, it was harder to pin down any change in Spivey's demeanour. She hesitated.

Without waiting for her answer, Mareka scrutinized the cards.

'It's just that I'm trying to get some timing going, some sense of how long it's been happening in that *way*. But it doesn't matter that much. The important thing is what you're going *toward*. You'll see as we go further along, I hope, where the timing is coming from. When was the last break or ending around you?'

Caught by surprise by this, Alexandra felt all at once almost unendurably bereft and was later to hear herself sound it when she finally played back the tape. 'Of any sort, do you mean?'

Mareka nodded.

'Three weeks ago.'

'And was it quite sudden?'

'Yes, it was.'

'And the one before that?'

A pause. 'No. No, I can't think of anything.'

'That's good, because that means we are in the near past. Now that break, is it creating quite a lot of change around you? It's just that they're saying plans suddenly go *awry* and even if you tried to get the plans back on track, it couldn't happen. So what you're going to find is that new decisions will have to be made, new thoughts will have to be followed.'

They were circling it. Alexandra decided to go for broke.

'When you say back on track, Mareka, I don't know how illuminating you want me to be. Would it help you if I was specific?'

'It would, yes, and if it's not what I'm getting, I'll tell you no.'

'All right. What has happened is that three weeks ago my husband was fired. It was a total bolt from the blue.'

'Ah! And he's left now?'

'Yes.'

'Then that's why the cards tell me that the plans can't ever go back to where they were. So now he's got to look at new areas. Good. I don't mean it in an uncaring way but it's as though because of what he symbolized where he was, he couldn't have gone on there for very much longer. He'd reached that sort of ceiling where the move on is going to mean much more open space for him. Spirit are very funny! If you are meant to do something and you get to be too comfortable where you are, which stops you doing what you're meant to be doing, they actually do push things to take away the comfortable feel and get you back onto what is actually the right track, not the easy track.' (Well, thanks, Spirit! thought Alexandra.) 'And that's where he seems to be at the moment, getting on to where he's meant to be. Shuffle the pack and take one.'

The sitting ground on in a general way for a further fifteen minutes, when, having laid down a line of cards, Mareka abruptly stopped. Frowning she stared at them. The silence was electric. 'Now *this* is interesting!'

The edge to her voice indicated that something of import was coming. Agog, Alexandra leant forward.

'The company that your husband was involved with—and I don't know why this would be showing because he's left now—there's a lot of mess coming up around that company. A *lot* of mess and part of it is that somebody's doing certain things they shouldn't be doing. And the fact that your husband isn't there is giving free rein to certain situations.'

Startled, Alexandra stared at Mrs Hemingway. At last she said, 'I wonder if this would explain why they got rid of him!'

'Yes, it would make sense because it's as if somebody couldn't do something or put something into practice because of his presence. But my God, there's a mess coming up there!'

'And is it going to become public?'

'In quite a big way!'

'Do you think that's soon, Mareka?'

'Well, I think what's going to happen is that you'll hear rumbles of it, you know how rumour starts. That's how it begins. Very shortly. Weeks to months rather than months to years. *Strange!*'

Alexandra said, 'I think it's unnerving!'

'It is, isn't it? All I can say is that *before* it happens, your husband is offered a job with another company and this other company actually benefits from the upset. Where he's going, he'll find himself in a bit of an odd position having to look at some of the people that are around the old company and taking a decision about *them.*'

Here Mareka paused and, inscrutably sibylline, looked directly at her client.

Revenge. Well aware of how sweet that would be, Alexandra narrowed her eyes. It seemed too much to hope for.

'Really! That would be very ironic, wouldn't it?'

'*Wouldn't* it! But really your husband doesn't have to worry for very much longer. However good he thought things were before, he's now going into a very good situation. You'll be concerned for another few months, but that's it. Or your husband will be concerned therefore you will be concerned. But I'm not getting anything long term, no major worry.

'That's about all I can tell you at the moment.'

Mareka leant back in her chair and smiled at Alexandra. There was a soft knock at the door. Mother reminding her that time was up.

She clicked off the recording machine and handed back the tape. Slipping this into its case before stowing it safely in her shoulder bag, Alexandra said, 'Thank you. That was marvellous.'

In the Italian restaurant afterwards, £60 lighter, Alexandra ran her eyes over the notes she habitually took in case the tape should fail. It's too much to hope all this will come to pass, she reflected, reading them, even though Mareka can be, no, normally *is*, extraordinarily accurate.

All the same, in spite of her scepticism it was with a lighter heart that she travelled home.

The following week a hot yellow sun shone on Oliver out of a darkly blue sky as he made his way along the dusty London pavement towards the headquarters of Stellar and a meeting with Toby Gill. Gill, whom Oliver had met several times before, was cordial. He operated from a comfortable office not unlike that which had been Oliver's own in the days when he still had one. There were paintings and flowers and two secretaries discreetly going about their duties in a room off it. The sense of all he had lost, or rather all he had had taken away from him, was forcibly brought home. Gill regarded Oliver, whom he liked and respected, with sympathy across his antique rosewood desk.

Gill said, 'What happened? I was astonished when I heard about it.'

'So was I,' responded Oliver drily. He recounted the details.

'And I'll bet Spivey told you that you're a natural number two, not cut out for the top job.'

Oliver was astonished. 'Yes, he did. How did you know that?'

'It's one of the most insulting things one can say to a manager and therefore par for the course where jealousy and animosity are involved. I had it said to me in what I suspect were fairly similar circumstances as, no doubt, have many others in the City. Tell me,

what's the setup like at Circumference? At board level,
I mean.'

Fully aware that he was about to be debriefed Oliver
said, 'Well, as I'm sure you know, there were rumours
of takeover sometime ago which they managed to see
off. Just. Since then Reg Spivey has managed to garner
more and more power for himself to the point where,
to all intents and purposes, he runs the whole show
and there are very few checks and balances, if any. So
the board is either weak or lazy or both.'

Gill stared into the middle distance. His telephone
began to ring and was ignored.

'What about the non-execs?'

'They appear to go along with it. I mean I was fired
and nobody seems to have delved too deeply into the
actual facts.' Oliver sounded weary.

'What's the City's view of Spivey?'

'The City is ambivalent. Reason being, as I'm sure
I don't have to tell you, that this is a conglomerate
which should be doing a lot better than it is and, as
things stand, the share price simply moves with the
market. Ergo it's not a very creatively managed company. Plus, even then it's only where it is because they
bought a tranche of that company brilliantly managed
by Maitland which had a fabulous run of success, no
thanks to our friend Spivey, so they're riding on the
coattails of that.'

Gill turned his chair so that he was staring out of
the window. The sunlight, by now of the mellow, rich
late afternoon variety, struck through the half unfurled
Venetian blind laying broad, bright bands across the

desk. The only sound in the room was that of a bee dashing itself against the glass of the window, oblivious to the fact that a foot below the sash was open. When Gill spoke again it was to say, 'I'll be perfectly frank with you, Oliver. I wish I had something I could offer you but there's nothing coming up at Stellar at your level of seniority. It's all already in place. And there's no point in putting a four-cylinder man into a two-cylinder job.'

'No there isn't. I understand that.'

Oliver stood up. They shook hands.

'Good luck and keep in touch,' said Gill. 'We'll split a bottle of champagne when you re-establish. Which you will.'

When Oliver had gone, Gill pulled up the Venetian blind and stood uncharacteristically doing nothing for ten minutes, looking out over St James's Park. The account he had just listened to took him back once again to his own traumatic firing. I've never forgiven it, and nor will Oliver Curtis, I'm willing to bet, he thought. I wonder what his wife is like and whether she's up to what lies ahead. I hope so for his sake. Clare had been. It was odd, he reflected, that calamity followed by two lean years had put them in tune with one another in a way that the preceding fat years never had.

Clare.

'Christ, I miss her,' said Gill aloud. 'I'm the great business success story and I'm so fucking lonely!'

He turned away from the window and buzzed through to his secretary.

'Get me Robert Maitland on the telephone, would you please?'

Their London house having sold surprisingly quickly at a deliberately competitive price, Alexandra was sorting out the logistics of the impending move to the country with Mr Muldoon. Mr Muldoon, whose family firm was based in Peckham, had moved the Curtises once before and liked Mrs Curtis. Wearing a loudly checked suit, whose trousers were held up by braces covered in small red hearts, he looked as though he had just wandered off a race track. Alexandra would not have been surprised to see him break into tick tack. In the event, he quietly followed her from room to room taking notes as he went.

'This time, so great is my confidence in you, Mr Muldoon, I don't intend to pack anything up myself. I'm going to leave it all to you. Most precious to me are the stipple engravings, the paintings, of course, and the blown blue Victorian meat plates. And the mirrors. And the clocks. Mustn't forget the clocks! Actually, it's all precious.'

'Bubble wrap!' pronounced Mr Muldoon. 'That's the answer. I'll send someone round in advance. Two days it'll take us to move this little lot. We'll have to pack it up one day, store it in the van in the warehouse overnight and then drive down to the country the following morning.'

He made some more jottings in the tattered notebook.

'You giving up your London life altogether, are

you? Hubby got a new job, has he?' He looked at Mrs Curtis, shrewdly divining that beneath her polite and apparently cheerful façade, she was not altogether happy about what was going on.

'That sort of thing,' replied Alexandra vaguely, unwilling to get into it. 'Oh, and I must remember to book a skip.'

A new life. Get rid of the detritus of the old. Start again.

'I think that's about it, isn't it? Until the day, I mean. As soon as you let me have the estimate, I'll organize the deposit.'

'No sweat,' said Mr Muldoon, putting his pencil behind his ear. 'You leave it all to me.'

Nigel Guest, advertising, rang Charmian to confirm their Wednesday evening tryst and to enquire whether she was free the following weekend.

What? Charmian was amazed. 'No, I'm afraid I'm not. I'm never free at weekends. But then, nor are you usually.'

'I know,' replied Nigel, 'but my wife is going to visit an old school friend of hers. So I'm on my own.'

Well, too bad! decided Charmian. For all he knows I'm on my own every weekend.

'Oh, come on,' wheedled Nigel. 'I know a smashing little country hotel—well, several actually, but this particular one has a brilliant chef. You'd love it.'

'Yes, I daresay I would,' said Charmian, who could not in fact imagine the urban advertising man that was

Nigel in the country at all. 'But I can't. I've already got something else arranged.'

'Is it a house party? Perhaps you could wangle me an invitation too?'

'It isn't a house party. Back off, Nigel.' Picturing the impact of the London advertising world and Nigel's dazzling ties in particular, on Giles's rural idyll, Charmian laughed silently to herself. Instead of just one, there would be two of them tripping over rakes and pulling up camellias thinking they were buttercups. 'If you're so desperate why don't you go to the country with your wife? Or doesn't she want you there?'

'Oh well, if you must know I had an affair with the friend a couple of years ago,' said Nigel, without a trace of shame, 'which ended rather acrimoniously. When I met you, in fact.'

'And she's never told your wife.'

'No, as I've said, they're friends.'

Funny idea of friendship he had, reflected Charmian, digesting this information. Thank God I'm not married to Nigel.

'Don't you think perhaps you ought to be there, if only to head off any alarming disclosures the friend might feel tempted to make?'

'I don't think that would happen. The problem is she wants me back.' He sounded fugitive.

'Well, aren't you the lucky one!' Charmian was unsympathetic.

'All right, Charmian! That's enough of that.' Nigel sounded sulky and then, brilliant and fickle butterfly of the ephemeral world of advertising that he was, almost immediately cheered up. Getting off the unsatisfactory subject of his own philandering, he said, 'There's a private view of the Poussin exhibition on Wednesday evening. Because I'm a Friend of the Royal Academy I can go and take a guest. Would you like to come? We could have dinner afterwards.'

'I'd love to!'

'Great! Let's meet there. Seven o'clock suit you?'

5

The house move took place at speed and as is the case with all such pack-ups, however well organized, it was stressful. It was impossible to think of everything and when Alexandra came to vacuum the floor in order to leave the place at least superficially clean in the wake of Mr Muldoon's departure, she discovered that the hoover was nowhere to be found, presumably because it was already on its way to the country via Peckham. This came as something of a relief but when she came to write an apologetic note, it also became apparent that there was nothing to write it on or with, and nothing to sit on either. The sooner I get out of here, the better, thought Alexandra. I'll have one more trawl through the house before I go, though. As she was doing it the telephone rang. Sitting on the floor to answer it she found herself talking to Charmian.

'Alexandra? You sound as though you are in some sort of cave!'

'I *feel* as though I'm in some sort of cave. Everything's gone, I'm only the echo. It's a relief to sit down for five minutes.'

'I'm sorry I couldn't be there to help you.'

'Don't worry about it! Nor could Oliver, in fact,

though he will be there tomorrow when the whole thing happens in reverse, which is when I'll really need him.'

'How is Oliver?'

'Slowly coming to terms with it all. He's in Manchester today consulting, arriving back by train tonight. Charmian, you've found Mareka very accurate, haven't you?'

'Very. What she predicts mostly happens in the end. Not always in the way one expects though, as I'm sure I don't have to tell you. Have you been to see her or are you just about to go?'

'I've been. I've meant to ring you but what with the chaos at this end never got round to it.'

This was a shame in the light of the events Charmian intended to try to initiate, starting by picking the brains of Dominic Goddard, whom she was meeting at six. Secret knowledge of the occult sort dispensed by Mrs Hemingway would have been very useful.

'She said some astonishing things,' continued Alexandra, 'about what she calls the old company. Obviously she doesn't know it's Circumference.'

Charmian reviewed the rest of the week, which was extraordinarily busy both in work and social terms. She thought, I really do need to see Alexandra and it looks as though the weekend is the only time available. I wasn't prepared to give up Giles for Nigel but I am prepared to do so for Alexandra. Aloud, she said, 'Look, you want to get off to the country, so I don't want to hold you up now...'

Pre-empting what she was about to suggest, Alexandra said, 'Why don't you come down on Saturday? Stay the night. The children will be back by then and they'd love to see you.'

Charmian made up her mind. 'Fine by me, but are you sure? I mean, won't you still be in a muddle? I don't want to get in the way.'

'You're my sister so you won't mind the mess and you won't be in the way either.'

'It's a deal. I'll materialize on Saturday, late afternoon. See you then.'

Charmian hung up.

Suddenly filled with optimism at the prospect of seeing her, Alexandra stowed the two traumatized Curtis cats in their respective baskets in the back of the car. Before finally leaving she closed the downstairs window shutters, walked around the house one last time and then let herself out, double locking the front door. Without a backward glance she drove away. Off with the old. On with the new. Whatever that might turn out to be.

Giles was extremely disappointed when Charmian informed him that she would not be able to see him as usual.

'Can't you see your sister some other time?' he asked.

'No, I can't, this week's absolutely hectic. Try to understand.'

'I do understand but it doesn't alter the fact that I shall miss you. Especially in bed.'

In the end he went to sit in Karen's kitchen and

bemoaned his solitary state. Listening to it, Karen said, 'Why don't you come and have supper here on Saturday night? And Charmian can come too if she changes her mind.'

Giles was embarrassed. 'I hope you didn't think I...'

'Was angling for an invitation?' she finished for him. 'No I don't. Or maybe yes I do. It doesn't matter. Look, do you want to come or not? Yes or no.'

'Yes.'

'Right then, that's settled.' She wiped her floury hands on her apron and then looped up a stray lock of her hair. She looked charmingly domesticated and at one with her kitchen in a way in which Charmian never would. Kitchens and Charmian did not, on the whole, go together. But the main difference, Giles saw, was that Karen was where she ought to be, where Charmian in the country was an exotic bird of passage and, as such, only a visitor. Decorative and desirable but with an indelible London gloss. Always only a visitor. To his secret surprise and shame, Giles found himself wondering what it would be like to let down Karen's long auburn hair and kiss her unpainted mouth.

It was not difficult to spot Nigel in the throng milling around in the gallery foyer. Nigel's tie was the size of a small painting and very colourful. The shirt it fronted was pink and the whole effect was only slightly toned down by a rumpled Armani suit which looked as though it was made out of brown paper. It must have been obvious to even the most casual observer that here was a creative person. He was standing talking to a tall, distinguished man also wearing a suit but of altogether more conservative pinstriped mien. Charmian waved. Nigel's thin clever face lit up at the sight of her as he beckoned her over. Running his hand through shiny black hair whose straight locks brushed his collar, he said, 'Charmian, allow me to introduce you. Charmian Sinclair, Toby Gill. Toby Gill, Charmian Sinclair. Now you can tell me that you've both met already!'

'No, we haven't,' they replied as one.

Toby Gill.

As she smiled up at him Charmian's quick brain computed the information, *Chairman, Chief Executive, Stellar,* from its social file. Attractive aura of power. Early fifties? His spare elegance made Nigel appear at best extrovert, frivolous definitely.

'Charmian is a colleague of mine,' Nigel was saying. Charmian, who was used to turning into a colleague when with a lover who encountered a friend who probably knew his wife as well, said nothing.

'Oh, really? Advertising as well?'

'No, not exactly. PR. I run my own little company. Very little.'

'I keep trying to persuade Toby to give us the Stellar account.' Nigel could see no point in letting an opportunity like this slip.

'Yes, you do, don't you?' This statement was followed by no hope of any kind, only a reptilian flick of the eye. After a moment's thought, Gill said, 'Why don't you have a crack at the Circumference account? Rumour has it that they're about to sack their agency.'

'They're always about to sack their agency,' said Nigel. 'The problem there is Reg Spivey, who is cordially loathed by most of those with whom he comes into contact in business. And probably socially as well for that matter. Still, maybe you're right. Business is business, after all.'

Gill had a faraway look in his eye. He wants to leave, join his party or whatever and go round the exhibition, thought Charmian. And so do I.

She was just preparing to suggest this when Gill said unexpectedly, 'I had Oliver Curtis in my office a week or so ago. Know him?'

Giving an appearance of polite interest, Charmian waited.

'No, not personally,' replied Nigel, 'though I read all about it. The dust-up, I mean. Rather underlines what I've just said.'

'Impressive!' murmured Gill, almost to himself. Charmian had the impression that here was somebody thinking aloud.

'So I gather,' said Nigel, who did not want to talk about Oliver Curtis. 'Are you on your own, Toby? Because if so…'

Forestalling the inevitable invitation, Gill said, 'I am but I'm going on to a dinner party afterwards.' He turned to Charmian with a half-bow. 'It's been a pleasure!'

'A mutual pleasure then,' responded Charmian, giving him the full force of her bright direct look. It was, she knew, the most potent memory he would take away with him, assuming that he had really noticed her at all. Gill moved away into the exhibition, an oddly lonely figure.

In the event, Charmian and Nigel followed him round. Like shoppers who had already met each other once in a supermarket, they avoided further contact, assiduously studying different paintings.

Nigel in the Poussin exhibition was like a child in Disney World.

'I love it, Charmian! Love it!' exclaimed Nigel. His particular favourite was *The Triumph of Pan*, and, standing looking at it, Charmian could see why. There was an irresponsible dance taking place involving nymphs and satyrs during the course of which floating draperies had slipped from white shoulders revealing round, pretty breasts and various unlikely liaisons looked imminent. Music played, wine flowed and the ground was littered with masks. Right in the middle of it all was a bemused goat wearing a collar and a bell. In short it was an adman's dream.

For herself, Charmian preferred *Cephalus and Aurora*. 'That is the one I would like to own,' said Charmian.

'I can't think why,' said Nigel, 'they aren't having half as much fun!'

'Fun isn't everything!' remarked Charmian, aware not for the first time that a little of Nigel could go a long way. Even to herself she sounded tart.

'Well, if you say so, then it must be so!' He was unabashed and apparently set on being relentlessly merry. 'All the same, I have to tell you that the catalogue doesn't rate *Cephalus and Aurora*.'

'Well, the catalogue can get stuffed!' Dreamily she stared at the painting. The handsome couple lay beneath a canopy. With flowers in their hair, the Hours attended Aurora and there were clusters of putti and even Zephyr embracing a plump, creamy swan. In the background poised for flight stood her chariot drawn by a pair of winged white horses and manned by two fat cherubs carrying flaming torches. Aurora was wearing red. All around her the golden flesh tints and dark browns and lush creams combined to produce an effect that was both rich and sinful.

Charmian was also wearing red.

Her sharply cut trouser suit, which had a short fitted jacket and was teamed with a ruffled shirt made her look like a page. On her feet were buckled shoes.

Though he was apparently admiring *Tancred and Erminia,* Toby Gill took time off to note the way Nigel slid his arm around Charmian's small waist. So, as he had suspected, more than just a colleague. Much more probably. She's wasted on Guest thought Gill. With something of a sigh he passed on into the next room and *The Seven Sacraments.*

Although her back was turned, Charmian was immediately aware that he had gone. It was extraordinary, she mused, only half listening to Nigel wax lyrical about *Bacchanale Before a Herm,* the impact certain people were able to make just by sheer presence. Gill intrigued Charmian on two counts: his reference to Oliver, and the air of splendid isolation which he carried with him. At the same time she had divined his probably fleeting interest in herself and been conscious of his gaze upon her as she and Nigel had moved through the exhibition in his wake. It occurred to her to wonder whether he really was going on to a dinner party afterwards or whether that hadn't been just an adroit social sidestep. She would never know and recognized that the moment he left the gallery he would probably forget her. Out of sight out of mind.

'Charmian. Charmian!' Nigel was saying. 'For Christ's sake! Wake up that girl at the back!'

'Oh, I'm sorry, Nigel, I was miles away! What were you saying?'

'I was saying, let's do the landscapes, skip the religious lot and go straight out to dinner!'

No longer apologetic, Charmian said severely, 'Nigel, stop being so *flighty!* I want to see it *all*. It's what I'm here for. Now come along and don't fidget!'

Travelling down to the country on Saturday, Charmian once again mulled over her brief encounter with the enigmatic Toby Gill. Some discreet research conducted in the days following the RA exhibition had established that Gill was a widower whose wife of twenty years had died comparatively recently of cancer. Temperamentally a loner, by repute Gill was a shrewd operator and ruthless with it, who, through the medium of Stellar had made himself a huge amount of money. A powerful force. And a powerful force who had met his own business Nemesis at one point in his extraordinary career in the shape of a firing just about as spectacular as that of Oliver and also from Circumference. She went once more through the bundle of cuttings and profiles which she had prevailed upon Dominic Goddard to ask his secretary to search out for her from his firm's library, before putting them away and going back to her novel.

As he waited for Charmian's train to arrive, Oliver was conscious of a resurgence of the old ambivalence to which he had long been prone where she was concerned. It had always seemed to him that whereas Alexandra had a centre of gravity, Charmian did not, and in her company he was alerted by a sense of hidden agenda and much left unsaid. How she passed the majority of her time when not actually running her business remained a mystery and Alexandra, though close to her sister, did not seem to know the answer to this either.

'You have to remember,' Alexandra said when they talked it over, 'that Charmian and I had very different upbringings. Hers has made her secretive, maybe aware of how hurt she could be. Living with our father can't have been easy, you know. I sometimes think although I can't forgive him for the act, that he deserted us early rather than late was a blessing in disguise. Anyway, there you are. She's my sister, and I love her and am totally loyal to her. It doesn't mean I can explain her infinite variety.'

No. Quite.

Now his sister-in-law came along the platform towards him. Her air of insouciant elegance caused heads to turn. Because he knew they were sisters, Oliver could see certain physical similarities between the two

of them, but these would almost certainly have escaped
a more casual observer.

'Oliver!' She kissed him.

'Charmian!' He kissed her back. 'Let me take your
case.'

'That's all right, thanks. I can manage it.'

She always had been very independent. A sudden
startling resemblance to his wife when she smiled up
at him took Oliver by surprise. He had never seen it
so pronounced.

'As you wish.' He took her arm instead. 'The car's
over here.'

Once they were on their way back to the house, it
was Oliver who brought up the sensitive subject of his
recent fall from grace, concluding with the words,
'You see, Charmian, I thought forward momentum
would protect my back!' Listening to it, it was astonishing to her that someone as sophisticated as her
brother-in-law could at the same time be so naïve. Of
course in one sense Oliver had been at Circumference
man and boy. How long had it been? Twelve years?
A long time and when one was as close to an institution for as long as that it was possible to underestimate
a change for the worse in the culture of what had once
been a paternalistic company. All the same, it was clear
that Oliver had been so busy going forward that he had
neglected to observe the old army rule to keep his flank
and his rear under constant surveillance. Charmian
doubted that he would make that mistake again. On the
other hand while she recognized that her upfront
brother-in-law would never be a diplomat there was no

reason why he should not succeed elsewhere provided he brushed up his politics and succeeded in putting the past behind him.

'I'm afraid,' said Charmian at last, 'you'd been with Circumference for so long you'd lost touch with what the real world is like.'

'Possibly,' countered Oliver, irritated by this remark, 'but business is all about strategy and profit. Nobody can deny that, while I may have put some backs up doing it, I managed that company successfully through one of the worst recessions we've ever had.'

No, it couldn't be denied. Which made the fact that he had been fired at all inexplicable. It just didn't add up.

'No point in looking back,' said Charmian. 'You have to turn away from it and move on.'

Swinging the car through the gate Oliver said, 'Yes, but where to?'

After dinner the two sisters sat out in the garden. The moon was high and full and very pale. Drifting through a starry purple sky, its muted radiance silvered the garden. The night was very still and a smell of mown grass and night-scented stocks infused the warm air.

'Where are the children?' asked Charmian. Their school had broken up for the summer holiday only that week and earlier they had been noisy and excitable.

'Off for a swim with Oliver, I think,' answered Alexandra absently, her mind apparently elsewhere.

'Sounds Spartan!'

'Yes. They're at that age where they don't notice it. As you know, I had that sitting with Mrs Hemingway.' She sipped her wine. 'I've been waiting until they were all out of the way to tell you about it.'

Charmian was immediately on the alert. 'Well go on! What did she have to say?'

Alexandra recounted the gist of it. 'Now what do you make of that?'

What *did* she make of that? Charmian frowned.

'On the face of it, it seems highly unlikely, though I'm willing to bet that a lot more fraud goes on in the City than ever comes to light and, of course, the higher up a company it takes place, the harder it is to uncover. The other observation I would make is that there's no reason why Circumference should be any more immune to it than anyone else. Oliver never caught a whiff of such a thing when he was there, did he?'

'No, never. I'm sure he would have told me if he had.'

'Have you told *him* what she said?'

'Heavens, no! I haven't even told Oliver I've been to see her. While he *says* he thinks clairvoyance is mumbo jumbo, at the same time he's wary of it and doesn't approve. So I keep quiet about it. It's my particular brand of therapy. It doesn't happen to be his. No, I wondered if Mareka hadn't picked up telepathically some wishful thinking on my part. Although, on the other hand, I have to say fraud had never crossed my mind.'

Interesting.

Charmian said, 'I should just put the tape away and

wait on events. It may all happen but as I've said before not quite in the way you were expecting. It strikes me that the most heartening news she had to communicate was that Oliver will re-establish. Let's concentrate on that for the time being. And see if any of her other predictions come to pass.'

A clamour at the end of the garden indicated that the swimming party was back. Alexandra watched her family, wrapped in towels which looked like togas, slowly move up the sloping lawn. Grey ground mist was rising and drifting around their feet so that, wraith-like and moonlit, they seemed almost to float. There was a sudden insubstantiality about them, a dreamlike quality as though they were not really there at all.

Alexandra shivered. She thought: so long as I know that my family is safe I feel that I can field anything. Watched by Charmian, who was aware that her action betokened in a curious way a need for reassurance, she rose and walked across the grass to meet them.

The following day, while Alexandra prepared lunch, Charmian took it upon herself to entertain the children. All were fractious because after the swim they had sat up late playing cards.

'Anyone for tennis?' enquired Charmian, inspired by the vague idea that exercise would cause them to snap out of it.

'Nick and I thought we'd have a game of croquet,' said Alice.

'I don't want to play croquet,' said Dan.

'Nobody asked you to,' said Alice.

'The croquet lawn isn't your personal property you

know, Alice! If I want to play, you can't stop me,' announced Dan, knowing that he was being unreasonable but disliking his sister's proprietorial attitude.

'You just said you didn't *want* to play!'

'Oh shut up, Alice. Isn't it your turn to water the garden tonight?'

'Yes, it is, and I don't need you to remind me, Dan, thank you very much!'

Charmian wondered if they bickered like this all the time. Tactfully she suggested, 'Dan, why don't you and I have a short game?'

'Great,' said Dan with alacrity. 'I'll get my sneakers and my racquet.'

'Maybe I *would* rather play tennis after all!' The speaker was Alice, clearly bent on making a meal of the whole thing. 'I can't make my mind up.'

Dan was outraged. 'Alice, you just want to play because *I've* decided to!'

Forestalling the inevitable 'The tennis court isn't your personal property, you know, Dan!' and out of patience with it, Charmian said, 'I should stick with the arrangement you've already made, Alice. If you don't, what's Nick going to do? He can't play croquet on his own. By the way, where is Nick?'

'Last seen helping Dad with the barbecue.' Alice looked as though she might be about to sulk.

'Right, I'm ready!' said Dan. 'Let's go!'

They went and when they arrived at the court, which was a five-minute walk away, discovered that between them they had forgotten the key.

'I blame you, Dan,' said Charmian, without any rancour. Neither felt inclined to go back for it. Charmian sat on the old garden seat which was strategically placed to accommodate lazy spectators. Its wooden slats felt warm against the back of her legs. Dan lay on the grass. The low evening sun gilded the two of them as they relaxed in easy silence for a while, savouring its benevolent warmth which felt like a benediction to Charmian as, eyes closed, she turned her face towards the light.

It was Dan who broke the spell. He said, 'Aunt Charmian, do *you* think Dad will ever get another job?'

Charmian opened her eyes. She stared down at Dan, who was lying on his back, one arm outflung, the other shielding his eyes from the dazzle. His hair spread itself in an aureole around his tanned face and his straight dark eyebrows, unusual for a blond, were drawn together. A golden child.

'Yes, I do.' Charmian had always treated the children as adults and saw no reason to deviate from this now. 'The question is *when*. It could be quite a while.'

'But what happens if he doesn't?'

Sidestepping this, Charmian asked, 'Haven't they talked the whole thing through with you?'

'When it all first happened they did, but now nobody says anything. And I don't like to ask. I do think about it, though.'

'Sure you do. We all do. And, Dan, I'm not just jollying you along when I say I think he will get another one. It's what I really do believe!' I'm going to have to talk to Alexandra about this, thought Charmian. What with her concern for Oliver and all the organization attached to the house move she hasn't noticed what's happening just below the surface. Aloud, she said, 'I think you'll find that what with moving house and your being away at school until the other day, Mummy doesn't realize how long it is since you've all had an update. Do you want me to touch on it with her, or would you rather do that?'

'I'd rather you did, if you didn't mind.' He clearly feared casting himself as the fool who rushes in where angels fear to tread. 'It's just that I don't want to upset her any more than she is already. Or Dad.'

'No, of course you don't.'

Charmian loved her niece and nephews and overt favouritism would have been unthinkable. All the same, in her heart of hearts, she knew herself to have a particularly soft spot for Dan. Dan cared. Dan wore his heart on his sleeve. He sat up. His introspective troubled look wrung her heart.

'What do the other two think about it?'

'Well, Nick just says there's nothing he can do so he's just going to look away from it and get on with his life.'

'What about Alice?'

Dan mulled it over. 'I think Alice worries more than she lets on.'

A bell began to ring. It was the hand bell Alexandra used to gather in the children at mealtimes rather than shouting herself hoarse. They got to their feet. Charmian put an arm around Dan. Through a loose white shirt his adolescent shoulder blades jutted like embryonic angel's wings.

'*Courage*, Dan,' said Charmian. 'It may take a while, but in the fullness of time all shall be well.'

Together they dawdled slowly back to the house.

Back in London later that evening Charmian put Alexandra's garden roses in water and then checked the answer phone. There were several messages, including one from Dominic Goddard concerning arrangements for the following evening. There was nothing from Giles. She threw open the windows, which made no difference to the temperature, but let in the summer night and the muted roar of the city. Let in life, in fact.

Charmian made herself a vodka and tonic, then after a certain hesitation which she could not explain she rang Giles's number.

No answer.

Restlessly she rose and selected a compact disc. *Così fan tutte*. The Trio. Elegaic, evocative, the voices rose and fell, replacing the sound of a telephone ringing in an empty room, reviving poignant memories of another summer night, another place, possibly by now another life. When it had finished, unwilling to go lonely to bed she slotted the copy of Mareka Hemingway's tape that Alexandra had given her into a small recorder and settled down to listen to it.

6

Marcus Marchant poured himself a second cup of morning coffee, scrutinizing the business section of the *Telegraph* and saying as he did so to his wife, Jane, 'The Circumference share price is very weak at the moment. I wonder why.'

'No idea. Why don't you ask Oliver?'

'He probably wouldn't know either. Oliver's right out of it for now.'

'Maybe the market's down.'

'No, the market's up. But you're quite right, it usually does follow that. I have to say I haven't heard any rumours. Maybe it's just a temporary blip.'

'Why don't you ring one of your City analyst friends?' suggested Jane, refilling her own cup.

'That's a good idea!' Marcus folded the newspaper and picked up his briefcase. 'You're a brilliant business brain.'

'No need to be patronizing,' said Jane, 'but while we are on the subject, why don't you take Oliver out to lunch? If he has re-established he'll want to tell you about it and if he hasn't he'll want to tell you about that too.'

'I am, on Thursday, and he hasn't.'

'That's a shame.' Jane was silent for a moment. 'It must be very hard on Alexandra.'

'Yes, I'm sure it is but she'll survive and so will Oliver. Oliver has determination and courage but although he's very professional in his business dealings, on a personal level he won't forgive what's been done to him. He'll want retribution. Put it this way, if I was one of the Circumference enemies I would make it my business to steer very clear of our friend once he's on his way up again.'

'You make it all sound very Jacobean!'

'It *is* very Jacobean. That's *just* what it is!'

He fished out his diary. 'Christ, my first appointment's in forty-five minutes!'

'Then you'd better run along,' said Jane sweetly, 'and,' taking the newspaper from under his arm, 'if I'm to maintain my reputation for business brilliance I can't allow you to hijack this either.'

'Touché,' riposted Marcus, kissing her. 'I'll buy another copy at the station.'

Dominic Goddard night came round again. This week, thought Charmian, I'm going to make them all sing for their suppers. I can't get Oliver his job back but I probably can put a spoke in Spivey's wheel if I set my mind to it. How, though, was the question which still needed addressing. She had already discovered that Dominic knew Spivey, although alas only peripherally.

'It's a pity,' said Charmian during the interval at the ballet, 'that you've lost touch with Reg Spivey.'

'Personally, I wouldn't say so,' replied Dominic. 'Why are you still harping on about him anyway? He's a thug. A successful thug, I'll grant you that, but still a thug.'

'I don't want him for his social graces,' said Charmian.

'Just as well,' said Dominic, 'because he hasn't got any.'

'No, I want him because he could be useful to me. I'd like to have Circumference as a client.'

'Oh, I see.'

He was aware of seeing part of it rather than all of it, and knowing Charmian as well as he did, suspected a hidden agenda.

'Of course I could approach them cold, but as I don't have to tell you I'm much more likely to get somewhere as a result of a personal introduction.'

There was no denying that.

The bell rang signifying the end of the first interval. Taking Charmian's empty glass and putting it on the side, Dominic said, 'Let's go back in before the crush starts.'

The ballet was *Manon*. For the moment Charmian put all thoughts of Circumference out of her mind and concentrated on the dancing. It was all there, innocence, love, venality and betrayal, more or less in that order. Watching Sylvie Guillem effortlessly express one after the other with consummate artistry, her boneless fluidity melding with the music to the point where the two were indivisible, Charmian was aware of being in the presence of greatness. I am privileged to have seen this woman dance, she reflected. Though he was also entranced by Guillem's ethereal rhapsodic performance, it was another of the dancers, namely the portly villain Monsieur G. M. who reminded Dominic of Spivey and gave him a good idea.

During the second interval he said, 'You don't necessarily have to meet Spivey, you know, to achieve what you want. What about the Circumference Finance Director, Neville Cruickshank?'

'You know him? What's he like?'

In his mind's eye, Dominic reviewed Neville and found him wanting. 'Thin, whippy, a devotee of wide lapels and kipper ties. He looks as if he's in a sartorial sixties time warp. The unfortunate word "natty" comes to mind. What worse can I say?'

'Would he have the same amount of clout, though?' Secretly elated, Charmian sounded deliberately dubious.

'No, he wouldn't, but he would be an entrée. Perhaps he could get you on their party circuit and then you could take it from there. If you'd like me to, I could organize a lunch.'

'I would like! Dominic, you're a sweetheart!'

They were summoned by bells once again.

'Drink up,' said Dominic. 'We're off.'

It was while she was standing up in the dress circle prior to taking her seat that Charmian saw Toby Gill in the stalls below. He appeared to be part of a group of six and was conversing with a tall blonde. Charmian wondered who the woman was and whether he knew that she, Charmian, was here. She was conscious of a desire to meet and talk to Toby Gill again, and next time she did so to be the focal point of his interest.

'Who are you staring at?' enquired Dominic.

'Nobody in particular,' fibbed Charmian. 'I was celebrity spotting in the stalls.'

'And did you?'

'What?'

'Spot any?'

'No. No, I didn't.'

They both sat down. The lights dimmed and the curtain went up on the last act. Betrayal, retribution and death. At the end of it all there was silence and then the audience rose to its feet with a surge of applause.

'Brava!' shouted Dominic. *'Brava!'*

Flowers cascaded onto the stage from one of the boxes. Taking her curtain call the prima ballerina picked one up, kissed it and dropped a graceful curtsy. Curtain call succeeded curtain call and when, finally, the lights went up Charmian saw with mixed feelings that Toby Gill and his party had gone.

Later that night, after an *après ballet* supper at Joe Allen's, the two of them went back to Charmian's flat.

'You don't want another drink at this hour, do you?' asked Charmian, throwing open the windows.

'Yes, of course I do! What have you got?'

In the kitchen Charmian opened the fridge. 'Dry white wine or the usual spirits.'

'Dry white wine.'

Dominic sat down on the large comfortable sofa which ran along one wall. He felt that he knew her small sitting room as well as his own. There was a bowl of sweetly scented roses on a side table. Their charming unsophistication proclaimed them garden roses as opposed to the more formal florist variety. Idly he wondered where Charmian had spent the weekend. Even if he asked her, he knew she would not tell him.

'You are my married lover whom I see and enjoy once a week and very nice too,' said Charmian, 'but what I do with the rest of my time has no bearing on us and therefore I prefer not to talk about it. It's irrelevant.'

Dominic had had other mistresses before he met Charmian. In the main, these had all begun by taking an independent stance and then, as time went by, had become clinging and finally sad, at which point they had *wanted* to tell him about their solitary weekends. All these relationships had been initiated by Dominic together with the statement that he loved his wife and had no intention of ever leaving her. After, as he saw it, this honest assessment of where it was all at, it was, Dominic reasoned, their lookout. Virtue was his. He had not pretended to be anything that he was not. When he trotted it all out for Charmian's benefit, she laughed out loud.

'For heaven's sake, Dominic, can't you do better than that?'

Miffed he said, 'I don't know what you mean.'

'Next thing you'll be telling me is that your wife doesn't understand you.'

'Well, she doesn't!'

More mirth.

He was mystified.

'Look, let me lay it on the line,' said Charmian when she had recovered her composure. 'I *want* you to love your wife and I *don't* want you to leave her under any circumstances. And whether you understand one another or not is between the two of you so I'd prefer you to keep your adulterous clichés to yourself. Most of all, I don't want to hear about your marriage. I would go further and say I'm not interested in marriage per se. So on that level we are at one. It remains to be seen whether we can achieve oneness on any other.'

That had all taken place six months ago and in bed they had achieved a different sort of oneness.

He stared around the room which, although stylish, an extension in that way of Charmian's own personality, was also comfortable, even intimate, a difficult combination to achieve. Her personality made itself felt in her choice of paintings, books and furniture but interestingly there were no family photographs of any kind. Not one. Dominic found this an odd omission. Occasionally he speculated on what would have happened if he had met Charmian before he met Laura, but was forced to conclude that, given the former's view of marriage, the answer was probably nothing.

His lover entered, bearing two glasses of wine and bringing his reverie to an end. She handed one to him and he sipped it before putting it down on the mantelpiece. He pulled her towards him and slipped down a strap of her black dress revealing one pale shoulder which he kissed. She said nothing. Grey eyes met brown. She waited. Archetypal Eve, she smiled. Unable to resist it, Dominic kissed her full, mobile mouth. He slid the other strap off the other smooth shoulder and the dress, which was of silk jersey, crumpled to the floor. There was something unclassifiable, ageless about her. Whatever it was she was quite right, it was aeons away from the bourgeois institution known as marriage and was probably what excited him about her. On the undressing front he discovered himself to be stopped in his tracks since beneath the little black dress she was wearing a basque whose cunning shape pushed up her creamy breasts, at the same time nipping in her already tiny waist. This and her sheer black tights gave Charmian the air of a principal boy.

Breaking into the basque proved as difficult as breaking into Fort Knox.

In the end: 'All right! I give up! How do I do it?' Demurely (he had the feeling that she was amused by his bafflement) she undid the first of a row of artfully concealed hooks which ran down the front of it from breast to waist. Feeling that he had not distinguished himself so far, Dominic undid the rest, releasing her small round breasts, and then, on his knees, peeled off the tights. 'Bitch goddess!' said Dominic, nettled by her evident amusement. 'Come to bed!'

Lying drowsily in her lover's arms afterwards, Charmian murmured, 'I do love fucking.'

Used by now to her practical, and as he saw it, very masculine approach to sex, Dominic was neither shocked nor surprised by this remark. There was a minuscule silence which she ended by saying, sounding altogether less sleepy, businesslike even, 'You won't forget to set up that lunch with Neville Cruickshank, will you?'

Tuesday. Gervase Hanson Night. Unlike Nigel Guest, Gervase liked modern art, which was why the two of them started the evening at a private view at The Gallery, a fashionable venue whose principal artist was the inspired though unreliable Jack Carey.

'Marvellous,' said Charmian. 'Though I can't pretend to understand any of it.' They were surrounded by lustrous oils whose depth and variety of colour were pointed up by the stark whiteness of the walls. Charmian could imagine herself co-existing with one of them, though not in her present flat. A Carey painting would demand a complete change of decor, possibly even a whole room to itself.

'I'm going to ask my wife to buy me one for my birthday,' said Gervase airily. 'I thought we could call it an investment.'

Gervase was very pragmatic on the subject of his marriage. He said, 'We have been married a long time and have joint children. I love my wife, who still has all the qualities for which I married her bar one. She no longer enjoys sex. As a result of this significant change, although I still love her, I am no longer *in* love with her. So what am I to do, Charmian?'

'Exactly what you do do, Gervase! Her indifference is my gain.'

'That's how I see it. I have to say that in my opinion one marriage in a lifetime is enough for anybody. Why have you never married, Charmian?'

'Marriage in the form in which it is commonly promoted in our society, especially where women are concerned, doesn't appeal to me,' said Charmian.

'Of course, I'm aware that you prefer not to talk about your private life outside our relationship and I respect that, but thinking about you in my idler moments I have come to the conclusion that your father was probably an incorrigible womanizer. Must have been to put you off permanence quite so conclusively. Or maybe your mother took lots of lovers and neglected you.'

Poor Mother. Chance would have been a fine thing, thought Charmian.

Not for the first time, though, she was dazzled by Gervase's perspicacity. However, she simply smiled mysteriously and said nothing.

By now they were standing in front of the most dominant canvas in the room. This was titled *Experiment in Reds*. Its soaring, wheeling shapes made Charmian think of infinite outer space and other universes. Or maybe, on a more abstract level, other universes of the mind. Whatever it is I could sit and look at that canvas for a very long time, reflected Charmian.

'Why don't you ask your wife to buy you this one? It's wonderful!'

Gervase ran his eye down the catalogue.

'No, I don't think even her trust fund would run to that one. Besides it's vast. A whole wall would disappear. It's more the sort of thing that one of our more august companies, Circumference or Stellar, for instance, might buy for their private corporate collection.'

Here it was. A heaven-sent opening.

'You don't know anybody at Circumference, do you? I only ask because I'm quite keen to have them as a client.'

'No. Although I'm currently acting for someone who used to be one of their top managers. Oliver Curtis. You may have read about the rumpus. Because he's a client, it's all confidential, of course, but since, force majeure, he's no longer there, that connection would be of no use to you anyway.'

Not registering surprise at this piece of intelligence was an effort but Charmian managed it. It had never occurred to her to ask Alexandra who was handling the legal side of Oliver's dismissal for them. Keeping her voice carefully casual, she said, 'I thought I might approach Reg Spivey. But obviously it's easier with an introduction.'

Gervase looked pained. 'Charmian, surely you aren't that hard up for business!'

Knowing the answer perfectly well, 'Why do you say that?'

'Spivey's a grade-A shit. It only took ten minutes in his company to enable me to work that out. I should steer very clear if I were you.'

They passed on to the next canvas.

Looking at it, 'Business is business,' murmured Charmian. 'Lots of grade-A shits in business. I deal with quite a few of them. But because they're all clients that's confidential, of course.' She shot Gervase a mischievous look.

Unruffled, he said, 'I may have sounded pompous, but you know as well as I do the importance of discretion. Even between the two of us.'

She took his arm. 'Yes, I do. Especially between the two of us. And just as well. What about Hugo Rattray-Smythe?'

'Well, I suppose he's notionally Spivey's boss but he doesn't get a very good press either, though for different reasons. Is it worth it? Why don't you forget about Circumference. Try Stellar instead. My guess is that the culture there would suit you better.'

That's my guess too, thought Charmian. However, all in good time. Changing the subject she said, 'What about this one for your birthday? *Horizontal Integration*. Perplexing title. Wonder what the artist had in mind. It's a manageable size though and those ethereal blues are sublime. But would your wife like it? That's important since she's got to live with it as well as you.'

Gervase was uncertain how to take that last remark. In the end he decided the best possible way was the answer, 'Good point. Perhaps I'd better bring her here to see it.'

'Perhaps you better had!'

Later that night, when Gervase had departed, Charmian reviewed the position. All she had achieved so far was the offer of a lunch with Neville Cruickshank who was several steps away from where she really wanted to be. On the other hand it had become evident from the small amount of research she had so far conducted that Rattray-Smythe was the one she should be aiming at. Maybe Cruickshank would have to be the conduit at the end of the day. All the same it seemed like a ponderous way of achieving her end. I need a direct hit, she thought. Maybe Gerald Stanhope, Thursdays, was the answer. Gerald was that odd combination, a landed Labour Member of Parliament. Noblesse oblige, said Gerald. Gerald hunted, shot and fished but also had a social conscience and a brain. Quite possibly he moved in the same social circles as Rattray-Smythe.

The arrangement was that they would meet in the foyer of the theatre. 'You know what the House is like. If I am delayed just go on in,' said Gerald, 'and I'll catch up with you during the interval.' Prophetic words as it turned out, and when there was no sign of him five minutes before curtain up Charmian went and found her seat, leaving his ticket with the box office.

At the first interval there was no sign of him either. It was beginning to look as if he had stood her up although, on the whole, Charmian thought this unlikely. Gerald was eccentric but he was not rude. The second interval came and went. Still no sign of him. Charmian enjoyed the play but would have enjoyed it more with company. When it was over she went to the box office on her way out.

'Nobody left a phone message for me, did they?'

'Your name is?'

'Charmian Sinclair.'

'No. No, they didn't.'

Intending to pick up a cab, Charmian walked down

Shaftesbury Avenue. All the theatres were disgorging their audiences and the streets were crowded. It was very warm and the heat of the day still rose off the city pavements. On the corner of Leicester Square she stopped and bought an *Evening Standard* but did not look at this until she was finally ensconced in the back of a black taxi. When she did, 'Oh, heavens!' exclaimed Charmian. 'Oh, no!' The headline read: 'MP Collapses On Floor Of House.' It appeared that rather than going to spend a frivolous evening at the theatre, Gerald had gone to meet his Maker instead. It sounded like a massive heart attack.

Tears welled. She switched off the light. Sitting in the darkness of the cab, Charmian silently wept. According to the newspaper report, which was mainly preoccupied by the prospect of a marginal by-election, it had happened at 5 p.m. Which is why, thought Charmian, I missed it. I came straight from the office to the West End.

She paid off the cab. Feeling bereft, she let herself into her flat where the two of them had been scheduled to have a cold candelit supper. In need of someone to talk to, Charmian rang Giles. This time he was there, but sounding oddly distant in manner as well as miles. Or maybe that was her imagination. She did not mention Gerald Stanhope, whose connection with herself Giles knew nothing about.

'I'll be on the usual train,' said Charmian. 'I've missed you!'

'I've missed you too.' The right sentiments but conveying, at the same time, an impression of restraint.

'Do you mind if Karen joins us for dinner on Saturday night?'

Ah!

Charmian discovered that she did mind.

'No, of course I don't.'

He had, it transpired, already asked his neighbour. A duo had become a trio.

Charmian travelled down on the train to Sussex with an unread book open on her lap and a heavy heart. She had always known that sooner or later she would have to relinquish her hold on Giles, and now it looked as though sooner might be better than later especially if, as she suspected, he was inclining towards a more conventional relationship with Karen. The trouble was that all her other arrangements no longer held quite the attraction they once had. Possibly Gerald's death had brought on this atypical attack of disenchantment, gloom even. Intimations of mortality, perhaps? The question was, would she be able to shake it off and carry on as before? Charmian suspected that she might not. She dreaded ending up old and alone.

Like Father.

The train drew into the station and Charmian stepped down onto the platform as she had done so many times before. At the barrier stood Giles's tall figure. She saw that someone was with him and that that person was Karen.

'I hope you don't mind,' apologized Karen when Charmian finally reached them. 'I hitched a lift into town with Giles this afternoon since both of us had things to do and he offered to run me back as well.'

'No, of course I don't mind,' replied Charmian easily. 'Why ever should I?'

But of course I do mind, she thought. I mind very much, more than I ever thought I would.

A fraction too late, Giles kissed her. Greeting the two of them as opposed to just her lover, Charmian felt like an interloper. She wondered whether they had ended up in bed together the previous weekend, although she was in no position to moralize. Whatever had happened, there was now a hairline crack in her relationship with Giles, she recognized, pointed up by the small but telling hesitation before he embraced her. It was as though Karen's presence held him back, neutralizing whatever there had been between them.

The car, when they got to it, was like an oven.

'Sorry about this,' said Giles, winding down a window. 'There was nowhere to park in the shade. It'll cool down as soon as we start moving.'

Charmian took the front seat besides Giles. She could have offered this to Karen, as their guest, *should* have offered it to Karen, but did not feel disposed to do so. The front seat could be hers when she, Charmian, had abdicated, not before.

Driving back the conversation was stilted. When they had dropped Karen off, Giles said, 'You don't like her, do you.' It was a statement, not a question.

'On the contrary, I like her very much!'

Impossible to explain that it was too soon to put a good face on what was happening. Even though she had always known it would happen eventually.

'Really! It appeared to me that you were offhand, hostile even!'

It seemed that Giles, not normally a combative person, was looking for a fight.

Charmian decided that a soft answer to turn away wrath was called for.

'I'm tired that's all. It's been one hell of a week. Come on, don't spoil it all by being cross.' She took his hand. Taking it back, getting out and going round to the boot of the car to unload her bag, he gave every appearance of being very huffed.

Inside the house, Charmian said, 'Giles, what is the matter? I mean *really* the matter?'

'This, if you must know!' He threw a folded newspaper on the table in front of her.

Charmian picked it up. It was an up-market tabloid, open at the gossip column page. Julian Cazalet's gossip column, she noticed. Right in the middle was a photograph of herself and Gervase Hanson at The Gallery private view.

Christ! I hope Mrs Gervase Hanson doesn't see this, was Charmian's immediate reaction. Aloud, she said, 'So what? He's a friend.'

'The way he's got his arm around your shoulders looks very proprietorial to me!'

Charmian took a second look. Giles was right. It did. Funny because she did not remember seeing anybody taking photographs. Nor had Cazalet been there. She was sure of that. Although it was just the sort of function he would cover. He must have sent a minion instead.

'I'm not sure why you're getting so steamed up,' said Charmian at last, 'and where did this newspaper come from anyway? It's not one you usually take.'

He looked uncomfortable. 'It's Karen's. I noticed it lying on her kitchen table.'

Open at this page, no doubt, Charmian guessed. Well, all's fair in love and war.

'I think it's time we had a talk,' said Charmian, 'but before we embark on it, I think I'd like a drink.'

Studying him over the rim of her glass, it was Charmian's surmise that Giles was aggressive because he felt guilty. Not so much probably because he had seduced Karen or (and more likely) Karen had seduced him, but because he sensed himself inclining towards the sort of stability and permanence which were not on offer from herself and, therefore, moving away from their affair. Which was why he had not rung her all last week.

Finally Charmian said, 'Giles, you never used to take the slightest interest in my London life, though you must have worked out that I do not spend five days of every week living like a nun. We deliberately never talked about it. So what's happened to change all that?'

The anger seemed to drain out of Giles. He looked wretched. After staring down at the table for a full minute, he raised his eyes and looking her straight in the face announced, 'I've fallen in love with Karen Wyndham. At least I think I have. But I'm still in love with you. Or rather I think I am.' His torment and confusion were evident. 'Oh, hell! I'm suddenly not sure of anything any more.'

'Well, what I'm about to say might clarify things. Do you want to marry Karen?'

'It's early days, but yes I probably do. Or you! It's certainly time I married someone!' This time he took her hand. 'Oh, Charmian…'

Gently disengaging, she said, 'It wouldn't work. Marriage between us, I mean. First because I like living in the city and you prefer the country, but secondly because as an institution the way it works simply doesn't appeal to me. I don't want to live in a small house with a small garden and have 2.1 children or whatever the average is. So you see there's no contest.' Listening to herself, Charmian felt suddenly bleak. The spectre of lonely old age confronted her yet again. There must be some other solution to my problem, she thought, but if so I can't see what it is. 'In fact, I think I'll leave the field to the two of you and travel back to London tonight.'

The end of the affair. Get it over with. Leave now.

The air between them suddenly cleared. Giles knew, had always known, there was no future for them as a couple but knowing it he still could not bear to see her go.

'Oh, not tonight. Stay here. One last time. Go tomorrow if you must, Charmian darling, but please stay tonight!'

He took her in his arms.

She wavered.

'If you're sure! One last time.'
'I'm sure!'

On her return to London the following day Charmian felt exhausted. She sank into the chair nearest the telephone and kicked off her shoes. First the death of Gerald Stanhope and now the defection of Giles. My life is beginning to disintegrate, she thought wearily. Out of habit she looked at her answer phone. Unusually the flashing light indicated only two messages. Charmian pressed Play. Nothing. Only the sound of someone moving about and then a long silence which indicated that the caller was wondering whether to speak or not. The machine passed on to the next communication which proved to be more of the same. A triple bleep indicated that that was the end. Maddening! No point in speculating about who it might have been. There was something unsettling about being in town on a Saturday when she should have been in Sussex. Charmian felt like a displaced person. There was a sterility about weekends in London, and Sundays in particular, which she did not experience during the course of the rest of the hectic, stimulating week. She sighed. One day it would just be the mute answer phone and herself.

7

Reg Spivey faced Hugo Rattray-Smythe across his desk. It was late on Tuesday evening and both his secretaries had departed for wherever they lived. He adjusted his tie and refocused on his chairman.

'I don't know what it is,' Hugo was saying, 'it just doesn't feel right. If there's a discrepancy, if there is, what are we going to do?'

'You're in charge, Hugo. I'll do whatever you say.'

It seemed to Rattray-Smythe that whereas normally Spivey held court, whenever a problem cropped up, he, Hugo, was back in charge in fact as well as in name. Responsibility for a possible wrong decision, about which he had known nothing, loomed. Flustered and frightened he lost his temper.

'Regardless of who's in charge make no mistake your head will be the first to roll if we are in trouble!' Puce in the face and shouting, he was aware of presenting an unedifying, panic-stricken figure.

Bushy eyebrows drawn together, Spivey shot his chairman a poisonous look. 'It's all above board. No need for anything to become public. There is no discrepancy.'

'But what about the auditors? It doesn't look right to me,' repeated Hugo.

'We are not doing anything the auditors will even notice. Nothing will become public,' intoned Spivey, 'unless you lose your head, Hugo. Just leave it to me and do as I say. Oh, and Hugo...'

'Yes?'

'...you're going to have to get a grip on yourself. Do you understand me?'

When Rattray-Smythe had gone, Spivey walked to the large picture window where his substantial presence blocked out most of the light. The temperature seemed if anything to be escalating day by day. The sky appeared to have been bleached almost white by the intensity of the sun and the air rising from the hot London pavements shimmered. Even at night the heat hardly seemed to abate, inducing a feeling of building pressure. And possible imminent explosion, reflected Spivey, reviewing his unfortunate exchange with Rattray-Smythe. For Rattray-Smythe, though now reassured that nothing was amiss, was a potential weak link. On the other hand he could probably be intimidated into subsiding if he raised the subject again. Thoughtfully Spivey tidied his desk. He glanced at his watch. Too late to ring Cruickshank.

He locked his filing cabinets and then let himself out of his office, closed the door behind him and locked that too.

Charmian went to Gerald Stanhope's funeral which took place at the church in the grounds of his small country estate. Gerald, it transpired, had been a Catholic. Though not a very good one, thank heaven, was Charmian's view. Odd that he had never mentioned the fact.

Mrs Gerald Stanhope, who was whipping in the mourners and who did not look very grief-stricken, sounded as though she was still on the hunting field.

'Connection?' she boomed at Charmian.

'A colleague,' Charmian meekly responded.

Relegating her to the back, and indicating a row of other colleagues (presumably) as she did so, 'Sit over there,' ordered Mrs Stanhope. 'Next!'

Obediently Charmian did as she was told, thinking my God, no wonder Gerald was driven into the arms of the proletariat and finally mine if this is what he had to endure at home. She concentrated on observing the little church, which was rapidly filling up. There were dead Stanhopes all over it. They covered the floor in the form of memorial stones and rose up the walls in the shape of ornate plaques. In a side chapel were two supine Elizabethan Stanhopes, marble ruffs pointing to heaven, hands joined in prayer, she with a small dog at her feet. By now there was standing room only, mostly taken up by Members of Parliament, all of whom seemed to have arrived at the last minute. Mrs Stanhope was scanning the rows. Watching her narrowly, Charmian thought, if she tries to take my seat off me in order to give it to one of them, I'm going to resist. In the event this did not happen, probably because time ran out and the organ struck up. She read the order of service which at the end generously informed all those present that they were invited to the house afterwards for refreshments. Though I probably won't go, decided Charmian, who felt that she had had more than enough of the widow Stanhope.

The sight of Hugo Rattray-Smythe, whom she recognized from press photographs, sitting three or four rows from the front caused her to change her mind. He appeared to be alone. It was too good an opportunity to miss.

The house, or rather that part that Charmian saw, had an air of grand neglect. Probably it had not changed much over several generations. Clearly the current Mrs Stanhope had little interest in interior design. Knowing no one, and clutching a sad sandwich and a glass of the sort of medium sweet white wine Gerald would never have countenanced had he still been alive, Charmian decided to join a group. She watched two women kiss one another on the cheek, slotting together the wide brims of their hats with practised ease as they did so, tilting one way and then the other. As she approached them with a view to introducing herself, Charmian heard one say to the other, 'So what brought you here today, darling?' The speaker might have been talking about a casual meeting during a walk in the park.

The other, who had a cadaverous actressy face, responded, 'I felt I really *should* come. After all, I *was* Gerald's mistress.'

There was a very short glacial silence which proved to be a regrouping exercise since it was followed by the starchy rejoinder, 'But so was *I!*'

And so, thought Charmian, inwardly laughing as she walked past them, abandoning any idea she might have entertained of joining them, was *I!* I'll bet Gerald was fucking everybody except Mrs Stanhope.

Unable to stand any more of it she put down her glass of wine in front of a bemused-looking bust of Plato and, as she did so, saw Hugo Rattray-Smythe enter the room. He paused and looked around, rather as she herself had done on arrival. She noticed that the two Stanhope mistresses had temporarily abandoned their acrimonious trip down Memory Lane and, very predatory, were both monitoring the Rattray-Smythe advance. Speed was plainly of the essence and Charmian wasted no time in the hi-jacking of Hugo.

'Do you mind if I talk to you?' asked Charmian. 'It's just that I'm here on my own and I don't know anyone.'

Rattray-Smythe, who had a lot on his mind, turned a fishy eye in her direction, preparing to be dismissive, liked what he saw and became avuncular instead.

'No, of course not. I'm Hugo Rattray-Smythe, what's your name?'

'Charmian Sinclair.' She smiled up at him.

Across the room one redundant mistress said crossly to the other, 'Who *is* that woman?'

'Now tell me, what's your connection with poor old Gerald?'

'Colleague,' replied Charmian, sizing up her man and coming to the conclusion as she did so that he would prefer talking about himself to talking about her.

There would be no need to elaborate on the word *colleague*. 'What about you?'

'Oh well, that's a long story!'

Charmian braced herself and prepared to listen.

'Gerald and I were at school together. First prep school and then public school. And then after that...' Twenty minutes later he was still telling her. '...So that's the answer to your question...er...'

'Charmian.'

'...Charmian,' he finally concluded.

'And what do you do?'

'Do? Well, I shoot and fish. You know the sort of thing. Keeps me very busy, I can tell you.'

Thinking, what a vacuous ass, Charmian said, 'Yes, but what I meant was what do you do professionally?'

'Ah!' He sounded as though a great light had suddenly shone all around, illuminating an unimportant corner of his life that he had so far forgotten to tell her about. Clearly work was the very last thing on his mind. 'I run Circumference,' announced Hugo grandiloquently, omitting to mention the pivotal role played by Reg Spivey in this operation. 'I expect you've heard of us.'

Very tempted to answer, 'Yes I have, in fact I'm Oliver Curtis's sister-in-law,' which would no doubt have taken the smile off his face, she said instead, 'Hasn't everyone?' and was just about to follow this up when he suddenly noticed a French ormolu wall clock.

'Good Lord! Is that really the time? I'm afraid I have to go. It's been a pleasure...er...'

'Charmian.'

'It's been a pleasure, Charmian!'

'A mutual pleasure…'

'Hugo.'

'A mutual pleasure, Hugo.'

She had lost him. He looked distant. Whatever he was leaving for was clearly important enough to have succeeded in briefly mobilizing even the Rattray-Smythe brain. Charmian wondered what it was. She had one last try.

'Are you going back to London? If so, perhaps I could give you a lift?'

'I am, but my chauffeur's standing by outside, thanks all the same.'

And to think, mused Charmian, watching him take his leave of Gerald's fearsome widow, that if I hadn't brought my car, as I very nearly didn't, *he* could have given *me* a lift back. And then I really could have consolidated! Ah, well, never mind. At least I've made contact.

She let him make his exit and then followed suit. On her way to the door, she once again passed the mistresses, still apparently engaged in sexual competition, for she heard one saying to the other, 'Forgive me but I can't see how you can have been with Gerald the night before he died, since *I* was!'

The reply to this was inaudible and probably just as well. They looked as though they might be about to lock hats.

Charmian shook Mrs Stanhope's hand.

'Thank you for coming, Miss…?'

'Sinclair.'

'Miss Sinclair. A colleague, I think you said you were.'

'Yes,' said Charmian.

'Quite a few of those here. Gerald was *very* popular, you know.'

'So I gather.'

Sitting in the back of his chauffeur-driven Daimler, Hugo Rattray-Smythe pondered the approaching meeting with Reg Spivey and Neville Cruickshank. It was billed as a strategy meeting, but he was aware that its real title might turn out to be a Humiliate Hugo meeting. There were days, quite a few of them, when Rattray-Smythe wished he had never encountered Reg. On the other hand, when not showing off in front of pretty women such as the one he had just met at Stanhope's funeral (what was her name? Something unusual. Chastity? No. Not Chastity. Ch...Ch...Charmian! Yes, that was it! Charmian) he was honest enough to admit that he needed Reg, now more than ever, certainly until after the audit. Maybe then he could put Spivey's name forward for the knighthood he had had the bad form to say that he so badly wanted, prior to retiring him, a euphemism for getting rid of him.

Which in turn raised the question of who would take his place. For someone would have to.

Rattray-Smythe was well aware that the shareholders, already restive, would revolt if he attempted to appoint himself Chairman and Chief Executive. Of course the obvious successor, in the fullness of time, would have been Oliver Curtis, whom Spivey had been hellbent on removing. 'Oliver is undiplomatic, abrasive,' pronounced Spivey, who was himself one of the most abrasive individuals it had been Hugo's bad luck to meet. 'He upsets the other subsidiaries.'

On and on he had gone, like a tap dripping.

Finally, in the midst of a particularly busy month during which Hugo was attempting to relandscape his country house garden and found these repeated requests to address the affairs of Circumference irksome, not to say distracting, just to get Reg off his back for five minutes, he recalled saying, 'All right, ALL RIGHT! Get rid of him! But *you* organize it. I don't want to know.' After which exchange he had gone back to the drawing of the proposed sunken garden.

The deed had been done a month later. By then the water feature was on stream. And Rattray-Smythe was aware than an independent spirit had gone, which left Spivey effectively running Circumference with no dissenting voices at all.

Hugo, whose own position was under intermittent severe examination, and who therefore knew himself to be vulnerable, was at a loss as to how to stop him. It was becoming clear, even to Hugo, that his Chief Executive was power mad—out of control, even.

The car stopped outside the Circumference building. Reluctantly Hugo got out and took the briefcase handed to him by his chauffeur.

'I should be back in about an hour, Denis. If this meeting looks like ending any earlier I'll contact you on the car phone.'

He took the lift up to the tenth floor. Spivey and Cruickshank were waiting for him in Spivey's office. Spivey was encased in the usual double-breasted suit so glove-tight that it put Rattray-Smythe in mind of a straitjacket. Pity it isn't a straitjacket, thought Hugo sourly. He loosened his tie, which was black in deference to the demise of Gerald Stanhope, and waited for what was to come.

They all sat down. Cruickshank, who was wearing a loud pin-stripe and a red tie with pink flowers on it, perched on one side of Spivey's desk so that the two of them faced Rattray-Smythe.

'Right, gentlemen, now we are all finally here,' (a not very oblique reference to the fact that his Chairman had turned up twenty minutes late) 'let's review the options.'

Spivey talked for forty-five minutes. Trying to follow what he was saying, Rattray-Smythe was conscious of incomprehension and a gathering headache. Throughout the monologue, Cruickshank nodded at regular intervals which presumably indicated that he did understand. Nodding appeared to be catching. Hugo found himself doing it too. So much so that at the end of the monologue the idea of saying, 'I haven't understood a word, would you mind saying it all over again, Reg?' seemed inconceivable.

'So you see, Hugo,' said Spivey in conclusion, 'all we're into is creative accounting. Now you see it, now you don't and finally, at the end of the day, now you do. The money's all there somewhere working for us. No need for you to worry.'

Like novelty dogs of the sort which can be seen within the rear windows of certain cars, Rattray-Smythe and Cruickshank nodded, their heads bobbing in unison.

'Is it? Isn't there?' Although he could not have said why, Hugo was uneasy. 'But what about the auditors?'

'*What* about the auditors?' Spivey was impatient. Hugo had auditors on the brain. In Spivey's experience, like building surveyors, most of the time auditors did not pick up one tenth of what was really going on.

'Well, won't they...?'

'They won't know. Provided you keep your mouth shut, that is, Hugo.'

Still groping towards reassurance, Hugo said, 'Why don't we do things the way we've always done them? If the money's all there, I mean.'

Spivey forebore to explain that ever since he had been Chief Executive of Circumference this was the way things *had* always been done and that the problem they were currently having was not so much with the method but with the fact that, for the first time, Hugo had noticed that things were not being done in the traditional way.

'As I say, the money is all there,' said Spivey suavely, 'it's just that it's working better for us in other areas and I'm reluctant to move it.'

The gamble paid off. Brow furrowed, Hugo said, 'If it's all above board and everyone does it, why are you asking me to keep my mouth shut? I mean, what does it matter?'

'It's too sophisticated. It's the same as when you are

filing your tax return. You don't want to attract their attention by being too clever, albeit *legally* clever because if you do they start investigating every penny. Better to be discreet!'

Well, yes. The analogy with his tax return struck a chord and he could see that that did make sense. Though still not clear what the decision he was taking was all about, Hugo took it anyway.

'All right. I agree. Is there anything else we should discuss?'

'No, that's it for the moment.'

When he had gone Neville Cruickshank spoke for the first time since he had greeted Rattray-Smythe on his late arrival. 'Do you think he understood any of it?'

Spivey carefully put the cap on his pen.

'No. Not one bloody word. Which suits us down to the ground.'

Outside, even though the sun was going down, the heat was almost tangible. After the air conditioning of the Circumference building it enfolded and stifled like cling film, sapping energy. In the west a darkly brilliant sky was shot with crimson, promising more of the same. Hugo undid the top button of his shirt. Where was Denis?

There was Denis! Piloting the Daimler prior to drawing to an obsequious door-opening, bag-appropriating halt. With relief, thinking, thank God that's over, Rattray-Smythe got in. This time he retained his briefcase and, when he had made himself comfortable, extracted some papers and opened these up.

Ah! Here it was! The next project. The gazebo!
'Home, Denis!'

As he had promised he would, Dominic rang Charmian to say that he had set up a lunch with Neville Cruickshank.

'Don't expect too much,' warned Dominic. 'He may be Finance Director of Circumference but that doesn't make him electrifying company. Though fly is a word which does spring to mind. I have to say, in common I suspect with a lot of other people, I still can't understand why they got rid of Oliver Curtis.'

'No,' said Charmian.

'Anyway, look, does Monday suit you?'

She looked in her diary. 'Yes, it does. Where?'

He named a restaurant. A very expensive one.

'Good heavens!' exclaimed Charmian. 'Who's paying?'

'Unless he offers, although there's no earthly reason why he should, I expect I am.'

'I wouldn't hear of it! You've set it up for me, I should pick up the bill.'

'Don't worry about it,' said Dominic. 'I'm going to charge it to expenses. There are certain things I'd like to learn about Circumference which it wouldn't be appropriate to ask at one of Neville's own soirées.'

'Oh, really?' Charmian wondered what those were. Dominic did not enlighten her and since she was bound to find out what his agenda was during the course of lunch, she did not push it.

On that particular Monday the weather broke with a cannonlike rumble of thunder. Prussian-blue clouds, which had been advancing all morning, massed over the City. The still, dense air felt as though it was charged with electricity. Like a dancer, forked lightning jumped across the sky. A following explosion of thunder caused the street to empty in seconds. Running along with her jacket over her head and succeeding in achieving the restaurant just before the deluge, Charmian was reminded of the very similar storm in Sussex just before she had met Karen Wyndham for the first time.

Dominic had got there before her but as yet there was no sign of Neville Cruickshank. Partly because of her precipitous entrance and partly because she was not wearing her contact lenses that particular day, Charmian did not spot Toby Gill, who was sitting partially screened by a large palm at the other end of what was a large room.

Gill did see her and caught his breath.

Charmian's hair was dishevelled from her sprint along the pavement and her cheeks were flushed. There was a vivacity about her which was infinitely alluring to someone like himself who, in spite of his business success, had felt as though he was existing rather than living since his wife's death. He looked to see who she was with. Dominic Goddard, someone he vaguely knew. Lucky fellow, thought Gill. He watched Charmian kiss her lunch companion on each cheek in what he considered to be the ridiculous Continental fashion before sitting down opposite him and beginning to talk animatedly.

Gill's guest arrived at the same time as Neville Cruickshank, who he was intrigued to see join Charmian's table. Interesting. He would have liked to have gone on observing them but felt obliged to concentrate on his own guest instead.

Watching Cruickshank make his way towards their table Charmian thought, good gracious, how very undistinguished. Funny suit and funny haircut too. Looks like a small-town barber. After the introductions were completed, she settled down both to evaluate and impress. She remembered something Alexandra had said the weekend Charmian went to stay: 'Cruickshank would stab his grandmother if he thought it would advance his own rise to power. Nice, he is not.'

No, it certainly didn't sound like it.

Mindful of why they were all here, Dominic said to Cruickshank, 'As I told you, Charmian runs her own PR company, which has some very prestigious clients, and although I'm sure Circumference has all that sort of thing sewn up, I still thought it might be a good idea if you met. After all you never know when you're going to need someone, do you? Shall we order?'

'As a matter of fact, we may need someone in the not too distant future,' said Cruickshank unexpectedly, picking up his menu. 'Because I'm sure that when Oliver's successor is appointed quite a few of the existing arrangements will be revised and that side of things may very well be one of them. New broom and all that.'

Neither Dominic nor Charmian spoke.

Encouraged by their silence, Cruickshank continued, 'As you probably heard, Oliver resigned very suddenly. The announcement came as a tremendous shock to everyone, including me I may say. He's an old friend of mine, you know.'

Charmian found this carefully edited lie with its sanctimonious delivery hard to stomach. He likes to be all things to all men, she reflected. In a word, he's creepy. Probably a perfect foil for Spivey.

'I heard fired, not resigned,' said Dominic, who knew a fudge when he heard one and for different reasons was not prepared to let his guest get away with it.

'Oh, really?' Cruickshank was bland. 'I'm afraid I can't comment on that.'

'You say he's a friend, so presumably you've seen him since it happened?' Charmian could not resist it.

'Not socially, no,' Cruickshank was forced to admit.

'When I was fired,' reminisced Dominic, 'my successor knew all about it in advance and had the balls not to deny it! He wasn't a personal friend, of course.'

This was getting altogether too close to the bone. For the first time Cruickshank looked restive.

'I hope you're not suggesting that I—'

Aware that however satisfying this game of cat and mouse might be it was in danger of becoming counterproductive, Charmian said, 'Getting off the subject of Curtis and back to my own neck of the woods, how likely is it, do you think that Circumference will want to retain someone? Because if so I'd be very interested and I'm certain we could do a lot for you.'

'*Very* likely,' said Cruickshank, grateful for the diversion from the vexed subject of the departure of Oliver Curtis. 'Let me have your card, Charmian, and meanwhile why don't you come to the private view of an exhibition Circumference is sponsoring at the National Gallery. You, too, Dominic, if you're free.'

'Depends when it is,' said Dominic sounding, to Charmian's acute ear, underwhelmed.

Cruickshank got out his diary. 'This Friday. The twenty-ninth.'

'I'm afraid you'll have to count me out.' Dominic was definite. 'Laura and I are off to the country.'

Friday—Fridays were normally sacrosanct but Charmian had not heard from Giles since their last meeting and now did not expect to. An empty weekend stretched ahead. The sort Charmian thought of as a typical mistress weekend. 'I could come,' she said.

Swallowing the last of his wine, Cruickshank wrote a note in his diary. 'I'll get my secretary to send you an invitation. No coffee, thank you,' (to a hovering waiter) and, to Dominic this time, 'I'm afraid I have to be on my way. I have a meeting at three.'

'I'd like a coffee,' said Charmian.

When Cruickshank had finally gone, Dominic said, 'Well, what did you make of all that? Strikes me that at least you got what you wanted out of it!'

'I did! Thank you very much. Now it's all down to me.'

'I couldn't resist pulling his tail over the Curtis affair.'

'I noticed! So you think he knew in advance what was going to happen to his (I quote!) friend?'

'Yes, of course he did. The man's a hypocrite. He wants to come out of it smelling of roses.'

Charmian drained her coffee cup. 'Ah well, whatever he is it's no business of mine. He's just a means to an end as far as I'm concerned.' That much at least was true. 'Dominic, I shall have to go too.'

He signalled for the bill. 'I'll come with you.'

Watching them leave together as he waited for the restaurant to return his credit card, Gill, who saw all the newspapers at Stellar, recalled the photograph in the Cazalet gossip column of Charmian and Gervase Hanson whom he slightly knew. It was one of two or three and had simply been captioned 'Guests Enjoy Themselves At The Gallery Jack Carey Private View'. Nevertheless he had recognized her straight away. Charmian Sinclair, it seemed, got around, as the saying went. Stellar had a couple of Carey paintings in its corporate collection, and as a result, this particular party was one he had very nearly attended. At the last minute he had decided not to go.

The waiter returned with his card on a plate together with the counterfoil. Gill put both away in his wallet and then he and his guest, a merchant banker, made for the door.

Outside the storm had passed, leaving a shining, revitalized city in its wake. Water gushed along the gutters and the wet streets reflected a paler sky whose faded blue looked as though the colour had been washed out of it. Gill dismissed his chauffeur. Temporarily released from the stranglehold of the heat, the air was fresh. Stepping out towards his office, Gill thought with an unaccustomed lift of the heart: maybe life is worth living after all.

8

Exiled to the country, force majeure, the alluring thought of re-establishing in London had occurred to Alexandra more than once and had been subsequently dismissed. This was mainly because their income could dry up at any time at which point the cash from the sale of the town house, currently accruing useful interest in a high-yield deposit account, would have to be pressed into service. It seemed that for the time being anyway, there was nothing to do but endure and wait. Wait, probably, for their luck to change. Superstitious where that sort of thing was concerned, Alexandra believed that nothing would go right for them until it did.

Once or twice a week she talked to Charmian on the telephone but Charmian did not sound on top of the world either and coded enquiries as to what, if anything, was the matter were not responded to. It was beginning to feel as though the whole family was embattled.

On impulse Alexandra decided that while Oliver was away on a consultancy assignment in the north of England, she would drive up to London and spend a few days there staying with friends. I'll explore the possibilities of more work for me and I'll also case out the property market, she decided, and most important of all, I'll do what Charmian wants and go with her to see Father. The prospect was both daunting and interesting, and having decided to follow this course of action Alexandra discovered, rather to her surprise, that her resentment against her father had evaporated. When this had happened she had no idea. Maybe, she thought, it's just that we all have a finite amount of energy for emotional issues and all mine has gone into shoring up Oliver and because there was none left to stoke up my resentment at the way Father treated Mother and me, that particular fire has gone out. Whatever the cause she felt oddly relieved, as though a long exhausting war was coming to an end and peace was about to break out.

She rang Charmian.

'I wish I could have you to stay,' said Charmian, who had no spare bedroom.

'Don't worry about it. I'm being put up for a couple of nights by the Marchants. In fact there's a lot I want to do and most of it is at their end of town rather than yours. What I've really rung up to say is that I'd like to come and visit Father with you.'

Tears came into Charmian's eyes.

'Alexandra, I'm so glad to hear you say that. It isn't really for him, he's...' here she hesitated, '...shall we say, the same in many ways. By which I mean even at this stage in his life he hasn't worked out the effect that his behaviour has on other people and so he can't understand their negative reactions to it. Still very selfish. But you aren't like that and I just think if you woke up one morning and heard that Father had died, you would be devastated. Because by then he would be truly out of reach.'

'Are you sure he really wants to see *me?*' Alexandra was suddenly confused.

Charmian was patient. 'As I keep saying, it's nothing to do with what he wants and everything to do with what you need. I don't know how to put it. Look, he's old and alone but at the same time so impervious to outside influence that he can't see himself in a universal context the way most other people do. And the predictable result is that while he's still the centre of his own universe, as he sees it, he hasn't taken on board that his audience has dwindled to one. Others would say he's sad but in fact he's so insulated by his own self-absorption that he simply hasn't noticed. In a nutshell he's managed to reach the age of eighty without learning anything. Quite a feat! I think I'm saying don't expect too much but do come.'

'I will come!' Alexandra was definite. 'Oliver's away for part of the week after next and I'll come then. When do you normally visit?'

'Thursday evenings at the cocktail hour.'

'I'll bring a bottle of champagne. Father does still drink it, doesn't he?'

'Yes, of course he does. Father wouldn't drink anything else if he had any money left, which he doesn't and, come to think of it, that's probably why he doesn't. What a brilliant idea. It'll take him back to his heyday when, according to him, *all* the girls were heiresses, and champagne flowed from the taps. The photograph albums couldn't do better.'

'The photograph albums?'

'Never mind. You'll see!'

When Charmian had rung off, Alexandra sat staring into space. Everything was shifting and changing and though, in kaleidoscopic fashion, it would eventually stabilize into some sort of pattern, that time was not yet. Meanwhile old loyalties were being underlined and old vendettas making way for new ones so that, on that level at least, some sort of emotional growth was flowering amid the material devastation of life as she and Oliver had once known it. Of course we will come through this, thought Alexandra, but after it neither of us will ever be the same again. Whether the resultant change will be for the better or worse remains to be seen.

Abstractedly she tucked a stray strand of hair behind one ear. Midday. The sun was at its zenith. It was another still, torpid day of which there had been so many lately. Outside there was no movement of any kind, everything seemed to be in a state of suspended animation, all activity arrested by the dead hand of the heat. On the window pane a butterfly, a peacock, drowsily sunned itself, its iridescent, fragile wings open, and in the garden the cats lay comatose in the shrubbery, coolly concealed by wilting, dusty leaves. For the first time in my life since I married Oliver, reflected Alexandra, I have nothing to look forward to. Only uncertainty. Worst of all, I feel powerless to do anything about it. Charmian is quite right. I have to look away from all our problems and cheer myself up by working. Only Oliver can organize his own rehabilitation though I can help by just being there, but *wanly* being there is of no use to anyone. It was true to say there were some days when Alexandra thought she had lifted herself out of the slough of insecurity and despond into which Oliver's dismissal had cast her and many others when she knew she had not.

Charmian had got to the heart of the matter. She said, during the course of one of their telephone conversations, 'Do you know, Alexandra, you *aren't* depressed, you are *angry!* It is suppressed anger that is dragging you down. In one sense it's a pity we don't live in the days of the Borgias because an elegant poisonous elimination of your enemies such as they took for granted in those days would do wonders for your morale. Honour would be satisfied and that would be that!'

Alexandra had laughed out loud. 'I'm sure that's right. Though Spivey has upset so many people that even in this civilized age he probably feels it necessary to employ a food taster.'

It wasn't a very good joke but they both laughed anyway.

All the same, she recognized a great truth when she heard one. Murder would definitely solve my problem and use up my aggression she thought. Unfortunately pinpointing the cause of the problem did not scotch it. If anything the recognition of a desire for vengeance in an inconvenient era which did not condone that sort of solution caused a different sort of frustration to build up.

During the following week the weather at last became cooler. Because he found commuting every day exhausting, Oliver declared his future intention of spending Monday to Friday staying in London with friends. This arrangement was only a temporary one but, he calculated, would take some of the pressure off. When it was due to end, at the beginning of November, Dan's godmother, who had a house in France and who was writing a travel book had offered them the use of her London flat while she departed for a six-week working stay there. It promised to be a fractured existence but at least, albeit in a very inconvenient way, Alexandra felt that life was on the move again. Oliver felt it too.

Oliver said, 'Do you know I have an odd sensation of things gathering around. I think maybe our luck may be about to turn.'

Alexandra fervently hoped so.

As scheduled, Oliver departed for the northern business trip and Alexandra prepared for her own journey to London. At the same time, she was aware of not feeling well. Not ill exactly but not well either. As though she was in a curious health halfway house. She had begun to wake up at 5 a.m. with monotonous regularity, after which getting back to sleep proved difficult. When she did succeed and the alarm woke her up at seven she felt unrefreshed and leaden and was conscious of having had crowded, harrowing dreams, the details of which she could not remember. Although Alexandra recognized that the day Oliver came into his kingdom with another job was the day she would begin to recover her old equilibrium, for the present there was no relief in sight. By habit a non-complainer on this sort of issue, she said nothing to anyone but soldiered on alone.

The trip to London brought the whole thing to a head. Travelling at seventy-five along the dual carriageway, Alexandra suddenly panicked. She felt short of breath and faint and found herself hanging onto the steering wheel for dear life, her knuckles white with the effort. Clearly it was imperative to slow down and get off the motorway as soon as possible. Her mind went blank. The car hurtled on.

Where was the brake?

Almost as soon as this terrifying memory lapse happened familiarity re-asserted itself, she located the pedal, dropped her speed and moved into the left-hand lane. A sign proclaimed that the next exit was one mile away. Mustering all her reserves, Alexandra limped the car towards it. Finally off the motorway, sweating with fear and shaking, she drew to a halt and switched off the engine. Exhausted and fraught, she closed her eyes and lay back in her seat. Alone, Alexandra grieved aloud for the past three months and the pain it had caused all of them.

When she finally opened her eyes she saw from her watch that twenty minutes had elapsed. For the first time she noticed that she had parked the car in a country road which ran through a wood. Apart from the occasional car which passed her own there appeared to be nobody about. Alexandra got out. Her limbs felt stiff. She walked into the wood where the leaves of the tall trees were just beginning to turn. Above her they arched, loftily forming a canopy of translucent colour. Where the sun was able to penetrate this it fell in straight narrow shafts as though shining through Gothic windows and where it touched the dark earth illuminated it with bright blocks of light.

Alexandra leant against one of the trees. On impulse she took off her shoes. The ground beneath her bare feet was curiously energizing and the tree itself, which had probably been there for at least a hundred years growing out of the quiet earth, communicated its own vibration of timelessness and endurance. She stood there for a long time. Finally, carrying her shoes, Alexandra went back to the car. She got in, noticing as she did so that she had forgotten to lock it, slipped Vivaldi's *Four Seasons* into the cassette player and, driving slowly and carefully, resumed her journey to London.

She finally arrived an hour and a half later than she had planned, located the hiding place of the Marchants' key and unloaded her small suitcase. Just being back in the capital gave Alexandra a rush of adrenalin and a deep certainty that while Oliver was as embattled as he was, here in London with him was where she ought to be.

The telephone was ringing when she entered the house. Preparing to take a message, Alexandra found herself talking to Charmian.

'Where on earth have you been?' Charmian wanted to know. 'You said you'd be there an hour ago. I've been worried about you!'

'Well, I'm here now.' For the time being Alexandra decided to say nothing of her unnerving journey up.

'Yes, you are. What's your agenda?'

'Tomorrow I'm doing the rounds of the house agents. I want to get a feel for the property market and decide whether we can afford a small flat.'

'I have to say I think that makes sense. Lurching along the way you are at the moment isn't helping anybody. Continuity is what you need. And a united front. Does Oliver know about this?'

'No, he doesn't. At the moment he doesn't want to put money into bricks and mortar. My own view is that we should but make sure we buy something we can quickly sell if we have to, and, if not make a profit, at least recoup our investment. There's more at stake here than just money.'

'You're right, there is. And then what?'

'I'm going to spend all day doing that followed by an evening with Jane and Marcus. The following day I'm going to see one or two old clients to try and drum up some work and in the evening, as you know, I'm seeing you and Father. Friday morning I'm taking in the new exhibition at the National Gallery and Friday afternoon I'm going back to the country. That's it.'

'Sounds very positive! See you on Thursday.'

Charmian rang off.

Dinner with the Marchants was a relaxed affair in the kitchen. Marcus said, 'How's Oliver bearing up?'

Alexandra sighed inwardly. 'He's okay. It's all far from ideal on almost every front at the moment but there's nothing to do except get on with it. I can't believe things can go on the way they are. There must be an upturn at some point.'

'There will be,' said Marcus. 'The key to it is keeping the nerve.'

'He still can't believe what happened.'

'Nor could we!' exclaimed Jane.

'I don't suppose he's still in touch with any of the Circumference lot?' said Marcus.

'One or two perhaps but in the main no, I don't think he is. Why do you ask?'

Marcus sipped his wine. 'Because as you know, I own quite a few Circumference shares and the price is exceptionally weak at the moment.'

'Apart from an all-time high a couple of years ago they never have done much,' Jane pointed out. 'I don't know why we don't just sell. Especially now they've hove out Oliver.'

'Idleness on my part mainly,' answered her husband. 'But what captured my attention was that the share price which has been at a two year low, has been showing signs of revival during the last fortnight. I just thought Oliver might have some idea about what was going on.'

'I doubt it,' said Alexandra. 'He's trying to move away from all that. Looking back doesn't help!'

'No, of course not. I made some enquiries of my own and apparently there have been rumours.'

'Rumours!' Remembering Mrs Hemingway Alexandra was alerted. 'What sort of rumours? What are they saying?'

'That's what I couldn't pin down. There's a feeling in the City that something's in the wind. Could be a takeover. And, of course, if it were, chances are the share price would shoot up and we would all stand to make a killing. I say all because on the day of his corporate execution Oliver told me that he still has a stack of share options which even Circumference wasn't stingy enough to take off him. I don't know. Nobody seems to want to say too much at present. It's all dark hints, but whatever it is there's *definitely* something.'

'There were takeover rumours a few years ago which gave them a fright, as you no doubt know,' said Alexandra. 'It concentrated their minds wonderfully, even Hugo Rattray-Smythe's.' She debated with herself whether to tell them about her session with Mareka Hemingway and came down against it on the grounds that the sceptical Marcus would think that sitting in the country waiting for Oliver to re-establish had caused her to go quietly mad. Instead she added, 'If you hear any more, Marcus, do let me know. There's no point in losing any more money courtesy of Circumference than we have to.'

'No, there isn't,' he agreed, 'though there may be nothing in it. The City rumour mill may have got it wrong.' Watching Marcus very narrowly as he spoke, Alexandra thought: but he doesn't think it has. His antennae tell him that something is up. If Mareka Hemingway is right it isn't takeover but something rather more sinister. 'However,' he resumed, 'whatever I glean, I'll pass on.'

'I'd be grateful,' said Alexandra, 'if you would pass it on to me because Oliver is so busy dealing with two consultancies, he's whirling like a dervish and doesn't have time to monitor that sort of thing right now.'

'Sure. I gather Gervase Hanson proved a useful adviser by the way.'

'I've never met him but according to Oliver, yes he did. Very useful. Apparently at the first session he punctured Spivey's *amour propre* so successfully that Reg balefully subsided for most of the rest of the meeting.'

'Gervase is very clever and very arrogant,' observed Jane. 'It's easy to underestimate him because he looks like a fop, but when he strikes he's deadly. And he doesn't suffer fools gladly.'

'Spivey isn't a fool,' said Alexandra, 'but he does like the sound of his own voice. Phrases such as, "I don't agree, Reg," or, worse, "You're wrong, Reg," constitute a capital offence. He feels threatened by debate. Which is all right within the walls of Circumference because all his luckless employees *have* to listen, but of course the Gervase Hansons of this world don't.'

'Sounds like a salutary lesson to me,' remarked Marcus. 'Possibly he could do with a few more like it. I've always assumed that was one of the imbalances in Oliver's relationship with him.'

'What?'

'Well, presumably to that sort of despotic mentality

Oliver's independence of spirit must have looked at best like lese-majesty.'

'Absolutely right. Oliver was his own man and thought for himself, both hanging matters, apparently.'

'He would probably have done better at Stellar. By all accounts Toby Gill is a despot as well but in a different way. There's no doubt who's in charge but provided he knows what they're doing he likes his managers to show initiative and use it. The fact that somebody else has a good idea doesn't make him feel insecure. The whole setup is more collegiate.'

'Yes, but there's a big difference,' said Jane. 'Gill is Stellar's major shareholder. Spivey's just a hired gun.'

'Do you know Gill?' asked Alexandra.

'Slightly. We've met a couple of times that's all, but he's frequently profiled in the business press.'

'Oliver went to see him at his request,' said Alexandra, 'but it didn't lead to anything. Or, rather, it hasn't as yet.'

'You never know. That sort of operator rarely does anything without a reason.'

'What are you doing tomorrow?' asked Jane, thinking that Alexandra looked suddenly drained.

'I'm flat hunting,' answered Alexandra. 'It's my view that we need a London *pied-à-terre*.'

'Well, all I can say,' said Jane, 'is that if we didn't have this one and I spent most of my time at Marchants I'd hardly ever see Marcus. So I'm sure that if you and Oliver can afford it at this juncture, it does make sense. I'd come with you if I wasn't delivering a lecture at the Tate.' Jane was an art historian. 'Does Oliver know you're doing this?'

Alexandra smiled. 'No, he doesn't. He'll probably need persuading so I thought I'd do some research first, get together some facts and figures and then do a presentation. What do you think?'

'I should go for it. Where are you going to look?'

'Clapham, Wandsworth, that sort of area.'

The following morning Alexandra rose early and put on a sundress and flat shoes prior to setting off on her property hunt. It was early enough in the day for the light to have a limpidity which would diminish as the sun rose higher and the heat increased, taking the edge off everything. For now there was a hint, though only a hint, of coolness in the air, a feeling that autumn just might be in the offing. On a crystalline morning such as this, London had the fine-drawn delicate quality of an aquatint.

Alexandra parked the car off the Northcote Road. Walking along towards the estate agent's office she felt a rush of optimism such as she had not experienced for months—not since before Oliver was fired in fact. The pleasure of doing rather than just enduring was intoxicating.

The estate agent was expansive and wearing a bow tie.

'Ah, Mrs...?' He was also unprepared.

'Curtis.'

'Now what sort of property are you looking for and at what sort of price?'

'I told you all that on the telephone when I made the appointment,' said Alexandra.

'My colleague, I'm afraid!'

'And he didn't pass any of it on to you, of course.'

He studied his acid-yellow lined A4 notepad. 'Er, no. No, he didn't.'

'Right. Start again,' said Alexandra. She hoped the other two were not going to be as dozy as this one. 'With only a finite amount of time at my disposal, I am looking for a three-bedroomed mansion flat. I do not want a garden. I already have a garden elsewhere. Also there must be both a viable kitchen and bathroom. I would not want to have to engage in major building works once I was there.' Anything else? She thought for a moment. 'Oh, yes. Very important! It must be quiet. Ongoing noise makes me neurotic. The area I had in mind is SW4 and, before you ask me, I have no idea what I should expect to pay for the sort of property I've just described, but if I do find what I want at a price I can afford, I would be a cash buyer.'

'I see.' He began to rummage in a filing cabinet.

'You wouldn't consider a small house?'

He must be deaf.

'Houses, even small houses, tend almost without exception to have gardens. I did say that I do not want a garden. I also used the words mansion flat.'

'Right.' Unlike certain house buyers he had encountered it appeared that this one had very definite ideas about what she wanted and was not about to compromise.

Regretfully he refiled four sets of details of properties which were not flats, did have gardens, were in need of extensive renovation and were proving very hard to shift. He returned to the desk with the remaining two.

'These might be just the ticket. Shall we take my car?'

Driving along to wherever it was, Alexandra scrutinized the sheets he gave her. Both were stats with smudged over-inked reproductions of the properties which might have been igloos for all she could see. Eventually he drew to a halt. They both got out.

'Where is it?' enquired Alexandra.

He pointed aloft. 'Up there.'

She could not believe it. 'But I expressly said that whatever I buy must be quiet!'

Lamely he said, 'People have different ideas concerning what is and is not noisy, and double-glazing is very efficient these days...'

A pantechnicon whose exhaust belched black smoke roared past them, followed by another and then another and finally a bus. The ground shook.

'This,' pointed out Alexandra very haughtily, 'is the South Circular, one of the nastiest, noisiest roads in London. I don't believe we're even in Clapham!'

'Borders of,' was the sheepish reply.

They both got back into his car.

'Don't you have any smallholdings in Westmorland to show me?'

Startled, he stared at her.

'What you've tried to interest me in so far bears so

little relation to what I've specified that I just thought you might have.'

He gathered himself together. 'Ha ha! Good joke! Maybe the next one will be more up your alley!'

On one level it was. It was a period flat and it did have three bedrooms. Just. The kitchen looked as if it might have been the original and so did the depressing bathroom. I couldn't live here without rebuilding both, which is out of the question at the moment, thought Alexandra, eyeing the gas meter in the hall which was one of the voracious variety which had to be regularly fed. The trick with buying property, she knew from previous experience, was to be able to look beyond the present incarnation, which in this case was one of peeling decrepitude, and visualize the potential. Though without original features such as cornices, doors, shutters and fireplaces any attempt at transformation was likely to prove unrewarding.

'You don't have any other flats for sale in this block, do you?' she asked the agent. 'Because this is the sort of thing I'm looking for, though in a better state of modernization, so that all it needs is a paint job and the odd carpet.'

'Not at present, but they do crop up fairly regularly and when they do they sell on very quickly.'

'How much for?'

He specified a price range. A very reasonable one.

'At last I think we're on the same wavelength,' said Alexandra, exasperation caused by his previous wilful disregard of her clear instructions ebbing. She gave him the benefit of her wide and friendly smile. 'You can put me on your mailing list anyway, but the moment another of these flats comes on the market I'd like you to ring me in Hampshire and I'll drive up to see it. You never know, we just might end up doing business together!'

This sudden exercise of her considerable charm mollified him, causing him to replace the word *Difficult* which he had so far felt inclined to apply to this particular client with *Discerning* instead.

'There's one more thing you should see.'

He beckoned, she followed.

At the back was a communal walled garden the size of a small park, mainly laid to lawn with shrubs and mature trees. Staring at this unexpected vision of vibrant green in the middle of south London, Alexandra thought, what a find!

The remainder of the day was more of the same though with different estate agents. Standing in dilapidated flats, old flats, poky flats, spacious flats and, finally, a modern G-plan horror, she resolved to pursue the idea of the Edwardian mansion block. I don't know what it is about that flat, reflected Alexandra, but it just *feels* right.

'Did you have any luck?' enquired Charmian when her sister arrived at her office, where they had arranged to meet.

'Yes and no!' was the cryptic answer. 'By which I mean that I've found the sort of block, the location and the right price, but not yet the specific flat. Now I have to persuade Oliver that it's the right thing to do.'

'I expect you'll succeed,' was Charmian's opinion. 'When do you have to be back for dinner? Have you got time for a drink?'

'Absolutely.'

Charmian extracted a bottle of Sancerre from her small office fridge. 'That's good because I'd like to brief you properly on Father and how he is.'

How he is.

Never mind how Father is, Alexandra could remember a great deal about how Father was.

Going to see him the following evening, Alexandra said, 'Where do you say he lives? Peckham? How on earth did Father ever land up in Peckham?'

'*I* don't know and he can't remember. Nor can I explain how he organized himself into a council flat but there he is. Although in a way there he isn't because, as you'll see when you meet him, Father is mentally in the South of France. The privet outside his window is not privet at all but bougainvillaea according to him.'

The flat was part of a rectangular grey block. The metallic lift in which they travelled to the third floor smelt of urine and was covered in offensive graffiti.

'Next time I'd rather walk up,' said Alexandra.

Charmian who, it transpired, had a key, rang the bell first and then let them both in.

He was sitting by the window. Age had stripped away flesh and had pared down almost to the bone what had been a sensuous face. There was little trace now of the dandy he had once been or of the style in which he had once lived, just a shrunken old man sitting in a council flat with his memories.

'Father,' said Charmian, 'Alexandra has come to see you.'

Alexandra sat down opposite him. She wondered whether to kiss him and decided not to. It was like meeting a stranger. She proffered the champagne. 'I brought you this.'

He took it and scrutinized the bottle. 'Veuve Clicquot. Excellent.' He handed it to Charmian. 'It's cold. Put it on the radiator, would you, darling?'

'The *radiator?*' They both stared at him.

'Yes, the radiator. Champagne ought to be served warm. Everyone knows that.'

His voice still sounded young. Unlike the rest of him that had not aged.

'No radiators on at this time of year so you'll have to take it as it comes,' said Charmian. 'I'll open it, shall I?'

Left alone with her father for the first time for years, Alexandra could find nothing to say. She felt immeasurably moved as though an emotional wheel had come full circle for her if not for him. He did not refer to their long estrangement but sat sunk in thought for a few minutes and then opened up the book on his lap and as though she had never been away began to take her through it. 'Look, Alexandra, this is Paris and this, this is Bayreuth. And here we are at the races. Longchamps, if I remember rightly. I won a packet that day.' Alexandra looked at the photograph in silence. There he was, top-hatted and tailed, standing beside some socialite or other whose hair was teased into a blonde roll under an extravagant hat and who was sporting a long cigarette holder.

Also looking at the album as she leant over his shoulder and handed him his champagne, Charmian thought, that must have made a change. Usually he lost a packet.

Sipping with appreciation he said, 'There was a time when this was all I used to drink. Those were the days.' He turned some more pages. Capital city after capital city and every so often elegant watering holes such as Antibes. Makes me wonder how he ever found time for two marriages, reflected Alexandra as the endless hedonistic progress was revealed snap by snap.

They finished the bottle. Time to go.

Reluctantly he shut the album. Impressively heavy and expensively bound in dark green morocco leather embossed with gold, it looked extraordinary in his small dingy flat, ill at ease, like an unwilling apport from a grand country house. There were two albums, Alexandra noticed. The other was bound in dark red. She went into the kitchen where Charmian was washing up the glasses.

'Why don't we take Father out to dinner with us?'

'Yes, all right,' replied Charmian, 'but he won't go anywhere unless it's very grand.'

'I don't mind taking him to the Ritz if you think it would please him. And by the way, it's my treat for both of you. He doesn't particularly deserve it, but you do.'

'I'll go and get him organized into a suit.'

It was years since either of them had been to the Ritz and decades since Father had. Diminished by the last enemy, age, he sat between his two daughters, drinking in the atmosphere, back in his element. The Ritz. Still the same. Well-heeled diners, the smell of expensive scent, damask tablecloths, silver cutlery and all that gilt. They studied the menu and it was while Alexandra was ordering the wine that Charmian felt a tap on her shoulder. She turned round.

Nigel Guest.

'Oh hello, Nigel!' Charmian was less than ecstatic to see him.

'Aren't you going to introduce me?'

It was the very last thing she wanted to do. Charmian hesitated.

Into the brief pause, with a surge of his old *savoir-faire*, Father said, holding out his hand, 'Austin Sinclair. And this is my daughter,' Charmian held her breath, 'Alexandra.' He did not add a surname. It occurred to Charmian that perhaps he did not even know she was married.

'I didn't know you had a sister!' Nigel was plainly very interested. Wishing he would go away, Charmian opened her mouth to reply, when once more her father butted in.

'Half-sister. Different stables, you know.'

The waiter appeared.

'Pâté de foie gras,' said Father, 'followed by lobster thermidor. Are you one of Charmian's lovers?'

'Yes, I am,' answered the irrepressible Nigel without

missing a beat, 'but since I'm married we try not to bruit it around?'

'Being married never stopped me doing anything.' It looked as though egged on by Nigel Father might be about to go from excess to excess. Charmian caught Nigel's eye, frowned and with an almost imperceptible movement of her head and eye, indicated that she wanted him to go.

'Charmian wants me to go,' announced Nigel, at his most irritating.

Charmian found herself forced into saying, 'No, I don't.'

'Yes, you do.' He was apparently not at all offended. 'Still on for next Wednesday?' and then, as she nodded assent, 'good, good, good!'

He went.

Alexandra raised her eyebrows.

Charmian shrugged.

Father, who could be relied upon to dot the i's and cross the t's, opined, 'Not sure about him, Charmian. Looked rather louche.' (Separately they both thought this was rich coming from Father.) 'His views on marriage are sound though.' He added incomprehensibly, 'Marriage is fine for women. Men need something to leaven the lump. Your mother could be very difficult,' and then, apparently deciding to spread it around: 'So could yours, Alexandra. Shall we order the wine?'

At the end of the evening he resisted all attempts to leave.

'Afraid I'll turn into a pumpkin, are you? What about a nightclub?'

They eventually got him home by midnight. Alexandra installed him in what she supposed must be his favourite chair.

Unexpectedly, beseechingly he took her hand. His signet ring tapped her wedding ring. 'Alexandra you will come back, won't you? Promise me you'll come back.' She was dismayed to see a tear slide down his cheek, followed by another.

Recalling the time when he himself had walked out without a backward look and had never come back, Alexandra said, 'Of course I will! Meanwhile I brought you this.' She handed him a picture of herself and Oliver and the three children. One more for the album.

They left him with a mug of coffee in one hand ('Coffee is such a boring drink, Charmian. Isn't there any more champagne?') and the photograph in the other. He did not look at it but instead stared through the open window, whose curtains were still undrawn, and out into the darkness.

9

On the Friday night, Charmian went to the Circumference private view at the National Gallery. She deliberately got there early in order to watch the other guests arrive. Otherwise, she thought, by the time the whole thing becomes a crush it will be impossible to move and hard to see who *is* here. Before setting off she had done her homework and felt confident that she was absolutely up to date on the careers and achievements of the three men she had in her sights, namely Rattray-Smythe, Spivey and Cruickshank.

Standing holding a glass of champagne and a canape, Charmian surveyed the growing gathering. The air resounded with shrill cries of 'Darling!' underpinned by the hum of brittle chitchat. They all seemed to know each other and nobody took any notice of her. It was extraordinary, considering how large her circle of friends was, that there appeared to be nobody she knew. Rattray-Smythe entered. She looked for Mrs Hugo Rattray-Smythe, but once again he appeared to be on his own. Perhaps like many men of his background he kept his wife stowed away in the country. Instead he was with a tall, portly individual who, from Dominic's description, she divined must be Reg

Spivey. Chins ebbed and flowed around his shirt collar. Unaware of her critical eye he preened, putting Charmian in mind of the pompous mayor of a very small town. All he needs is one of those hats and a chain resting on that gross stomach and he's all the way there, she decided. Here it was, the chance to make a breakthrough and kill two corporate birds with one stone. She was just about to move across and buttonhole the two of them before someone else did when Neville Cruickshank emerged from the throng and accosted her.

'Ah, Charmian! So glad you could make it! Have you been round the exhibition yet?'

'No. No, I haven't,' replied Charmian, one eye on Rattray-Smythe and Spivey who appeared to be having an intense discussion. 'I thought I would try to talk to one or two people first and then enjoy the paintings.'

'Business before pleasure, eh?' Cruickshank clasped both his hands together in an oddly feminine gesture and massaged one with the other. 'In that case why don't I introduce you to my Chairman, Hugo Rattray-Smythe?'

Following in his wake it was obvious to Charmian from their body language that Rattray-Smythe and Spivey did not want to be disturbed. Rattray-Smythe half had his back to them so he did not see their approach. Spivey did, however. His rage at being interrupted was silent but palpable. Charmian wondered what on earth they had been talking about which could not have been discussed during the business day.

Impervious to nuance, Cruickshank pressed on.

'Hugo, may I introduce you to Charmian Sinclair whose company may be coming on board as our new PR agency.'

Extraordinary thing to say! Charmian thought, startled. He's showing off. He's met me once in the company of Dominic Goddard. Beyond that he knows nothing about me or my company. And as I understand it, it isn't in his gift anyway.

Spivey's extraordinary eyebrows bristled. He appeared to swell. Ignoring Charmian he said, 'What's the matter with the old one?'

Stranded halfway through his introduction, Cruickshank digressed to say uncertainly, 'Since in my view they're one of Oliver's less felicitous appointments, I thought—'

'Curtis didn't appoint them, I did!'

In the face of this irretrievable faux pas, Cruickshank's own visage was ashen. His eyes darted. It was obvious from his anguished look that he was desperately searching for a way to minimize the damage. He's terrified of Reg Spivey, thought Charmian, witnessing this. He watched the flexing of managerial muscle which culminated in the axing of Oliver and he knows that it could also happen to him. Unwittingly, in the way he no doubt did a lot of things, Hugo Rattray-Smythe came to the rescue. Hugo had been staring at Charmian with furrowed brow.

'Poor old Gerald's final farewell!' he finally exclaimed. 'That's where we met.'

'How clever of you to remember,' flattered Charmian.

'And you're going to be our PR agency!'

'According to Neville but not according to this gentleman,' said Charmian, indicating Spivey. 'So probably not.'

Cruickshank had hoped the subject had been dropped and now here it was again. He flushed.

Shooting his subordinate a disenchanted look, Spivey announced, '*I* haven't been introduced to Miss Sinclair.'

'Charmian Sinclair, Reg Spivey, Reg Spivey, Charmian Sinclair,' intoned the hapless Cruickshank.

Shaking Spivey's hand, Charmian pictured him firing Oliver.

Hugo was saying, 'Yes, Charmian and I met at Gerald Stanhope's funeral, you know, the landowner and M.P. I was at school with him.'

Impressed by this evidence that Charmian moved in the same exalted social circles as did Hugo Rattray-Smythe, Spivey prepared to be affable. Watching the transformation, Cruickshank hoped that his PR gaffe might be forgiven if not forgotten. Better to let Spivey run with this particular ball now.

'Can I get you another drink?' said Cruickshank to Charmian.

'Yes, that would be very nice.' She handed him her glass. He went, intending not to return until Spivey should have taken himself elsewhere. Spivey registered the fact that Hugo appeared to be very interested in Miss Sinclair. Feeling his nose to be out of joint here, he said, 'Perhaps I'd better go and mingle with our guests.'

'So should I,' said Hugo, suddenly remembering that he was the host. 'Why don't you let me introduce you to one or two other people, Charmian, and then, when this little soiree is over, perhaps you'd permit me to take you out to dinner?'

In Sussex Giles thought a lot about Charmian. Several times he picked up the telephone receiver to ring her, only to replace it. For what was to be gained? Perhaps it would have been better if their relationship had never had the sexual dimension so that the two of them could have gone on seeing one another as friends in spite of his liaison with Karen. Unfortunately, because this was not the way it was, he felt himself incapable of seeing Charmian without wanting to make love to her. Better not to meet in that case. It all made sense but still he languished. He wondered what she did to pass her time at weekends now that she no longer came to Sussex to see him, and shied away from the answer to this.

The first time he made love to Karen, Giles was astonished by her beauty. There was a dignity, even gravity, about her which humbled him and at the same time was combined with a passive sensuality which was very seductive. And that, Giles decided, was the difference between the two women in his life. Charmian took what she wanted. Karen waited for it to come to her. Both, when they got what they wanted, in their different ways knew what to do with it.

Giles never did pick up the telephone and neither did Charmian. Later, though much later, Giles recognized, the two of them probably would meet again but by that time other commitments and other loyalties would have distanced what had once been a very passionate affair and still was but in memory only. He was astonished to find how little in material terms he had of Charmian. No letters, no keepsakes, no photographs even, just the memory of her walking along the station platform to greet him carrying her small travelling bag. Which was the key to it all. Charmian travelled, *liked* to travel, but never really arrived.

He raised himself on one elbow and looked at his lover who lay deeply asleep beside him. Karen's face was serene. Cloudy and dark, her hair spread all over the pillow, her breathing was imperceptible. She was half covered by the white cotton sheet and the early morning sunlight filtering through the curtains bestowed a light golden bloom on round breasts, tracing and highlighting at the same time the graceful line of shoulder, neck and cheekbone and burnishing her auburn hair. She stirred and without opening her eyes reached out for him. Giles remembered that somebody had once said that the art of a successful marriage was not to choose the one you could not live without but the one you could live with. In that instant he resolved to look away from the past. Forget it never, but move on. *Oh Charmian!* He took Karen in his arms.

At the end of the private view, Charmian was taken out to dinner by both Reg Spivey and Hugo Rattray-Smythe. Watching them interact she came to the conclusion that they really were an extremely odd couple.

To begin with it was plain that each considered himself to be using the other. Spivey appeared deferential but at the same time plainly, and rightly in Charmian's opinion, considered himself to be in charge. Rattray-Smythe patronized Spivey and generally behaved like a toff but in the end did what he was told. It was, no doubt, a microcosm of their joint business life. There was an unspoken competition between them for her attention, even it seemed to Charmian, her approval. Which was tough on Reg since she had already decided that Hugo would be the winner.

'Tell me,' said Charmian ingenuously, 'about Oliver Curtis.'

Spivey's mouth became a thin little line and turned down at the corners. In his mind's eye he saw once again both the glamorous Curtises cutting a dash at various Circumference functions to the point where he, Reg Spivey, had felt upstaged. Himself a partner in a marriage which had long ago gone stale, the sight of them, easy and affectionate together, caused him to review his own situation and find it wanting. Where women were concerned he considered them to have only one role apart from organizing the household and that was flat on their backs. 'Dad, you're an unreconstructed male chauvinist!' said his daughter, a modern girl who had more spunk than her mother. 'Yes, I am,' he remembered replying, resisting the impulse to give her a clip on the ear for cheek, 'and proud of it!' But not too proud to make a tentative play for Alexandra Curtis. Who thought so little of him that she had apparently not even noticed he was doing it. Or had she?

Whether she had or she hadn't, the humiliation still rankled.

Aloud and very mean-spirited he opined, 'Ah yes, Oliver Curtis. Oliver has many qualities, but I'm afraid his character is fatally flawed.'

Not like yours, of course, thought Charmian listening to this.

'Yes,' resumed Spivey, 'there was so much I could have taught him, *did* teach him, but he thought he knew everything.'

'Whereas now,' said Hugo gloomily, 'until the appointment of the next MD, we've got nobody. And when he does finally arrive we have the learning curve.'

Nettled, Spivey said, 'It doesn't matter, Hugo. I'll guide the new incumbent.'

Yes, but where to? mentally queried Charmian, mindful of the lacklustre Circumference share price and the equally lacklustre comment in the business press concerning the company's pedestrian management and apparent absence of anything that could be described as a coherent strategy.

'But surely,' observed Charmian, 'you're too busy to be in the position of overseeing the managing directors of all the Circumference subsidiaries?'

'Reg likes to know everything that is going on. He doesn't like to delegate and when he does he reserves the right to interf—' Rattray-Smythe stopped himself just in time, amending it to, 'offer helpful suggestions.'

Quite so. Anxious to get off the subject of Oliver in case she said too much, Charmian said, 'Assuming there are some, why don't we discuss the PR opportunities?'

At the end of it all, comfortably seated in the back of Hugo's car as his chauffeur drove it in the direction of her flat, Charmian said, 'What's happened to Oliver Curtis?'

'No idea!' Hugo shrugged. 'For all I know he's still on the beach. He always struck me as a high-flyer, but Reg said not. In the end I let him have his way. No point in having a dog and barking yourself!' Any moment now he would be saying that you couldn't make an omelette without breaking eggs. It occurred to Charmian that life incarcerated in the country all week away from her husband and his platitudinous observations must come as a great relief to Mrs Rattray-Smythe. With disgust, she thought, Oliver, who's worth more than Reg and Hugo put together, worked there for twelve years and added millions to the value of that company and they simply couldn't give a damn.

Rattray-Smythe was still talking. 'Of course Reg isn't One Of Us,' said Rattray-Smythe, heartlessly consigning his Chief Executive to the outer regions of the socially damned and conveniently forgetting his own father's recent arrival on English shores as he did so. 'He'd like to be but he isn't. He's Latvian! I have to decide whether to put his name forward for a knighthood. Do you know he actually *asked* me to! Height of bad form!'

Reflecting that he seemed more exercised by this social faux pas than by Spivey's activities at Circumference, Charmian said, 'And will you?'

'I haven't decided,' said Hugo portentously, feeling almost in charge for once. The car drew up outside Charmian's mews flat. He took her hand. His felt soft and plump and limp. A pampered, lazy hand. 'What about a nightcap?' suggested Hugo hopefully. 'I could send Denis off round the block.'

'Er, not tonight, Hugo. I have to be up very early tomorrow for a client meeting.' He looked unconvinced. 'I have to leave the house at seven a.m.'

'Good Lord!' Hugo, who never rose before nine and usually did not arrive at his office until after eleven, was visibly shocked. 'Isn't that above and beyond the call of duty?'

'Not for me, no,' replied Charmian. She pressed his hand encouragingly, prior to taking back her own. 'Thank you very much for the private view and dinner, Hugo.' She extracted her keys from her small gold sling bag and prepared to get out. Denis opened the car door.

'What about lunch next week?' proposed Rattray-Smythe, anxious to regain the initiative. 'Thursday?' Due to the death of Gerald, there was now a Thursday evening slot available. Charmian briefly entertained the idea of suggesting dinner instead and then dismissed it. Better keep Hugo on the lunch circuit for as long as she could. Charmian gave him her card.

'I'd like that very much, Hugo.' With it she sent him a flirtatious smile. Hugo was dazzled.

'I'll ring you after the weekend!'

He and Denis watched her let herself into the house.

When she had finally gone, Hugo said, 'Charming! Absolutely charming! Didn't you think so, Denis?'

'Yes, sir,' affirmed Denis, more to keep the old boy quiet than anything else, since he had not in fact thought anything beyond hoping that tonight he would get home before midnight.

Inside her flat Charmian threw open the windows and then switched on her answer phone. She checked her watch: 11.30. There were four messages. The first was from Gervase Hanson.

'I thought you'd like to know that we bought the painting,' said Gervase. *Horizontal Integration.* Charmian laughed inwardly. 'Hope we're still on for Tuesday night. I thought we might take in the French film at the Curzon. I'll ring again on Monday.'

It was followed by another from Dominic Goddard.

'Dominic speaking, Friday evening, eight p.m. Look, Monday's out of court this week because Laura is unreasonably insisting that I accompany her to a parents' evening at the school.' He sounded very peeved. 'What about Thursday instead? I know the answer to any deviation from the usual arrangement is probably no, but I thought I'd ask anyway on the off chance. Incidentally, did you get anywhere with Circumference and the oleaginous Cruickshank? Give me a ring back.'

Laura's absolutely right. Dominic *should* go to the parents' meeting, thought Charmian, passing on to the next. It proved to be another of the Shall I/Shan't I variety, which culminated in no message. The silent uncertainty of the caller lasted for all of thirty seconds before the terminal click. It was Nigel Guest who picked up the baton.

'Hi, Charmian!' He sounded his usual effervescent self, one of life's eternal grasshoppers. 'I've had an invitation from Stellar to go to an orchestral concert they're sponsoring at the beginning of November at the Queen Elizabeth Hall. And guess what? It's a Wednesday, Charmian! Drinks at the interval and we get supper afterwards. Black tie. I've assumed you'll want to go and have accepted. I'll give you a bell to finalize the details. *Ciao!*' Nigel usually spent his family holidays in Tuscany.

Remembering Toby Gill, Charmian said aloud, 'I would like to go. I'd like to go very much.'

The tape announced the end of the messages and proceeded to rewind itself. No message from Giles. I know the score with Giles and yet I still feel bereft, admitted Charmian to herself. It's absurd. Whatever happened to logic?

Unable to answer this, she switched off the light and went to bed.

With the advent of October a suitably benign autumn blew in after one of the hottest summers on record. It brought with it warm breezes and the air, which had enervated and exhausted throughout the parched months, became invigorating. Under sapphire skies, the trees flamed yellow and orange, rose madder and vermilion. Alone in the country all week, Alexandra was conscious of order, tranquillity even, returning to her days and with them optimism.

At the end of September Oliver had gone to Japan on a very lucrative consultancy assignment. Having something to do even if it was not exactly what he wanted, restored his confidence and some of his old zest. Home for a long weekend, the children noticed the difference.

Nick said to Dan, 'Dad's on the way up again.'

'Yes, but he still hasn't got a job. Aunt Charmian said it would take him about a year.'

'What does she base that on?'

'*I* don't know!' Dan was irritated by his twin's dismissive tone. 'She just said he would have to get over the shock before he could move on.'

'I think she's right. You saw what he was like when it happened!' The speaker was Alice. 'After half-term he and Mummy are going away together.'

'Why?' asked Dan.

'Why do you think, dimwit?' Alice was scathing. 'Can't you see Mummy's tired out?'

Both the boys who were at an age where they really only noticed their mother when she was not on tap for the next meal, exclaimed as one, 'Is she?'

Alice cast her eyes to heaven saying as she did so, 'Ye gods!' a habit she had picked up from Alexandra. She suddenly shivered. They were all sitting in the shade of the august copper beech which presided over the end of the garden. Now that the sun was sinking in a blaze of gold there was a perceptible chill in the atmosphere. 'Yes, she is. Very tired. And she doesn't like us all being separated either. It upsets her.'

'Where are they going?'

'Sicily.'

'Where?'

'*Sicily.* You know, "The big boot of Italy kicked little Sicily…"'

'All right, Alice, no need to show off.'

As the purveyor of interesting news, Alice was smug.

Nick was moody. 'I wish we hadn't sold the London house. The country's all right, I suppose, but there's nothing to do.'

'What do you *want* to do?' As usual his little sister went straight for the jugular and as usual he didn't have an answer.

'I don't know, but I just don't want to be miles from anywhere all the time. There isn't even a cinema near here.'

Dan stared at his brother for a few seconds in silence and then observed, 'I don't suppose we can afford two houses any more.'

'Given what they did to Daddy,' said Alice, 'we're lucky we've got one! I'm going in.'

They all stood up. As they turned to face the cottage the last low rays of the sunset struck the glass of the windows causing them to refract into squares of solid gold. Walking up the garden, the three of them were separately aware that life would never be quite the same again because what had happened to their father, and more importantly, the *way* it had happened, had pushed them out of the security of childhood and into the outside adult world as it really was.

* * *

Alexandra and Oliver had a What We Do Next discussion.

'It's a question of where we base ourselves,' said Alexandra.

Her husband was silent for a moment. 'So what are you proposing?'

'I'm proposing that we re-establish in London and buy a *pied-à-terre.* Something which we could sell easily in a hurry if we had to. After all, we've got the money in the bank at the moment.'

'Yes, but how long for? There's no security of any sort in what I'm doing at present. I'm flying by the seat of my pants.'

'Darling, we *all* are, so we might as well do it together.'

Oliver had to concede that she had a point. Nevertheless, with the housing market in its present sluggish state he was reluctant to tie up capital in something which, albatross-like, might prove impossible to get rid of. It was yet another of those 'on the one hand and on the other hand' situations with which they had both become all too familiar lately.

Finally he said, 'I don't want to take a decision until we have to and we do have a few weeks' grace before it gets to that.'

Alexandra said, 'That's true, but if we do decide to go that route I have to find somewhere. I think what I'm saying is that it would be a great deal easier to flat search while house-sitting in W2 from next month rather than lurching up from the country all the time.'

Well, yes, he could see it would.

'Where is it?'

Alexandra gave a guilty start. 'Where is what?'

'The flat you've found. You're not going to tell me that you haven't already reconnoitred.' Knowing his wife as well as he did, Oliver would not have been surprised to hear that she had not only found it but had put a deposit down as well. 'Come on, darling, you might as well tell me.'

Flushed out, Alexandra stared at her husband. Very severe he stared back. They both burst out laughing.

'All right! It's a fair cop. I'll come quietly. I have been looking, and though I haven't found a flat as such I have found the block. Honestly we've plainly been together for too long. You can read me like a book. Don't you get bored with the same old story?'

'No, I don't. I love you to distraction, you know that.' He kissed her. 'Why don't you go on looking, or get your tame agent to go on looking for you? If something comes up that you think will fill the bill, we'll both go and see it.'

'I know exactly where I want to be!'

He was amused. 'Yes, I'm sure you do.'

'I wouldn't be pushing for it if I didn't think it was the right course of action.'

'I know. And I think at the end of the day you're probably correct and it *is* the right thing to do. It's just that it's so hard to plan anything in a vacuum. Christ, I wish this period of our lives was over.'

'We have to look forward not backward.'

'I realize that, but it would be a lot easier with something to look forward *to*.'

'I know.' Finding nothing further to say that she had not said already Alexandra took Oliver's hand and held it, twisting his signet ring round and round his finger, thinking as she did so: Dear God, *please* let something come up for him soon.

Lunch with Rattray-Smythe had proved to be more interesting than Charmian might have expected, mainly because he was so indiscreet. He appeared to have no conception of reticence at all and no conception of what he sounded like either. In many respects the outside world seemed to have passed him by and, very like her father, he talked as though he were the only person on the planet. Though there were contradictions. In spite of the fact that he was a fully paid-up member of the hanging and flogging brigade, he was also, it transpired, addicted to the gentle art of gardening. Or, rather, the more lordly gentle art of telling someone else how to do it for him. Which gave Charmian an idea. Giles is always strapped for cash, thought Charmian, listening to Rattray-Smythe rambling around the subject of his water feature. Hugo doesn't like the fellow who's helping him design his garden at the moment, ergo, I should do Giles a good turn and recommend *him.*

She was just opening her mouth to suggest it when Rattray-Smythe said without warning, 'What did you make of Reg Spivey?'

Charmian was at a loss for words.

'I…well…I hardly know him,' she parried. 'Why, what do you think of him?'

'I'd like to get rid of him,' replied Hugo with devastating candour, 'but I can't.'

'Why not? You're the Chairman of the company, aren't you?'

'Yes,' said Hugo, who might have added the word, *just.* 'I would have liked to be Chairman and Chief Executive, you know, but the shareholders and nonexecs wouldn't have entertained the idea, which is where Reg came in.'

'Then you're stuck with him,' observed Charmian, who had heard this story already. Was it from Dominic Goddard? 'Or with somebody very like him.'

'I'm stuck with him.' Hugo looked and sounded morose. 'Circumference used to be very paternalistic, relaxed. Reg runs it like a concentration camp. People who upset him disappear practically overnight.'

'Like Oliver Curtis?'

'Like Oliver Curtis.'

Since frankness seemed to be the order of the day, Charmian said, 'So his aim would be to replace the people who aren't his men with toadies who are with the result that, at the end of the day, all avenues of power would lead to him. You want to be careful, Hugo, his next bite could be you!'

Plainly alarmed Hugo jumped and, to her surprise, instead of dismissing such an eventuality out of hand took her point seriously. 'I don't think the board would let him get away with that. In fact I'm sure they wouldn't. My mother's family had a major stake in the company and I'm still the major shareholder.' He made the Rattray-Smythes sound like gods on Mount Olympus and clearly believed in divine right. The fact that Circumference was a publicly quoted company with people called investors appeared to be irrelevant.

'What about your wife? What's her view on Reg and the running of the company?'

He had no difficulty with that one.

'She can't stand him. Says he's exactly like one of the characters in the endless soap operas she used to follow.'

Charmian was entranced. A mental picture of Mrs Hugo Rattray-Smythe sitting in the country in baronial splendour, watching proletarian life unfold amid the homely surroundings of, say, The Rover's Return, was irresistible.

'But does she take much interest in your day-to-day problems with the running of the company? Listen and give wise counsel, that sort of thing.'

For once in his life Hugo was succinct. 'No, she doesn't.' He sounded snappy. 'Truth to tell, Charmian, my wife and I are divorced. We used to have a very satisfactory arrangement until she blew the whistle. She lived in the country, where I went at weekends, and was a pillar of the local community and I spent all week in London.'

Thinking, if I was unlucky enough to find myself married to Hugo, *I'd* want to blow the whistle too, Charmian remarked, 'Ah well, I daresay that gives you more latitude,' and waited for the inevitable.

'Yes, you see she never really understood me, not in the way you do. I think I'm right in saying you and I really do understand each other, aren't I, Charmian?'

He covered her hand which lay on the table with his own.

Charmian gave him a candid yet at the same time opaque look.

'Yes, I'm sure we do, Hugo!' But be that as it might, the next question was, having now made contact with him and established some sort of rapport, how did she get what she wanted out of him without going to bed with him? For I really couldn't stand it, thought Charmian. Not even for Alexandra could I do that.

Anxious to get off the topic of mutual understanding, she said, 'By the way, on the subject of your landscape gardening project, I have a friend who does it. If you'd like me to, perhaps I could put you in touch with one another?'

Mulling over the meeting afterwards Charmian came to the conclusion that any favours to be exacted from Hugo would have to be obtained by means of a promise of treats to come rather than on delivery. I shall have to find out about the honours system, thought Charmian, how it all works and when names have to be put forward by. She wondered who to ask. Of course the obvious candidate would have been Gerald Stanhope, but Gerald was now beyond all such frivolous things. Eventually she hit on the idea of contacting his former secretary who presumably still worked in the House and who could perhaps tell her who might be able to help her. Of course, mused Charmian, it's just possible that Hugo will decide off his own bat not to put Spivey's name forward but he's such a wimp where confrontation is concerned that I doubt it. She pulled a notepad towards her and began to make a list of all the things she had to do tomorrow.

The Maitlands invited the Curtises to the opera. *Don Carlos*. In the palmier days of a high-powered job and corporate entertaining they had both attended either the opera or the ballet at least twice a month and Alexandra looked forward to this particular performance, seeing it as a cultural oasis in what for them currently was a desert of the arts. I really do want to get back to having a place in London, thought Alexandra. The plan was that she would meet Oliver in London at the Royal Opera House.

Because the day in question was a Thursday, it occurred to her that it might be possible to fit in a visit to Father beforehand. She rang Charmian in advance to suggest this. Charmian said, 'If the opera starts at seven, you'll have to leave Peckham at six o'clock latest in order to arrive on time and park, which means I'll probably get there just as you're leaving. Never mind, it will be a bonus for Father to have both his daughters dancing attendance.'

Driving to London, Alexandra was aware that she was still in a vulnerable nervous state although it was nothing like as acute as the last time. The thing to do is to take the pressure off all around, decided Alexandra. I shall leave in plenty of time, no rushing and go straight to Peckham. En route she stopped off at an off-licence and bought the mandatory bottle of champagne.

When she arrived, Father was sitting in his usual seat by the window, with the red album open on his lap.

'Ah there you are, darling?' he said, for all the world as if she had never been away. Champagne was received as a right rather than as a gift. 'Do you remember Gstaad? 1951? The snow was wonderful that year. Who was I with?'

Not mother, that's for certain. She and I were left behind while you gallivanted! thought Alexandra. 'No idea!' she said aloud.

'Ah well, never mind.' He turned a few more pages. The doorbell rang and Charmian appeared. 'I got away earlier than I expected,' she said, 'and I brought some champagne.'

'So did I,' said Alexandra. 'Have a glass of mine.'

She poured it and was just handing it to her sister when they heard their father exclaim, 'Blow me down if it isn't Charlie Rattray-Smythe!' As one, both women stopped what they were doing and went to look over his shoulder. Father pointed to a small black-and-white snap edged with white. The races again. Rattray-Smythe senior was standing in between a statuesque brunette and a large horse whose bridle he was holding. It looked like the winner's enclosure.

'Married an old girlfriend of mine.' Remembering her parent's energetic past, Alexandra thought, probably most people did. 'Not that one,' he elaborated, pointing to the woman in the photograph, 'another one.'

'I didn't know that you knew the Rattray-Smythes,

Father,' said Charmian, looking at Alexandra over his bowed head.

'Know them? I should say so. Charlie was a mucker of mine! Course when I first met him he was fresh from the Antipodes and his name was Smythe. Bit too close for Smith for comfort, so when he and his wife married they also joined their names together thereby becoming double barrelled. And, of course, with Fiona Rattray came a large chunk of Circumference. Charlie really fell on his feet there.'

'Oh really?'

'Yes really. Charlie was thick as two planks,' pronounced Father, calling to the fore the diplomacy which had caused all his friends to desert him in the end. 'He wouldn't mind me saying that. He knew he was!'

Reflecting that there was a world of difference between Charlie saying it about himself and Father saying it, Alexandra said, 'What were the Smythes like? Before they became Rattray-Smythes I mean.'

'Like?' he thought for a bit. 'The first one was all right, the one who made all the money in Australia, but after that it was downhill all the way. They got thicker and thicker. What's the current one like?'

'He's useless too,' replied Charmian.

They all stared at Charlie who bore a startling resemblance to Hugo.

'Have they still got a part of that company?'

'Just hanging in there by the skin of their teeth,' said Charmian.

'Hugo Rattray-Smythe recently sacked my husband,' said Alexandra.

'What does your husband do?' asked Father.

'Nothing at the moment,' said Alexandra. 'I told you, he's just been fired.'

'They never could keep staff,' was Father's only retort to this.

She looked at her watch. 'I'm going to have to go, I'm afraid. I have to be at the Royal Opera House in forty-five minutes.' She kissed him on the cheek. 'Would you like me to bring the children to see you during the next school holiday?'

'Are they noisy?' Father sounded fugitive.

Giving up on it, Alexandra said, 'Think about it. You can let me know another time.'

She went.

'Alexandra and Oliver are going through a very difficult time,' said Charmian when she had gone.

'Oliver? Oh, the husband. Well, that's marriage for you,' he said dismissively. 'Couldn't abide it myself.'

'Nothing to do with marriage!' Charmian was curt. 'Oliver was well and truly shafted by the son of your old friend Charlie Rattray-Smythe.'

'Doesn't surprise me,' said Father, bored by the whole subject. 'Like Father, like son. Charlie always was a shit.'

10

Because she had the good luck to find a parking place straight away, Alexandra arrived at the Opera House early. Even so, it was already beginning to fill up. She bought a programme and a glass of dry white wine and then moved to the back of the foyer to read up on the first act. It was while she was doing that that she heard a voice at her elbow saying, 'Alexandra! How very nice to see you! Is Oliver here?'

Cruickshank. She remembered something she had said to Charmian, *appears to have the hide of a rhinoceros*. There were two other people with him, a man and a woman.

Alexandra stared at him for thirty glacial seconds in silence before saying, 'There must be some mistake. I'm afraid we've never met!'

She went back to reading her programme.

He persisted. 'Oh, come now...'

Once again she raised her eyes from the text. 'Please stop harassing me. I do not know who you are!'

Oliver arrived just in time to hear the last exchange.

'I don't know who you are either. Push off and leave my wife alone.' He took Alexandra's arm and steered her in the opposite direction. 'The Maitlands have just arrived, darling, they're over by the stairs.'

Watching them leave together, Cruickshank turned to his two mesmerized guests.

'I thought you said you were still on good terms with the Curtises,' said one of them.

'I thought I was,' said Cruickshank, lamely mendacious. 'Shall we find the rest of our party?' He hoped they would not be sitting anywhere near the Curtises.

As the two of them made their way towards the Maitlands, Oliver said, 'They're all here! Spivey, Cruickshank plus wives *inter alia*. It's like a works outing. Unless they've taken a box, we're bound to run into them in the interval.'

'I see your old sparring partners are in the audience. Though not Rattray-Smythe. I haven't seen him,' said Robert Maitland when they had exchanged greetings, 'but I have just indulged myself in the inestimable pleasure of cutting Reg Spivey dead. They went in the direction of the stalls and we're in the dress circle so hopefully we won't have to meet them again.'

But they did all meet again. In the crush bar at the first interval the two parties came face-to-face. Unwilling to incur further humiliation, Cruickshank hung back, and so did Robert Maitland who felt he had made his point already. There was a lull born of bated breath. All around, the other opera-goers boomed and brayed and laughed. With apprehension Mrs Spivey watched Alexandra Curtis, who was holding a glass of red wine which she was thoughtfully swilling around in its goblet. Oliver's wife had been known to be very impulsive

and she was well aware that if Alexandra tipped Beau-
jolais all over Reg, she, Shirley, would have to endure
the filthy rage this would provoke for months to come.

Stony-faced, Oliver said nothing. Alexandra stepped
forward. Minimally acknowledging Shirley as she did
so, she advanced on Reg. Reaching him she leant towards him as though about to kiss him on the cheek.

There was a universal sigh of relief from the Circumference cortège. I always thought Alexandra Curtis
was a very *civilized* girl, reflected Shirley.

Oliver watched his wife with astonishment. What on
earth did she think she was doing? Alexandra did not,
in fact, kiss Spivey but appeared to say something to
him instead. Nobody could hear what this was. When
she had finished she stepped back a pace and smiled
at him.

So *very* civilized. Shirley was full of admiration.

It was disconcerting, therefore, to see her husband's
face become dark red the way it did when he flew into
a rage, which was quite frequently. The colour rose
above the wing collar of his white dress shirt and
moved slowly up his face as though somebody was
topping him up with blood. Alexandra drank her wine
at a swallow and, turning away, said to Robert as she
did so, 'If there is any room, would you mind if we
stood out on the balcony for a while? It's suddenly
very hot in here!'

'Not at all.' The Maitlands led the way.

As they followed Oliver said to Alexandra, 'What
on earth did you say to him? I thought, no, *hoped,* he
was going to have a fit.'

'I said, "You're a treacherous bastard and, by the way, I know what's going on at Circumference. You won't get away with it! The secret's out!"'

He stared at her. 'Yes and you clearly struck a nerve, but what did you *mean* exactly? What secret?'

'Oh, just something a little bird told me.' They caught up with the Maitlands. 'I'm sorry you were subjected to that,' apologized Alexandra. 'I think we should now agree not to mention Circumference for the rest of the evening or ever again, if you prefer. Tell me all about India. Was it wonderful? How long were you there?'

In the gentlemen's lavatory where they had both gone for a pee, Spivey said to Cruickshank, 'She knows. Alexandra Curtis knows that something is going on. Which means that Oliver Curtis knows as well. *I* haven't let the cat out of the bag.' He pointed an aggressive accusing finger. 'So it must have been *you!*'

Zipping himself up, Cruickshank protested, 'I haven't said a word to anyone! You'll find Rattray-Smythe's been shooting his mouth off!'

'Hugo couldn't have, he doesn't understand what's happening. It *must* have been you!'

Reg was clearly in a very nasty mood indeed. Panicking, Cruickshank began to bluster. 'It wasn't me, Reg. I *swear* it wasn't! I've got just as much to lose as you have!'

This at least was true.

'Well, who was it then?'

Neither of them could come up with an answer to that.

'Perhaps Alexandra was just guessing.'

'Why would that sort of thing cross her mind at all? Circumference's reputation is of the highest. Blue chip!'

Neither of them could come up with an answer to that either.

'What did she say precisely?' asked Cruickshank.

Omitting the words *treacherous bastard,* which still rankled, Spivey told him, 'She said "I know what's going on. You won't get away with it. The secret's out!"' He was clearly rattled.

'And that's all she said? She could mean anything, Reg. She can't know what's going on. I haven't told her or anyone else, you haven't and we are the only two who know.'

An announcement informed them that *Don Carlos* was about to recommence. Flapping his programme to right and left so that other opera-goers parted to let him through, Spivey cruised like a giant squid towards his seat in the stalls. Trailing glumly along in his self-important wake, Cruickshank, who did not like opera, reflected that not only was he being subjected to a very long evening of awful music but now he had had a row with his Chief Executive as well. Well aware that Reg was dangerous when upset and had an unlovely habit of neither forgiving nor forgetting, he mentally resigned himself to a future of watching his step very carefully.

Toby Gill, who was also in the audience that evening with his very ancient Aunt Harriet, whose birthday it was, witnessed the encounter between the Spivey contingent and the Maitland party with a certain amount of sardonic amusement. In common with everybody else who saw it, he wondered what Mrs Oliver Curtis could possibly have said to produce such an apoplectic reaction. He would probably never know. The lights dimmed and the orchestra struck up.

'We're off!' said Aunt Harriet adjusting her hearing aid.

During the next interval it had been Gill's intention to catch up with the Curtises and the Maitlands. In fact the first person he ran into was Reg Spivey.

'Toby!' exclaimed Spivey, hailing him as one would greet an old friend.

'Reg!' said Gill. 'Allow me to introduce my aunt, Mrs Harriet Gill.'

Harriet debated whether to say, 'Not Mrs Gill, Harriet, please!' and then, sizing up her man, decided not to.

'Reg Spivey, Chief Executive of Circumference,' proclaimed Spivey, shaking her hand, and sounding as he said it like a major domo announcing himself. 'Neville Cruickshank, my Finance Director.' Their wives, who had gone off to the loo reappeared necessitating another round of introductions. Impatient to get away, Gill stared past Spivey's head but could see no sign of Oliver Curtis and his wife.

'We're about to crack a bottle of champagne,' said Spivey munificently. 'Why don't you join us?'

'Thank you, but no,' replied Gill politely but without warmth. 'We have the remains of a bottle of Chablis over there and I think we had better catch up with it.'

He nodded and turned away. Feeling that he had been casually treated and uncertain why, Spivey watched him move through the throng until he stopped and talked to Robert Maitland from whom both he and Mrs Gill did accept a drink, finally engaging in animated conversation with the Curtises. Still smarting from the treatment meted out by Maitland earlier in the evening, Spivey felt himself to have been on the receiving end of another snub. On top of that he felt himself upstaged all over again. This evening, which had promised so well, was turning out to be unsatisfactory. With apprehension Cruickshank watched the face of his boss set into an increasingly familiar mould of discontent and was conscious of the fact that working for someone with quite such an unpredictable capacity for high dudgeon meant that in spite of his recent gratifying promotion, for which he had angled tirelessly and disloyally during the months leading up to it, he Neville, could be said to be skating on very thin ice indeed. Being singled out for high office by Reg was feeling increasingly like being singled out for high office by Henry VIII.

As he talked to Alexandra Curtis, Toby Gill was struck by two things about her. The first was her apparent ability to rise above what he knew from personal and painful experience must have been a colossal and humiliating blow for her and her husband, and the second was a sense of recognition which would not go away, a feeling of *déjà vu* and yet, at the same time, he was certain that he and she had never met before. So what was it? For the moment he gave up on it.

They prepared to go back to their seats for the last act.

Allowing her nephew to settle her into her seat and retrieve her programme for her which had slipped to the floor, Harriet said, 'I hope you won't mind me saying so, but that was an absurd man.'

'Spivey, you mean, or should I say Reg Spivey, Chief Executive of Circumference!' He shot her a droll look. 'You're quite right, he is absurd. Powerful though.'

Harriet rummaged in her small black velvet evening bag for her opera glasses.

'And has nobody ever told him that wing collars are naff?'

When the evening was over Alexandra and Oliver drove back to Hampshire together. It was 1.30 in the morning and the roads were empty. Skimming along the motorway at that hour as though they were the only people on the planet was exhilarating. Disillusion and disappointment fell away and were replaced in Alexandra's case anyway by a sudden surge of optimism and hope. The night sky was clear and a tilted crescent moon rode queenly and high. One day, thought Alexandra, I will look, *we* will look back on this period and say, it all seemed so important and so catastrophic at the time and yet, look at us now. We have achieved what seemed impossible and passed beyond the rage and the grief and gone on to something better. None of it has the power to touch us ever again.

She turned her head and looked at her husband.

Keeping his eyes on the road as it unwound before them to the horizon, Oliver said, 'There's no need to say anything. I feel it too!'

Alexandra was struck by the sudden upturn in morale. The improvement had been happening for some time but here she sensed a quantum leap forward, almost as though that evening's encounter with Spivey and Cruickshank had been cathartic because, just by meeting them as a duo, Oliver had been forced to jump a fence which up till now he had found too high, and now he had done it, knew that he could.

'Fuck them!' said Oliver. 'I'll show them!'

Their unexpected arrival at the cottage dispersed a horde of rabbits and put up a deer. There was a slight breeze which stirred the tinder-dry leaves still on the trees and blew those on the ground hither and thither with a faint rattle. The cool air smelt of earth and old stone.

Letting them both into the house, Oliver said, 'Oh, by the way, I meant to tell you and forgot. Toby Gill asked me what was going on at Circumference. A City analyst who's a chum of his reckons that something is going on there but nobody seems to know quite what. Or, and more likely, if they do know they aren't saying. Apparently the share price instead of bumping along the bottom has been bucketing about a bit lately for no discernible reason.'

'How very odd,' answered Alexandra after a pause. 'I say that because Marcus Marchant received exactly the same impression and he couldn't pin it down to anything in particular either. He thought maybe a takeover might be in the air. I meant to keep an eye on the share price and what with one thing and another haven't done it. I will now though.'

'Too much to hope for, of course, but it would be wonderful if there was an upset there.'

'Wouldn't it!'

11

Dominic Goddard had surprising news for Charmian the next time they met. As they idled their way through Soho after lunch, Dominic said, 'I'm going abroad. At least, that is Laura and I are going abroad.'

This speech was delivered with an apocalyptic air. They turned into a small London garden square and sat down.

'Not to France again, surely?' enquired Charmian, mystified.

'No. Hong Kong.'

'*Hong Kong!* What are you going to do there?'

Dominic sighed. 'Same as I'm doing here only for more money. I would have turned it down but Laura, who wants me out of London, insisted we take it. She's in a terrific bate.'

'What about?'

'She found some letters!'

No need to ask what sort of letters.

'Well, I'm innocent! I've never written you any!'

'No, from your predecessor!'

'Nicely put! You don't really mean to tell me that you keep all your adulterous love letters in the house! Whatever happened to bank vaults?'

Dominic was silent.

'You do! Don't tell me! Tied up with pink ribbon and secreted at the back of your sock drawer.'

'Thanks a lot, Charmian, I knew I could count on you to sympathize. It's no laughing matter, you know.'

No, Charmian could see that it was not.

'Why Hong Kong?'

'Partly because I've been seconded to a top job there and as you know after my career accident I've never managed to re-establish at the same level, but mainly because Laura feels she can't trust me out of her sight. It's to be called A Fresh Start. I don't suppose there's any hope of *you* moving to Hong Kong, Charmian, is there? Lots of opportunity, I'm told.'

'No, there isn't, I'm afraid. And it wouldn't be A Fresh Start if I did, would it?' Thinking as she said it, it's beginning to look like a fresh start for me too. First Gerald fell by the wayside, then Giles defected and now Dominic. That only leaves Gervase and Nigel, though I have to say that on all sorts of levels Nigel is beginning to get on my nerves.

With an effort she turned her attention back to Dominic, who was saying regretfully, 'Yes, I thought you'd say that. Anyway, the idea is that we'll throw a farewell party for friends before we leave and naturally you'll be invited. Do say you'll come!'

'Of course I will! How long are you going for?'

'Two years, possibly longer.'

'What about the children?' Charmian was conscious of sounding more like a wife than a wife.

'They'll come too.' Dominic looked embattled.

'Oh come on! *Courage!*' Charmian was mischievous. 'Not everyone gets the chance of The Fresh Start you know. But, more importantly, *when* are you going?'

'Soon. Because it's a secondment I don't have the inconvenience of working out my notice here. It's all been arranged. Laura will follow me out at the end of the school term.'

'So the party is…?'

'Exact date to be decided.'

Charmian felt suddenly sad.

'I'll miss you,' she said, meaning it. 'On the other hand it's probably time my life took a different turn as well.'

Since she never talked about the way she passed her time when not with him except in the most general terms, Dominic was intrigued and emboldened to ask, 'Why, what's the matter with your life? I thought you were happy with things as they were. You always used to say you were.'

'I was. But things aren't as they were any more. For one thing I'm getting older and for another there are changes happening all around which are beyond my control. Like you going to Hong Kong. But as I say, it's not just you, it's all around. I know that nothing will ever be the same again and half of me wants it and half of me doesn't.'

Never having heard her talk like this before, Dominic was at a loss as to what to say. One statement had altered the balance of their relationship, or maybe it was true to say that there never had been a balance for it was suddenly plain to him in the light of her last sentence that Charmian had no centre of gravity and had possibly only just realized this fact, which meant that there had been an inherent instability which nobody, not even herself, had known about. Perhaps it was just as well he was going to Hong Kong, for while Charmian brilliant and independent presented one face, Charmian introspective and insecure presented quite another. In his childhood Dominic had had a nanny who had been fond of saying, 'Handsome is as handsome does.' Another favourite platitude had been, 'All good things come to an end.' Though the first of these trite utterances had seldom, if at all, impinged much on Dominic's life, it now looked as if the second one was about to make its mark. And it was with the end in sight that he looked afresh at his mistress wondering, as he did so, how differently he would see her if they had been married for years, as had he and Laura, to the point where familiarity had bred, not contempt or even boredom but certainly predictability. Laura felt secure enough in her marriage to display less endearing facets of her personality such as tiredness and bad temper after a day at home with the children. Because he had only ever spent what the Americans call prime time with Charmian until today Dominic had never seen her anything but well groomed and in good spirits. It was easy, he saw, to maintain this front and have a spurious superiority over somebody such as Laura who, apart from the joint joys of parenthood, had a great deal of dross to contend with and not as much fun. In spite of the very unpleasant row they had just had he felt a sudden remorse and tenderness at the thought of his wife. Maybe A Fresh Start was the answer after all. He stood up, consulting his watch as he did so. Two fifteen. The little park was beginning to empty.

'Better get back,' said Dominic. 'I've a lot to do and not very much time in which to do it.'

He held out his hand and pulled Charmian towards him. For all to see he kissed her goodbye, something he never normally did. And it *was* goodbye. Eyes closed, arms by her sides, Charmian let him. The warm sun of autumn fell on her face. A light air stirred the fallen leaves, shortly to be swept up by the park keeper. All my life, thought Charmian, I was positive that I had what I wanted and now, now I'm no longer certain what that is.

Registering a difference and with it his lover's uncharacteristic inertia, Dominic released her.

'As soon as I can, I'll let you know the time and venue of the party.'

They went their separate ways.

Regardless of whether he wanted to or not, Alexandra decided to insist that Father meet the rest of his family. The prospect made him fretful and he said as much to Charmian.

'Oh, come on, a day in the country will do you good. Don't you want to see your grandchildren?'

'No, not particularly,' said Father.

Out of patience with it, Charmian said, 'Well, they

do want to see *you*. You never know, you might enjoy yourself.'

'Doubt it. What's Alexandra's husband like?'

Since he had never before shown the slightest interest, Charmian was encouraged.

'Oliver? Oliver's an old Harrovian and has, or had, the impervious self-assurance endemic to that particular breed. I say had, because as you know he's been fired, so mind you don't say anything tactless.'

'As if I would!' was Father's unselfaware answer to this. 'Do you like him?'

'*Quite!*' Charmian was uncertain how to answer this. 'And he *quite* likes me. What we have in common is Alexandra, whom we both adore.' She thought for a moment. 'Oliver's intelligent and very ambitious. I think my reservation in so far as I have one, is that he's good company on his day but not witty company. On the other hand if he'd had a lighter touch it's possible he wouldn't have got as far as he did career-wise.'

Father sniffed. 'Doesn't sound to me as though he's currently anywhere career-wise.'

'No, he isn't, but it's a racing certainty that he will be. Meanwhile Alexandra's there for him in the same way that he has always been there for her.'

Speaking these words, Charmian experienced a poignant and unaccustomed pang of regret. *For at the end of the day there is no one there for me.*

'Huh!' said Father.

'You're jealous!' retorted Charmian.

'Jealous? Of course I'm jealous!' replied Father. 'I

don't want other men around my girls while I'm still here to protect them!'

Good God, you've got a nerve, was Charmian's mental reaction to this, mindful of all the years during which they had seen neither hide nor hair of Father.

'But, I'm sure you'd agree that it's always useful to have a reserve,' she said aloud.

'Yes, I suppose so,' he agreed, deciding as he said it to be oblivious to ironical intent.

'How do you want to travel down?' asked Charmian, in order to avoid, by just assuming that he would go, a lot of pointless discussion. 'I usually let the train take the strain when I go to the country, but if you would prefer to go by car I'm quite happy to drive you.'

'Go by public transport?' He looked horrified. 'Definitely not! Car if you please, Charmian. What sort of car is it?'

Before starting to field this one Charmian consoled herself with the thought that at least she had coaxed him to the starting gate as far as going at all was concerned.

'It's *my* car. That's all you need to know.'

The day in question dawned fair. By now it was nearly the end of October. The following week, at the end of half term, Oliver and Alexandra were due to fly to Sicily before commencing their house-sitting London incarnation. Father and his photographic albums sat in the front seat of her car beside Charmian. Her unpredictable parent was unexpectedly animated, verging on cheerful and, for once, seemed to have his mind firmly fixed on the present.

The old devil, thought Charmian, inserting herself into the heavy motorway traffic from the slip road, after all that complaining and prevaricating I do believe he's looking forward to today but typically would die rather than admit it.

It was mid-morning when they arrived. Alexandra and Alice came out to greet them.

'The men are playing tennis,' said Alexandra, kissing her father and then Charmian. 'Father, this is Alice.'

'How do you do, Alice?' said Father, in Olympian mode. 'And how old are you?'

Reflecting that Father never had had a clue where children were concerned and that he sounded like a royal touring a factory, Charmian heard him get his comeuppance.

'Don't you know, Grandfather?' said Alice.

The new relation winced. 'Not *Grandfather,* Alice! *Never* Grandfather!'

Perplexed, Alice stared at him.

'You may call me Austin!'

With one eye on her mother, 'Thirteen,' said Alice. 'Nearly fourteen.' Father cocked his head to one side and waited. 'Austin.'

They all followed Alexandra into the house. As they did so, Charmian heard Austin say to Alice, 'And what do you hope to do when you grow up, Alice?' followed by Alice replying in kind, with starchy dignity, 'I am nearly fourteen! I *am* grown up, Austin.'

Which was more than one could say for Father.

Listening to it Charmian thought, Father's really fallen on his own sword this time. If he hadn't been too vain to allow *Grandfather,* deference would have been his lot. As it is he's landed himself with equality instead. Turning back towards the car for something she had forgotten she heard Father in dreadful arch celebration of this piece of intelligence say, 'Fourteen, eh? Ah ha! Won't be long before we have to find you a duke, eh, Alice? What a pity all my old address books are out of date.'

Alice's reply to this was inaudible. Later on, at the tennis court where she had been dispatched to tell the twins that lunch was ready, Alice said, 'He wants us to call him Austin.'

'Who does?'

'Grandfather does.'

'Austin!' They spoke as one.

'Why doesn't he want to be called Grandfather like everyone else and where's he been all this time anyway?' The speaker was Dan.

'Search me!' Alice shrugged.

Back at the house in the kitchen, Alexandra was saying to Oliver, who had returned from the tennis court in advance of the boys, 'Father wants the children to call him Austin.'

Taking off his tennis shoes, Oliver said, 'Why can't he just be Grandfather like everybody else?'

'Search me!'

'Anyway, never mind about that. Time we met. Where is he?'

'Out in the garden sitting under the apple tree with Charmian.'

Lunch with Father, also known as Austin, turned out to be an education for them all, for Father, elegant, silvery-haired, perfectly mannered Father revealed himself to be a social terrorist. He did not care what he said, scathingly dissecting family, friends and foes with impressive impartiality, laying waste such old-fashioned virtues as discretion and loyalty without a second thought.

It was not, however, until the children had all left the table and the rest of them were enjoying their coffee that Father made his significant contribution. He said to Oliver, 'Alexandra tells me that you've been shafted by Charlie Rattray-Smythe's son. Well, hear this. The Rattray-Smythe art collection is composed mainly if not totally of copies. And that probably goes for the odd painting in the Circumference corridors as well. I'd like a brandy with this if you don't mind, Alexandra.'

'How do you know? Are you sure he wasn't having you on? You've never told me that before!' said Charmian.

'Never needed to! Charlie spilled the beans one night when he was in his cups. *In vino veritas.* Of course he always was a gambler and not a very fortunate one. After my money ran out I used to stand around in Crockfords watching him lose his. But it wasn't just that. It was girls and horses and yachts. All the usual little extravagances. Anyway finally, like mine, his cash ran out but Charlie never told anyone. A refill would be appreciated, Alexandra. No, he never told a soul but started sending the paintings, some of which were masterpieces, off for cleaning and restoration. They went to that fellow Van something or other. To cut a long story short, what went out was not the same as what came back. Presumably most of it went to private collections to afford certain individuals their own private gloat. I wouldn't know, but suffice it to say he went on doing it for years—and I'll bet one or two important company paintings didn't escape his attention either.'

'But surely, although I can see that he could get away with it in his own house, *surely* the company canvasses were looked after by experts?' protested Charmian.

'No, they weren't,' said Oliver. 'They were taken completely for granted. The top echelon of Circumference are Philistines almost to a man.'

'In Charlie's day the company was run like his own private fiefdom. I used to wonder how he laundered the huge amounts of money he must have been getting. Swiss bank account I guessed, or maybe he kept it in an old pair of Elizabethan tights under his four-poster. Though I don't suppose it was allowed to sit around for long. Of course, after he died there was no sign of any of it and, because Charlie had always been assumed to be fabulously wealthy, there was a sensation when the will was published, though not among his old muckers who had all watched him pouring money into the Crockfords coffers for years.' Father gave a sardonic smile. 'Another little refill, please, Alexandra. What's the current one called?'

'Hugo,' said Oliver. 'He's a complete shit.'

'So was Charlie, God rest his soul.'

'It raises the question,' said Oliver, 'of what Hugo did for money in the wake of this disaster. I wouldn't have thought Charlie was the sort to salt money away for a rainy day, so what about death duties and so on?'

'You'll probably find he's living off a massive loan secured by the paintings,' said Alexandra.

'Well, he must be living off something, but I have to say given the fact that along with everybody else I had always presumed there was loads of Rattray-Smythe money in the bank, it did often occur to me to wonder why he continued coming into Circumference when it was plain that the whole work process bored him so much. Now we know why. He needed the cash.'

'But why do you think *he's* never tried to sell a painting or two to take the pressure off?'

'God help him if he does,' forecast Father.

'Either he knows they are fakes or he isn't allowed to sell under the terms of a family trust. If Charlie had had the wit to organize such a thing it would have insured that the fraud continued to remain a secret,' said Oliver.

'Charlie wasn't a great brain, but he could be devious as we've seen. Alexandra, what about another little—'

'There isn't any left!'

'Why have you kept quiet about this till now, Father?' asked Charmian.

'Nobody to tell really. They're all dead.'

And then suddenly querulous again, 'Where's Alice? I want Alice. I want to show her my photograph albums. Oh, there you are, Alice. Come and sit by me. Now look, Alice, this is Cap Ferrat and this, this is Monaco. Those were the days, Alice!'

Driving Father home afterwards, Charmian brought up again the subject of the paintings.

'I don't know why you're so interested,' remarked Father, 'but since you are, Charmian, all I can say is that Charlie wouldn't lie about something like that. Besides which, it was exactly the sort of thing he would have done. "Why not, Austin?" he said to me, "It's my art collection, I can do what I like with it!"'

'Yes, quite so,' agreed Charmian, 'but passing fakes off as originals and raising money by doing it is fraud!'

'Not if you don't get caught, it isn't,' said her delinquent parent, who appeared to have no moral dimension at all. Charmian decided to give up on that aspect of it. He was never going to change now. She decided to concentrate on the practical instead.

'What if you'd told somebody else?'

'I'd known Charlie for years. Charlie had enough on me to be certain I wouldn't breathe a word.' Startled, Charmian looked sideways at Father. Of course she knew that he had never been too scrupulous in his affairs with the women in his life, but this sounded like something else entirely. Better not to ask. She concentrated on the road ahead.

It seemed he was going to tell her anyway.

'We used to do business together. Deals.' Without a trace of false modesty he followed this up with, 'I had the brains and, before he lost it, Charlie had the cash.' No problem about losing money with Father in the offing, was Charmian's view as she negotiated a roundabout. He never had had the faintest clue about business either come to that.

'What happened to all the money you made? Assuming you did actually make some.'

'Well, we did make some but then we lost it all again.'

Tell me the old, old story, thought Charmian digesting this. 'But getting back to the paintings, wasn't Charlie afraid of being found out?'

'No,' pronounced Father, 'he wasn't. Charlie thought it was all a lark. Said to me that by the time anybody found out what he was doing, he'd be pushing up the daisies and he was right.'

'But what about his son and heir? Wasn't he concerned for Hugo's sake even if he didn't care about the company?'

'Charlie only ever cared about Charlie,' opined Father with searing honesty. 'When I was in Queer Street he wouldn't advance me so much as a shilling. Imagine that, Charmian, and he was a friend of mine!'

It appeared that even after all these years this omission still rankled. Charlie must have seen the light.

'What did you say happened to Alexandra's husband?'

'Do you mean Oliver, Father?'

'Oliver,' said Father reluctantly, and then in a burst of peevishness: 'It's too bad. I don't see my daughter for all those years and then when we do finally meet up again I can't have her to myself because she's got a husband in tow.'

'Yes, Alexandra's very thoughtless like that,' agreed Charmian demurely. 'Getting back to your superfluous son-in-law, he was fired by Rattray-Smythe's employee, Reg Spivey, so to all intents and purposes by Rattray-Smythe himself.'

Father mulled this over and then lobbed another little hand grenade into the conversation. 'Charlie was never sure that Hugo was his son! Yes, room for doubt there. Fiona Rattray-Smythe was a goer. She's in the photographic album!' He chortled knowingly.

Charmian froze.

'You're not saying that you and…?'

'No,' said Father. 'Though many were called *and* chosen, I was not one of them. At least I don't think I was.'

'Can't you remember?' Charmian was severe.

'No, I'm pretty sure I wasn't. It was a long time ago, you know, and you have to allow for the fact that there was a lot going on. I was busy, busy, busy!'

Busy doing nothing more like, thought Charmian.

'Besides,' continued Father, 'she wasn't really my type. Very bossy. Never could stand bossy women. Lots of money though.' He sounded wistful. Unreassured by the vagueness of his answer, Charmian made a mental resolution to look up Hugo's date of birth in *Who's Who* and then conduct a trawl through the photograph albums to try to discover where Father had been nine months earlier. With a bit of luck the answer would be indulging himself abroad on one of his lengthy sojourns either in the sun or on skis, depending on what time of year it had been.

When she had dropped him off, Charmian drove back to her own flat, thinking about Hugo. For now, assuming her unreliable parent had been telling the truth, there was no need to butter up Hugo since she had the lever with which to make him do anything she wanted. Or, rather, anything which only he and she knew about. Where the reinstatement of her brother-in-law was concerned, for instance, Hugo would have to explain himself to Reg Spivey and the board. After which there would be uproar, without a doubt, but no change for Oliver.

Back at home Charmian took off her shoes and went through the familiar ritual. A message from Dominic informed her that he was unable to see her on Monday as usual. There was no explanation for this, just a commitment to telephone her the following day. Dominic, it appeared, was slipping away.

Hard on the heels of this communication came the well-rounded vowels of Hugo Rattray-Smythe. Hugo was apparently not at ease with the answer phone. There was a certain degree of throat clearing and uming and ahing before he even managed to achieve the date and time of his call and who he was. There was then a baffled silence, followed by a sudden rush at the message. With no secretary to do it for him he must have been marshalling his own thoughts.

'What I wondered,' said Hugo, 'was whether you would like to come and spend the weekend in Gloucestershire. I could show you the sunken garden and the water feature?'

Well, yes, she supposed he could. If that was what he had in mind, it was certainly a new departure in seduction. And I'd like to see the Rattray-Smythe pile, Charmian suddenly decided. Spend a weekend in the country. The silence from Giles had been total.

Having got the bulk of it off his chest, Hugo was now circling around the Arrangements, apparently assuming that she was able to come. 'Perhaps Denis could pick you up and drive you down,' speculated Hugo, who seemed unable to make a decision about anything.

On the whole, Charmian thought this a bad idea. Just in case it all went wrong, she would need the security of an escape route in the reassuring form of her own transport. There was no indication as to the absence or presence of his wife.

'I'll telephone you tomorrow to finalize things,' promised Hugo.

It was interesting that he seemed certain of her acceptance.

The following day, Charmian set aside half an hour before lunch to try to track down somebody who could tell her how the honours system worked, and on what sort of timescale. The first person she rang was Gerald

Stanhope's old secretary, Miss Pettit. Miss Pettit, who had never been quite sure that she approved of Miss Sinclair, sounded wary. In the course of arranging Gerald Stanhope's various assignations for him (all of which, including those with Miss Sinclair, had gone into the diary as official lunches, dinners, etc.) she had more than once found herself on the wrong side of the terrifying Mrs Stanhope. Of course Gerald was dead and Miss Pettit was now working for somebody else, but nevertheless the voice of Charmian Sinclair raised some old ghosts. There had been one memorable occasion when Mrs Stanhope had confronted her, Miss Pettit, concerning her husband's extra-Parliamentary activities and had subjected his secretary to what Miss Pettit later referred to as the third degree. Between the hammer and the anvil had been another description.

It therefore came as a great relief to discover that Miss Sinclair was not, in fact, conducting an affair with Miss Pettit's current boss, or at least not yet anyway, but wanted to know all about the honours system and how it operated.

'I'm afraid I can't help you,' answered Miss Pettit, 'but I can give you the telephone number of an office that can. One moment, please.' There was the sound of leafing. 'Here it is. Have you got a pen?' She dictated a number.

Writing it down, Charmian said, 'Thank you. And how are things with you?'

Prune-faced and very prim, Miss Pettit replied, 'Oh really, I can't complain. And with you?'

'No, I can't complain either,' said Charmian, entering into the lacklustre spirit of the thing. 'That's very helpful, Miss Pettit. I'll ring them now.'

Going back to the Dictaphone Miss Pettit wondered what connection there could possibly be between Miss Sinclair and the honours list.

The office in question was very informative, even offering to send a proposal form. It transpired that the next list which would be the Birthday Honours was due to be published in June. 'But ideally we require names to be submitted a year in advance,' said whoever it was.

'And then what happens?'

'The recipients are informed two months in advance but the sponsors do not find out if their recommendations have been accepted until the list appears. That's it, really.'

'That's all I need to know,' said Charmian. She hung up and proceeded to count backwards. It was possible that she was too late. Although, she thought, in spite of the fact that they say a year, I'll bet they're still receiving suggestions up to six months ahead. I'll ask Hugo this weekend if he's done anything about it.

The week was a hectic one and by the time it drew to its close Charmian found herself looking forward to getting out of London. It was still unusually warm, and in Charmian's small office suite in Covent Garden, particularly airless. Even the cool waxen lilies, bought only the day before, looked flaccid. Not for the first time, she wished she had air conditioning.

It was on the Friday morning before her trip to Gloucestershire that the letter arrived from Mother.

This was surprising because Mother, who lived in Ibiza where she ran a bar with a Russian and who was not a renowned correspondent, had written just the week before. It must be bad news. It was.

Charmian, stated Mother, *I am writing to tell you that Vlad* (the Russian) *is dead. Heart attack. Out like a light. There one minute, gone the next.* Put like that, it sounded heartless but Mother's style of writing always had been staccato and seemed to have got worse as she got older. She was a born writer of telegrams. Charmian, who had never liked the Russian, which was why she had seen so little of Mother for the past few years, read on. *Time to sell up and come home.* Oh, heavens! This was the bad news. Her eyes glazed. Now it looked as if she was going to have not just one difficult parent on her hands but two. *No living next of kin. I get all of it. Money of my own for the first time since the divorce. Can't wait to get out of here! Chelsea, I thought. Don't tell the O. R. Love, M.*

That was it. End of letter. *O. R.* Old Reprobate. Don't tell Father.

Try as she would, Charmian could not imagine the lean, walnut-coloured, gin-swilling ex-pat that was now Mother back on the chilly shores of England at all, let alone in SW3. Of course you never know, thought Charmian, without much hope in her heart, it might never happen.

Travelling to Gloucestershire on the Saturday morning took her mind off it. Charmian drove very fast with the hood of her little sports car down. The sheer exhilaration of speed and the wind streaming through her hair lifted her spirits and, as she drove, she thought about the elusive, attractive Toby Gill.

12

The entrance to the Rattray-Smythe grounds was guarded by two ornately impressive iron gates, which stood open, presumably in anticipation of Charmian's arrival. Beyond them the tree-lined drive swept in a languorous curve and continued in this serpentine fashion for at least a mile. Charmian was just beginning to wonder what had happened to the house when she turned another corner and there it was. Though substantial, it was not as big as might have been expected from the length of the drive. Georgian, thought Charmian, and very pretty too. Its buttery stuccoed fascia seemed to absorb the sun rather than reflect it. Mellow was the word that came to mind. Behind, the land rose, protectively cupping the house like a pale square citrine in the hollow of a hand. Slowing right down in order to look at it, Charmian could quite see why Hugo was so obsessed with his mansion and its setting.

She speeded up, still concentrating on the view, and nearly ran over someone who was slowly ambling up the drive on foot. She put her hand briefly on the horn. He turned round.

'Good God!' exclaimed Charmian.

It was Giles Hayward.

He was equally astounded. 'What are *you* doing here?' said Giles.

'I'm here on business,' replied Charmian, 'in a manner of speaking.' And then, knowing the answer perfectly well, 'What about you?'

'Hugo Rattray-Smythe rang me out of the blue. He wants me to help him redesign his garden. I've no idea how he found out about me.'

'I recommended you,' said Charmian. 'I told him not to tell you. He must have forgotten. Efficiency is not Hugo's middle name.'

'So I've noticed,' said Giles, 'and I've only spent half an hour with him so far. He doesn't seem able to make his mind up about anything. I'm just down for the day. What about you?'

'I'm here for the weekend.'

'On *business*? For the whole weekend? When his wife's away?' Giles was firstly incredulous and then put out.

'She's always away. They're divorced. Look why don't you get in?'

'No, thank you. I'd rather walk!'

'Giles, don't be stupid…'

'Oh, and if you're really here on business as you say, *if* you are, you'll be required to park at the back of the house. Tradesman's entrance and all that.' He turned away. He was clearly very disapproving. Considering that he stood me down in order to see more of Karen, reflected Charmian, driving the last little bit at ten miles per hour in deference to the sign which asked her to, for Giles to start being grumpy and possessive really takes the bun!

She ground to a halt at the front in a scatter of gravel, thinking: And I'm not parking at the back for anyone!

Hugo materialized at the head of the steps.

'Ah, Charmian! Here you are!' He took her grip. 'Did I see you talking to our gardener chappy? What did you think of him?'

Hoping that Hugo was not going to continue in this patronizing vein when Giles finally deigned to join them, Charmian said, 'Hugo, I already *know* Giles Hayward. It was me who suggested that you get in touch with him!'

'Good Lord, was it? I'm all at sea when my secretary isn't with me, you know!'

'Oh, and by the way, Giles is not any old gardener, he's a very talented garden designer, particularly good at landscape. Like Capability Brown. But prickly as befits the artistic temperament.'

'Yes. Capability Brown was prickly,' reminisced Hugo. 'I know…'

Startled, Charmian said, 'How do you know? Bit before your time, wasn't he?'

'He designed the park belonging to an ancestor of friends of mine. They kept a garden book. Wrote it all down. That's how I know. Very difficult. Threatened to quit every time one of the family had the temerity to make a suggestion about their own land.'

'Well then, you know what a minefield the gentle

art of gardening can be,' said Charmian. 'Here comes Giles now.'

Giles was the sort of sulker who was able to operate on two levels. That is, he was pleasant to Hugo but able to exude *froideur* in Charmian's direction at the same time as appearing to be polite.

There are times when I think Giles needs to grow up, thought Charmian, seething.

Oblivious to any atmosphere, Hugo prattled on.

'I gather you two already know each other,' said Hugo.

'Yes, Giles and I met a couple of years ago and have kept in touch ever since,' said Charmian, giving her ex-lover a meaning look. Disliking the way this was phrased, which made their relationship sound Platonic if not pedestrian, and sensitive to the fact that, for whatever reason, Charmian wished to keep their long love affair a secret from Hugo, Giles said, 'Kept in touch is certainly right!'

He experienced a treacherous resurgence of the old desire. Charmian was wearing jeans and a loose white shirt through which it was just possible to detect the shape of her round high breasts. Circling her neck was a gold chain that he, Giles, had given her the Christmas before last and on her narrow brown feet were sturdy leather sandals whose dependable look was undermined by the frivolous red of painted toenails. I'm behaving badly, thought Giles. I know I am and I just can't stop myself. The fact remains that I would like to take Charmian's clothes off and make love to her, *now*. Giles, Karen? Giles, Charmian? Karen, Giles,

Charmian. *Oh, Christ!* No. No, it had to be Giles, Karen. He felt ashamed of himself and at the same time very jealous.

Charmian shot him a furious look.

'Yes, I get on very well with Giles's fiancée, Karen Wyndham!'

'Oh good,' said Hugo vaguely, and then, suddenly interested, 'Any relation to the Norfolk Wyndhams?'

'Not as far as I'm aware.' Giles was short. 'Why are Norfolk Wyndhams special?'

'Been there for centuries,' observed his host and prospective employer.

'I think you'll find that's the case wherever Wyndhams crop up,' said Giles, very crisp, 'whether they're yours or somebody else's.'

Giles will lose this commission if he carries on like this, thought Charmian.

Bored with the subject now that it had been established that Giles Hayward's wife-to-be was not a Wyndham who mattered, Hugo suggested, 'What about a general tour of the park first? And then I thought we might have a brainstorming session over a cold lunch.' The idea of Hugo having a brain-storming session over anything was risible. In spite of herself, Charmian sent Giles a droll look. 'Has to be cold, I'm afraid,' continued Hugo, 'I've given the staff the weekend off!'

Oh, had he! So no Mrs Rattray-Smythe and no servants either. All alone with Hugo.

Giles raised his eyebrows and sent Charmian a speculative look back. Are you sure you know what you're getting yourself into? queried the look.

Where Hugo had left it alone, the park was magnificent. To Giles's eye it appeared that the original eighteenth-century landscaping was more or less intact. It was near the house that the compulsion to tinker had become irresistible. The sunken garden in particular was a disaster. It was crossed by a bridge reminiscent of old Peking. The spirit was there but the execution was right over the top. Watching Giles silently looking at it, Hugo said with pride, 'I designed that myself!'

'I thought you might have,' said Giles.

The observer of this exchange, Charmian, gave up on it. She need not have.

Oblivious, Hugo responded, 'If you like that then wait until you see the drawing for the gazebo! We'll have a look at it over lunch. On to the water feature!' He pointed the way.

The water feature, unfinished, turned out to be a medium-sized lake, which was a curious kidney shape. It put Charmian in mind of certain dressing tables. Watching Giles suck in his breath, she had to repress a wild desire to laugh.

'Unusual, eh?' said Hugo.

'Very!' said Giles. 'Where were you going to put the gazebo?'

'Here, of course,' said Hugo, indicating the inside curve of the kidney.

'Of course,' said Giles.

They walked back to the house. Charmian's grip was

still standing in the hall. 'Hugo, I wonder if I could just see my room and maybe freshen up before lunch.'

'*Mea culpa!* I meant to show you up to it before the tour.'

She followed him upstairs.

Left to his own devices, Giles wandered around the drawing room whose swagged decor was predictable. There was a clutch of family photographs on the grand piano which was a Broadwood. There were several of, presumably, Hugo's wife. One looked like a studio portrait, or maybe it had been done for *Country Life* and depicted the sitter plump, smiling and guileless in pearls. The one which looked the most recent could have been of a different woman, apart from the nose and chin which were unmistakable. No smiles now. Very thin. Narrow-eyed, intractable and wearing the sort of sad sundress espoused by certain English gentlewomen, Mrs Rattray-Smythe squinted into the sun. There was (here Giles searched for the *mot juste*) a disappointed look about her, a feeling of iron having entered into the soul. He transferred his attention to a large silver-framed sepia print at the back of the group. The fellow in question was like Hugo, had the same slippery, glassy look as though a cod were wearing a collar and cravat, but at the same time had a jaunty quality of the sort conspicuously lacking in Hugo. There was an air of the man who broke the bank at Monte Carlo. Without knowing it, Giles was looking at the untrustworthy Charlie Rattray-Smythe.

Upstairs, Charmian was repairing her lipstick in her room while Hugo hovered outside the door. Odd behaviour, thought Charmian, taking her time. Why on earth didn't he go downstairs and show Giles the gazebo plans? The bedroom had two doors off it. One led to a small en suite bathroom and the other into a medium-sized room with a single bed in it and a large mahogany hanging cupboard. In one corner was a wash hand basin and a shelf covered in gentlemen's shaving paraphernalia and expensive aftershave and cologne. There was yet another door. Quietly opening it Charmian discovered that it led into what, judging by its grandeur, was the master bedroom. So the room in whose doorway she was currently standing must be Hugo's dressing room. She retraced her steps and checked the door which connected it with her bathroom. There was a lock but no key. Giles was right. It was beginning to look as if she might be in for a sticky evening.

By the time Charmian emerged, Hugo had given up and gone. Descending the stairs, she could hear him holding forth to Giles in the drawing room. Into a brief lull, she heard Giles asking what had happened to the last garden designer. 'We had a contretemps over the gazebo,' was the eventual answer. 'In fact,' elaborated Hugo, 'it was one long contretemps! Fellow couldn't seem to see what I was getting at.'

Amid an unsurprised silence from Giles, Charmian entered.

Over some very good cold salmon, prepared in advance by Hugo's invisible cook, they studied the drawing of the gazebo. It was pagoda-shaped and together with the bridge looked like a refugee from a willow-pattern plate.

'Have you ever been to China, Hugo?' asked Giles at last.

'No,' said Hugo. 'What do you think, Charmian?'

'Charmian doesn't know anything about gardens,' said Giles, thereby letting her off the hook by making the first helpful remark since her arrival. 'So there's no point in asking her. I have to say I don't think it's quite right for the period. And I'm not sure about the shape of the lake either.'

Hugo was crestfallen. 'What about the bridge?'

Praying for Giles to say something tactful, Charmian was to be disappointed.

'Well…' Giles's voice trailed away. Charmian suppressed another mad fit of mirth. There was something exhilarating about the way this was all going so spectacularly wrong.

Giles thought for a minute. He thought: I really could do with the money this project would bring in, but unless Rattray-Smythe's prepared to countenance a rethink and then begin all over it's a non-starter. After a moment's hesitation he said most of it aloud.

'Out of the question,' said Hugo. 'I've already spent a mint.'

'Perhaps you need a more rococo designer,' suggested Charmian. 'Giles has always been very *linear*.'

'Maybe Charmian can think of someone,' said Giles, giving his lover a Fuck You Too look as he did so. He drained his coffee cup. 'Anyway, I think I'd better go. I'm supposed to be back in Sussex by six. Thanks for lunch, Hugo, and if you change your mind, let me know. Goodbye, Charmian.'

Laughing and casting her eyes to heaven as she did so behind Hugo's back, 'Goodbye, Giles,' she said.

When Giles had set off down the drive in his battered old Deux Chevaux, Charmian turned to Hugo and said, 'Since I thought you might have affairs of state to attend to this afternoon, I thought I might drive around the countryside a bit, explore the nearest town. That sort of thing.'

'Yes, I do have certain things I have to attend to, so maybe that is a good idea,' said Hugo, who had in fact been wondering how to entertain his guest before dinner. After dinner would be a different matter, he hoped.

Travelling back down the drive half an hour afterwards, Charmian wondered how she was going to stave off Hugo later on. I'll simply tell him no, decided Charmian. I'm his guest and he'll just have to accept it. The other question was how to bring up the subject of Spivey and the honours list. There seemed to be no answer to this. Probably better to play it by ear.

When Charmian arrived back, Hugo was nowhere to be seen and his car was not there, but the front door was open. This was a welcome release.

Before getting changed for dinner, Charmian embarked upon a tour of the house. It was odd to think that Father had probably spent quite a bit of time here all those years ago and even odder to think that, according to him anyway, the paintings, some of which were quite magnificent, were copies, albeit very good ones.

When it came to deciding what to wear, Charmian chose severe but chic Jean Muir. There seemed no point in exciting Hugo since she had no intention of coming across.

In the event, her host did not get back until seven and when he did arrive, smelt of spirits. They finally sat down to an elegant cold dinner at eight o'clock. If it had not been Hugo Rattray-Smythe sitting opposite her the whole thing would have been very romantic. The woman from the village who filled in when Hugo's regular cook was away appeared to have thought of everything. There were flowers and candles and silver and creamy table linen and the dining-room doors open onto the floodlit terrace. Hugo raised his wine glass. 'To us, Charmian! To us!'

They both sipped, and then: 'Now, why don't you tell me why you're really here? Because I think I know.'

The strike was so sudden that it took her breath away.

Not so stupid after all.

There seemed little point in prevarication and Charmian did not even attempt it. Cries of I *don't know what you mean,* accompanied by coy simpering, would have been demeaning in the circumstances and would have rendered the whole weekend a pointless exercise.

Leaving herself a little loophole for flattery later on should he appear receptive to it, Charmian said, 'I'm partly here to ask you not to nominate Reg Spivey for an honour in the Birthday List.'

There now, she had said it.

To say Hugo was thunderstruck would have been an understatement. It was clearly the last thing he expected to hear.

Oh Christ! She need never have told him!

'Why?'

'Let's just call it a personal vendetta,' said Charmian, feeling the whole thing sliding out of control.

Hugo was disbelieving.

'But I thought you didn't know Reg. I thought the pair of you met for the first time at the private view!'

'We did.'

'I have to say I don't understand any of it,' complained Hugo. 'What is it that you have against Reg?'

'I prefer not to go into detail. I know he wants a title because you told me and I know he has asked you to sponsor him. Height of bad form, you said. I just don't want him to have it and I'm prepared to go a long way to stop it.' This last caught Hugo's attention, causing him to wonder: how far? and refocused his mind on seduction.

'After all,' continued Charmian, 'you don't have to do anything. It's what you don't do here that counts. You haven't sent the form in, have you?'

'No, but I ought to get it off. I've been meaning to do it for months.' Dilatoriness exposed, Hugo looked uncomfortable.

'But *why?* You think he's a shit as well. Why do it?'

'He *is* a shit and I'm trying to get rid of him,' protested Hugo. 'Once he gets his K, which is what I think he's hanging around for, I think I'll be able to persuade him to go. He might even go of his own free will.'

Some hope, thought Charmian listening to this. Hugo stood up and made his way unsteadily round the table until he was standing behind her chair. He put his hands on Charmian's shoulders and leant over her. 'You said you'd go a long way to stop him. How far?' The hands slid down to her breasts. She tried to push them off but he persisted. It was intolerable.

'No, Hugo—' Aiming to get away she slid sideways, half slipping off the chair as she did so. Hugo stumbled, lost his balance and nearly fell into the remains of the galantine of chicken. He swore. Scrambling to her feet, Charmian attempted to make a dash for it. Surprisingly quick for one so drunk, he lunged at her and caught her by the floating sleeve. The Jean Muir chiffon, chosen not to inflame, tore. Hugo spun Charmian round, inserted one hand within the remainder of the modest neck of the dress and wrenched. Modest no longer, and thinking: I can't believe this is happening to me! Charmian cried desperately, 'No, Hugo, no!'

Hugo slapped her face. The shock was immense.

'Yes, Charmian, yes! You know it's what you want!'

Now he was dragging up her skirt. The feeling of powerlessness was truly terrifying. In desperation Charmian screamed at the top of her voice. 'I know all about the paintings! I know they're fakes!'

The effect of this was electrifying. Hugo let go of Charmian so abruptly that she fell to the floor. His face was ashen.

'What did you say?'

'I know about the fraud. My father's name is Austin Sinclair. He was a great chum of your father, Charlie. Charlie told him.'

Charmian slowly got to her feet. Arms crossed to protect herself, she clutched the shreds of what had been a very pricey dress to her body.

'What do you want?' All aggression gone, Hugo appeared to be shell-shocked. He did not trouble to deny it, she noticed.

'I've told you what I want. There's nothing else.'

'How do I know that you won't tell anyone else?'

'You don't. But I won't. I couldn't care less if it was all painted by numbers.'

'All right. You can have it!'

He turned away from her and walked out of the room. Charmian sat down on the nearest chair. Her face felt as though it was on fire. She looked at her watch. It was still only 9.30. She picked up her shoes, which had fallen off in the fracas, and went to the door. The hall was totally silent; there was no sign of Hugo. On stockinged feet Charmian very quietly mounted the stairs. Back in the bedroom she threw her belongings into her small case and then went down again and let herself out.

She covered up her disarray with a mac she habitually kept in the back of the car and drove to a small pretty pub with hanging baskets, which she had noticed on her way into the local town that afternoon. She went inside. A familiar voice greeted her entry into the tiny saloon bar.

'I've been expecting you,' said Giles. 'I could see what was coming. All those lascivious looks. I felt like punching him. Good God,' leaning forward to get a better look at her, 'what's happened to your face?'

'*He* punched *me*. I honestly think Hugo Rattray-Smythe has a screw loose. He's one of those downtrodden not very bright individuals who if not being bullied is doing the bullying himself. He said something to me which, looking back I now think I misunderstood, probably because I had a guilty conscience. I thought he had in some way latched on to the reason why I was there and in fact I think all he was fishing for was a compliment on his manly attractiveness followed by a come-on.'

'What *were* you there for?' asked Giles, mystified.

'Nothing I'm at liberty to talk about,' replied Charmian. 'What about a large drink? I feel I need one. A vodka and tonic please, Giles.'

He ordered it.

'At least,' she remarked, 'I got what I wanted!'

'Yes, I daresay you did but was it worth it?' Giles was dry. 'I wondered at the time if you thought you knew what you were doing. It's why I'm still here.'

Charmian felt suddenly shaky.

'I should have known better,' she admitted at last, tears in her eyes. 'Rattray-Smythe's to the right of Genghis Khan and holds the view that when women say no they really mean yes. Which must mean that he finds himself forced to attack every woman he takes out. I feel quite ill just thinking about it. I think I'm going to have to go to bed.'

'Share mine,' said Giles. 'Once more. For old times' sake.'

That night they did not make love and as Charmian sobbed herself to sleep in his arms, Giles was revisited by a familiar sorrow where she was concerned. Even if she would let me look after her it wouldn't work, thought Giles, and yet there is part of me that would die for Charmian. Stroking her hair and kissing her tear-strained face he said, 'Try to get some sleep, darling.'

When, fraught and exhausted, she finally did drift into unconsciousness, he lay awake for some time beside her, tenderly and protectively staring at her lovely, bruised face between whose brows there was the faintest trace of a frown, before eventually putting out the light.

In the morning, staring at the tattered remains of the Jean Muir, Giles said, 'You could have Rattray-Smythe for assault, you know.'

'What's the point?' Charmian had got up, pale but composed. Probably the stormy weeping of the night before had been the best thing. 'There would be horrendous publicity and my role in the whole thing would be comprehensively misunderstood.'

Still wondering exactly what her role had been but resigned to the fact that if he asked her she would not tell him, 'He'll do it to somebody else,' pointed out Giles.

'Then let *them* complain,' said Charmian.

Kissing her goodbye before they drove to their respective homes, Giles knew that this was the last time.

They would meet again but never as lovers. And that was how it should be. Resolutely, he turned his face towards Sussex and Karen Wyndham.

On her arrival back at her flat, Charmian was intercepted by the porter, who beckoned mysteriously. His small office was full of dark red roses. There must have been at least four dozen.

'Are you sure these are for me?' Charmian was amazed. Carrying them upstairs, she wondered how the flowers had been organized on a Sunday. Tucked inside one of the boxes was an envelope which contained a cheque for £500. That was it. Compensation for the Jean Muir. He doesn't want a fuss! Charmian's first impulse was to tear this into small pieces and drop it into the bin, where it would shortly be joined by the dress itself. As she prepared to do this a thought struck her. Hugo had told her, apropos of heaven knew what, that he could not stand cats, was allergic to cats. It was symptomatic of their marriage that Mrs Rattray-Smythe, of course, had liked cats. Charmian tucked the cheque into her wallet. Tomorrow she would pay it into her account. She considered the roses. It seemed a shame to throw these away. Probably the trick was to give them to somebody for whom they had no history and therefore could be appreciated for what they were. In the end, she drove them to a hospice. Handing them Cellophane box by Cellophane box to an astonished receptionist, Charmian said, 'These arrived for me this morning. Unfortunately, because I am going abroad they are of no use to me. Perhaps you would

like to give them to those patients whom you think
would most appreciate them.'

Brushing aside thanks with a smile, she turned and
left.

13

On reflection, Reg Spivey decided that he had probably over reacted to Alexandra Curtis's sotto voce attack at the Royal Opera House and was even inclined to give Neville Cruickshank the benefit of the doubt, though generosity was not his usual mode. Rather it suited him to assume that in fact nothing was amiss. In his mind, phrase by phrase he went over it again.

Treacherous bastard.

Well, she would say that, wouldn't she? reasoned Reg to himself. Misguidedly loyal to her husband, a man who had not been prepared unreservedly to recognize the business genius of Reg. It was a pity that Alexandra had never seen the light either where he, Reg, was concerned. With a woman like that on my arm, fantasized Reg, the sky would have been my limit. Dissatisfaction swept over him as he contemplated Shirley, his wife of thirty years. Shirley had not aged well, Reg was aware, and there were days when he thought she had done this deliberately in order to spite him. Scowling, he stared into the middle distance, wondering what on earth had happened to the girl he married who had had good legs and a trim figure. Gone, all gone. With an effort he dragged himself away from the contemplation of domestic disaster and went back to the matter in hand.

I know what's going on.

Well, of course she did. Oliver had been with Circumference for twelve years, so on that front Alexandra knew exactly what was going on.

You won't get away with it.

With what? Well, the sacking of her precious husband naturally. But I have got away with it, thought Reg, mainly due to the laziness of Hugo, the inertia of the board and the fact that the only person around here who knows what he wants and goes for it now Curtis is no longer here, is me.

Her parting shot had been harder to explain away.

The secret's out!

For it raised the question: what secret? Maybe she meant the secret of his own curdling dislike of Oliver, though in the early days Reg had contrived to mask this for the most part. Or maybe she meant the fact that Oliver had become too obvious a successor for his own job. The prospect of retirement to the country with Shirley held no attractions for Reg and without an obvious successor in the offing it would be just that bit easier for him to stay on beyond retirement, to look indispensable. And even if he did not, assuming Hugo came through with the honour, hopefully a knighthood, as he had promised he would, then, as Sir Reginald Spivey, business elder statesman, august ex-Chief Executive of Circumference, plum non-executive posts would be his for the picking. All the same, he had a niggling doubt.

Because he did have a secret and one which would destroy him if it ever got out. Spivey did not think Neville had been lying when he denied that he had committed any indiscretion, for they were in this together and short of divine intervention there was no other way news of their joint activities could have leaked out. On the whole, then, he thought himself to be safe and whatever Alexandra had been talking about, it wasn't that.

Dismissing the matter for the moment, he pulled his diary towards him and summoned his secretary.

On her return from Sicily, Alexandra rang Charmian.

'We're back!' announced Alexandra, sounding more like her old positive self. 'What about lunch?'

'Not this week I'm afraid,' said Charmian, who did not want her sister to see the bruise on her face. This was in the process of fading into a cloudy yellow and by the weekend would, with luck, be gone.

'Next week is what I had in mind. By then I'll be back in London with Oliver, house-sitting in Bayswater, which is when I'm going to blitz the estate agents. I've persuaded my reluctant husband to bite the bullet and we are going to buy a London *pied-à-terre*.'

'Oh, *good!*' Charmian's heart lifted at the prospect of her sister coming back to London.

'And that's not all. Oliver's been offered another job. That's the good news.'

'What do you mean? What's the bad news?'

'It's not really what he wants. There's a debate currently going on as to whether it's better for him to get his knees back under a desk as soon as possible or go on refusing to compromise until exactly what he *does* want comes along.'

Charmian was cautious. 'Without a crystal ball I wouldn't know about that! What about Mrs Hemingway? What does she have to say?'

'Just that he'll re-establish. She doesn't say how.'

'How very Delphic,' observed Charmian. 'While we're on the subject, I've had my own indeterminate piece of news.' Here she paused for effect. 'Mother's coming home!'

'What, with the Russian?'

'No, he's dead. So, without the Russian but with the Russian loot. A woman of means.'

'Well, that's all right, isn't it?' Alexandra's own mother had died five years ago.

'No, it isn't! You've never met her. She is *so* difficult. Which means I'll have two of them on my hands.'

An idea occurred to Alexandra. 'Can't she and Father be difficult together?'

'You would think so, wouldn't you? Mother needs—no, *demands*—constant company, which is where I will come in until she achieves it elsewhere, and since she mentioned buying in Chelsea, it sounds as though she's coming back with a stack of cash. Father's equally on his own with only the photograph albums and without a bean. She used to be dotty about him until he bolted, of course.'

'Yes, but he's not about to go anywhere these days, I shouldn't have thought,' was Alexandra's opinion.

'That's only because, incarcerated as he is in Peckham, he doesn't get the opportunity, so I wouldn't bank on it. Heaven knows what would happen if we let him loose in the King's Road. But I think Mother's had it, anyway. After ten years of being the tragedy queen after Father's departure, she's now, with the aid of the Russian, turned herself into gritty ex-pat Señora Sinclair who runs a bar and likes a gin. Which would give Father a lot of opportunity, not to say ammunition, for his fastidious and hypocritical tut, tut, dear oh dear, your mother's gone to the dogs, act. His own part in the whole affair would, naturally, elude him. No, it wouldn't work!'

'Put like that it certainly doesn't sound like it! Maybe she'll decide not to come.'

Charmian was gloomy. 'Ask not for whom the bell tolls, it tolls for me. I'm sure she'll come!'

A telephone call in the wake of the letter confirmed this prophecy.

'Charmian? Coming. Definitely,' announced Mother's upper-crust bark.

'When?' asked Charmian. Terseness appeared to be infectious.

'Soonest possible,' came the unreassuring reply. 'Lot to do here. Slowly getting through it. Going to need somewhere to live when I get back, though.'

Here it was.

'Want you to find me a house, Charmian. Got a pencil?'

Charmian, who was expecting a client for a meeting at any minute, decided to stand firm.

'I really don't think that's a good idea, Mother!'

There was a silence at the end of the line. Impossible to tell if it was a huffed silence or just a silence.

'The reason being,' continued Charmian, 'that, as you know, I'm running my own business and therefore won't be able to devote the necessary time to looking. Moreover, I don't know what you want. Only *you* know what you want. If I find something and you don't like it, it's a waste of everyone's time.'

Mother was not about to give up.

'Week's holiday would do it. I'll tell you what I want!'

Charmian stared up at her office ceiling and then counted to ten. Better to ignore that last remark and carry on. 'Much the best thing, in my opinion,' intoned Charmian, 'would be for me to book you into a central hotel and then, with the aid of a good estate agent during the week and myself at weekends, you can fan out from there.'

'Looking is so boring,' complained Mother.

'Quite!' agreed Charmian through gritted teeth, 'but only you can do it. Ah, my secretary has just let me know that the client has arrived which means that my next meeting is about to start. I'll have to go. Ring me as soon as you know what the timing is. Lots of love! Goodbye, Mother.'

It was at this point that Mother, clearly miffed, took brevity to its logical conclusion and did not reply at all but simply hung up.

Gathering up the papers she needed, Charmian sighed. That evening she and Nigel Guest were going to the Stellar concert at the Queen Elizabeth Hall. Her bruise was healing rapidly and could be camouflaged completely with makeup. Her heart quickened at the prospect of meeting Toby Gill again. On the other hand he had probably forgotten all about her.

He had not. There was a champagne party in a private room for a select few in advance of the concert itself. Toby Gill stood by the door greeting his guests.

'You remember Charmian, don't you?' said Nigel.

'I do,' said Gill. 'The Poussin. I remember it very well.' It was unclear whether he meant his first encounter with her or the exhibition.

They shook hands.

It was the first time they had touched. His hand felt hard and dry. Briefly his fingers closed around her own and once again she looked up at him, willing him to really notice her. As she did so and their eyes met, Charmian was aware of something else passing between them. The spark which she had noticed during their first brief meeting ignited and she knew in that instant a connection had been made and that the implications for both of them would be profound. Years later, she was to say, 'It was mutual recognition. I knew straight away that I might love Toby Gill or hate him but there would never be anything in between. It would be one extreme or the other and whichever it was it would be very important.'

Nigel divined that something had happened too, and

without knowing exactly why became uneasy, proprietorial even. 'Come on, Charmian, the receiving line's
building up behind us.'

'Oh, I'm sorry.'

If only Nigel weren't here, she thought.

She lowered her eyes, broke the contact, and turned
away after him into the crowd. Watching her go, Gill
knew with certainty that he would see her again after
tonight and was aware that she knew it too. This
knowledge was all he needed. For the moment there
was nothing further to be done. He shook the next
hand. 'So pleased you were able to come,' said Gill,
meaning it.

Eyes closed, Charmian let the music flow over her
and through her. Sound was everywhere, insulating her
from responsibilities. She was conscious of feeling
elated and, at the same time, very tired. So tired.
Maybe it was fallout from the Rattray-Smythe episode
but, on the whole, she did not think so. It felt more
like the useful French expression *ennui,* an unaccustomed sensation of life having gone stale.

Dinner afterwards was a buffet affair. Without appearing to watch Charmian, nevertheless Gill did watch
her and although he solicitously circulated among his
other guests he did not gravitate in her direction. There
was no need and besides, that evening she was with
Nigel Guest. Charmian wondered how and when she
would hear from him again. Effervescing as usual, Nigel was concerned for his lover who seemed to have
lost her usual sparkle.

'What's the matter?' he said, as they moved from

one group to another. 'Been burning the candle at both ends?'

'Mmm, that sort of thing,' agreed Charmian absently, 'or maybe I'm sickening for something.'

Love? The worst disease of all.

To Nigel's acute ear this did not sound too promising for later on.

'My place or yours afterwards?' enquired Nigel, more to refocus his lover's attention than anything else. He was right. It was not promising. For the first time in the history of their relationship, Charmian said, 'Forgive me, Nigel, but I think neither tonight. Or, rather, mine for me and yours for you. I don't know what it is. I just feel drained suddenly.'

Nigel was disappointed but because he was intrinsically a kind man, albeit a shallow one, did not make a fuss. Rising above this was probably made easier by the fact that, although he had a deep affection and high regard for Charmian, he was not in love with her, for the only person Nigel was truly in love with was Nigel, a fact taken on board years ago by a formerly enamoured but now largely indifferent Mrs Guest. Let him write his slogans and go to bed with my best friend if he must, was Mrs Guest's attitude, so long as he carries on paying the bills and keeps out of my hair. Although he glided over the surface of most things, Nigel's social antennae were very sensitive. Probably they had to be to enable him to survive as he went on his irresponsible way. Whatever the reason, it was by this means he intuited that something had happened between Charmian and Toby Gill. What that was, was another matter. There had been no overt sign, just a vibration, a charge in the atmosphere. All the same, Nigel would have put money on the fact that he was right. Chalk to the other man's cheese, Nigel had always thought of Toby Gill as cold. On the other hand there was a controlled intensity there, a ferocious condensation of energy allied with an analytical brain which had taken the City by storm. Gill was a paradox, Nigel saw, for with his remoteness went an easy urbanity on a purely social level which women probably found very attractive.

Nigel looked at his watch. It was already eleven o'clock.

'Why don't I take you home now?' suggested Nigel, reflecting as he said it that another of what he referred to as his squeezes might still be up and about. Toby Gill was nowhere to be seen and in the end they went without saying goodbye to their host.

'I'll write,' said Charmian.

'Don't worry, it was my invitation, I'll do it.' Nigel led the way. Outside they walked along by the river to where Nigel had parked his car. There was a chill vibrance in the air, as befitted November, but no wind at all. The Embankment lights traced the serpentine course of the Thames and their fragmented reflections shot to and fro in the black, slow-moving water under an indigo night sky. As they walked, Nigel ruminated aloud about the evening.

Finally he said, 'As you know, Charmian, I have not been a good husband and there have been a fair number of girls down the years, but, without a doubt, you have been the best. If only my wife had been more like you…'

It was impossible to let him get away with that and Charmian did not.

'Wives and mistresses are quite different,' said Charmian. 'The job description, everything. *Everything's* different. There can be no comparison. If I was your wife and she was your mistress, you'd be saying what you've just said to me to her. Most of the time I suspect it's the terms of employment that are wrong, not the person at all.'

She pulled her coat around her and slotted her arm through his. It might after all be the last time. They reached the car. Which was a good thing, thought Nigel, who was not keen to start an analysis of the terms of employment of his own wife at the end of which he would probably be found wanting.

'Well, you know what I mean,' said Nigel, glossing over the whole thing as he opened the door for her. 'I'm trying to pay you a compliment, dammit!'

'I know you are.' Charmian smiled to herself in the dark before modestly adding, 'And I'm flattered to be judged the winner. I expect the standard was very high. Thank you, Nigel!'

'Just watch it with Toby Gill,' said Nigel, taking his revenge as he let out the clutch.

Charmian had left the flat before the post arrived in the morning and now there was a heap of mail on the carpet. She picked the letters up and sifted through them as she walked along the small hall and into the sitting room. 'Bill, bill, circular, unclassifiable, possible invitation, bank statement, and oh, heavens, letter from Mother,' said Charmian to herself scrutinizing each envelope in turn. She consigned the dross to the top of her small kneehole desk and proceeded to open the rest.

The possible invitation turned out to be just that. *Laura and Dominic Goddard who are about to move to Hong Kong invite you to their farewell party...*and so on. Unclassifiable proved to be from the Cat Protection League. 'My dear Ms Sinclair, We confirm with great pleasure that, as you requested, we have written to thank Mr Hugo Rattray-Smythe for his generous donation of £500,' enthused the letter. Charmian pictured Hugo going puce over his morning cup of Earl Grey as he read that one.

That only left Mother. Reflecting that this was unlikely to tell her anything new since she had spoken to Mother that morning, Charmian slit open the envelope. Mother's pointed, spiky handwriting was as staccato as the clipped way in which she spoke. I'm sure Mother never used to be quite so short, mused Charmian. Probably cohabiting with the monosyllabic Vlad, whose English had been minimal when they first met, had exacerbated an existing trait.

She went back to the letter. And discovered that it was the purveyor of new information after all. 'Good Lord!' exclaimed Charmian, reading on, hardly able to believe her eyes. 'I wonder if she's got this right.'

14

The Curtises moved to London and Alexandra usefully employed the house-sitting period finding them somewhere of their own to live. The fact that within a comparatively short time she found what she wanted at more or less the price she wanted, indicated to Alexandra that maybe their luck was beginning to turn. And not before time. Sitting on crates currently being decanted from Mr Muldoon's removal van, she and Charmian reviewed the battlefield. At this stage of the proceedings the chaos was comprehensive.

'It's years since I lived in a flat,' said Alexandra with something of a sigh. 'The last time was when I was at art school.'

'I remember it,' said Charmian, for whom that flat had become something of a haven during a particularly rootless period of her life. 'You ought to give up picture restoring and go back to painting, you know. When the dust finally settles and Oliver has reestablished. Dan tells me *he* would like to go to art college. But you probably know all about that.'

'No, I didn't know.'

Charmian stared at her sister in surprise. Alexandra looked guilty. 'Do you know I've been so embattled, what with shoring up Oliver and organizing another house move that I haven't had a lot of time left over for the children.'

She did not tell her sister that a letter had arrived from his school concerning Dan that morning. Just thinking about it, Alexandra's brow furrowed.

It has been impossible to pin Dan down this term on the work front, wrote the housemaster, *and I fear dire exam results as a direct consequence of this lack of application.* Desperation mounting, he continued, *Dan is an intelligent boy who is currently not doing himself any favours. I have consulted with my colleagues and, with the sole exception of the Art Department, we all take the same view. His Latin master is particularly exercised. Detentions and punishments in the form of writing out very long, very dull* Times *leaders instead of playing rugby have been of no avail. Passive resistance seems to be the order of the day. Unless Dan pulls his socks up, I predict GCSE disaster next summer. It is possible, however, that a change of attitude, provided it takes place now, could avert this. I feel it is imperative that we have a meeting to talk this situation over as soon as possible.*

Reading it and wilting, Alexandra thought: how come matters have come to this with Dan without me noticing that something was wrong?

Knowing none of it, Charmian remembered Dan lying on the grass that hot summer afternoon by the tennis court, with his aureole of blond hair, one arm shielding his eyes from the sun and the other flung wide, telling her basically that he was insecure and lost in a situation that was not his fault, the reasons for which he did not fully understand, yet which, nevertheless, affected him deeply. Alexandra's very like Father, thought Charmian, in that she treats children as though they are miniature grown-ups, expects them to be able to work out what's happening and cope on their own. Probably because it's what we both had to do. But it's different for these three who up until now have never known anything but security. And it's ironic too that, whereas she's got three children and I don't have any or want any, yet I think I empathize much better with them on certain levels than she does.

'I think it's time you stopped fretting about Oliver quite so much,' said Charmian at last. 'At this juncture the children need you more. Oliver's on the up again. He's consulting, he's got a job offer or two on the table. It's all beginning to happen for him, and now that you've got a breathing space of sorts it strikes me that it's their turn for reassurance. Especially Dan. The other two are more...' here Charmian searched for the word, finally coming up with, 'robust.'

Unexpectedly, at the end of this well-meant speech, her sister took offence.

'I hope you're not insinuating that I'm neglecting my children!' This was said very starchily and probably indicated that she herself thought she was. The temperature dropped. Alexandra stood up abruptly. 'I'm afraid I must get on. I'm sorry I can't even offer you a cup of coffee, but you can see the problem.'

Charmian could. Nevertheless...

'Would you like me to drive down and see Dan?'

'Just leave it, Charmian, would you please! I am perfectly capable of sorting out my own family!' By now *froideur* had become distinct irritation.

'Yes, of course you are. I'm sorry! Anyway, look, I'd better go. If there's anything I can do to help just let me know.'

'Yes. Thank you.' Her sister was unmollified and therefore short.

With an uncomprehending shrug, Charmian went. Her departure coincided with the after lunch return of the removal team, bow-legged under the weight of a pine chiffonier but still whistling.

'In here,' said Alexandra, leading the way, 'and against that wall over there, please.' She pointed. Through the window of the sitting room she could see her sister, a solitary windswept figure, walking away across the common through the drifts of leaves. Watching her go, Alexandra felt remorseful and recognized that the flare-up had occurred partly because of the letter she had received that morning (which she had fully intended to talk over with Charmian anyway) and partly because with Oliver currently away, she was tired and probably spread far too thin. 'Damn, damn, damn!' exclaimed Alexandra, going back to the supervision of the mechanicals, thinking as she did so. I'll ring Charmian up tonight, say I'm sorry. And I'll contact the school first thing on Monday morning. Probably Oliver and I should both go down next week.

The following day, which was Sunday, Alexandra drove to the local, so-called, superstore in order to fill up her empty kitchen cupboards and was amazed at what she found. Sunday appeared to be fruitcake day. The whole place was full of the sort of eccentric whom she never normally encountered in such mundane surroundings. Rangy six-foot blacks with streaming dreadlocks, brilliant clothes and the narrowest hips Alexandra had ever seen, queued alongside etiolated gaunt girls in fashionable tatters, who might have been models. The aisles were equally outré and while attempting to select free-range eggs Alexandra was very nearly run down by a trolley piloted by someone on roller skates. Faintly familiar people, second-rate television actors abounded, rooting inconclusively among the potatoes and carrots. The whole lot looked as though they might break into song and dance at any minute. All in all this was a revelation, and raised the question of where these people hid themselves all week. Oh, I love being back in London, thought Alexandra. I'm simply not ready to be put out to grass yet.

Later that evening, having had a snack supper, Alexandra moved a pile of odds and ends off one of the sofas and sat down at last. As yet there were no curtains at the windows. In the distance, across the common, the lights of the traffic could be seen like a torchlight procession marching slowly around the perimeter. Rain had begun to fall and the road beyond the front garden of the flats was shiny black like PVC except where the streetlamps shed their pale fluorescent radiance. Alone in the flat, looking out at the inky starless night she experienced a heady premonition that they were now on the brink of something and the move back to London was the first step towards it. The knowledge that nobody apart from her immediate family knew where she was was oddly luxurious, like temporarily stepping out of the line of fire. The sound of the doorbell therefore came as a not altogether welcome surprise. Wearily Alexandra got to her feet. The doorbell rang again.

'Who is it?' said Alexandra into the answer phone.

It was Dan. Amazed, she let herself out of the flat, passed out into the passage and flung open the main front door of the block. Outside the rain was now driving in diagonal gusts, showers of silver arrows caught in the halo of light around the porch. Drenched and shivering, her son looked exhausted. Wondering what on earth could have happened, Alexandra took Dan in her arms and then, without speaking, led him inside.

So much for the lull in the battle.

Elsewhere, Charmian was being entertained by Gervase Hanson. This was a departure from the norm since it was a Sunday, but since for whatever reason he was on the loose in London and she was free there seemed little point in wasting the opportunity.

When they came out of the cinema, the rain had stopped but there were still no cabs immediately to be seen.

'Let's walk to the King's Road,' suggested Charmian. 'I could do with some fresh air.'

At that time of night on a Sunday, Sloane Street was practically deserted. Presumably the sort of person who lived round here went to the country every weekend as a matter of course. They passed the black tower of the Carlton Tower Hotel on their left and then a small park whose saturated, dripping trees bore witness to the force of the downpour and replicated the sound of falling rain. The sky above the city was no longer as dark as it had been and rags of cloud floated around the remains of a dimmed and sulky moon. Loping along shod in suede, Gervase made no sound but Charmian's heels clicked on the London flags. A city girl through and through.

As they walked, Gervase put his arm around her shoulder enquiring as he did so, 'Do you know who I mean by Marcus Marchant?'

'Vaguely,' replied Charmian, whose only connection with him was through her sister, a fact she did not want to divulge. 'He's a barrister, isn't he? High profile.'

'That's right. I had a drink with him the other evening and he suddenly started talking about Circumference. It was Marcus who put Oliver Curtis in touch with me, of course. They've been friends for years. Anyway, to cut a long story short, he tells me the City is awash with rumour that there might be a takeover bid in the offing.'

'Really!' Charmian was immediately alerted.

'And it occurred to me to wonder if you...'

'Had any luck getting them on my books as a client?' finished Charmian for him.

'Yes.'

'In a nutshell, no.'

'But you did manage to infiltrate the top echelon?'

They crossed the road into Sloane Square.

'Yes.'

'What did you make of the setup there?'

'Why are you so interested, Gervase?'

'Curtis is still my client, though I think I've probably done as much as I can for the moment. Do you want to grab a cab from the rank or shall we carry on walking?'

'Carry on walking. What do I make of them? Well, Rattray-Smythe's a lethal chump, by which I mean he's dim with a nasty streak. Spivey's just lethal and then there's a finance director called Cruickshank, who you've probably met, who oils around both of them trying to advance himself, one of whose unofficial functions is to be used as a verbal punching bag when Reg is in a bad mood. All in all it could not be called the most harmonious of setups. There's a veneer of civilization with Hugo notionally in charge, but when Reg says jump, Hugo jumps. Though Hugo, on the other hand, who is a colossal snob, takes his revenge by looking down on Reg from a great social height and has never invited his Chief Executive to the Rattray-Smythe mansion.'

'My, my! You did pick up a lot of information in a short time!' Apparently congratulatory Gervase was, at the same time, sly. Avoiding his keen eye, Charmian stared ahead. By now they were at Walpole Street. A gauzy drizzle had begun to fall and the streets and buildings glistened with its fine sheen.

'Rattray-Smythe was involved in a scandal a few years ago which was successfully hushed up,' said Gervase, 'by which I mean it never hit the papers, though it was common gossip among certain members of the legal profession at the time.'

'What sort of scandal?' As if I really need to ask, thought Charmian.

'A woman. Someone perfectly respectable who suddenly found herself being ravished by Rattray-Smythe in the conservatory while his wife, who was in the house at the time, was lying upstairs with a headache. It seems enthusiasm outran judgement and he misunderstood the signals. Could happen to anyone, of course, but the difference here was that according to my source, on being informed of his mistake he carried on ravishing.'

'*No, Hugo, no!*'

'*Yes, Charmian, yes!*'

Charmian shuddered.

'How did she succeed in getting away? Or didn't she?'

'No, I believe she did. Maybe she was a black belt. Nice fellow! Cab?'

'Cab.'

Back at her flat Charmian put her feet up while Gervase mixed them each a Campari and soda. Sitting watching him do it, she thought about Hugo. I was naïve, was Charmian's verdict. Maybe I've just been lucky up till now with the men I've met, but I've never experienced anything like that before. She became aware that Gervase was at her elbow with her drink. 'Aren't you going to listen to your messages?' queried Gervase, watching with fascination the flashing red light which indicated that there was quite a few of them.

'No, I wasn't planning to!'

'Because I'm here.'

'Because you're here.' She smiled at him over the rim of her glass, tantalizing and narrow-eyed. The damp weather had caused her hair to wave and it undulated away from her face, exposing high cheekbones which would probably stand her in good stead until the day she died. Although she professed not to like them, there was something of the cat about Charmian, a languorous watchfulness underpinned by a very independent spirit.

She lowered the glass.

Eyeing with admiration her curved, painted mouth which, he noticed, had left a perfect impression of itself like a small scarlet etching on the edge of her glass, Gervase was conscious of an overwhelming desire to make love to her. He savoured the thought for a moment and then: 'Why don't you come and sit over here,' he said.

Later on, as they lay in bed together, Gervase said, 'What would you say if I asked you to marry me, Charmian?'

'I'd remind you that you are already married and then I'd say, don't be so greedy!'

'But supposing I wasn't!' He kissed each rosy nipple.

'I should say no,' said Charmian without hesitation. 'You're not a good bet, Gervase! Look at what you're doing with me.'

Gervase laughed. He rolled over onto his back and ran a languid hand through his hair.

'You're probably right!'

'I'm sure I am!'

When Charmian finally got round to listening to them the first message on the machine proved to be from Father and the second, appropriately enough, was from Mother. Neither of them had anything very much to say. Mother's contribution as usual did not waste any time on the niceties. Mother said 'Hello, Charmian. Furniture. Storage. What do you recommend? Ring back soonest!' 'What do you recommend?' did not mean what do you recommend at all. It meant: could you please organize the removal of my furniture from Ibiza and its storage in London until we find me somewhere to live? Alexandra's Mr Muldoon came to mind. Deciding that she really could not face this sort of push you pull me that night, Charmian passed on to the next, which was from Alexandra.

'Alexandra, Sunday night, ten-thirty, and the message is: sorry!' said her sister, without preamble. 'I don't know what's the matter with me lately. I seem to have lost my sense of proportion. Look, something unexpected has happened and I need to talk to you, tonight if possible. If not tonight tomorrow morning first thing would do it, but it is quite urgent!' Charmian was alerted by this communication. It took her back to the night Alexandra told her that Oliver had been fired. She consulted her watch: 1.30 a.m. Too late. And then her diary. No breakfast meeting tomorrow. Better to ring then. She passed on to Nigel, who wanted to know about the Wednesday assignation, and finally Dominic, who appeared to have been effectively grounded by Laura. 'No hope of a meeting before the party, I'm afraid,' announced Dominic. 'Curfew is at seven every night. If I can slip under the wire I will, but otherwise look forward to seeing you on the twenty-eighth.' Disappointingly there was no message from Toby Gill, who could have got her number from Nigel, she thought. Charmian went to bed.

In the morning she rang her sister.

'Hang on a minute, would you, Charmian?' said Alexandra. There was the sound of a door being closed.

'What's going on?' asked Charmian when she returned. 'Not another crisis with Oliver, I hope!'

'No, not this time. It's Dan. He turned up on the doorstep last night, wet through and absolutely exhausted.' Alexandra spoke in an undertone.

'Where is he now?'

'Spark out. As I say, he's absolutely exhausted.'

'Does the school know he's here?'

'Apparently not. I'm going to ring them when I've finished talking to you. He told me that he took off on impulse. "I just couldn't stand it any more" was the phrase used, ''and I'm not going back!'' and then he broke down.'

Although her heart was wrung listening to this, Charmian was not surprised to hear it.

'And what I didn't tell you yesterday was that I had a letter from the school saying that he's not doing any work of any kind and they are at their wits' end.'

'What are you going to do?'

'Heaven knows! *I'm* now at *my* wits' end. Obviously I'll have to confer with Oliver about it when he gets back tonight, but my instinct is probably to take Dan out. What do you think?'

'Look,' said Charmian, 'you're embattled at that end. When he wakes up, why don't you send Dan into my office later on today? He can loaf around the West End and come and see Father with me in the evening and then I'll take him out to dinner.'

'I thought you always went to Father's on Thursdays!'

'Normally I do, but I got an imperious message saying could I make it Monday instead this week.'

'To which you naturally replied, ''Your wish is my command, O Sultan!'''

'Naturally! Tell Dan I'll expect him around five.'

Father was in top iconoclastic form. Father opined, 'You don't want to worry about anything as mundane as exams, Dan old boy. I never did and it never held me up! I had the time of my life!'

Certainly did, thought Charmian. At everyone else's expense. Aloud she said, 'There just aren't enough

Vanderbilt heiresses to go round these days, Father, and anyway Oliver and Alexandra don't move in the sort of circles where Dan is likely to meet one. So I'm afraid there's nothing else for it. One way or another Dan will have to get his GCSEs and then his A levels. Very few people can afford not to work these days.'

'What did you do?' Dan found himself unable to call Grandfather, Austin.

'As little as I could get away with!' came the uncharacteristically self-aware answer. 'Nine-to-five work is demeaning. Don't have anything to do with it, Dan.'

'Absolute rubbish! It's what I do!' exclaimed Charmian. 'How would I pay my rent if I didn't? And what's more, I enjoy it. Father's joking. Take no notice of him, Dan.'

She frowned at Father, with a slight shake of the head. Perfectly capable of picking up this sort of signal, her parent decided to be impervious.

'Never been more serious in my life. Don't get on the treadmill, old boy, you'll never get off it. And while I'm on the subject, don't get married either. Is there any more of that champagne, Charmian?' He proffered his glass.

'Yes there is, although you don't deserve it!'

Father, who liked being cast as an *enfant terrible*, albeit one in his eighties, smiled incorrigibly.

Dan said, 'I'd like to go to art college!'

'Art colleges?' Father sniffed. 'They're full of yahoos and weirdos.'

'No they aren't,' said Charmian. 'Alexandra, your impeccable daughter, attended one.'

'Yes, and I blame her mother. There's no point in educating women that I can see. Just gives them ideas above their station!'

For the first time that evening, Dan laughed. 'You don't really believe that, do you?'

'Of course I do. Doesn't everybody. Giving them the vote was bad enough.'

'Try telling Alice that,' riposted Dan. 'Alice is very egalitarian. Alice wants to go into politics.'

'A young girl like Alice shouldn't be worrying her pretty little head about things like that.' Father was quite shocked. 'But don't fret about it, I'll sort Alice out. Make her see sense.'

Charmian thought: if I didn't know Father as well as I do, I'd think he was just showing off for Dan's benefit. As it is, he really is the blinkered product of a certain era and some—no, *most*—of his opinions are quite appalling. Heaven knows what his views on race are. On the other hand it was highly likely that it would be Alice who sorted *him* out. Better leave it to Alice.

She stood up.

'Were you ever able to use that information that I gave you about Charlie?' suddenly asked Father, getting off the unsatisfactory subject of women's rights.

'Yes,' said Charmian. 'Though not in exactly the way I expected!'

'Splendid!' said Father, losing interest. 'Before you go would you bring over the albums, Charmian, please, and just put them on the floor by my chair? Thank you!'

'I thought we'd eat Italian if that's all right with you,' said Charmian to Dan, as they drove away from Peckham, 'and while we do so we can talk over your problems and maybe you can help me out with some of mine!'

'I think I'm going to go back to school after all,' said Dan unexpectedly, 'just until I finish my GCSEs.'

Charmian, who had been wondering how to counteract the undermining effect of Father's irresponsible advice, was startled. Perhaps the sight of the man who despised qualifications and had ended up in a shabby flat in Peckham when looks and rich women ran out had clinched it. Whatever it was she decided to capitalize on a sound decision.

'Well, if you can hack it it probably does make sense. Depends how unhappy you really are,' said his aunt. 'I mean you've only got another few months and then you're shot of the place and can go to art school or whatever. Though Nick likes it there, doesn't he?'

'Yes, but although we're twins we're quite different. Nick doesn't give a stuff what anybody else thinks so it's possible for him to exist outside the system without caring. Whereas I...' He hesitated.

'Do give a stuff,' finished Charmian for him. 'I know, and because you do, you'll go on to do great things. Just believe in yourself, Dan, and don't lose heart.'

She finally dropped him back at the mansion block at 11 p.m., where it was Oliver who opened the door to them. He embraced his son, saying only, 'We'll talk it all through tomorrow.'

Dan went to hang up his coat. Oliver turned to Charmian. 'Thank heavens you're back. We didn't know where to find you.'

'Why, what's the matter? And where's Alexandra?'

'She's at King's College Hospital.'

'*What?*'

'It's your father. He's had a fall. They think he may have broken his hip.'

'Oh no! How did it happen? Do we know?'

'Apparently,' said Oliver, 'he tripped over the photograph albums.'

'I'd better get over there,' said Charmian, thinking as she did so, I always knew Father's past would catch up with him sooner or later.

15

'It never rains but it pours, wouldn't you say?' declared Alexandra, greeting her younger sister.

'How is he?'

'Currently in X-ray. I may say they've already worked out that here is not an easy patient.'

'What *are* we going to do? He'll need nursing when he comes out. I haven't got a spare room and you need yours for when the children come home.'

'How long will they keep him in, do you think?'

'For as short a time as possible, I should have thought, given the way he's behaving!'

They stared at one another. 'We'll just have to play it by ear,' said Alexandra at last.

The thought of Mother briefly crossed Charmian's mind and was dismissed. No joy to be had there.

Father arrived back on a trolley wheeled by a very harassed-looking nurse, with a medical attendant in tow. Together they ladled him back into bed.

'When's my room going to be ready?' grandly asked Father, who was currently on the ward.

'As far as I'm aware, Mr Sinclair, this *is* your room and please keep your voice down. It's midnight and the rest of the ward is asleep. The doctor has prescribed a sedative.'

'What about a painkiller? I'm in pain, you know!' said Father, for whom stoicism seemed to be a foreign concept.

'I was just coming to that!' The nurse was admirably stern. 'But firstly I'd like to take your temperature. While I'm doing it the Night Sister would like to see you in her office, Miss Sinclair.'

They both went. Sister was a nice woman who looked about their own age. Reflecting on her demanding parent, Charmian thought: what Father needs is not a humane, saintly carer like this one, Father needs one of those starched sprung-heel autocratic matrons of the sort which don't exist any more.

'What happens next?' asked Alexandra.

'That depends on the result of the X-ray,' said Sister, 'and whether he's going to have to have an operation. If, as we suspect, he has broken his hip, at his age we could be into quite a long haul before he's properly mobile again. But the consultant will be able to give a much more accurate prognosis than I can. He usually does his rounds in the morning, but before you ask me I can't give an exact time.'

It struck Charmian not for the first time, that being in a National Health Hospital was like being in another country—the outside world of work might as well not have existed. Mentally she went through tomorrow morning's diary.

'I'll stand by to spend the morning here,' offered Alexandra. 'It's easier for me since I don't have a full-time job and one of us has obviously got to talk to him.' They both stood up. Looking at her watch, Charmian saw that it was 12.45. It would be 1.15, probably nearer 1.30, before she got home tonight and the following day was due to begin with a breakfast meeting at 8 a.m. On their way out they went back to the ward. Father was asleep.

'He asked me to give you this,' said the nurse. The note said: 'Don't forget the albums when you come tomorrow and my shaving tackle and so on. But most of all don't forget to bring a bottle of the best painkiller of all, plus glasses!'

Reading this Charmian said crossly, 'If it wasn't for those bloody albums, he wouldn't be here in the first place. I'll sweep by his flat on my way in to see him at six and collect whatever he needs. He's bound to come up with some additions before then.'

In the hospital car park, for once almost empty, the two sisters wearily embraced before setting off in their different directions.

Opening his post, Hugo Rattray-Smythe was puzzled to find a letter from the Cat Protection League. It must be for his wife who liked them and was not allergic to the furry little monsters as he himself was. He checked the envelope. It was definitely addressed to himself. He went back to the letter. As he read it, his head shot forward in astonishment like that of a tortoise coming out of its shell after hibernation. Apparently he, Hugo Rattray-Smythe, had donated £500 to the greater good of cats. Also among that morning's post had been a bank statement. Hugo normally filed this sort of communication away until he felt strong enough to face it. Today, however, he broke the habit of a financial lifetime and slit open the threatening cream envelope. He ran his eyes down the column of figures. There was only one payment of £500, and that was to Charmian Sinclair. Clearly some old dear at the Cat Protection League, probably suffering from senile dementia, had made a mistake. A phone call would no doubt clear the matter up. It came as something of a relief to see that Charmian had cashed the cheque he had sent her, though. The last time Hugo had sent a similar cheque for a similar reason it had not been cashed but preserved as evidence and the upshot had been a narrow escape from a prosecution by way of an out-of-court settlement to a charity which had cost him a lot more than that. Such high-mindedness was not discernible here and raised the question of whether Charmian Sinclair would keep her word concerning the fraud that was the art collection. While waiting to find out, Hugo felt he had no option but to tear up the nomination form he had been preparing to send to the Honours Secretariat featuring Reg Spivey as nominee and had, in fact, already done this. Not for the first time he wondered what Reg could possibly have done to Charmian to evoke such enmity and, at the same time, was keenly aware that once Reg realized he had been passed over, life at Circumference would not be worth living. Whatever it was Reg had or had not done to deserve this deprivation, it was, Hugo recognized, a refined but highly effective revenge. It was a pity that he, Hugo, would be caught in the fallout. I'll just have to lie, thought Hugo. The whole honours system is so shrouded in secrecy that he'll never find out that I didn't do a thing about it. This was comforting as far as it went, but did not resolve the question mark over whether Charmian would keep her side of the bargain.

More to take his mind off this than anything else, and to sort out a ludicrous error on somebody's part, he dialed 192 for Directory Enquiries.

'Could you get me the number of the Cat Protection League?' said Hugo.

Toby Gill was in no hurry to contact Charmian Sinclair. Because, like her, he knew that whatever happened next would profoundly affect both of them, though whether for good or ill was in the lap of the gods, he wanted to savour the prospect. Gill was not a man to rush his fences and was also aware that, now she knew he was interested, delay would heighten both anticipation and interest. Also, *force majeure,* after Clare's death, business for the last few years had become his *raison d'être,* a habit that was hard to break, especially in the light of the fact that he was currently planning a coup the delicacy and complexity of which demanded a cool head and no distractions.

Business first, pleasure later—when I can relax into it—was Gill's view.

All the same, Charmian entered his mind more than he cared to own and the thought of her out there leading her customary London existence while at the same time *knowing* that one day he would come and find her, just as *he* knew he would, was oddly luxurious. There was no point in forcing the pace of the inevitable. For the time being, Gill was content to concentrate his acute brain on the strategy and tactics of his next business move, unaware as he did so that what he hoped to bring off would prove to be as close to her heart as it was to his own.

Christmas loomed. Mother, who had still not succeeded in extricating herself from Ibiza and the various complications surrounding the Russian will, and who was due to move to England in February, at her own suggestion made a preliminary foray to London to reconnoitre. It was during the course of this visit that Charmian brought up the subject of the Russian windfall.

'Mother, are you sure you've got it right? It's a huge amount of money!'

'Huge!' Mother was complacent. 'Didn't know he had it, either!'

'But where did it come from?' Charmian did not say so, but was privately of the opinion that there was a smell of illegality about the whole thing.

'Who cares?' Mother waved a dismissive hand. 'It's mine now! Question is what I do next.'

'What *I* have to do next is visit Father,' said Charmian, looking at her watch, 'who's currently in hospital.'

'What's the matter with him?'

'He fell and broke his hip. He's had an operation and he's now in plaster and driving the staff mad. Next comes physiotherapy followed by a spell of recuperation in a nursing home. After that I don't know what we're going to do with him.'

'I'll come with you!' unexpectedly offered Mother.

'I thought you said you didn't want to see him!'

Mother ignored this. She was conspiratorial. 'Not exactly. It's the money. Don't mention the money!'

On entering the hospital, it occurred to Charmian that maybe meeting Mother again unannounced after all these years, might be a shock to Father's system. With this in mind she was just about to suggest that she went in first and primed him when, as they left the lift, she was buttonholed by Sister. Mother strode on into the ward. Too late.

'How's the patient today?' enquired Charmian.

Sister cast her eyes to heaven.

'He's had two nurses running ragged, plus your sister on the go all day. Nobody else gets a look in. I'm thinking of giving him his private room just so that the ward can get back to normal.'

'All right, no need to tell me any more,' said Charmian hastily. 'However, you may be pleased to know that he's about to get his comeuppance. Ahead of us is his ex-wife whom he hasn't seen for years and isn't expecting.'

Father, who had been dozing, opened his eyes and then quickly shut them again. He must be dreaming. *Must* be dreaming. Or perhaps he had died. For the person standing at the foot of his bed looked very like someone from another incarnation. Very like Violet, in fact. But of course it couldn't be her. He partly based this opinion on the fact that if it was her, she had changed colour. Violet had been pale, reproachful and monosyllabic. The visitor, who was walnut-coloured, when she spoke revealed herself to be still largely monosyllabic.

'Hallo, Austin,' said the apparition.

It *was* Violet.

'I'm back!'

Self-evidently. Father, who had taken no further interest in the doings of his wife after he had left her, briefly wondered where from. For once in his life he could find nothing to say. Transfixed, he lay there. There was an aura of confidence about Violet which had been conspicuously lacking before except maybe at the very beginning of their partnership. Then as now, though Father did not currently know this, she had had independent means. Staring at the grounded Austin in silence, Violet felt very powerful and not as though she was about to make the same mistake twice. This time she would hang on to her own money.

'Been in the wars, then?'

'Yes. Hip!' said Father, finding as had Charmian before him that her verbal economy was catching.

Charmian arrived.

Thank God, thought Father.

'Sorry about that!' said Charmian. 'Sister—'

Disregarding what she considered to be wittering, Mother interrupted. She said, 'After the nursing home he can live with me.'

Father's eyes widened in panic. 'Oh, I don't think—'

'I'm on my own. He's on his own. Makes sense!

You find me a house, Charmian, I'll take him on! Twilight years together. Austin instead of Vlad.'

Who? Never mind. Pinned to his bed, 'No, no...' beseeched Father.

Neither of them was listening. Because he was lying down while they were both standing up it seemed that he had in an odd way dropped below the level of their consciousness. Flabbergasted, Charmian was not about to show it. Every so often, though hardly ever, there came the answer to a prayer and this was one of those moments.

'Done!' said Charmian. 'It's a brilliant idea!'

'No, it *isn't!*' Father had one last try. Nobody noticed. They carried on disposing of him.

'And you're quite right,' she continued, 'you'll be company for one another.'

'Soon have you on your feet, Austin,' announced Mother, suddenly remembering the object of their discussion. She spoke slowly and loudly, as though having a fractured hip had affected his brain, and sounded very bracing. Father let his head fall back on the hard hospital pillow and closed his eyes. Maybe when he opened them again it would be to find that this *was* simply a bad dream after all. He fervently hoped so.

Charmian rang Alexandra and told her the news.

'I wanted to tell you before you see Father,' said Charmian. 'Father's preparing to do his I'm-just-a-poor-old-man, nobody-cares-what-I-think routine and, of course, it's possible the arrangement won't work. In case it doesn't, I think we should keep on the Peckham flat for the time being without telling him. If he knows it's there he won't try. Meanwhile the deal is that I find a suitable house for them both in Chelsea as minutely specified by Mother.'

'It's much more Father than Peckham,' observed Alexandra, 'but what if he won't go?'

'He'll have to go. It's an offer I'm not prepared to let him turn down and anyway there isn't anywhere else. He can't go on living by himself, it's out of the question.'

'That's true! What on earth made her offer?'

'She doesn't want to live alone. She needs somebody to snipe at and Father, with his antisocial habits, is the perfect target.'

Alexandra laughed. 'Of course, you know her and I don't, but it could just be that she still loves him a little bit, despite his behaviour? Anyway, I'll take your word for it. And if you're going to be stuck with the house hunt, I'd better volunteer to take them both on for Christmas in the country, assuming Father's out of the convalescent home by then and your mother's over here.'

'Alexandra, you have the heart of a lion,' was Charmian's response to this.

16

Probably tired of waiting for the inevitable, Fate took a hand in the affairs of Charmian Sinclair and Toby Gill and they met again at the Goddard leaving party. Neither had any idea the other was going to be present.

For the occasion Dominic and Laura had borrowed a vast Albert Hall Mansions flat which belonged to a friend who had not yet moved in. So, whereas there were carpets on the floor, no curtains hung at the lofty windows and the only furniture in evidence was what the caterers had imported. Light was supplied by chandeliers, whose multi-faceted, diamond-shaped lustres scintillated like shards of ice. The whole effect was grandly surreal.

Laura was not what Charmian had been expecting at all. Laura was a petite blonde with an hourglass figure. The unfortunate word *fluffy* came to mind, though there was an officiousness about her which probably stemmed from regimenting the copious Goddard children. It was while exchanging pleasantries with Laura, prior to passing on into the rest of the group that Charmian looked over her shoulder and saw Toby Gill. Moving on from her hostess to greet Dominic, Charmian said, 'I didn't know you were a friend of Toby Gill!'

'Only very peripherally,' answered Dominic. 'It's a Laura connection. Laura was at school with his late wife, Clare. Shall we go over and say hello?'

'No, not right now,' said Charmian, discovering as she said it that she was irritated by the fact that Gill had not contacted her after the Stellar orchestral concert. Let Gill catch up with her if he wanted to.

The slight toss of Charmian's head as she looked in his direction told Gill exactly what she was thinking and he realized that if he did not follow up tonight's advantage he might not be afforded another opportunity. For the first time she appeared to be on her own, presumably because Dominic Goddard was one of her lovers. Gill's mind went back to the day he had seen her in the restaurant with him and Neville Cruickshank and once again he wondered what the purpose of that lunch had been. Currently heavily embroiled with his own agenda where Circumference was concerned he could only speculate on what Charmian's might be.

Politely he disengaged himself from the group he was with and moved in her direction. Sensing rather than seeing him coming, Charmian herself moved on. Cat and mouse. A few guests had turned into a throng. In spite of the time of year someone had opened one of the massive, arched windows and the cool draught which slipped in as a result caused the chandeliers to sway and the lustres lightly to touch one another, producing a delicate chiming ripple of sound as they did so. In common with many of the women there, Char-

mian was wearing black and once or twice, despite her
height, Gill lost sight of her.

Finally the room they were in began to empty as the
other guests gravitated towards the food. Charmian did
not move with the herd but remained where she was,
standing by the open window. She did not turn round
as he approached. Outside an occasional flake of snow
drifted down and the temperature of the drawing room
in which they were now the only ones left had fallen.

Charmian shivered. She felt both feverish and cold
at the same time.

'Get your coat,' said Gill. 'We're going.'

Outside in the street the air was electric blue and the
pavement was slippery underfoot due to a light cov-
ering of the first snow of the winter. It was very still.
Gill took Charmian's elbow.

'Do you have your car?'

'Yes,' said Charmian. 'What about you?'

'I walked,' answered Gill briefly. 'I live near here.'

They located her car, which was parked opposite the
Albert Memorial, and got in. Charmian started the engine. It was still snowing. Caught in the headlights
large flakes spiralled slowly down and began to settle.

'Where to?'

'Chelsea Green. Monkeys Restaurant. It's a favourite of mine. I'll direct you.'

He did not, she noticed, ask her if she would prefer
to go anywhere else. As Charmian drove, Gill admired
her profile and the length of her neck which was en-
circled by a pearl choker. On impulse he pushed the

tape already in place into the player. The upshot was a surprise. Expecting something popular, he found himself listening instead to the haunting purity of a counter tenor.

'The fresh streams ran by her, and murmured her
moans;' plaintively observed the singer,
'Sing willow, willow, willow;
Her salt tears fell from her and soft'ned the stones
Sing willow, willow, willow
Sing all a green willow must be my garland!'

'What is this?' asked Gill.

'"The Willow Song"', replied Charmian, concentrating on the road. She did not elaborate.

'I called my love false love;' complained the
singer, *'but what said he then?*
Sing willow, willow, willow!
"If I court moe women, you'll couch with moe
men."'

It occurred to Toby Gill that in spite of her active social life there was a mental isolation about Charmian Sinclair which matched his own.

'Where now?' asked Charmian.

'Turn right here and then straight on,' instructed Gill. 'Park anywhere you can at the end.' She did so and they both got out. Charmian swept her cloak around her and pulled up its large loose velvet hood.

By now the snow was beating down and they arrived inside the restaurant frosted with it.

As she sat opposite Toby Gill, just the two of them at last, Charmian felt elation, as though this were the end of a very long journey and she had finally come home. He raised his glass. 'To us!' said Gill. He turned to the menu. 'But for the moment I want to hear about *you.*'

As they ate, she told him more, much more, in fact, than she had ever told anyone before. True to form, though, she did not tell him quite everything. She did not, for instance, say that her sister was married to Oliver Curtis, whom he knew. If pressed as to why she did not, Charmian would probably have said, 'Because secret knowledge is potentially the most powerful kind. It is not just my future that is at stake here and *I* don't know what is going to happen next.' Besides which, there was plenty of other information to be going on with. Gill listened intently, interjecting the odd question here and there and, also true to form, he did not tell her all he might have either, probably for very much the same reason. The other thing he did not do was to proposition her.

Later on, chastely back in her own flat, Charmian reviewed and evaluated the evening which had been extraordinary by any standards. She had anticipated a pass and had debated what to do about this when it occurred. In the event there was no decision to be taken since no such thing happened. It was difficult to know whether to be relieved or piqued. However, what *did* occur, towards the end of their meal, was that Gill suddenly said, 'What are you doing for Christmas?'

Christmas? Charmian sighed at the prospect. 'Going away if I can.'

'Excellent. Then you can come to Rome with me!' Once again she noticed that he was not asking her but telling her. 'Separate rooms though. No strings. I want to get to know you, see how we get on together.' He might have added, though in the event he did not, that at this stage to have embarked straight away on a hot affair would have obscured the view. The real view, that is.

There was no question of her not agreeing to go, of course, but all the same, 'I'd like to think it over,' replied Charmian.

'Yes, of course you would,' agreed Gill, smoothly in step with this ritual dance. 'But while you are doing so, perhaps I had better book anyway.'

'Perhaps you better had,' she concurred, shooting him a look both naughtily seductive and humorous over the rim of her wineglass. 'After all, if necessary, you can always cancel!'

Caught in its beam, and thinking that Charmian Sinclair really was a knockout, it occurred to Gill to wonder if he was going to have the self-control necessary to conduct the early stages of this relationship in the way he had envisaged.

'Yes, I can always do that,' said Gill.

Charmian decided to sack the two remaining lovers. In its way this was a statement of intent by herself to herself, though not one that Toby Gill was ever supposed to know about.

Their reactions were predictable and, when she came to think about it, in character.

Gervase was intrigued. He said, 'What's the matter, Charmian? Are you unwell? Or perhaps you just need a sabbatical?'

'No, it's none of those things,' replied Charmian and then surprised herself by saying, 'I may decide to get married.'

'Oh, is that all? Then I confess I can't see the problem. Why should that make a difference? I mean, look at me! I'm married. Besides it seems an odd thing to do considering all you've had to say on the subject.'

There was no denying this.

'I know! It's a grand passion.'

Gervase was unimpressed. 'Oh, one of those! They don't last, you know.'

'I'm not sure about that. But be that as it may, the other half of this possible arrangement isn't about to condone playing away and I'm not about to push my luck, not even for you, Gervase.' She shrugged. 'That's it.'

'Who is it anyway?'

'You don't really expect me to tell you that, do you?'

'No, I don't,' he conceded, 'but it was worth a try.'

'All the same, I'll miss you!' As she said it, Charmian was aware that she was burning her boats, possibly prematurely, and in the light of that fact hoped that monogamy would suit her. On one level, therefore, Gervase's next words were heartening.

He said, 'Well, when it all collapses, you know where I am. Maybe I'll hold off finding a replacement for a while.'

'Gervase, you're too kind,' murmured Charmian, 'but what I really appreciate is your optimism.'

Nigel, on the other hand, did not waste any time dissecting his lover's plans for the rest of her life. Where Gervase had been philosophical, Nigel fell into a decline.

'I just don't understand it,' he mourned. 'Haven't I given satisfaction? Aren't I amusing enough? What am I going to do on Wednesdays? It's very thoughtless of you, Charmian. We've had such fun together. Haven't we had fun?'

'Oh, we have,' replied Charmian though, truth to tell, the fun side of it had been wearing a little thin lately where Nigel was concerned.

'I mean,' said Nigel pursuing it, 'if you'd only *told* me about this sudden need to get married, I could have organized it!'

'Organized it?'

'Yes. Fired my current wife, who's not amusing anymore, and then you could have married *me!*' He was clearly very put out.

Marriage to Nigel! Ye gods what a prospect!

'Nigel, our relationship wouldn't stand marriage. We've survived very well on one day a week. But that's it!'

'Yes, and now I've got to survive on no days a

week!' Not born to be miserable, Nigel was getting mopier by the minute. 'It's not fair. It's not fair at all.'

Charmian laughed out loud. The sight of her animated face revived hope that she might relent and he briefly cheered up. Like a moth mesmerized by the flicker of a flame he drew closer. And was singed.

'If the worse comes to the worst you'll just have to spend time with your wife or, if that doesn't suit you, you could advertise the fact that there is a Wednesday job vacancy. I'm sure you'll be deluged with applicants.'

Nigel clutched at the only straw that appeared to be left. 'What if this marriage doesn't come off? What then?'

'Quite likely,' said Charmian.

'Then we could go back to where we were!'

'No, we'll never do that.' Speaking the words, Charmian discovered that Nigel and his reaction had crystallized the way forward. That might be with Toby Gill or it might not. Either way it would not be with Nigel Guest.

'So I'm redundant!' Unaware that in the not so distant future he was to hear the word again, once more applied to himself but this time with regard to the removal of his lucrative job, Nigel grinned. It had apparently only taken him the space of their short conversation to plumb his own shallows. The only way now was up. 'Well, I expect I'll get over it.' Even his tie, not such a gaudy one as usual, seemed to light up with this surge of positive thinking. 'Though it will probably take a while.'

You're over it already, thought Charmian, watching him. No need to worry about you!

'What about one more Wednesday? For old times' sake! Oh, go on, say yes!'

'No more Wednesdays,' Charmian was quite decided. Another Wednesday would mean that she would have to say the whole thing all over again, Nigel's grasp on reality being as fickle as his personality. 'It wouldn't be the same. This is the last one. Let's quit while we're ahead.'

Momentarily disappointed, Nigel rose above it.

'Oh! OK! But I don't promise not to ring you up.' He moved forward to say his farewell and found himself demoted to kissing her hand which today was embellished with a fine, large cameo ring whose profiled classical face made him think of Ancient Rome. There was a pagan sensuality about it and as Nigel's gaze lingered for a moment, he was aware that in spite of the time they had spent together he had never understood Charmian, never really known her. Perhaps she did not even know herself.

With the dismissal of her lovers, the answer phone went into decline, its red light flashing less frequently these days, the messages it did convey altogether less interesting and in so far as a machine could, it appeared to sulk. A week after her last meeting with Gervase and Nigel it came briefly back into its own.

'Charmian!' said the first message. 'Toby. It's seven p.m. on Friday the eighth. All is in place vis-à-vis Christmas. It only remains for you to let me have your decision.' That was it. There followed what was, presumably, his home telephone number. Writing it down, Charmian passed on to the next. This proved to be from a very indignant Hugo who had finally solved the mystery of the Cat Protection League and did not like what he had discovered. After the usual hesitant start, he launched into a long harangue apparently impervious to the part he himself had played in the feline windfall. Indignation mounting, Hugo said, 'I thought there must be some mistake!' Dictating this communication into Charmian's machine, he remembered with displeasure the unsatisfactory exchange between himself and a crisp upper-class female voice with no signs of senile dementia at all. There was no doubt who had come off worst and there was no doubt either who had set this particular train of events in motion. Worst of all from Hugo's point of view, there was no offer to return his £500.

'*You* may have changed your mind, Mr Rattray-Smythe,' said the voice, without incidentally a hint of gratitude, 'but *our* arrangement was with Miss Sinclair, so if you wish to vary it I suggest you talk to *her*.'

Click.

By now fuming, that was exactly what he had tried to do and his mood was not enhanced by the sound of her unruffled clear voice telling him that she was not there. His furious bafflement was risible. Listening to it, Charmian pictured Hugo's glassy eyes bulging, and smiled. For her personal satisfaction she listened to it all once more, prior to wiping off the tape.

Let him whistle for his money.

Dismissing the whole matter, Charmian picked up the telephone receiver and dialled the number of Toby Gill. He answered. In the background she could hear music playing. Opera. It sounded like Mozart, though not the Trio this time. *'Il mio tesoro.'* Don Giovanni.

'It's Charmian,' said Charmian.

'One second. I'll just turn the music down.' There was an unmistakable heightening of interest in the voice, a sudden vibrance. He did so. 'Well?'

'The answer's yes. As you knew it would be.'

'As I *hoped* it would be,' gallantly corrected Gill. 'We probably won't meet again until the day we leave but I'll be in touch to finalize the details.'

'Fine,' said Charmian. 'I'll wait to hear.'

She hung up the receiver, and reflected as she did so that in spite of having conducted her own survey down the years concerning men and what they had to offer, she had never met anybody quite like this one.

17

Stiletto silver, Reg Spivey's Mercedes, driven by Denis, slipped between the ribs of the traffic. Congestion was heavy that afternoon. In, out and in and then out again, Denis deftly manoeuvred his way across London. Lunch had apparently been a rich one and Mr Spivey was claret coloured and late for his board meeting at one of the subsidiaries as a consequence. Driving would be easier once they reached the outskirts of the city.

It was a relief not to be driving Mr Rattray-Smythe for once, though. Mr Rattray-Smythe talked incessantly, mainly thinking aloud but also expecting the odd response which meant that Denis could not allow his mind to wander, one of the great pleasures of driving as far as he was concerned. Mr Spivey was quite different, being either silent or shouting into the telephone.

Denis relaxed into it.

By now, they were in South London, Clapham to be exact, and although Spivey was not aware of the fact, only a couple of hundred yards from where Oliver and Alexandra Curtis now lived. There were still isolated pockets of snow on the common, preserved by the hard frost of the night before, but most of the rest of it had gone. Black skeletal trees lined the road. A weak sun had come out, causing the day, diamond-like, to sparkle.

Sitting in the back seat and taking up most of it, Reg Spivey felt himself to be insulated, inviolable, a powerful man being driven along in a powerful car. In business terms, apart from the ineffectual Hugo, king of all he surveyed.

The impact of another car hitting them therefore came as a colossal shock. The noise of the crash was tremendous and the impetus of the collision stove in the side of the Mercedes. Pinned by his seat belt and very nearly strangled by the cord of the car telephone, even if he had seen the danger coming, Spivey could not have got away. As it was, the small executive world of the walnut-veneered, leather-upholstered back seat exploded as though struck by a meteor. Like a fountain erupting, glass shot high in the air catching the sun before showering like water in a graceful curving arc all around. With perfect timing the bonnet shot up as the glass fell.

Dazed and also still wearing his seat belt, Denis sat there. Where on earth had it come from, whatever it was? He was suddenly aware that smoke was pouring from the engine. Better get out! Galvanized into action he half fell out of the driving seat and staggered to the back of the car where he flung open the opposite door to the one which had been pushed in by the force of the collision. In the middle of the wreckage, Spivey appeared to be asleep. To Denis's profound relief stertorous breathing indicated that his boss was still alive. Although given Mr Spivey's unforgiving nature maybe it would have been better for the future of Denis's job if he had not been.

The question arose as to whether to move the injured man, which might only exacerbate the damage, or leave him where he was. On the other hand if the Mercedes caught fire a particularly nasty death would be the upshot. Wildly Denis looked round and discovered that a crowd had collected.

'I should leave him where he is,' offered one of the observers, noting Denis's indecision. 'There's an ambulance on its way.' And the police, no doubt. Denis took off his jacket and wrapped it round the unconscious Spivey and went to look at the rest of the damage. The other car, which was old and battered and pea green looked as though it had fused with the Mercedes. There was no one in the driving seat. Denis looked around and spotted the culprit standing swaying on the edge of the pavement. He appeared to be talking to himself.

'That's him,' said one of the onlookers helpfully. As Denis watched, the man, who was rubbing his head, buckled at the knees and collapsed slowly on to the flags. Closer inspection revealed a strong smell of liquor.

'Drunk as a skunk!' ejaculated Denis, with disgust, prodding the supine body with his foot. It was at this point that the ambulance turned up. As if in a dream, Denis watched Spivey being stretchered into the back of it and then settled down to wait for the police.

* * *

Bush telegraph ensured that the news of Reg Spivey's accident shot around the Circumference building immediately. Denis telephoned the news to Hugo Rattray-Smythe's office. When Neville Cruickshank heard the news, without outwardly revealing the fact, he was engulfed with panic. Without Reg to tell him what to do concerning their unorthodox financial manoeuvrings he was totally at a loss. Should Reg die, he, Neville would be left to carry the can. The good news from the hospital when it eventually came was that Reg was not about to expire, and the bad news was that a complete recovery from, among other injuries, a punctured lung and a broken jaw, could take months. Probably *would* take months.

'I'll take up the reins of Reg's job,' proclaimed Rattray-Smythe self-importantly, 'I know I can do it.' He was aware as he uttered the words that, whereas the notion of being totally in charge was gratifying, the actuality might not be quite so enjoyable. He would have to arrive at the office earlier for example and leave later. It would be hard to escape doing a full day's work.

Fervently Cruickshank wished that Hugo had comprehended his and Reg's financial arrangement so that he was not having to face the future alone. He felt exposed and vulnerable and, if he was honest about it, frightened.

'When do they think Reg will be well enough to receive visitors?' Cruickshank faintly asked Hugo.

'No idea,' replied Hugo, 'but with a broken jaw, not

for the foreseeable, I would have thought. Should it be flowers or fruit?' Then, answering his own question, 'Flowers, probably, for the same reason. What sort does he like, do you think?'

Unable to imagine Reg evincing any interest whatever in flowers, and reflecting that getting Hugo Rattray-Smythe's mind off the minuscule was going to prove one of the more arduous tasks ahead, Cruickshank said, 'No idea. But I'll organize it, shall I? Or, rather, my secretary will.'

'That's right,' said Hugo vaguely, dismissing the matter, 'you do it. Poor old Reg!'

'Yes, poor old Reg!' echoed Cruickshank insincerely, wishing as he spoke the words that he had never encountered Reg Spivey.

The first time Reg Spivey opened his eyes after the crash it was to find that he was lying in a darkened room he did not recognize in a bed he did not recognize either. Pain predominated. At the periphery of his vision he could discern a dark shape which appeared to be wearing some sort of hat. There was a rustling noise, as of wings. The angel of death perhaps. He tried to lift his head and a series of small explosions like miniature fireworks ignited and erupted within his brain. Fighting off waves of nausea, Spivey groaned. His head fell back.

The dark shape advanced on him and the rustling was revealed as starch. Not the angel of death but a nurse.

Unoriginal in his discomfort and confusion, 'Where

am I?' Spivey tried to say, although in the event no
words emerged.

'Try not to speak,' said the nurse. 'You've had a car
accident. You're in hospital.'

A car accident? He could remember none of it.
What was the woman talking about? Heavily sedated,
he could feel consciousness coming and going and, at
the same time, was aware that there was something he
should have done or, maybe, had begun but not completed, which was of the utmost urgency. Dimly he
wondered what day it was and how long he had been
here. Perhaps it was all a bad dream. Once again he
tried to speak and could not.

'Go to sleep now,' said the nurse, bending over
Spivey but nevertheless impervious to his agonized
look. She probably saw a lot of them. 'Your wife has
gone home now but she'll be in again to see you tomorrow.'

Shirley. But it was not Shirley that he needed to see.

'No other visitors though for the time being. Only
nearest and dearest,' continued the modern version of
the lady with the lamp, scotching any hopes he might
have nurtured on that front as she said it. 'You need
plenty of rest, Mr Spivey, and we're here to make sure
you get it.'

18

The Curtis household did not jubilate when they heard the news of Reg Spivey's accident nor were they particularly sorry. Oliver learnt of it through two sources—an ex-colleague from Circumference with whom he was still on lunching terms, and Marcus Marchant.

'I've been expecting some sort of upset at Circumference,' said Marcus, 'but not one like this. A lot of different rumours have been doing the rounds and as I expect you saw, the share price took a hefty tumble when the news was announced.'

'I thought the City didn't rate Spivey any more!' exclaimed Oliver.

'They don't but they rate Hugo Rattray-Smythe even less and *faute de mieux* he's now the one in charge. And their misery has been compounded by not one but two sell orders.'

'Good!' said Oliver. 'I hope they go bust!'

'Yes, but not until we've made a profit. You are keeping an eye on the shares, aren't you?'

'Off and on. To be perfectly honest I'm heavily into high-level talks with a rival concerning a top job and I'm trying to look away from Circumference.'

'Glad to hear it,' said his friend, 'but don't take your eye off the ball entirely, will you? Because the rumours I've been hearing, or some of them, predict takeover and there's no point in missing out on that sort of killing.'

'No, there isn't,' agreed Oliver. 'On the other hand rumours of takeover have been surfacing intermittently for years. Who's the predator supposed to be this time?'

A vision of Toby Gill sitting in his Stellar office and talking about Circumference passed before Oliver's inner eye and was gone. He did not say anything about this to Marcus.

'No idea, but all I can tell you is that until Spivey got in the way of a car, the share price was very strong indeed. According to my broker the City's been buzzing with it!'

Oliver was thoughtful.

'You're right,' he said at last, 'I should be keeping my ear to the ground. And will. But you keep me posted too. Strikes me you're more in the thick of it at the moment than I am.'

'Maybe,' said Marcus. 'All I knew is that there's something in the offing and, having sensed it, the City is all agog, though I'd be surprised if anything happens before Christmas.'

He was quite right. Nothing did, though a great deal of a more domestic, mundane order was on the move, notably Father going into a nursing home complaining every step of the way.

As the nurses watched him rolling off down the corridor in a wheelchair pushed by one of his daughters, the other bringing up the rear with a small case and the photograph albums, Sister observed, 'You know I really can't say I'm going to miss Mr Sinclair.'

'No,' concurred Staff with feeling, 'neither can I.'

'Imagine his ex-wife *volunteering* for the job of looking after him!'

'What do you mean? She's an absolute Tartar. Imagine him *accepting!*'

Outside, when the sisters and Father reached the car, Charmian said, 'You're going to be allowed out of the nursing home for Christmas in the country with Alexandra.'

'What about Violet?' Father was suspicious.

'She's coming home from Ibiza to spend Christmas there too.'

'And what about *you?*' Father stared severely at his younger daughter. 'You're not going to desert me over Christmas, are you?'

'I always desert everyone over Christmas, you know that,' replied Charmian. 'I'm going abroad.'

'Huh!' said Father. 'It's all right for some!'

Alexandra was unable to contain herself any longer. 'Do you know, Father, if I didn't know you as well as I now do, I'd think you didn't *want* to spend Christmas in the country with me!'

Father opened his mouth to say something, caught Charmian's eye and subsided.

'Whatever gave you that idea? Of course I do,' he said.

* * *

Toby Gill and Charmian Sinclair arrived in Rome a week before Christmas. As he had promised, separate rooms were the order of the day. Charmian was delegated the task of sorting out an itinerary and did so. Although it was out of season, quite a few of the more famous monuments and palazzos were open. To begin with, despite the fact that it was very cold, the weather was settled with high light skies and weak sunshine. Gill and Charmian went everywhere together, had breakfast, lunch and dinner together but did not sleep together. Gill was courteously friendly, solicitous even, but apart from taking her elbow when they crossed a particularly busy *corso,* did not touch her. Curiouser and curiouser, was Charmian's view of this. It's as though Toby is proving something to himself and, at the same time, to me. There was no point in pushing it with a man like this, Charmian recognized. Better just to take each day as it came and go with the flow.

As time wore on, it became apparent that they had a lot in common. The fourth evening in Rome, Gill began to talk about his wife.

'I hope you won't mind me doing this,' he apologized, 'but Clare was a very precious part of my life for a very long time. She's dead and I've come to terms with that. These days my marriage feels as though it was part of a different incarnation. All the same, I want you to know all there is, and from me. Not from anyone else. So that there is nothing hidden between us. After which there will be no need to talk about her again. I loved her and she's gone. That's it.'

His words were almost identical to those of Karen

Wyndham who had also had a happy marriage cut
short by death and who had also reached a point where
she could talk about it. Listening attentively, Charmian
wondered how much she should tell Toby in return. It
was hard to decide but made easier when he suddenly
said, 'I don't want to know about lovers past or present, by the way. They don't signify. But a marriage
such as mine was *does* and has to be got out of the
way, neutralized if you like, before something else can
take its place. Otherwise there will always be a feeling
of the past shadowing the present. You do understand
that, don't you?'

'Yes,' said Charmian. 'I do.'

And she did.

The following morning as they ate breakfast together
after yet another Platonic night, Charmian said, 'Today
I've earmarked the Villa Borghese. I've never seen it.
The last time I came to Rome it was closed for some
endless Italian repairs.'

Gill's face lit up. All at once he looked boyish, as
though thirty years had miraculously dropped away,
the narrow face smiling with pleasure beneath the grey-
ing sweep of his hair.

'It's wonderful! And that means I can be the one to
show it to you for the first time.'

They took a cab as far as the gates and then proceeded to wander through the park towards the villa.
That morning the weather had broken and a leaden sky
lay low over the tops of the cypress and pine. The
darkness of the morning gathered around baroque
fountains, bringing out the lustrous pallor of the mar-

ble. Suddenly striking through a gap in the cloud a silvery uncertain sun slipped along the hedged walks, highlighting old stone and bestowing its own brief brilliance on classical statuary so that this shone, luminously creamy, through the bare winter trees.

I shall remember today for the rest of my life, thought Charmian, turning up the collar of her coat against the cold. She was conscious that Gill had put his arm around her shoulders. The sensation was like that of a small electric shock.

'There are three things in particular I want you to see. After that it's up to you.'

The first turned out to be a Cranach *Venus* who was not, in Charmian's view anyway, particularly beautiful but was distinguished by the fact that she was wearing nothing except a spectacular hat from beneath the brim of which she slanted a knowing, enigmatic smile at her audience. There was something indefinably sinful about her, a decadence compounded by the presence of Cupid at her feet, holding a honeycomb.

'I wouldn't have said she was your type,' observed Charmian to Gill, 'but perhaps I'm wrong!'

'No, you're right. She isn't. It's the hat!'

Charmian laughed and at the same time was intrigued.

'What next?' She followed him. Together they admired Canova's statue of Pauline Bonaparte. Exquisitely haughty and very *grande dame,* albeit nearly naked, with the aid of her sculptor and through the medium of marble, Pauline had succeeded in vanquishing old age, the greatest female enemy of all.

'Isn't she beautiful?' said Gill. 'I have to tell you that I am deeply in love with her. The more so since I once saw her *chiaro di luna,* an echo of the way Canova used to exhibit his masterpiece to the privileged by the light of a single candle.'

This little tour of Toby's three favourite Borghese works of art really is surprising, mused Charmian, and it's illuminating, too. For what it tells me is that Toby Gill, ruthless, powerful Toby Gill, is a romantic.

'Where now? Whatever it is I assume it's the *pièce de résistance!*'

'It is!'

It was *Amor Sacro e Amor Profano,* Titian's *Sacred and Profane Love.* Charmian drew in her breath. She had, of course, seen it reproduced many times but nothing could possibly do justice to the magnificent original. In an odd sort of way, it mirrors my own life, she reflected, studying it. For there they both sat in the limpid light of a pastoral landscape, Amor Sacro, staidly dressed and exuding disapproval as she resolutely looked away from Amor Profano, who in common with Gill's other ladies, painted and otherwise, was unselfconsciously wearing virtually nothing at all except a scarlet robe which was thrown back, the better to frame an alluring body. As Nigel Guest would have put it, there was no doubt as to who looked as though they might be having more fun.

Charmian became aware that Gill was staring at her intently, as she in her turn admired, and at the same time in an odd way felt herself to be confronted by, the Titian.

'It encapsulates my own dilemma,' Charmian was astonished to hear herself say aloud.

'I know!' said Gill.

He knew? No wonder he hadn't been interested in the other lovers. It seemed he knew about them already.

'So what is it to be, Charmian?' said Gill. 'Sacred? Or Profane?' there was no immediate answer to that.

On Christmas Eve, though neither was religious, purely for the spectacle they decided to go to one of the great Roman basilicas for Midnight Mass. Within the church the lights were low and candles flared and died, appearing to gutter and then flared again, their fitful flames enhancing the golden, glowing mosaics above the high altar. All around, Ionic columns soared heavenwards, their capitals lost in the shadows. Head tilted back Charmian appeared to be lost in a dream, her profile delicately outlined in light. There was a fragility even ethereality about her which deeply touched Gill's heart and at the same time caused him pain. It occurred to him that, regardless of how much he wanted it, learning to live again in the wake of bereavement was not an easy thing to do. All the same, I am fifty, thought Gill, with, God willing, half my life again ahead of me and I *must* go forward.

The church was full. All around them sound surged through the incense-laden air, worship ebbing and flowing, amplified by the extraordinary acoustics of the basilica. Isolated within it, but not of it since they were not emotionally part of the Mass, for its duration Gill and Charmian had thoughts only for each other.

The music died away. Mentally released, Charmian became aware of Gill's eyes upon her. She turned towards him. And smiled. There was nothing remotely flirtatious about the smile. It was a secret smile. It said, I recognize you, just as I know you recognize me. There is no need to say anything. The rest is up to you.

Christmas Day. Outside, all the bells of Rome pealed together.

Unable to resist it, he took her small chin between finger and thumb, tilted back her head and kissed her on the lips.

Christmas in the country in England was by no means as harmonious. Invited by Mrs Sinclair to call her Violet, Alexandra did so. Violet and Father in the same room caused her to feel permanently on edge. There was an unnerving and ultimately exhausting feeling that anything could happen next.

'After all, Christmas is fraught enough already without having to cope with an ongoing dogfight as well,' complained Alexandra to Oliver in the blissful privacy of their own bedroom. 'At his age Father really should know better!'

'If I've got Austin worked out correctly, he's *never* going to know better,' said Oliver. 'It's not in the nature of the horse. Does Violet ever talk to you about the Russian lover?'

'No, she doesn't,' said Alexandra. 'Vlad has been transmuted into Father or Father has been transmuted into Vlad. I'm not sure which but whatever way you look at it, Violet's all right. She's got the money of one of them and the neutralized physical presence of the other, and I'm right in the thick of it. The sooner Charmian finds them a flat so that gladiatorial combat can commence without me having to be a part of it, the better.'

'What do you think the kids make of it all?'

'Alice engages Father in spirited discussion concerning women's rights. You must have heard her!'

'Yes. I have to confess I'm on Austin's side on that one.'

'Very funny! For God's sake don't encourage him, even in jest. What was I saying? Oh yes, and the boys look upon Father and Violet as being like two dinosaurs in that their views and the way they both behave bear no relation to the modern world at all.'

'Talking of the modern world and modern women, or, rather, one in particular, who do you think your mysterious sister is spending Christmas with?'

'So mysterious is my sister that I have to tell you I have no idea at all!'

'I wonder if it's anyone we know.'

'Might be!'

The sound of raised voices on the floor below made them both sit up.

'They're at it again. I think I'd better go and separate them,' said Alexandra. 'Read the riot act.'

'I should let them slug it out. This is, after all, only a practice run for the real thing. Come and make love to me instead.'

* * *

While Alexandra spent Christmas morning wrestling with a large turkey in England, hampered rather than helped by Violet and accompanied by streams of advice from Father, Toby Gill and Charmian enjoyed a late Christmas Day champagne breakfast in Rome. Gill handed Charmian a small square box.

'This is for you.'

It was a ring. A large solitaire diamond. Pale fire. No embellishment. None needed. Perfect taste.

Wonderingly and, for once, at a loss of words, Charmian just looked at it.

'I really couldn't...'

'Accept it? Of course you can! I'm asking you to marry me,' exclaimed Gill, sounding impatient.

'Are you usually this precipitate?'

'I'm not precipitate at all. I think things through very carefully. This was bought in London before we left.'

Really!

'But it might all have been a disaster!'

'Yes, it might! That is why I had to spend time alone with you without any distractions, work and sex being the main two I had in mind. Look, my darling, I'm a businessman. Once I take a decision that's it. I don't think about it again. I go on to the next item on the agenda. That is how I live. The next decision, however, isn't mine, it's yours.'

'Yes and I've taken it. The answer is yes!' Charmian was not tempted to tantalize.

Gill took her in his arms. 'What about all those lovers?'

'I also think things through very carefully. I fired the lot before embarking on this trip.'

'You're obviously cut out to be a directrice of industry! But let us be very clear, Charmian, if you are ever unfaithful to me I'll kill you!'

He probably would too.

Kissing him and in love for the first and, as it turned out, last time in her life, Charmian said, 'I'll never be unfaithful to you.'

19

When Toby Gill and Charmian got back to London, they had a discussion concerning where they went next.

Gill said, 'I want to leave the wedding until a project I'm currently working on is finished. After which I want to devote some time to you. Or, rather, to us. But that could be four or five months away.' He did not specify what the project was and although she was curious, Charmian, who had enough secrets of her own to respect other people's, did not ask. 'Do you mind, darling?'

'No,' replied Charmian, meaning it. 'So long as we're together it doesn't matter when the wedding is, but that being the case I'd prefer not to go public until then.'

Gill gave her a searching look but did not query this odd request. Clearly his wife to be had her own agenda and whatever this was he was prepared to trust her with it. In fact, Charmian could not have said exactly why she did not want to announce their liaison until she absolutely had to. Possibly instinct underpinned by habit was the answer.

'I shall, of course, put my flat on the market. It's the

one Clare and I lived in all our married life and because of that you wouldn't want it.'

'No,' Charmian conceded. 'No. I wouldn't.'

'So I suggest that you keep yours on for the moment and meanwhile start looking at the property market.'

'I already am,' said Charmian, reflecting as she uttered the words that one might as well be searching for two abodes as one. 'As I told you my mother is about to come back from Ibiza and my parents, long since divorced, are about to join battle under the same roof once again. I'm currently supposed to be house-hunting for her.'

'You can spend in the region of' (here he named a heroic sum) 'and it must be spacious. Small interiors don't suit me. And central. I'm an urban animal. I suggest you start immediately.'

He appeared to think that she had nothing else to do.

Charmian gave him a half-bow. She said meekly. 'I shall do my best to fulfil your every whim.'

Gill put down the book he was browsing through and gave her a penetrating look. 'Are you telling me in the nicest possible way that I sound dictatorial and insensitive to the fact that you also lead a busy professional life?'

'Yes,' said Charmian. 'You and my mother have a lot in common on that front.'

'This flat will be an integral part of our life together. It's therefore very important.'

'Exactly! And that is why you should carve out the time to come and look for it with me. Apart from anything else it's obvious to me that you are going to be very hard to please and I could waste an awful lot of time chasing up the wrong thing. I'll contact some agents, get details and we'll sift through them together. How about it?'

'Okay. It's a deal! But I have to say I'm beginning to wonder why I didn't fall for one of those pliable accommodating women!'

'No, you're not! You know perfectly well why you didn't!'

He took her in his arms.

'There's still time to pull out if you really want to,' said Charmian mischievously, 'though it's my considered opinion that you wouldn't know what to do with a surfeit of pliability.'

'Witch! Come to bed!'

Because achieving an audience with Reg was proving impossible, Neville Cruickshank rang Shirley Spivey at home.

'I want to go and visit Reg, take him some fruit, that sort of thing, but I can't get past Sister,' complained Neville. 'She's a battleaxe.'

'It's not her you can't get past,' said Shirley, 'it's me!'

There was a dumbfounded silence at the end of the line which Shirley, with a certain amount of satisfaction, allowed to become prolonged.

'Why?' queried Neville at last.

The real answer to this was that Shirley had seen herself in hot competition with the office for years and, as the loser in the battle for Reg's attention, blamed Circumference for the indifferent state of her marriage. Now, with the unwitting connivance of Sister, and in the guise of protecting Reg, she was in the happy position of being able legitimately to keep Neville Cruickshank, whom she had never particularly liked anyway, at bay.

In fact, what she said was, 'Quite apart from the physical injuries he suffered, Reg was deeply shocked as a result of the accident and his memory of events preceding the crash is still hazy, though the consultant is hopeful that, given time, this will improve. Meanwhile, because he finds remembering difficult, any mention of company matters makes him very frustrated and therefore very agitated. That is why it is better if, for the time being, he doesn't receive visits from colleagues.' Most of this was true, but what she did not say was that it was the absence of such visits which might have thrown light on the dark areas of his brain, rather than the opposite which was making her husband apoplectic.

('Why does no one from Circumference come to see me?' fretted Reg, all too conscious of the transience of power when one was no longer there to exercise it.)

Listening to this, Cruickshank's heart sank. The words *his memory of events preceding the crash is still hazy* left him an even more isolated figure concerning the conspiracy in which he and Reg had been partners. For what if Reg never fully recovered? What then?

In desperation and with a humility which had been conspicuously lacking down the years in his dealings with Shirley, whom he had considered to be only a corporate wife and therefore of no account, Cruickshank beseeched. He said, 'Shirley, it's very important! I'm *begging* you to let me see Reg.'

'Ah!' She was on to it in a flash. 'So not just a social visit then?'

Cruickshank saw that he had made a serious strategic error.

'A social visit? Well, yes of course but—' It was too late to correct it.

'No!' Shirley was stern. 'No! His need is greater than yours!' She was vaguely aware that she was misquoting someone or other. Feeling very powerful (this must be what it felt like to be Reg), she continued, 'I will let you know when my husband is ready to receive visitors. Until then you will have to be patient, Neville. And now I have to go. It is time for my own visit.'

God damn and blast the woman. Fuming, he hung up.

While this unsatisfactory exchange was taking place, in another part of London Toby Gill was instructing his secretary to ring up Oliver Curtis.

'Ask him if he would be free to have a drink with me one evening this week,' said Gill. 'Let's say seven o'clock at the Savoy.'

When they finally met, each man noticed a difference in the other. As he appraised Oliver Curtis, who had been frankly shattered the last time they had encountered one another, it was obvious to Gill that the rehabilitation process was well under way. The haunted look had gone and while he had not yet re-established it sounded as though he had quite a few irons in the fire plus some lucrative consultancy assignments. To Oliver's discerning eye, there was a lightening around Gill almost as though a change of personal climate had taken place. This assessment was both shrewder and closer to home than he realized.

Exchanging pleasantries while they ordered their drinks, Oliver informed Gill that he and Alexandra had spent Christmas in the country with his father-in-law and his father-in-law's divorced second wife, who had fought like cat and dog but who were nevertheless about to attempt to live together again. This produced a faint echo in Gill's mind of another conversation, causing him momentarily to frown in an effort to remember. He gave up on it. Oliver in his turn learnt that Gill had spent Christmas in Rome and was just about to say, by way of making small talk, what a coincidence, so did my sister-in-law, Charmian Sinclair, when the waiter arrived back and after this interruption the conversation moved on to something else.

Well aware that Toby Gill was a man who never did anything without a good reason for it, Oliver patiently waited for him to come to the point. Helping himself to a cashew nut, Gill said, 'I expect you're wondering why I invited you here.'

'I have to say it did cross my mind.' Oliver was dry.

'You recall the time we met in my office when I said I had nothing for you?'

Oliver nodded.

'Well, in a manner of speaking, I still don't but there

just might be something coming along and I wanted to find out what your current situation is.'

'Am I allowed to ask what the something might be?'

'No,' said Gill. 'It's too sensitive, but suffice to say if it comes off it would be right up your alley.'

'Really!' said Oliver. 'In that case my situation is as follows: I'm currently leading a plural existence which is making me plenty of money and keeping the wolf from the door. However, be that as it may, I don't like it. What I want is a hands-on-the-steering-wheel job; I want to be out there running something. Consequently for the past two months I have been having talks with another large conglomerate with whom it looks as though things might be moving to a head. On the other hand, as I don't have to tell you, appointments at that level can take months to finalize.'

'No,' replied Gill, recalling his own experience, 'you don't.' He thought for a moment. 'Look, I think what I'm saying is could you possibly keep me in touch with where you're at. Don't accept anything without giving me first refusal.'

'All right. What sort of timescale is your project on?'

'Hard to say. Three months maybe. Could be less, could be more. I see, by the way, that your corporate assassin is in hospital.'

'Yes,' said Oliver. 'What a shame. Couldn't have happened to a nastier individual.'

'No,' agreed Gill, 'it couldn't. What about another drink?'

'One more and then I must get back. We have people coming to dinner.'

Luxuriating in the prospect of Charmian in his bed that night after dinner for just the two of them, Gill said, 'I understand.'

He signalled to the waiter.

Violet Sinclair finally came home from Ibiza and prepared to take possession of the flat Charmian had found for her.

'It's just right!' said Violet. 'Told you you couldn't get it wrong. Not with those instructions.'

'Don't you think you should let Father see it before finally deciding?' ventured Charmian.

'No,' said Mother. 'It's my flat. Not Austin's. Most important thing is that he's got a room with a TV to sulk in front of when he gets difficult. Which he will. We both know that.'

'Yes, we do.' There was no point in trying to defend Father on that front. Or Mother either, come to that. Charmian wondered whether to mention her impending marriage and, for the moment anyway, decided against it. Nor had she told Alexandra. Knowing nothing of the meeting Toby had just had with her brother-in-law, she wondered what, if anything, might be happening on that front. It transpired that she was to find out sooner than she thought.

Gill and Charmian had fallen into the habit of eating together every evening, after which he would usually stay the night in her bed. Days were divided between his office in the Stellar headquarters and his own spacious flat where he had a large study. Charmian was destined never to see this particular apartment and did not want to. Analysing her own feelings on the matter, she came to the conclusion that she did feel competitive where Clare was concerned. It sounded as though Clare had been a paragon of domestic virtue, though she had never been required to hold down a full-time job. On the whole Charmian decided it was preferable to steer clear of the memory of her predecessor, for if I don't, she decided, I'll end up trying to second-guess her all the time on the household arrangement front which she was much better at than me. However well the Toby/Clare formula had worked, this was the Toby/ Charmian formula and therefore completely different. On the other hand, in love for the first time, Charmian discovered that domesticity could have its charms. Frequently Toby, who was used to staying on at Stellar long after the staff had gone home, arrived as late as nine, and sometimes nine thirty. On the whole this suited Charmian, who had her own office detritus to clear up every evening. It was a precious and secret time, during which the two of them slipped into an easy intimacy aided by the fact that nobody else knew about their love affair. The solitaire, symbol of a further stage in their commitment to one another, had been sent off to be resized and currently reposed in Charmian's jewellery box until they should finally decide to announce their intentions to the world. Those who saw the two of them occasionally dining out together, of whom one was the gossip columnist Julian

Cazalet, assumed the relationship to be of the business variety.

The night Toby had a drink at the Savoy with Oliver, he got back to Charmian's flat sooner than usual. He kissed her. Mixing him a drink, 'You're early. What happened? Did she stand you up?' teased Charmian.

'Not this time,' replied Toby. 'I've been having an informal meeting with ex-Circumference executive Oliver Curtis. At the Savoy.'

Taken by surprise, Charmian saw that there were only two ways to play this. The first was to maintain the fiction that she did not know Oliver and the second to admit that she did and to divulge her own connection. Charmian decided on the second.

'Oliver Curtis is my brother-in-law,' said Charmian. 'Oh, and by the way, I found a flat today!'

Toby stared at her. There was a short, loaded silence.

'What did you say?'

'I said I found a flat today.'

'Never mind about the flat for the moment. Did I hear you say that Oliver Curtis is your brother-in-law?' His eyebrows drew together. He was suspicious and then suddenly furious. 'Why haven't you told me this before? What's going on?'

The belligerence of his sudden attack took her breath away.

Why hadn't she?

'Because,' said Charmian finally, 'it takes me a long time to trust and it wasn't just my life that was involved here. Apart from that there's nothing going on.'

'You really expect me to believe that?'

Regrouping and angry too, Charmian said, 'I don't expect to be accused of lying!'

He disregarded this. 'Does Curtis know about you and me? Does he?'

'No, he doesn't!'

Toby looked at her for a minute in silence. 'I don't believe you!'

The storm had blown up so quickly that Charmian was totally unprepared for it.

'But, Toby, there's no deep-laid plot here. I don't know what your agenda is where Oliver is concerned, I don't even know what the master plan you're currently working on is. All I know is that it appears to be the most important happening in your life, to the point where it comes before our wedding!'

Toby was silent for a moment. He remembered meeting Alexandra Curtis at the Royal Opera House. Studying her he had been conscious then of an elusive echo but had been unable to pin down what it was. Now he knew. Further he recalled this evening's talk with Oliver Curtis and the mention of the disparate in-laws who were about to try to co-exist again under the same roof, and the similar disquieting feeling of having already been part of the same conversation. Toby hated to be made to look a fool and hated even more the idea that he had been taken for one and manipulated. In that respect he had been conditioned by his firing at the hands of Hugo Rattray-Smythe which he had not seen coming.

Thinking: why the hell should I put up with this? Charmian protested with vigour, 'May I point out that there are no doubt many things you have not told me but I am not making the sort of paranoid scene with which you are seeing fit to indulge yourself!'

'And may I point out to *you* that I am involved in a business deal of the greatest delicacy and importance which your devious machinations, whatever they are, could no doubt comprehensively dish if you put your mind to it. I don't know what you're up to, Charmian, but I don't like it and I don't trust it! Next you'll be telling me that Hugo Rattray-Smythe is a bosom friend of yours.'

Clearly this was not the moment to describe her acquaintance with *him*. All the same, it was the last straw.

'I'm not up to anything!' shouted Charmian, finally losing her temper. 'But if that's what you really think then perhaps you had better go!' She felt nauseous and confused and aware that she had seen the dark side of Toby Gill who was so determined to feel betrayed that he appeared incapable of listening, let alone rationally appraising what she was trying to tell him. Considering his power, his vulnerability was astonishing.

Deeply wounded but at the same time aware that this farcical misunderstanding had to be stopped by one of them and he was incapable of doing it, on impulse Charmian put her hand on his arm. 'Toby…'

He brushed it off. 'You're right. I should go. You can keep the ring.'

He went. The front door slammed.

Left alone in her silently reverberating flat, 'Bastard!' cried Charmian. 'Arrogant, unreasonable bastard!'

Distraught and weeping, she threw herself on the bed.

The following morning she awoke to the sound of rain. Fine and light it fell, the perfect foil for her own sombre mood. Charmian took the solitaire out of its box. She placed it on her finger and looked at it. There was a certain candour about diamonds. Other gems such as emeralds, had always struck her as much more sinful, something to do with the depth of their colour, perhaps. She slipped it off, slotted it into its own small square box and proceeded to wrap this up, finally putting it in a jiffy bag. She picked up the telephone receiver and dialled a number. When it answered Charmian said, 'I have a small package which I want delivered to Mr Toby Gill personally.' She gave the address of Stellar. In answer to the next question she replied, 'I know it's early, but he will be there. It's the time of the morning when he goes through all the papers.' Listening to herself, she vaguely wondered why on earth she was bothering to pass on such a pointless piece of information to a taxi firm who could not have been less interested in the personal habits of Toby Gill. 'When you have delivered it, I should like you to ring me and tell me,' said Charmian.

She pressed the receiver rest and then rang her assistant.

'It's Charmian. I shan't be in today. I'm ill. Nothing

serious but I would be grateful if you could hold the fort. Hopefully I'll be in tomorrow.'

She hung up.

With the post came an invitation to the wedding of Giles and Karen. Reading it with a leaden heart, Charmian found the timing of its arrival ironic. She propped it up on the mantelpiece and drew her wrap around her. Then she crossed the room and sat down on a chair by the window where she remained for a long time without moving, watching the falling rain.

20

Reg Spivey's memory of events before the car crash filled out a little but not radically. During one of their meetings the consultant said to Shirley, 'The mind is a very unpredictable thing. It could all suddenly come back to him. Once he's at home in familiar surroundings among familiar possessions you'll probably notice an improvement.'

Reflecting that home was rather peaceful without Reg, Shirley asked, 'When do you expect to discharge him?'

'Shouldn't be long now,' replied the consultant, in the manner of doctors everywhere managing to sound reassuring without committing himself. 'Of course I understand that you're anxious to have him back.'

'Mmm,' said Shirley also non-committal, by no means sure that she was. For apart from his unreliable memory, Reg was very much himself again, which is to say that he was ungratefully dismissive of the stalwart role she, Shirley, had played in his recuperation and, without a conglomerate to terrorize, extraordinarily autocratic about the smallest happenings. It was no longer possible, for instance, to 'shield' him from Circumference, which was why Neville Cruickshank had at last succeeded in achieving an audience that afternoon and Hugo Rattray-Smythe was expected to visit the following day. It was, Shirley recognized, the beginning of the end of her brief omnipotence.

When he was finally allowed to enter Reg Spivey's hospital room, Cruickshank was struck by the way in which certain people were able to retain their aura of menace while wearing the most unlikely clothes. Reg was sitting up in bed wearing maroon pyjamas piped with white and with the *Daily Telegraph* business section open in front of him.

'At last!' exclaimed Spivey, with unmistakable aggression.

At last?

Cruickshank gave his Chief Executive an apprehensive look. Clearly there was a need to mend a fence, though the fact that he had not materialized at the end of the bed before now was not his fault.

'I would have come sooner,' apologized Cruickshank, 'but Shirley said you weren't up to it. She wouldn't allow it.'

Giving his Finance Director an are-you-a-man-or-a-mouse? look, Spivey said, 'Bollocks! Anyway, now you're finally here, get on with it!'

Cruickshank launched into his catalogue of woe. The audit. What to do next? More to the point, *how* to do whatever was supposed to happen next while Reg, the brains behind it all, was *hors de combat* and the blissfully ignorant Hugo Rattray-Smythe was in charge. Spivey heard him out. The relief for Cruickshank to have some guidance in the offing was immense. And destined to be short-lived.

'I don't know what you're talking about,' said Reg at last. 'That is, some of it rings a bell, but most of it doesn't. I simply can't remember. It might well suddenly come back, according to the consultant.'

But not soon enough. All hope dashed, Cruickshank looked speechlessly at Reg. It was becoming apparent that the day the auditors moved into Circumference, he, Neville, might as well purchase himself a ticket to Rio de Janeiro.

'*Try* to remember!' beseeched Cruickshank. '*Try!*'

'I *am* trying!' Spivey was irritable. 'But at the moment I don't recognize any of it. Are you telling me that you and I between us were perpetrating a massive fraud?'

'Yes!'

Recollection hovered on the perimeter of Spivey's memory and then was gone. He experienced the oddest sensation of being as near as dammit to knowing what Cruickshank was on about, while at the same time being a long way away. So near and yet so far.

'You'd better take me through it all again,' said Spivey at last. 'Slowly.'

When he took delivery of the small package, Toby Gill knew exactly what it was. He extracted the diamond. There was no note, just the ring. In the palm of his hand it scintillated, reminding him of Charmian's own sophisticated sparkle. Eventually he put it in his office safe, entered the combination and then, bleakly, turned back to his desk.

That evening Gill went home late. There was, after all, nothing particular to go home for. It was when he was standing in front of the full-length mirror in his dressing room, loosening his tie that he thought he saw Clare. Just for a fraction of a second she stood behind him, a pale wraith reflected among the shadows in the depths of the old glass. She gave a slight characteristic shake of her head just as she used to in life when for one reason or another he was making an ass of himself, and then she was gone. Aloud, to his dead wife, Gill said, 'It's no use. Where I can't trust, I can't love. You know that!'

Even as he spoke them the words had an unconvincing ring.

Answer came there none.

Hungry for the sound of her voice, Gill dialled his lover's telephone number. Listening to the tone and then her voice telling him that she was not there he remembered the times he had done this before, after their first encounter at the Poussin when he had not left a message but through the medium of the machine felt himself to be with her in her flat, which he had not, at that point in time, yet seen. Why had he never left a message? Because, thought Gill, I didn't want to make a mistake. I wanted to know it was *meant*, I wanted that sense of the inevitable. I wanted whatever was going to happen next to come after me. And it did. All those sightings, the opera, the restaurant, the concert, she was moving nearer all the time. Lastly the Goddard party clinched it.

He wondered where she was tonight and, more to the point who she was with. Sexual jealousy was the worst kind.

Oh, Charmian. Clare's right! I've been the worst kind of fool!

He groaned.

With morning came a hardening of the heart, a chilly unforgiving recognition of the fact that Charmian had been less than frank. The worm of distrust gnawed on, causing Gill to reverse the decision he had just made, which was to seek a *rapprochement* with his lover. Instead he decided to look neither to right nor left, but concentrate on work and most especially on the spectacular coup he was currently aiming to bring off.

In spring Oliver Curtis received the letter he had been waiting for. It informed him that the job he had been pursuing was his if he wanted it. This brought to the fore the question of Toby Gill and his mysterious plans. As requested he rang Gill up and then, on being invited to do so, went to see him.

Sitting opposite the other man, it was Oliver's impression that this meeting was not as cordial as their last one. There was nothing he could exactly pinpoint, just the sensation of distance between them. The lightening he had noticed the last time he had seen Gill was no longer in evidence and had been replaced by an aura of altogether gloomier aspect. Unable to believe that this atmospheric shift could have anything to do with him, Oliver felt he had no alternative but to ignore it. He apprised Gill of his own position and then sat back and waited.

Gill stared out of the window. The day was a grey one. Rain drifted rather than fell and the pavements had a snakelike sheen. April already. Gill sighed. The timing was a bugger for he was still not in a position to make Curtis an offer. And then there was the other matter, which Gill had resolved to settle today. Normally a man who did not mix sentiment with business, here he felt he had no choice. Accordingly he sprang his little trap. Gill suddenly said, 'Have you ever met a woman called Charmian Sinclair?'

Oliver laughed. 'Of course I have. She's my sister-in-law! How do you come to know her?'

The candour of the Curtis response revealed to Gill as nothing else could that the conspiracy theory was wrong. I've made a mistake, thought Gill. Whatever Charmian's agenda had been it was not that. He was filled with relief. He smiled across his desk at Oliver who was once again aware of a change of climate and at a loss as to how to account for it. Ignoring the last question, Gill said, 'Can you dead bat the other lot for a while? Keep them in play but not take a final decision?'

'Yes, but not for very long,' replied Oliver. 'As I'm sure you understand, I don't want to end up with nothing.'

'I do understand. Three more weeks would probably do it.'

'OK. I'll do my best,' said Oliver. 'When are you going to be able to tell me what this is all about?'

'Very soon now,' replied Gill.

After he had taken his leave, it occurred to Oliver that he had never received an answer to his question concerning his sister-in-law.

That evening, Toby Gill rang Charmian Sinclair's number. This time she answered. He could hear music playing in the background. The Trio. *Cosi fan tutte*. Gill did not say a word but simply hung up. Without wasting any time he went outside and hailed a cab.

The sound of her bell took Charmian, who was not expecting anyone, by surprise. She opened the door and found herself confronted by Toby Gill. He stepped forward over the threshold, took her left hand and slipped the solitaire on to her finger.

'Forgive me!' he said.

21

The upshot of the public announcement of the forth-coming wedding of Toby Gill and Charmian Sinclair was not unconfined joy.

'Why couldn't you have tipped me the wink?' grumbled Julian Cazalet. 'My editor's been complaining about my page lately and that would have given me a scoop.'

'I'm not getting married after all this time on the loose to provide gossip column scoops,' was Charmian's answer to this. Hugo Rattray-Smythe, still smarting from his munificent unintended donation to the Cat Protection League, was very put out as well, but was not afforded the opportunity to say so personally. In adman's land, Nigel Guest was uncertain as to whether he should preen since he had been the (albeit unwitting) cause of these two coming together or sulk because no one had kept him abreast of events and he had had to learn about them from his newspaper. Finally he decided to tell nobody that this had been the case thereby insinuating that he had been in the know all along, and preened anyway. In Hong Kong, putting his back into his new job and, intermittently, his marriage, Dominic Goddard was wistful. He remembered irresponsible Monday evenings off the leash in Charmian's stimulating company and even more stimulating and irresponsible nights in her bed and regretted their passing.

Gervase Hanson rang his ex-lover up.

'What can I do but salute you Charmian? Half of female London would have liked to have been the next Mrs Toby Gill and you pulled it off. It's a veritable coup!'

'I know,' said Charmian modestly, 'but it's not just that. I'm in love!'

'Well, I've already told you what I think about that!'

'Yes, you have.'

'However, I see I shall have to set about finding a replacement since, as things stand there is no point in keeping your old position vacant for you.'

'None whatsoever,' said Charmian.

On the family front opinion was divided. Initially astonished, Alexandra took the view that Gill was probably the ideal partner for her unconventional sister. 'Marriage will give her security while at the same time keeping her in the urban social swim. But best of all she's so *happy!*' Oliver, it had to be said, was ambivalent. On one level he was pleased for his sister-in-law and on another, knowing as she had that he was having talks with Toby Gill, felt that she could have confided in the two of them.

'You know Charmian,' said Alexandra indulgently. 'She's the cat that walks alone.'

'So's he,' was Oliver's reply to this, 'so it probably *is* a good idea that they are marrying each other. They can be solitary together. I still have no idea what he has in mind for me. Or whether the fact that he's about to become a member of the family will have an adverse or a positive effect on what does or doesn't happen next.'

'Legend has it that Gill is very professional. My guess is it will have no effect one way or the other. If he thinks you're up to whatever it is he has in mind, you'll get it. If he doesn't, you won't.'

Father, on the other hand, was affronted by the development of events and seized every opportunity to say so.

'Nobody asked me!' He sounded very discontented. 'Who is this fellow, anyway? I've already lost one daughter to marriage, now I'm about to lose the other. It's too bad, Violet, too bad!'

Violet wasn't having it.

'Don't be so selfish, Austin. You've still got me!'

Her partner's moodiness was not alleviated by this statement of fact.

'Yes I know!'

'They're coming to see us tomorrow evening so mind you behave yourself.'

'As if I wouldn't,' said Austin.

Violet and Austin had settled into a sort of *modus vivendi* which suited both better than Austin was prepared to admit. Violet Sinclair looked up old acquaintances and began to give dinner parties.

'You're a much better cook than when we were married,' observed Father grudgingly.

'Since you were hardly ever there to eat it, I'm not

sure you're qualified to give an opinion,' was Violet's smart retort to this. Removal from the constant company of the monosyllabic Vlad had rendered her almost fluent, he had noticed with alarm.

When Toby Gill first met them he was struck by how unlike either Charmian was. If anything this came as something of a relief. Austin Sinclair he marked down almost immediately as an upper-crust drone, a man who felt the rest of the world, and that included his nearest and dearest, owed him not just a living but total allegiance as well. Mrs Sinclair ('you may call me Violet, Toby') was harder to fathom, probably because the ex-pat years with the unsatisfactory Russian had blurred her stereotype and of the two of them, Gill found her the more interesting. Also invited to dinner were Oliver and Alexandra. Without appearing to do so, Gill studied all of them. The resemblance between Alexandra and her sister was hard to pin down. It came and went and probably owed more to expression and voice timbre than physical similarity. But then they were half-sisters. In his mind's eye he once again saw Alexandra at the opera (*Don Carlos*, wasn't it?) and remembered the odd little incident he had witnessed when she had said something to Reg Spivey which nobody else had been able to hear and which had caused the man to look as if he might be about to have a fit. He resolved to ask her what it was she had said, and when Charmian went off to help Violet in the kitchen and Austin, precariously propped up by two sticks, was sorting out the drinks, he did.

'What did I say?' Alexandra laughed. 'I said,

"You're a treacherous bastard and, by the way, I know what's going on at Circumference. You won't get away with it! The secret's out!'''

'What did you *mean?*' asked Gill curiously.

'To tell you the truth I'm not sure, although his reaction was such that he knew what I meant.'

'But you must have had something in mind.'

'Well, if you must know, I went to see a clairvoyant who told me that there was going to be a massive upset at Oliver's old company. She doesn't know it's Circumference, by the way. And part of the reason for the upset would be that someone there is doing certain things they shouldn't be doing. It sounded like fraud.'

'You never told me about this!' Oliver was startled. Listening, it occurred to Gill that the Sinclair women appeared to specialize in keeping their men in the dark.

'I thought you wouldn't approve.'

'I don't! Anyway, since you went ahead and did it notwithstanding, what else did she say?'

'Oh lots of things.' Alexandra was deliberately vague because she did not wish to divulge too much in front of Toby Gill at this precise moment. 'Better not to recite from memory, I'll only get it wrong. You can listen to the tape, if you like.'

There's a tape is there? Never mind about Oliver, *I'd* like to listen to that tape, thought Gill. I wonder if Charmian knows about this. Aloud he said, 'How accurate is this woman?'

'On past form, very,' said Alexandra. 'Although I have to say I thought she might have over-reached herself here. Like them or loathe them, and I loathe them in view of what they did to Oliver and, more importantly how it was done, Circumference is a very prestigious company and so far as I'm aware there has never been the remotest suggestion of such a thing!' Though what about the paintings, on the other hand? Watching him, she saw the same thought cross her husband's mind. She caught Oliver's eye and tacitly they both decided to say nothing about that. Father might, after all, have got that wrong.

'You'll find more fraud goes on in the City that you'd ever expect and in some very unexpected places too,' said Gill, unconsciously echoing the opinion Charmian had expressed when Alexandra had first told her about Mrs Hemingway's intriguing prophecy.

The return of Father, together with Violet and Charmian and the drinks, caused the conversation to take a more general turn. For the time being, Gill put all thoughts of Circumference out of his head and concentrated instead on the family. Later on he would have the opportunity to ask Charmian about it. The time had come for both of them to put all their cards on the table.

In the event it was neither Charmian nor Alexandra who divulged the secret concerning the paintings, but Austin Sinclair himself at one of Violet's dinner parties. All those present had heard of Circumference and their rapt attention while he told the tale was gratifying. Before, incarcerated as he had been in Peckham, there had been no one to tell this particular story to. In two days it was all over the City.

When this rumour reached Gill's ears, which was almost straight away, he related the fact to Charmian, who once again found herself in the position of having to admit that here was one more thing which she could have told him but had not. The reason for this had been the promise of silence she had made Hugo Rattray-Smythe in exchange for Reg Spivey not being nominated for a knighthood. On the other hand she, Charmian, had kept her word and what had since happened was scarcely her fault. And the fact enables me to tell Toby everything, she decided. Otherwise my past will keep catching up with me in this inconvenient and frankly rather threatening way. Accordingly, over dinner one evening, she related the whole story. Gill listened attentively without interruption. Her account of the Hugo Rattray-Smythe weekend caused his face to darken, but that was all. When she had finished he sat for a while in silence. Finally he said, 'It struck me the other day that the time had come for total frankness and in the view of what you've just said, I'm going to pay you the same compliment. That is, I'm going to tell you exactly what I'm doing, thereby letting down my guard totally, something since Clare's death I have never done with anybody. Never felt I could *afford* to do with anybody.'

When he had finished, Charmian sat back in her chair and looked at her husband-to-be with undisguised admiration.

'Do you really think you can bring that off?'

'I don't see why not! As they say: nothing ventured,

nothing gained. But never mind about that for the moment.'

He raised the glass. 'Here's to us.'

In turn she raised hers. 'To us!'

The following day a letter arrived for Toby Gill. Scanning it, he said aloud to himself, 'Well, I'll be damned!' He put it in his briefcase and when he got to Charmian's flat much later on, handed it to her.

'Read that!' he said.

Unable to stave it off any longer on the pretext he was not yet well enough, Shirley had taken Reg home. Without enough to occupy him, and still without most of his business memory, though maddeningly things of little consequence were beginning to come back, Reg was a snort-tempered convalescent. As she had feared would be the case, a steady stream of personnel from Circumference came and went. The house, which had been hers for several weeks, was now very firmly his and Shirley was treated as though she was his outer office. Of all the visitors, the one most in evidence was Neville Cruickshank who seemed to get more despondent by the day.

It was now May. The weather was warmer and the hedgerows bridal with blossom. Shirley took to going out for drives in the country on her own, just to get away from Reg for a while and achieve some peace and quiet. In the mornings he was particularly neurotic, practically waiting on the doormat for the post to come, and when it did scrutinizing each envelope in a wild-eyed, hungry way which Shirley found positively unnerving. Then the blow fell. Reg learnt from one of his corporate peers who was to receive an MBE that the honours list letters had been sent out a week ago. It seemed that he had been passed over, not just for the coveted knighthood but everything else as well. The explosion of disappointment and ire was pitiful to behold and that day Shirley went for a very long drive indeed.

The following afternoon Hugo Rattray-Smythe was scheduled to pay his Chief Executive a visit. Because he was the subject of them, none of the rumours vis-à-vis the Rattray-Smythe collection had reached Hugo's ears and since, although gossip was rife, the business press had dared not to print them as yet, Spivey knew nothing about the stories going the rounds either. Neville Cruickshank did but was so embattled on every other front that, ostrich-like, he decided to ignore them in the hope that the whole thing would simply go away.

When Rattray-Smythe arrived, Shirley let him into her sitting room which had been commandeered as Reg's office, and discreetly withdrew.

Hugo, who knew this was going to be a sticky one, had marshalled his thoughts for once and he it was who brought the subject up.

'I'm told the letters have gone out,' said Hugo. 'So is it congratulations then?'

'Don't you know?' Spivey was snappy.

'No, they inform the recommendee but never the recommender.'

'And you did recommend me?' Reg was plainly very suspicious.

'Yes, oh yes,' lied Hugo blandly, 'I said I would and I did but, as I don't have to tell you, recommend is *all* I can do. The actual award is in somebody else's gift. What a shame! Dear, oh dear. Bad luck...' There seemed very little he could add to this. His voice faded away.

Based on he could not quite have said what, Spivey did not believe his Chairman. There was no way of proving it one way or the other, of course, but he took the only revenge open to him anyway. 'I intend to be back in the office on Monday,' said Spivey, gimlet-eyed. 'Without fail.'

Although in some quarters the news was not unexpected, the family was taken by surprise by Toby Gill's knighthood which was one of the services to industry variety.

'Goodness,' said Alexandra to Oliver, 'won't my sister be grand! Lady Gill, no less. I wonder who put him up for it.'

'No idea,' replied Oliver, whose mind was more pre-occupied with what was going to happen next at Stellar than with Toby's title. 'What does Austin think about it?'

'Since, as you know, he's the most monumental snob, Father's tickled pink, talks of nothing else and longs to publicly brag. Which he's not allowed to do until the list is published. Mother can be heard saying at regular intervals, ''*Do* shut up, Austin!'''

'Considering he didn't approve of the marriage, I think that's rich.'

'He approves of it now. Total reconcilement is the order of the day and he doesn't like reminders of his initial stance either. In short, he can't wait to give his daughter away.'

'Never mind what my future brother-in-law's intentions are vis-à-vis Charmian,' said Oliver. 'I need to know what they are vis-à-vis myself. As it is I'm running out of further negotiating points with the other lot and if I'm not careful they'll smell a rat and I'll lose it.'

'Why don't you request another meeting?'

'Because I don't want to look too eager.'

'Then it's an impasse.'

'Not quite. I think I can finesse one more week's grace. Let's see what happens.'

22

Charmian went to the wedding reception of Giles and Karen. This time there would be no one to meet her off the train so she drove. She did not take Toby Gill with her. The bridal pair had erected a marquee on the lawn and by the time Charmian arrived this was crowded. Giles and his wife were at the entrance greeting their guests. He was plainly very moved to see her. Karen stood by, gravely watching the two of them as they chastely kissed.

'I'm very happy for you,' said Charmian simply. 'No, I'm not. I'm very happy for you *both*.'

She smiled at Karen, who smiled back. Karen was wearing a long skirted suit whose short, fitted jacket was trimmed at bodice and cuff with rough creamy lace. The neckline was low, though not too low, and emphasized the length of her neck round which she had tied a wide black velvet ribbon on which was pinned a large oval bloodstone rimmed with gold. In her hair, which was up and from which escaped floating spiralling tendrils, was one camellia. Karen really *is* straight out of Thomas Hardy, thought Charmian, admiring her stylish turn-of-the-century country simplicity which both epitomized this garden wedding and, at the same time, proclaimed her queen of the day. A May queen.

The two women kissed. And stood back.

'Do I gather that ours is not the only celebration?' said Karen.

'If you mean that am I shortly to be married too,' replied Charmian, 'that's right.'

'Are you?' Giles was amazed. Clearly this was the first he had heard of it. Karen had known but had not told him. 'Who to?'

'A man called Toby Gill.'

'Good God!' said Giles, 'You mean…'

'Yes,' said Charmian. 'That's who I mean.' She was conscious that the old restraint between herself and Karen had evaporated. 'Here come more guests. I'd better leave you to it.'

The two of them parted to let her pass. Looking back before mingling with the crowd she saw Karen also look back. The light from the entrance of the tent traced a luminous line around the figures of her and Giles binding the two of them together. A duo. No longer the trio. Karen fractionally inclined her head and so did Charmian. It was a tacit admission of mutual respect. Charmian accepted a glass of champagne and moved on.

Later on there was dancing. Giles danced first with his wife, then with several of the other ladies and finally with Charmian. With his arm around her waist for what would probably be the last time he said, 'So you're finally going to do it. But not with me.'

'Not with you and rightly so,' answered Charmian, 'for all the reasons we discussed. You and Karen are perfect for one another. You know that.'

Giles was silent. In his heart of hearts he did know that. All the same, part of him still yearned. A vision of her naked in the garden the day of the thunderstorm passed briefly before his inner eye and was gone. It was all past history now. The music, which was being played by a local band, stopped.

'I think perhaps I'd better reclaim my wife,' said Giles. They both looked across at her. Karen's hair was beginning to come down becomingly in long looped drifts. She was dancing with an uncoordinated person whom Charmian presumed to be the local vicar. Her colour was high and her face animated. She looked at ease with herself and her surroundings and very happy. And deserves to be, decided Charmian. How funny that I am marrying a widower and Giles has married a widow. Though Karen was no longer a widow but once again a bride.

'I'll come with you to say goodbye.'

Marcus Marchant and Oliver Curtis met for lunch.

'With one definite job offer under your belt and a couple of possibilities, I should say things were looking up for the Curtises,' observed Marcus. 'What's stopping you taking up the first?'

'Strictly between ourselves, Stellar is on the tapis!'

'Christ! Well, since your sister-in-law is about to become Mrs Toby Gill, I should have thought that was a cinch.'

'Not necessarily,' said Oliver. 'Gill doesn't work like that, which is probably one of the reasons why he has been so inordinately successful. All I know is that he's about to make an acquisition of some sort and if he does, I'm in the running for one of the top slots. More I cannot tell you at this stage. The man is obsessively secretive. What I don't want to do is to lose the other.'

'No, you don't. I take it you've heard the rumours about Circumference, by the way?'

'What rumours?'

'Gossip in the City suggests that Hugo's art collection is composed largely of copies and that the same might apply to one or two of the Circumference paintings.'

Oliver was startled. 'How on earth did that get out?'

'What! You knew?' Marcus was incredulous.

'No, not while I was there. My delinquent father-in-law suggested quite recently that that was the case.' He recounted the story. 'Alexandra and I decided not to tell a soul since it sounded inherently unlikely. Austin's an old man and it seemed to us that he had probably got it wrong.'

'True or false, somebody's let the cat out of the bag.'

'Well, I don't know who it could have been. Maybe Charmian did, although I'd be very surprised if so. Charmian plays her cards even closer to her chest than Gill does. No, the candidate I think I'd put my money on is Austin himself, who's never heard of the word discretion. Though he might be about to learn the meaning of the word slander if he doesn't watch himself.'

'Well, well!' said Marcus. 'All I can say is that, coupled with all the other doubts vis-à-vis the company's performance, it hasn't helped the share price. Though I gather Spivey's back at the helm.'

'Just in time for the auditors. Impossible to leave that sort of thing to Rattray-Smythe. He doesn't know his arse from his elbow.'

'No, I don't suppose he does. What about a coffee?'

Back in his office at Circumference, and unaware that he was being talked about in a fashionable Covent Garden restaurant, Reg Spivey grappled with the problem of his fluctuating memory. More and more was coming back but there were still huge gaps. The frustration caused by this shortfall was immense. Shirley in particular was glad her husband was once again in harness and as she luxuriated in the repossession of her sitting room, her petrol bills fell.

Neville Cruickshank, whose fervent prayer for the restoration of Reg to his former self (something he had never expected to ask for) remained unanswered, looked haunted. It was apparent to Cruickshank that unless a miracle happened, he and his fellow conspirator were heading for a fall. The thought of the money in the Swiss bank account did not cheer him up the way it once had. Blissfully oblivious to what was going on right under his nose, and what the City rumour mill was saying about him behind his back, Hugo Rattray-Smythe went back to his old indolent ways and the design of his grounds. Noblesse oblige, was Hugo's view, surveying his domain in which yet another garden designer was glumly interpreting his ideas. This was what Hugo would bequeath to posterity. He was aware that Reg Spivey was still far from all right but found it convenient to ignore this fact for the time being since he was now heavily engaged on a grandiose Sir Humphry Repton-style relandscaping of the park. It did, however, occur to him that if things did not improve it would be possible to insist on invaliding Reg out of Circumference. He said as much on dropping into Neville Cruickshank's office.

'Poor old Reg,' said Hugo. 'I'm afraid he's not the man he was.'

'No,' replied Neville through gritted teeth. 'He isn't.'

'Funny thing, the mind,' ruminated Hugo, feeling profound as he uttered these words. 'He can't remember an awful lot, you know!'

'I know.' Panic, a familiar emotion these days, overran Cruickshank. 'The problem is that the auditors move in next week and there are certain incomplete transactions which only Reg understands. Maybe we should postpone the audit...'

Rattray-Smythe was surprised. 'Auditors aren't stupid, you know. Let's get it out of the way. What worries me is not the state of the books but the state of Reg. We can't lurch on for very much longer with a chief executive who can't remember anything. Though I gather it could all come back.'

Mentally once again on his knees before his Maker,

though without much hope in his heart, Neville silently petitioned that it would, and soon.

For the nth time Neville Cruickshank tried to explain to his Chief Executive what they had been doing together before his accident.

'That can't be right,' said Spivey. 'That would be fraud!'

Cruickshank felt close to suicide. The car crash appeared to have selectively removed all recollection of their joint nefarious endeavour and replaced it with the sort of probity normally foreign to Reg. Every so often there was a small breakthrough, which indicated that the knowledge was all there somewhere but, so far without exception, these had come to nothing. The audit was due to start on the following Monday. Without the ability of Reg to put into action whatever master plan it was he had had in mind, they were lost. And it was probably too late anyway. Sitting alone in his office on Thursday night, Cruickshank saw clearly what he must do. He seized the telephone and dialled a number. When it finally answered, informing him that it was Iberia Airlines: 'Put me through to reservations, would you please?' said Neville.

When the call was concluded to his satisfaction, Cruickshank opened his desk drawer and extracted his passport. All was in place, including a visa, since he anticipated being in Brazil beyond the mandatory ninety days. Staring disaster in the face, he had had all the recommended innoculations as well. He opened his office safe and then his briefcase, into which he transferred several wads of notes leaving the safe empty before closing the door. After doing this and with nothing but the clothes he stood up in and his briefcase, he let himself out of his office and, wishing to be as anonymous as possible, walked to the nearest underground station into which he disappeared without trace. Because he was an accountant and therefore had an orderly mind, Neville left his office in its usual tidy state with the result that there was nothing to suggest that he had gone for good. When he did not appear in the office the following morning, it was assumed that he was ill. Considering his generally wan appearance over the past month or two, nobody was too surprised by this.

The sound of Molly Cruickshank's voice on the line wondering where her husband was therefore came as a shock. As he disclaimed any knowledge of his Finance Director's present location, Reg Spivey was nevertheless alerted and possibly it was this concentration of mind which caused the shifting fragmented kaleidoscope of recent elusive events suddenly to begin to form a coherent pattern. Spivey promised to ring Molly back if he received any news and then heaved himself out of his chair and walked down the corridor to Neville's office. He let himself in. Everything looked exactly the same as usual, even down to the photograph of Neville's worried wife and unworried children. The room smelt stuffy and its one pot plant, a yucca, was wilting. Spivey opened the window, allowing an infusion of warm air. Idly, he opened the top drawer of Cruickshank's desk and examined the contents. He was immediately aware that something was missing. But what? Perplexed, he stared at it for a moment or two. Finally, his memory, which was still stubbornly refusing to release important information while at the same time having no such inhibition about trivia, deigned to reveal the fact that Neville's passport was not in its usual place. Reg knew that Neville always kept his passport at the office because he, Reg, had told him to. The reason for this was that Neville had once failed to catch the flight they were both supposed to be on in order to attend an important business meeting in Germany, due to the fact that his passport had been sitting in outer suburbia along with Molly instead of in his briefcase where it should have been. Spivey peered at the passport-sized space. It was inconceivable that Neville was being insubordinate. Subservience was one of the reasons Neville was where he was in corporate terms. Maybe the absent document was away being renewed. Dismissing it, he shut the drawer and went back along the corridor to report to Molly that he had nothing to report.

There was probably a perfectly rational explanation for the non-appearance of Neville but, all the same, it was odd.

Molly did not take this view. She went to the police. The police, who encountered in the course of their duties multitudinous bewildered deserted spouses who had been impervious over the years to the mounting desperation of their partners within the confines of stale marriages, were politely unhelpful.

'But my husband wouldn't leave, just like that,' said

Molly. 'My husband was steady, reliable. My husband was an *accountant!*'

Forbearing to observe that in his experience accountants were frequently the most unreliable of the lot, the officer she was talking to suggested, 'Maybe you had a tiff, Mrs Cruickshank? A little falling out, shall we say? We all have them, you know.'

Molly was firm. 'Neville and I *never* disagreed with one another. We've been together twenty-seven years and never a cross word.'

Observing her as she sat opposite him, matronly in Crimplene and peep-toed sandals, an essentially decent, unimaginative woman, it was his view that here was just one more atrophied marriage.

'Did your husband take anything with him?'

'Well, that's the funny thing. No, he didn't. I mean he had his credit cards and chequebook but he always carried those, of course. He just went off to the office as usual with his briefcase and never came back. I just don't understand it!'

No, they never did, thought the police officer. It was beginning to sound like a classic.

'What about his passport?'

'He always kept that in his desk drawer at the office.'

Molly was silent for a few seconds, remembering the awful row which had ensued over the passport and its whereabouts the day Neville had missed his flight to Germany.

'Had your husband been behaving strangely lately? I mean had he been depressed, that sort of thing?'

Well, yes he had. Molly had noticed it. There had been a faraway look in Neville's eye, as though he was preoccupied by something and a tendency not to listen to what she was saying so that she had to say whatever it was three times. And his mood had been uneven too lately, alternating between despondency and snappiness, possibly because he was drinking more than usual. Not a reader of the *Daily Mail* for nothing. Molly had ascribed this to the male menopause and had got on with polishing her G-plan furniture and making her toad-in-the-hole (one of Neville's favourites) in the belief that, in the fullness of time, it would all pass.

'What should I do next?' Her shoulders slumped. She sounded defeated.

'Nothing you can do but wait, Mrs Cruickshank. He'll probably turn up. They mostly do, you know. I'm afraid unless we think a crime has been committed, there's nothing much we can do either except register your husband as a missing person.'

He stood up and so did she. Watching her go, he shook his head slightly and then turned back to the paperwork on his desk.

On his way to Brazil, Neville Cruickshank mulled over the strange twist his life had taken. As the plane took off, lifting him beyond his troubles and taking him in the direction of a new life, euphoria was Neville's primary emotion. Through the plane window he watched sulphurous clouds, shot with gold, mass and surge. He slipped his hand inside his briefcase and felt the reassuring dry brittleness of wads of banknotes. This heady rush of excitement did not last long. It lasted for one glass of champagne to be exact. For he, Neville, had now comprehensively burnt his boats. There could be no going back. Not if he could help it, anyway.

By now Molly would know that something was amiss.

Molly.

Over the years his marriage, except in so far as it constituted practical backup, had ceased to have much emotional significance. In its place, habit and convenience had loomed large with the result that had Neville been asked if he was happily married it would have been hard for him to answer this. On the whole, though unelectrified, he supposed he was—or rather had been. Neville was ambivalent about doing without Molly's unquestioning support, if not her body, but not ambivalent about doing without toad-in-the-hole, of which he had tired about ten years ago. Nor was he ambivalent about seeing the back of Reg Spivey, on whom he blamed all his misfortunes. Although *were* they misfortunes? Here he was, off to Rio, fancy-free, Neville told himself, with stacks of cash. Although not quite fancy-free, because what about his children on whom he doted? Both were at university. As a result of this he did not see that much of either of them, unless they needed money or a bed for the night, which in the outer suburbs had been hardly ever. All the same, for the foreseeable future cutoff was going to be total.

This caused him to wonder how long it was likely to be before his whereabouts finally became known. The scandal, when it broke, would be immense and in its wake would come hue and cry. There was only one change of plane and that was at Madrid. Cruickshank had chosen Iberia deliberately because the connections were quick and the idea of hanging about en route to safety was insupportable.

On the last leg of his odyssey, he enquired of the stewardess the arrival time. On receiving the answer 05.45 he decided to try to get some sleep for tomorrow would have to be spent locating an anonymous hotel and a sharp lawyer, in that order.

In London, more days passed without the rematerialization of Neville Cruickshank. Molly rang up Reg Spivey again, this time sounding tearful.

'I went to the police,' said Molly, 'and they said people go missing all the time and unless there's a suspicion of foul play, there's nothing they can do. They wanted to know if his passport was still there.'

The passport.

'No, it isn't,' replied Spivey. 'I assumed he must be getting it renewed.'

'It's only just *been* renewed,' quavered Molly. 'I organized it for him myself. He was neurotic about that passport.'

And with good reason, thought Spivey, remembering the German débâcle. All the same this was beginning to look serious. Furthermore his memory of things past was beginning to improve as though the rags and

tatters of recollection were being invisibly mended.
What was coming back was not reassuring and Cruickshank's defection, if that was what it was, rather underlined this fact. Spivey decided that, until things clar-
ified, damage limitation, regardless of whether there
actually was damage or not, was the name of the game.
Accordingly the first thing he did was to corner Neville's secretary, Rosa, and instruct her to say nothing
about her boss's absence.

'Mr Cruickshank hasn't been feeling too well, Rosa,
and he's having a few days off. I'd be grateful if you
didn't tell anybody else,' said Reg.

Awed by his sheer size, 'Yes, Mr Spivey,' replied
Rosa, deciding not to mention the fact that she had
already told two other secretaries, who were friends,
that Mr Cruickshank had gone missing and that Mrs
Cruickshank had been on the phone three times a day
sounding fit to be tied. 'What would you like me to do
with his mail?'

'You deal with the dross and send the important
stuff through to me. And remember, Rosa, not a word
of this outside this room!'

'Yes, Mr Spivey. No, Mr Spivey.'

The next person he went to see was Hugo Rattray-
Smythe.

'Gone? What do you mean gone?' Hugo was thunderstruck. '*Where's* he gone?'

'For all I know, to the carnival in Rio,' spat Spivey,
unconsciously partly accurate and very irritable. 'All I
know is that nobody's seen him since last Thursday,

including Molly. It's now Wednesday, there's still no sign of him and his passport's missing. I want to halt the audit and go through the books myself!'

Aghast, Hugo said, 'You don't think Neville...?'

The last vestiges of this particular piece of the past marshalled themselves and fell into line.

Not Neville, but Neville and Reg. And Neville had bolted, thereby blowing the whole conspiracy wide open. Spivey saw with great clarity that his only hope of survival was the postponement of the audit.

Hugo could hardly believe his ears.

'Postpone the... Why should we do that? They're in the middle of it! Beside, if Neville has had his hand in the till we need to know about it!'

It was beginning to look as though Hugo's very denseness, which had been the main reason for Spivey's elevation, was also going to be the main reason for his fall. 'Yes, but, if so, we don't want everybody else to know about it as well.' Reg felt desperate. 'Credibility, Hugo. The share price!' The idea of a team of auditors moving inexorably through the books towards the black hole at the centre of the Circumference was horrific. What to do about it was another matter. He was to receive no help from his Chairman.

'No,' decreed Hugo finally, enjoying the spectacle of Reg's discomfiture without knowing the reason for it and mindful of many past verbal humiliations. 'No. The audit must go ahead.'

23

The dawn raid raising Gill's stake in Circumference to fifteen per cent was mounted with clinical efficiency and took everyone by surprise, except Charmian Sinclair and those on the Stellar takeover team. Unknown to the world at large, Toby Gill already had a substantial stake in his rival, bought through a nominee company and was also the possessor of two highly detailed reports assessing the value of his quarry. For months a fleet of merchant bankers and lawyers, whom Gill thought of as his foot soldiers, had been working on the mechanics and feasibility of a possible bid. Timing was the key to it and instinct told him the time was now. Sitting in his office in his shirtsleeves, Gill reflected that so far things were looking good.

The news of his hostile move swept through the City with the speed and urgency of a forest fire. Bid fever. As trading got under way, the Circumference share price rose sharply. Gill rang Charmian.

'Are you keeping up with it?'

'What do *you* think?' replied Charmian.

'So far, so good,' said Gill, deliberately missing her point, 'is what *I* think.'

'What happens now?' asked Charmian.

'Let's see the quality of their defence,' said Gill. 'If it's effective when we make the bid we may have to raise the offer. In the end it will be down to the shareholders to vote for or against. Should they accept, which I wouldn't expect, then we would be home and dry.' In his mind's eye Gill saw the whole scenario unfurl. There would be high-profile interviews. He, Gill, would be the businessman of the moment. If the quality of the Circumference top management was what he perceived it to be, there would be some skirmishes but not much more. Cat and mouse. On the other hand it had to be said that the threat of takeover often concentrated the minds of sleepy boards and their merchant banks wonderfully, and underestimating the opposition would be an elementary mistake. It was not one Gill had any intention of making.

'How about Oliver?'

Out of habit, Gill sidestepped this question.

'He's coming in this afternoon.'

'You know he's got a stack of Circumference stock options?'

'No, I didn't, but if he has then he's about to make a killing,' said Gill. 'My next meeting has just arrived. I'll see you tonight. Put some champagne on ice.'

Marcus Marchant rang the Clapham flat in a state of high excitement and got Oliver.

'Time to cash in,' said Marcus, without preamble, 'and it's beginning to look as though you might get Reg Spivey's head on a platter as well, if the rumours going the rounds are correct.'

'Well if what you mean is that his and Rattray-Smythe's will be the first to roll if and when Gill ultimately gets it, I probably shall.'

Oliver did not reveal that he was scheduled to meet Gill later that day.

At Circumference the disarray was total. Reg blamed Hugo, Hugo blamed Reg and both blamed the cowardly Neville, who appeared to have vanished without trace. A hurriedly convened board meeting got them nowhere. It was all too late. Meanwhile, like ants scavenging, the auditors crawled slowly and painstakingly over the books. For Spivey it was beginning to feel like the last days of the Third Reich, with his office in Circumference setting the scene of the bunker.

'Can't we head it off?' cried Hugo.

The answer to this in ordinary circumstances could have been yes, but Spivey's secret knowledge of dire news from the auditors in the offing caused him to shake his head.

'There isn't *any* way we can head it off.'

There was an unusual air of defeat about Reg which baffled his Chairman.

Desperate and therefore unusually creative, Hugo said, 'Can't we get into bed with someone else? Fight them off that way?'

With a return to his old acerbic self, Spivey said shortly, 'Who do you think is going to hold the line in the light of the offer Gill is dangling? Nobody is the answer to that. And especially not now.'

Thinking of Toby Gill and remembering the day he had fired him, Hugo failed to pick up the mysterious implications of that last remark. It occurred to him that if this was his revenge Gill had waited a long time for it and was not about to give up now. Chickens, it seemed, were coming home to roost.

Reg Spivey suddenly felt very weary. Everything that could go wrong had gone wrong. He felt himself to be slowly moving in the direction of destruction and was at a loss to know what to do about it. Possibly because the pressure was too great, his memory, recently sharply focused, treacherously began to blur and then to fragment again. Spivey felt fearful and the fear was made worse by the fact that he could no longer remember exactly what it was he was afraid of.

'Do you think it's a vendetta?' asked Hugo, pursuing his thoughts aloud.

'Well, you did sack the man,' replied Spivey very irate, thinking: in the same way as I sacked Oliver Curtis. He wondered what Curtis was doing now. Whatever it was, he would no doubt enjoy what was going to happen next. Finally he turned his attention back to his Chairman.

'I've got the merchant bank working on it,' Hugo was saying, getting more frantic by the minute. 'Advice! That's it! We need some very good advice! Perhaps we could revalue our assets. Secure the help of a white knight! Sell the crown jewels even! There must be something!'

Longing to see the back of him, Spivey said, 'Didn't you say you have a meeting with the auditors at three? It's nearly that now.'

'Yes, they want to discuss something urgently. If

you feel up to it, I'd like you to sit in on it,' said Hugo, though privately of the opinion that Reg appeared to be hardly here at all in actual fact.

Spivey had a strong intuition that Nemesis was at hand. He stood up. Might as well get it over with. Like a sleepwalker he followed Hugo from the room.

When Oliver entered Toby Gill's office, Gill was on two phones at once but, with one tucked under his chin, he still managed to shake hands. He was in shirt-sleeves and his tie was loosened. There was a danger-ous aura about him, almost one of exultation. The very air felt electric. For the first time Oliver noticed that one of the paintings looked like a Van Gogh. Probably *was* a Van Gogh. In an odd sort of way it reflected the energy of its owner. Broadly brushed, hectic clouds rushed across the sky, yellow cornfields bucked to-wards the horizon and in the foreground blue-green cypresses undulated and shimmered like gas flames. All was movement. In what should have been a peace-ful country scene nothing was still.

'Congratulations,' said Oliver. 'How long have you been stalking them?'

'Long enough to make sure I'd done all my home-work,' replied Gill. 'After that it was simply a question of timing.'

'When you finally launch the bid, what do you ex-pect the timing to be?'

Gill shrugged. 'Depends upon the opposition. It could be a two- or three-month battle or it could be over quite quickly.'

He waved a dismissive hand. 'Anyway, let's stop beating about the bush. When I get Circumference, I want to offer you Reg Spivey's job.'

Noticing that he said *when,* not *if* Oliver said with alacrity, 'And I'd like to accept!' Then, more cautiously, 'What if you don't get it?'

'That's a gamble you'll have to take. It's the way I live my business life. There are no guarantees.'

No, there weren't. As he, Oliver, had lately learnt to his cost.

The telephones, which had been silent for a while, presumably blocked by Gill's secretary for a finite time, began to ring together. Gill took all the calls at once. Watching him listening, assessing, taking decisions and then issuing orders, Oliver thought: this man is in his element and it's an element I'd like to share. Oh, what the hell! If I don't take a flyer on this offer there won't be another one because he will dismiss me as not having the balls to take a chance and I'll regret it for the rest of my career.

In the brief lull which followed this spate of action, he said, 'Okay! You're on! I'll come along and if it turns out to be only for the ride, too bad.'

'Good man! I don't think it will, incidentally,' said Gill. 'But even if it does, we'll have some fun on the way.'

Alexandra was visibly upset when Oliver told her his news that evening.

'But unless Toby brings this off, he's got nothing to offer. We don't know what's going to happen and nei-

ther does he. And by the time we do know the other
job will have slipped away. We could end up with
nothing all over again. I just want this uncertainty to
end. Doesn't he realize the position he's putting us in?'

Oliver was silent. His own view was that Gill knew
perfectly well but did not consider it to be his problem.
There was a magnificent selfishness about the man
which was no doubt one of the reasons why he had
got as far as he had. At the same time his audacity was
alluring and particularly appealed to Oliver who, in
spite of the consultancy assignments he had been doing, felt he had been out of the real action for far too
long.

'I've done it now,' he said at last. 'It never occurred
to me that you would be so upset.'

'I *am* upset. Whatever happened to discussion? I really think you might have talked to me first!'

'Look, this is a marvellous opportunity—'

'Possibly!'

'*Certainly!*' Always hot-tempered, Oliver turned on
his wife. Frustration, born of months of living from
day to day tilting at desirable jobs which, for one reason or another, had all slipped away, rose to the surface. With it came a resurgence of corrosive anger at
the way in which he had been treated by a company
to whom he had given twelve years of his working life.

'Look, I will not settle for second best,' shouted Oliver, 'and if that's what you really want you shouldn't
be married to me! It's support I need at the moment,
not criticism!'

'Oh!'

After all she had endured with her husband and for him, Alexandra felt this injustice keenly. Enraged, she slapped Oliver's face hard and then, weeping stormily, ran from the room. Seconds later he heard the front door slam.

'Oh, *fuck it!*' exclaimed Oliver. He sat down and put his head in his hands.

Tears streaming, and narrowly missing being hit by a car, Alexandra darted across the road and set off blindly across the grass. It was a pearly, warm evening. The sort of evening during which, had they not just had a very unpleasant fight, she and Oliver would have sat in the garden sharing a bottle of wine over a late dinner. Although the common was already darkening, the sky was high and light and washed with rose, betokening another fine day tomorrow. Eventually she found herself at Clapham Common tube station, which raised the question of what to do next. Normally she would have rung her sister but this was out of the question since Charmian was no doubt in the company of the odious Gill, whose fault all this was. Alexandra's tears had stopped falling but she was still furious. The thought of going back was inconceivable. All the same, better to keep this particular upset within the family. On impulse she decided to go to see Father and Violet.

'Good gracious, Alexandra!' exclaimed Violet, who opened the door. 'We've just had Oliver on the phone asking if you were with us, and now here you are.'

'Well, if he rings again please tell him I'm not here!'

Father materialized behind Violet, saying hopefully, 'Alexandra darling, have you left your husband?'

'No, not for good, just making a point,' replied Alexandra. 'May I come in?'

They parted to let her pass. Tactfully, unwilling to pry, Violet said, 'Why don't you let me get you a drink?'

'Thank you, Violet. I'd like a stiff gin, please, if you have one.'

'If we have one?' exclaimed Father. 'I should think we do! Violet drinks it all the time and I mean *all* the time.'

'Yes, I do,' agreed Violet, impervious to this sarcastic shaft, 'so we've got plenty. If you really want to know, it's what keeps me alive. Since you have so much to say on the matter, Austin, perhaps you would be kind enough to get it. Get me one while you're at it.'

When he had gone she looked directly at Alexandra. It was Violet's view that her stepdaughter looked exhausted. Encouraged by the fact that no questions were being asked, Alexandra provided some answers. She said, 'We've had a massive row, that's all. We do from time to time.'

'Oliver sounded very worried on the phone,' observed Violet. 'Are you sure you don't want to ring him? Tell him you're here. Put him out of his misery.'

Alexandra discovered herself to be still burning with resentment.

'Quite sure.'

Arriving with two gins and about to go back for a third, Father said, 'Give him his marching orders. I've always said my girls don't need husbands with me here to look after them.'

Violet was terse. 'Don't be such a fool, Austin. Sit down and shut up. You couldn't organize your way out of a paper bag. *They've* been looking after *you* for the last ten years.'

Alexandra blinked. Was this how they carried on all the time?

Father did sit down, beside Violet, but did not shut up.

'Marriage is a Great Mistake,' he opined, undeterred. 'I've always said so.'

'Since it's a Great Mistake you've made twice and, for all I know, more times than that, I think we can safely say: no you haven't always said that.'

'Huh!' said Father, unable to think up anything to refute this undeniable truth. Sitting side by side in companionable crossness, they both sipped their drinks.

The telephone rang. 'If it's Oliver, I don't want to speak to him.'

'Well, I can't very well tell him you're not here when you are, Alexandra,' said Violet.

'No, but I can,' interjected Father, who had no such inhibitions where telling the truth was concerned. While they were debating the point the phone stopped.

Into the silence which followed Violet said to Alexandra, 'Why don't you spend the night here? I could make you up a bed on the sofa.'

'I was going to check myself into a hotel,' said Alexandra.

'Seems like a very expensive way of conducting a

marital disagreement to me,' was Violet's answer to that.

Later that evening, when Father had retired to bed, the two women sat up in the kitchen, talking. Violet, whose life had had its own ups and downs, most of them caused by Father, proved to be a surprisingly good listener and perceptive with it.

'Do you know what I think is happening?' announced Violet. 'I think you and Oliver have had a very rough year. Rough for him and especially rough for you, and while it looked as though there was no way forward there was no question of either of you cracking up. Now the end is in sight, you both are. It's like battle fatigue.'

'I don't know if the end is in sight,' replied Alexandra. 'As I said to Oliver, we could end up back where we started.' It occurred to her that this was the first time she had really poured her heart out to anyone. The relief was enormous and with relief came guilt.

'You see,' continued Violet, 'Oliver is the sort of man who has to follow his star. I think he's very similar to Toby in that way. A lot of people don't mind what their job is so long as it brings in the money. Neither of those two is like that. You could put the pressure on and persuade him to turn his back on the Gill opportunity but he wouldn't thank you and he wouldn't be happy. He would always think he had missed out. And if Toby's bid for Circumference is successful, he'll *know* he missed out, and where would your marriage be then? So I say Hold The Nerve, Alexandra!'

Alexandra was stung by this into saying, 'I *have* held the nerve, but when Oliver starts insinuating that I'm not supportive enough, I can't forgive it.'

'Yes, you can,' pronounced Violet. 'Look, both men I've lived with didn't do anything, with the result that they *couldn't* be fired. I was married to Austin who didn't know what work was and didn't want to, and I then fetched up with Vlad who, apart from providing the bar, didn't do any either although somehow (don't ask me how) he made a lot of money not doing it. Most of the hard grind breadwinning in both houses was done by me. So I think you're lucky. You've got someone who knows what he wants and is prepared to go all out to get it. You should celebrate, not make a fuss. And regardless of what he says when he's in a temper, you should go on being supportive. He's a *man*, for God's sake. They're all like five-year-olds! Rap his knuckles certainly, but don't cramp his style. What about another gin?'

'Oh heavens, no more for me, thanks,' said Alexandra. 'I think I might just go to bed.'

'As you please.'

Violet did help herself to another one and when she was reasonably certain Alexandra was asleep, telephoned Oliver.

'Violet speaking,' she said sotto voce. 'Alexandra's here. She turned up after you telephoned.'

'I telephoned a second time but there was no answer.'

'That's because we were all arguing about what to say to you. Your wife wasn't prepared to speak to you.

I must admit you don't seem to have been very tactful, Oliver. Strikes me that you've managed to alienate your staunchest ally with a few ill-chosen words. Alexandra feels taken for granted and under-appreciated but it still goes without saying that she's totally on your side.'

'I know. I was an absolute bastard.'

'No need to be complacent about it,' said Violet.

Oliver decided to ignore the last. 'Look, why don't I jump in the car and come and fetch her?'

'Because she's asleep now. Tomorrow morning will be soon enough. And she *knows* you ought to go for the Stellar option but the way you handled it was all wrong. She felt disfranchised.'

'Thank you, Violet, very much,' said Oliver, thinking as he uttered the words that he could have enough of Violet. 'By the way, the Stellar offer is highly confidential!'

'I'm aware of that, though if you can't talk to your family, who can you talk to? But be that as it may, I shall say nothing to Austin, who is monumentally indiscreet, as we all know. What time shall we expect you?'

'It'll have to be early. Let's say eight. I'm due at Stellar at nine. Give Alexandra my love. Good night, Violet, and thanks!'

'Don't mention it! Good night, Oliver.'

The same evening Toby Gill arrived very late at Charmian's flat.

Mixing him a drink, Charmian said, 'Alexandra and Oliver have had a massive row.'

'What about? It's all on the verge of turning up trumps for them. And anyway, how do you know?'

'Because Oliver rang me earlier this evening to find out if Alexandra was here. When I said no he was clearly very disappointed.'

'Extraordinary! They should be jubilating. I offered him a job today and he accepted.'

'What job?'

'Reg Spivey's job.'

'But Toby, you haven't got Circumference yet. What happens if you don't succeed?'

'I will succeed. Only one of the bids I've made hasn't succeeded and that was because I took too much as read and they mounted a very foxy defence. I won't make that mistake again.'

'I repeat, what if you don't?'

'That's a chance Oliver's got to take. From my point of view it's a test of his mettle. If he's not prepared to take a risk, he's of no use to me. I didn't get to where I am today by hedging all my bets.'

'But he's my brother-in-law and therefore he's about to become your brother-in-law!'

'And this, my love, is business.'

Charmian pursued it. 'I'll bet he went home to Alexandra, told her that he was going to pass up on the other position he's been offered because he'd decided to accept your currently non-existent one and she erupted. With Oliver out of work for so long, Alexandra's been under terrific strain. The prospect of it going on like that just when it looked as though he was about to reestablish must have seemed insupportable.'

'Ah!' said Gill. 'What do you think I should do about it?'

'You could be a little more flexible. Take him on board regardless of whether or not the bid succeeds, and take the pressure off them by telling him so.'

'Look, there's no point in my treating Oliver any differently from anybody else on a business level and, if I've read the man right, *he* wouldn't want it.'

'It's Alexandra I'm concerned about rather than Oliver.'

As Charmian spoke the words the telephone rang. It was Oliver.

'Charmian? Alexandra is found. She's with Austin and Violet.' He sounded very relieved.

Charmian said, 'Oliver I've got Toby here wanting to talk to you.' She handed over the receiver with a meaning look.

Taking it, Gill said to Oliver, 'I don't know what Charmian meant by that but never mind. I'll look forward to seeing you in the office tomorrow at nine.'

Ringing off, he said to Charmian, 'Much as you'd like me to, I'm afraid there's nothing I can do about it. We'll just have to wait and see how the dice fall.'

24

Because she had sized Alexandra up as being very stubborn, Violet did not tell her of Oliver's impending arrival the following morning. Let it be a *fait accompli,* was Violet's view, and then if either of them tries to start another fight, I'll be here to referee. In the event this did not happen. The appearance of Oliver on the doorstep was regarded by Alexandra as a capitulation by him.

Lurking in the sitting room, and praying Austin did not get out of bed before his usual hour of 10 a.m. and sabotage the whole thing, Violet heard Oliver play the required scene perfectly. She couldn't have done it better herself. Oliver said contritely, 'Darling, I'm sorry. That was entirely my fault.' She pictured him hanging his head and scuffing his shoe. This was followed by Alexandra graciously deigning to forgive. There was a brief silence during the course of which they presumably embraced and then the door opened and they both came into the room. Violet was well aware that this was one of the rare occasions when interfering had actually worked and that she had been lucky to pull it off without both the warring parties turning on *her*.

When they had finally gone, she reflected briefly and

without self-pity that it was a shame that sort of marriage had never been on offer for her. Although maybe it could have been. Violet had come a long way from the young, unsophisticated girl who had been dazzled by the man of the world she believed Austin to be. She had learnt the hard way that, on the whole, people meted out the treatment they were allowed to get away with. Perhaps if I had stood up to Austin in the early days it would have worked, reflected Violet. On the other hand perhaps not. It was water under the bridge now in one sense and yet here they were back together under the same roof. One thing was absolutely certain and that was that Life moved in mysterious ways. What the point of it all was, was another matter altogether. Giving up on it, she seized a vase of wilting flowers, took these through to the kitchen where she dropped them into the bin, and prepared to commence her day.

Negotiating his way in and out of the rush-hour traffic, Oliver said, 'What on earth made you go to Austin and Violet?'

'I didn't want to go public on the fact that we'd had a quarrel, and since, for obvious reasons, it wouldn't have been politic to land myself on Charmian, that left only Father.'

'You could have come home to me,' said Oliver.

'After what you said to me, I couldn't possibly have gone back to you. That would have been too demeaning!' Alexandra suddenly felt furious all over again.

Noting the fact, Oliver said hastily, 'No, no, of course you couldn't. How very silly of me even to think that you could. I understand why you were upset about the job. I realize it's a gamble but it's all to play for and gut instinct tells me not to pass this one up.'

His wife's brow remained clouded. 'I just hope he brings it off.'

'I think he will, but how he'll do it is anybody's guess. Toby's a tycoon and they don't operate the way the rest of us do.'

'The children could do with some heartening news. Can I let them know there's something in the offing?'

'I should write and tell them the fact but not the detail. Nobody outside the immediate family is aware of the Stellar offer and I'd prefer to keep it that way until it's clear what's going to happen one way or the other.'

Oliver brought the car to a halt outside the Stellar headquarters and then kissed Alexandra and got out. She watched him walk up the steps and disappear into the building and then slipped over into the other seat and drove back to Clapham.

The following day, able to bear the suspense no longer, Alexandra went to Charmian and Toby Gill's new flat where her sister was trying to sort out packing cases.

'Makes a change to see someone else doing it,' remarked Alexandra. 'Can I give you a hand?'

'No, I'm about to sit down now. I'm afraid I can't offer you anything because I don't know where anything is.'

'I don't want anything on that level,' said Alexandra. 'To be honest I've come to find out if you know whether Toby's going to go ahead with the bid. Because if he doesn't it's disaster for us. We're back where we started!'

'I know.' Charmian had anticipated this conversation and frankly dreaded it. 'And the answer is: I don't know. Toby is completely compartmentalized. For him there's business and there's family and the two mostly don't mix. Where they do overlap, as in Oliver's case, there is no sentiment, just a hardheaded business decision. I have to say that it's the side of him with which I least empathize.'

'Are you sure you're doing the right thing marrying him?'

'Absolutely certain. After all, there must be aspects of Oliver that you aren't keen on and they haven't stopped your marriage being a happy one.'

'There are and no, they haven't,' admitted Alexandra.

'I tried to intercede,' Charmian said, 'But Toby didn't want to know. He simply said that if the bid succeeds there's a job for Oliver, and if it doesn't there isn't as things stand at the moment. Nothing would budge him. He said Oliver was the sort of man who wouldn't want any special favours anyway.'

'That's true, but Oliver need never have known. Surely Toby feels some responsibility for persuading him to pass up the other opportunity?'

'He didn't persuade, he just set out the options,' pointed out Charmian wearily. She foresaw a family rift. Aloud, she said, without much hope in her heart,

'Let's just pray the whole thing goes through without a hitch.'

'If it doesn't I don't think I'll be able to forgive Toby,' stated Alexandra.

'No,' said Charmian. 'But before striking extreme attitudes, let's just wait and see what happens next.'

In the event, the way the dice fell came as a surprise. Quite a few of Rosa's friends were also secretaries who worked in the City and one was employed at Stellar as a subordinate of Gill's vigilant secretary, Mildred. In this fashion Gill learnt ahead of everyone else outside Circumference of the defection of Neville Cruickshank. Gill remembered Mareka Hemingway's prophesy. Alarm bells rang. His reaction was immediate. If the rumours were true there could be no question of launching a bid. Gill rang his broker, whom he had earlier instructed to mop up as much Circumference stock in the market place as he could, and instructed him to put all further share purchases on hold. Damage limitation was now the name of a very expensive game.

In the wake of all this the story began to rumble and reverberate round the various institutions as though communicated by jungle drums, with the result that the Circumference share price fell steeply. It was beginning to seem like disaster all round.

In Brazil, Neville Cruickshank languished in a second-rate hotel, chosen for its anonymity rather than its amenities, and waited for the balloon to go up. For quite a while nothing happened. Nobody appeared to be looking for him. The British business press was full of a possible Stellar bid for Circumference. There was no mention of any spectacular financial shortfall in the accounts and nor was there any further mention of the rumours that had been circulating concerning the authenticity or otherwise of the Circumference paintings. On that front things seemed to have gone very quiet. Perhaps, thought Cruickshank, Reg had come to his senses and managed to pull it off after all. In which case what was he, Neville, doing sitting in a seedy hotel room in Rio? On the whole, though, he doubted it. He wondered how Molly was and how she was passing her days without him, and discovered that he missed her. Though had he been able to enjoy himself more and spend some of his money without drawing attention to himself, this feeling of isolation might have been less acute. There was no doubt that a high profile was out of the question for the moment, perhaps forever. As the days dragged by, Cruickshank began to ask himself if he wouldn't have been better off staying at home and facing the music.

Then the scandal broke.

Settling down to read all the Sunday newspaper financial sections first, as was his wont, Cruickshank was transfixed by the headlines. With trembling hands he spread all the papers out. Serious Fraud Office called into Circumference. Missing Finance Director sought by Interpol. Stellar bid stalls. Sir Toby Gill says, 'We're keeping our options open!' It was the lead story in every one. Columns of incredulity ran on down the page. The share price had gone through the floor.

That evening, on the eat, drink and be merry principle, Cruickshank took himself out for an expensive meal, drank a lot of wine with it and when he got back to the hotel afterwards, knowing that he shouldn't, rang Molly. There was no answer. Although he was not aware of the fact, Molly had gone to stay with her sister in order to escape the posse of journalists of both the broadsheet and tabloid variety who were currently camping outside her garden gate. Alone and embattled as he was, it seemed there was nothing for him to do but go to bed.

It was easier for Hugo Rattray-Smythe to run the gauntlet of the press with the aid of Denis and the Daimler, but not much. Hugo wished that his car had black windows like those of certain pop stars. Reg Spivey avoided all unwelcome investigative journalistic attention by going back into hospital where a combination of Shirley and Sister fended it off.

The investigation ground on and, accompanied by his background dirge, two things happened next. The first was the not entirely unexpected resignation of Hugo Rattray-Smythe and the second was the tracking down of Neville in Rio by the tabloid press. In a futile effort to evade them, Neville changed hotels not once but twice. Limpet-like, the journalists clung to him and in the end he gave up on it and, in between visits to his lawyer, he got into the habit of drinking with them. This assuaged his loneliness and, as they eagerly wrote down his maudlin but largely unilluminating ramblings, gave the hacks a good excuse for staying longer in Rio.

Molly went into print. 'Come home, Neville,' ran Molly's headline, 'We'll fight this together!' An unlikely Boadicea, she was pictured wearing a two-piece suit and sensible shoes opposite the page three girl who was wearing hardly anything at all. Neville's heart yearned for Molly, for her unquestioning loyalty and even, in the face of some of the food he was being forced to endure, her toad-in-the-hole. From the newspapers he learnt of the resignation of Rattray-Smythe (for which read firing, thought Cruickshank) and that Reg Spivey had also been sacked but, following the current corporate fashion of those caught out doing what they shouldn't have been doing, was reputed to be too ill to be interviewed. Cruickshank wished that it might have occurred to Molly, never famous for her adventurous spirit, to get on a plane and come out to South America and console him. Now that the tabloids had found him, they had vacated Molly's doorstep and she had felt herself able to go home again, and because of this Neville was able to talk to his wife on the phone. The sound of her voice made him feel quite tearful. In fact Molly sounded different—cool, as though, in the light of further reflection, the *We'll fight this together!* spirit had evaporated and had been replaced by a question mark over Neville's own loyalty to her.

'Why didn't you tell me what was happening?' Molly wanted to know. 'Why did you abandon me without so much as a note? Didn't you care what happened to me? And what about the children? I'm afraid that's it, Neville—I've had it!'

'But Molly, what about—'

'I didn't write that headline. They did.'

He detected her sister's feminist input here. Neville had never got on with Molly's sister to the point where latterly he had refused to have her in the house at all. It was his belief that she undermined his authority, thereby causing his wife to become difficult. All the same there was no answer to these probing questions. In advance of his flight, if he was perfectly honest with himself, Neville had not fantasized about Molly and himself amid the fleshpots of Rio, but about himself and dark South American beauties, none of which had materialized amid the same fleshpots. At the end of the day very little had materialized, not even a decent hotel.

'I panicked, Molly,' said Neville humbly. 'I'm very sorry. I feel I've let you down.'

'You have!' replied the new unforgiving incarnation of his wife. 'And it sounds as though Reg has let Shirley down as well. It's all over the papers, though nobody seems quite sure exactly what you both thought you were doing. I'm mortified, Neville. Mortified!'

'Yes, Molly.' There was a short unhappy pause. 'What's happened to Reg?'

'Reg is indulging himself in the luxury of a nervous breakdown and can't be interviewed,' said Molly dismissively. 'Why did you let yourself be taken in, Neville? I always knew that man was poison.'

She hadn't of course, though at this juncture it was

more than his life was worth to say it. At the beginning, in the wake of Reg's own rise to power, had come promotion and much more money resulting in a grander mock-Tudor house for Molly and in spite of the frequent manifestations of the less lovable side of Reg's personality, from the point of view of Mammon they had both deemed him to be a good thing. Neville sighed.

Finally into her baffled silence he said, 'What's happened to the Stellar bid?'

'If I understand it correctly, they never got as far as making a formal offer,' said Molly, 'and just as well since the stock they've bought to date and are stuck with has turned out to be a pig in a poke.'

Neville was silent. She was right. Caveat emptor. As things stood the odds were that Gill was going to take a bath. Neville didn't relish the fact that he had upset Gill. It looked like woe all round.

Unaware that in Rio he was the subject of Cruickshank speculation, Toby Gill surveyed his situation. There was, on one level, no way he could have foreseen the black hole at the heart of Circumference though, on the other hand, had he applied more concentration where the entrails, as presented by the Delphic prophesies of Mareka Hemingway, were concerned he might not be in the position he was in now. Gill was no stranger to reversals, but after a string of successes found the fact that this particular calamity coincided with his knighthood and his imminent wedding, embarrassing. The cost of mounting a bid was phenomenal, even a bid which never reached full term—or rather *especially* one which never reached full term. Although it was also true to say that as a result of a successful takeover a predator sometimes could be worse off, at least until some of the assets had been sold. But at the end of an apparent triumph, Pyrrhic or not, prestige and pride were enhanced, egos massaged. Not so here. At the end of this débâcle, it looked as though he would be locked into a lot of (possibly) practically worthless stock, plus sustaining a large dent where his credibility was concerned in the City, and last, though by no means least, facing an in-law rift of epic proportions. As was his habit, Gill put family considerations to one side. Either Charmian was for him or she was not. While he appreciated the Curtis dilemma, he felt there was not a lot he could do about it. Oliver, whom he perceived to be very professional, would, in Gill's opinion, rise about this setback but he was by no means so sure about Alexandra, his volatile sister-in-law-to-be.

Gill shrugged. Too bad. The financial blow to Stellar would be severe but not mortal. All the same, Gill would have liked to have closed the book on that particular old score, to have settled it once and for all. And so no doubt would Oliver. Gill's wedding was scheduled to take place in a fortnight's time and he was not hopeful that things would clarify on the Circumference business front before then. It would, however, be essential that he kept his finger on the business pulse while he and Charmian were on honeymoon in India. He buzzed through to Mildred.

'Mildred, could you possibly bring in the holiday itinerary, please?'

Mildred entered and handed it to him. She thought her boss looked depleted. The energetic dazzle which had been on display when takeover excitement had been at its height and success looked certain had all gone. It was as though a light had gone out. Gill, who had never been to the south of India, frowned at the schedule.

'Apart from Madras and Bangalore I don't know where any of these places are,' said Gill.

'Miss Sinclair worked out the route,' replied his Secretary. 'She says it's very cultural and mostly miles from anywhere.'

Mildred, who had followed her boss from Circumference, liked Charmian. She had liked Clare too, but recognized that since his wife's death, Toby Gill was not the same man. His reaction to the biggest separation life can inflict had not been philosophical but rather one of savage disappointment followed by a perceptible hardening of the emotional arteries. Charmian was totally different from Clare but it could be said that she was marrying a totally different man. It was Mildred's view that Gill needed to get his mind off business and the Circumference vendetta for a while and that the unconventional, spontaneous Miss Sinclair was the one to do it. After Clare there had been other women. Because she organized Gill's diary Mildred knew all about them and most of them had come into the office at one time or another but none had had the lightening effect that Charmian had on him. Over the past few weeks, watching Gill watching his new love with a possessive intensity, almost as if he could not believe in the reality of her presence, Mildred thought: he's happy again for the first time since Clare. And *deserves* to be. I hope to God she doesn't let him down.

Aloud she said, 'Why don't you try just going away and enjoying yourself? Forget about business for two weeks. It'll still be there when you get back.'

'Exactly,' agreed Gill, 'and that's why this is the wrong time to be going away. It's imperative that I stay in touch.'

'It's *never* the right time,' stated Mildred. 'And there's more to life than just business, you know!'

Gill gave his secretary a wintry smile.

'Yes, I know that now. All the same it's been my *raison d'être* for so many years that it's hard to change.'

'Nobody's asking you to change,' countered Mildred bluntly, with the forthrightness earned by years of faithful service, 'just to introduce a sense of proportion. And if you're not willing to do it, I'm willing to bet Miss Sinclair is! How did Mr Curtis take the news that you're not going to launch a bid after all?'

'On the chin,' replied Gill. 'After the news broke about Cruickshank's defection he worked it out for himself. It's tough on them, the Curtises, I mean. He turned something else down, you know, in the hope that this would work out.'

'And you let him?' Thoughtfully Mildred took a hairpin out of the loose bun she wore at the nape of her neck, tucked in a stray grey strand of hair and pushed the pin back in. She shook her head slightly. Sometimes it seemed to Mildred that Gill was determined to sabotage his private life come what may.

'What else could I do? I wanted him on board. How could I have foreseen what was going to happen next?'

'You could have told him to take the other position and then poached him back if and when your own coup was successful,' retorted Mildred. 'All's fair in business, as I don't have to tell you!'

'Sometimes, Mildred, I feel you've been with me too long.'

'You'd never find another secretary as competent or as loyal as I am.'

'No, you're right! I wouldn't!'

When he heard the news, Marcus Marchant rang Oliver again.

'I gather the bid's off but at least you made a killing on the shares, I hope!'

'Yes, at least I did that.' Oliver sounded flat.

'What's happened about Stellar vis-à-vis yourself? You said you thought Gill might have something for you.'

'It's fallen through.' Oliver did not elaborate.

Marcus frowned. 'I'm sorry. How's Alexandra taken it?'

'Better not to ask. She and the future Lady Gill are on non-speakers.' Toby's knighthood was common knowledge now.

'Why don't you leaven the marital lump, come over here for dinner one evening?'

'I don't think it would be a very convivial evening since Alexandra's barely speaking to me either. She's also refusing to attend the wedding. What should have been a celebration is shaping up to become a cat fight.'

'What's Gill's stance in all of this?' asked Marcus.

'Olympian!' replied Oliver. 'But I have to say that apart from what turned out to be misplaced confidence in the shape Circumference was in, something he couldn't have foreseen, he was straight down the line about what was and was not on offer. And, of course, he burnt his financial fingers badly too. Though, on the other hand, he can afford to.'

'Was the job offer something to do with all of that?' Marcus was curious. 'You never did tell me exactly what it was.'

Oliver hesitated. This was, after all, one of his oldest friends. Caution won. Trust no one.

'Do you know, I'd prefer not to talk about it. It's gone. Nothing to do but look forward.'

'Yes,' agreed Marcus, intrigued but deciding not to push it, 'that's right. Nil desperandum. Of course, you never know what else might be in the pipeline.'

All the same, he reflected, hanging up the receiver, the Curtis corporate exile in the wilderness was turning out to be a longer one than any of them might have expected.

25

Nigel Guest rang Charmian up.

'I wondered if you might be free for lunch,' said Nigel. He sounded subdued, very unlike his usual effervescent self. Charmian leafed through her diary.

'I can't do a single day this week, Nigel.' She went on turning the pages. 'Or the next week come to that.'

'Ah!' He sounded very bereft.

'Is it urgent?' asked Charmian.

'Not so much urgent as just that I need someone to talk to. But if you're too busy it doesn't matter.

Wondering why on earth he couldn't talk to his wife, which was presumably one of the reasons he had married her in the first place, she said, 'I've got a gap between meetings tomorrow afternoon. Why don't you drop by the office for a cup of tea? Shall we say at about four o'clock?'

Because she knew Toby to be a jealous man, Charmian decided to tell him that evening about Nigel Guest's impending visit. He would probably never have found out about it, but, on the other hand, life being what it was, it would have been the one day of the year that Toby also decided to drop in on her for a cup of tea.

Toby was not pleased.

'I thought that was all over!'

'It is all over on one level but that doesn't stop Nigel remaining a friend,' pointed out Charmian. 'Come on, he's hardly likely to chase me round my own office desk in the middle of the afternoon. Too much like hard work for Nigel.'

'I wouldn't be too sure about that,' observed Toby.

'If you want to come and chaperone me you're perfectly welcome,' said Charmian slyly.

'Of course I don't want to come and chaperone you! Your secretary can do that. Or, better still, maybe I'll send Mildred.'

They both burst out laughing. 'On a more serious note, have you spoken to Oliver and Alexandra lately?'

'I hardly ever hear from Oliver anyway and Alexandra *won't* speak to me because I'm marrying you, whom she regards as the devil incarnate.'

'For the nth time I couldn't have been expected to—'

'*I* know that, but *she* doesn't. Obviously if the bid had gone ahead and Oliver was firmly ensconced as Managing Director of Circumference you would be the hero of the hour. As it is you're the villain instead. I'll be devastated if she doesn't come to our wedding but as things stand I very much fear she won't. Once Alexandra makes up her mind, that's it!'

Listening to it, Toby made his own mind up to go and see Violet Sinclair the following day. Maybe she could persuade his intransigent sister-in-law-to-be to see reason.

* * *

Nigel turned up in Charmian's office wearing a sober grey suit and a black tie.

'Good gracious, you don't look like yourself!' exclaimed Charmian. 'You look as if you're in mourning.'

'I am in a manner of speaking,' said Nigel. He took a copy of *Campaign* from beneath his arm and handed it to her. 'Here, read that! I could do with something stronger than a cup of tea, too, if you've got it.' She made him a whiskey and soda and then sat down and opened the magazine.

'Page four,' said Nigel.

There it was. 'Guest parts company with Babcock Winton Brown.' There followed a short report which began with the words: 'The unexpected resignation of creative Director Nigel Guest surprised his colleagues yesterday...' thereby effortlessly conveying the unmistakable message that Nigel had in fact been fired.

Mindful of Oliver, Charmian said, 'What are you going to do? Can you freelance until you land another job?' Freelance work presumably was the advertising world equivalent of the sort of business consultancy her brother-in-law was currently doing. 'I've probably got some contacts who could be helpful and you must have a good solicitor. Do you know Gervase Hanson...?'

Her voice trailed away. He did not appear to be listening. It was as though someone had trodden on him, the butterfly that had been Nigel was crushed. There was a discreet knock at the door. Her next appointment must be there.

Charmian picked up the phone of her desk, buzzed through to the outer office and said, 'Five minutes.'

She turned back to Nigel.

'What does your wife think about it? Is she being supportive?'

'I haven't told her!' came the astonishing reply.

'What! You've told *me* but you haven't told *her!* Nigel...!'

'Because she isn't there to tell. She left me just before all this happened. I haven't seen her or the kids for a month.'

'Listen, Nigel, you must go and see her and tell her. You need your family now.' Another discreet knock on the door. 'Look, I have to get on. I hope you're coming to the wedding.'

'You don't want me there. Spectre at the feast and all that!'

'On the contrary, I *do* want you there. All the other spectres will be there and you can't let the side down. Exhume one of those extraordinary Armani suits and a very gaudy tie and come.' The mention of outré suits and loud ties appeared to cheer Nigel up.

Getting up to go, he said, 'OK, I will!'

Gill did go to see Violet but did not tell Charmian that this was his intention. His hope that for one reason or another Austin would not be there was doomed to disappointment. It was, in fact, Austin who opened the door.

They shook hands.

'Come in, come in!' invited Austin with alacrity. 'I expect you're here to try and defuse the latest family row. I've seen some in my time but this one strikes me as a humdinger! Violet!'

'I'm here,' said Violet. Gill was struck by the change in her. Violet was wearing a bottle-green crepe dress of becoming cut, and pearls. The mahogany-coloured suntan had faded and she had had her hair cut into a swinging iron-grey bob. Gill detected a marked resemblance between her and Charmian never formerly discernible. He suddenly saw that in her hey-day Violet must have been a beautiful woman. Now she was still handsome, the remains of her good looks underpinned by an aura of resilient self-containment.

Gill kissed her on the cheek.

'What can I get you to drink?' asked Austin.

'Champagne, of course,' said Violet.

'I didn't know we had any!'

'No, because if you had known there wouldn't be any now. It's hidden at the back of the fridge, Austin. Perhaps you'd like to get it.'

He went.

Settling back in her chair and unwittingly echoing Queen Mary, Violet observed, 'Well, here's a pretty kettle of fish. What are we going to do about it?'

'That's what I'm here to ask you,' replied Gill.

'I thought you were the man with all the ideas!' She gave him a sidelong look. He was conscious that he was being gently mocked.

'*Some* of the ideas! Look, Violet, I'm in love with

your daughter and I want to make her happy. If her sister doesn't come to the wedding the day will be spoilt for her. Regardless of what she thinks of me, I'm here to ask you to persuade Alexandra to come for Charmian's sake!'

'I'll persuade her. Don't worry about it,' said Austin, hearing the last sentence as he entered with the champagne.

'No you won't, you'll keep right out of it!' ordered Violet. 'Your input into this sensitive situation is all we need.' Turning to Gill, she said, 'I'll try, but it won't be easy. Alexandra feels that you used Oliver for your own ends without any consideration for their situation and then, when things didn't work out for you, you left them high and dry!'

'I did,' Gill freely admitted, 'but if I'd brought that takeover off she wouldn't be complaining. That's business. You have to take the rough with the smooth.'

'Quite so! And since you didn't bring it off, she *is* complaining and *you* have to take the rough with the smooth too.'

Gill took a sip of champagne. She had him there.

Violet continued, 'I'll do everything I can, but I don't want to hear any more dreary platitudes of the "that's business" variety. It seems to me they give carte blanche to some very selfish behaviour! It should be perfectly possible to make moral judgements *and* be a successful businessman. What do you think, Austin?'

Her partner was startled. His eyes glazed. 'Morality has never been my strong suit, Violet!'

'Well, that's certainly true and nor has business now I come to think of it, so you're probably the last person I should be asking. However, that's another story.'

Turning to Gill she said, 'I'll go and see her tomorrow but all I can do is my best. I can't guarantee success.'

'I realize that,' said Gill, draining his glass, 'and I'm grateful.'

'No! no! no!'

The speaker was Alexandra, who looked as though she might have been crying.

'Oliver keeps trying to persuade me as well. I love Charmian, I'd do anything for her, but the very sight of Gill gets my goat. He's arrogant and self-satisfied and at the end of the day doesn't care about anyone except Toby Gill.'

Although this was not a view Violet shared, it seemed easier for the moment to let it pass.

'Well, yes, I can see what you mean,' said Violet soothingly, 'but it's not Toby we're talking about here, it's Charmian and I think her day will be ruined if you don't show up. Don't put her in the position of having to choose between you and her husband. It isn't fair.'

'It's my view that she's making a mistake marrying him in the first place!'

'There you'd be wrong. Those two are made for one another. He may not be your type—'

'Certainly isn't!'

'…but he's a hundred per cent right for Charmian and she knows that. Alexandra, you're angry and worried and justifiably so, but can't you rise above it for just this one day? *Please!* It's so important to her. There's no need to speak to Toby afterwards ever again if you don't want to.'

'I *don't* want to!'

'No,' said Violet, wondering if Alexandra's mother, Austin's first wife, had been as uncompromising as this. 'But you will *think* about coming, give it some consideration, won't you?'

'Do you know, Violet, listening to you has made my mind up for me!'

Here was hope. 'So you will come after all?'

'No, I won't come after all. Not even to hearten Charmian. As things stand I'm not prepared to appear to endorse Gill.'

'And that's your last word.'

'That's my last word!'

'I have to say I think that on reflection you'll regret it.'

'It's a matter of principle,' answered Alexandra. Violet, who knew that when the word principle raised its head in a discussion it usually meant that the debate was over, gave up on it.

Later that afternoon she rang Gill at his office.

'No dice, I'm afraid,' said Violet.

Four days before the wedding was due to take place, Oliver received a phone call from Robert Maitland.

'Are we still on for a game of squash at lunchtime tomorrow?' asked Maitland.

'Yes, we are!'

'That's good because I've just come from a long crisis meeting with the Institutions and, more importantly, the Banks and there's something I want to sound you out about.'

'Really? Can you tell me what it is?' Oliver was immediately on the alert.

'I'd prefer not to talk about it on the open line. Perhaps on second thoughts it would be a good idea to cut out the exercise and concentrate on lunch instead. If I can get a table, what about The Gavroche? At one.'

'Fine by me,' said Oliver. He was conscious of a surge of adrenalin coupled with a feeling that things were suddenly on the move again.

'Excellent! See you there.'

26

The bride wore red and carried no posy, only a single rose.

There was a certain amount of tutting from elderly cousins.

'*That's* my girl!' said Father.

'Quite so,' said Mother.

The ceremony itself was to take place in a registry office attended only by immediate family. Nick, Alice and Dan, who had had a conference of their own and had decided their mother's stance was unreasonable, were all there. Gill looked sideways at Charmian and was surprised by the depth of his own emotion, which was one of fiercely protective love. I would lay down my life for this woman, he thought. Later Harriet Gill was to say that his second wedding day was the beginning of the rehumanizing of Toby. Chin high, Charmian stared straight ahead. Divining her distress and knowing the reason for it, without much hope in his heart, Toby looked round.

And saw Alexandra and Oliver standing at the back of the room. They must just have arrived.

Gill leant towards Charmian and murmured, 'Alexandra's here!'

Charmian turned her face towards him and he saw that her eyes were full of tears.

'Darling, don't cry. Not on our wedding day!'

'I won't. Not now!'

When the short ceremony was over, unable to believe his luck, he kissed his wife.

Despite herself Alexandra also had tears in her eyes. As Toby and Charmian moved on to sign the register, the two sisters came face-to-face and embraced. Neither felt the need for words.

When Toby and Charmian had departed for their new flat, where the reception was to be held, Violet caught up with her stepdaughter.

'Whatever made you alter your mind? You seemed so adamant.'

'Let's say a sea change,' mysteriously replied Alexandra.

None the wiser, Violet was nevertheless aware that the sea change, whatever that was, had wrought a more profound effect than a simple heart change with regard to attending a wedding. Alexandra appeared radiant like someone who has been suddenly, unaccountably healed.

'Whatever it was, you did the right thing,' said Violet. 'It meant such a lot to her.'

'I know.'

She was further mystified at the reception to see Alexandra kiss Toby on the cheek, presumably offering congratulations as she did so. Curiouser and curiouser, was Violet's view of that.

Drawing up the guest list, Charmian and Toby had had a discussion about the Lovers.

'You don't mind, do you?' Charmian said. 'It's my way of saying goodbye to the past and, after all, it's you I want!'

Truth to tell he hadn't been happy about it but put like that it had been hard to refuse without sounding stuffy, not to say bourgeois.

'All right, but don't forget it's me you're marrying!' She kissed him. 'As if I could.'

They all came. Even Dominic Goddard had managed to wangle himself a business trip back from Hong Kong. Dominic found himself talking to ex-Circumference Oliver Curtis and was astonished to learn that he was Charmian's brother-in-law. Remembering the lunch he had organized for her with the disgraced Neville Cruickshank, Dominic was at a loss to account for the fact that she had never revealed this at the time.

'So how do you come to know Charmian?' Oliver was saying, 'Or are you part of the Gill entourage?'

Accepting a canapé, at the same time speculating about the hidden agenda of the new Lady Gill, 'My connection is with Charmian. I'm a colleague of hers,' replied Dominic, 'Although perhaps I should say ex-colleague.'

On the other side of the room he could see her, animately talking to Julian Cazalet, the gossip columnist. The short-skirted scarlet suit became her and had no doubt caused a few raised eyebrows. On her dark head she wore a very chic, small, red toque. With a pang, Dominic remembered all those Monday assignations and was aware that he mourned their passing.

Charmian introduced Nigel Guest to Cazalet. 'Julian, this is Nigel Guest. Nigel is in the process of setting up his own advertising agency!'

Am I? Nigel was startled. He caught Charmian's eye. *Yes, I must be!*

Aloud: 'Yes, I am.'

'Really?' said Cazalet, interested. 'Called?'

Rising to the occasion and aided in this by the fact that he was wearing one of his most outrageous ties plus a Thierry Mugler suit probably designed with the twenty-first century in mind, Nigel said, 'It's early days yet, so I'm afraid it's all under wraps at the moment...'

His own agency! It suddenly seemed like a very good idea. Nigel mentally reviewed the list of other ad-men with whom he was acquainted who had also been fired. Maybe three or four of them could get together.

'Let me know when it's all out in the open and maybe I could give you a puff,' said Cazalet.

Charmian said, 'Would you excuse me? I've just seen someone over there I must speak to.'

As he watched her go, it occurred to Nigel that his ex-lover had possibly done him a very good turn indeed.

'What's your connection with Charmian?' asked Cazalet.

'Only a colleague, I'm afraid!' replied Nigel. 'Ex-colleague, actually.' With a sigh he took another glass of champagne.

The someone turned out to be her husband.

'Happy?' asked Gill.

'*Very!*' replied Charmian.

'I have to salute your sister over the way she rose above her disapproval of me!'

They looked across the room to where Alexandra was talking to Gervase Hanson, accompanied by Oliver. It struck Charmian, as it had struck Violet earlier, that there was a bloom about Alexandra which had been conspicuously missing over the last year, almost as though she had been recharged, and that this appeared to encompass Oliver too. Perhaps they had both had some good news. She hoped so.

To Toby she said, 'Come with me. I want you to meet Dan.'

Observing Dan and Charmian together, it was immediately apparent to Gill that here was a special friendship. Dan was wearing the sort of distressed suit which was a result of his own rapid growth and the fact that his mother saw little of him from the beginning of the term until the end, and when she did see him the suit had been left behind so that its state of repair could not be monitored. The trouser bottoms were frayed where Dan had pulled the hems down himself rather than waste his own valuable time and that of Matron by asking her to do it. Sudden sprouting had caused the jacket to become a bum-freezer of the type with which Gill was familiar from his own school days.

Business tycoon and schoolboy shook hands.

'Do you like school, Dan?' suddenly asked Gill, employing the technique of the unexpected which he often used when interviewing potential executives.

'No, I don't. But,' said Dan, after a fractional pause, 'I've decided to tough it out in order to get to where I want to be.'

'Which is where?'

'Not sure!' said Dan decisively.

Charmian was standing behind Dan as he spoke. Catching sight of her merriment at the end of this last speech, Gill, who had no son of his own, said, 'Well, when you do know where you want to be, get in touch with me. It's just possible that I may be able to help you.'

'I'm going to leave you two men together while I circulate among my guests,' said Charmian, who had just caught the eye of Gervase Hanson.

'You never told me that Oliver Curtis was your brother-in-law,' said Gervase when she finally arrived at his side.

'Oh, didn't I?'

'You know damn well you didn't! And by the way, that's a very becoming hat. I've always had a thing about hats.'

You're not the only one, thought Charmian, mindful of the Cranach Venus.

'But getting back to Circumference and remembering your sudden interest in the company round about the time the axe fell on Curtis, I don't suppose you could have been into some sort of refined revenge, could you?'

'Refined revenge? How very dramatic you are, Gervase. No, of course not and when you consider what they've done to themselves there was no need for me to interfere was there?'

'Regardless of other inauspicious influences, the temptation to wreak personal retribution is usually, in my experience anyway, irresistible.' He gave her a speculative look. 'You're a dangerous woman, Charmian. I wouldn't like to upset you.'

'Luckily you never have! Ah, here comes Giles Hayward.' Then, knowing the answer perfectly well, 'Have you two met each other? No?' She introduced them and, having done so, temporarily left them while she went to sort out Father's empty glass. Together with no point of mutual reference, Giles said to Gervase, 'What's your connection to Charmian? Or is it Toby Gill?'

'No, it's Charmian,' replied Gervase. 'The answer to your question is colleague. Quite a few of us here. What's yours?'

'Lover,' said Giles, who saw no point in beating about the bush. 'Or, rather, ex-lover.'

Amused, Gervase said, 'Well, I think we're all agreed that Gill is a fortunate man!'

'A very fortunate man,' agreed Giles, 'almost as fortunate as I am. Allow me to introduce you to my wife.'

In another corner of the room, Father said to Alexandra, 'I think it would be appropriate if I made a speech, don't you?'

Alexandra shuddered and succeeded in catching Violet's eye.

'Father seems hellbent on making a speech.'

'Well, he can't. The Gill decree is: No speeches. I anticipated this particular crisis and asked him. He says he has to listen to interminable speeches all the time in the course of his job and doesn't want to have to listen to any more at his own wedding. So that's that!'

When the last guest had gone, Toby and Charmian surveyed the debris.

'The caterers will clear it up tomorrow, supervised by Mildred when we've gone,' said Toby. 'This evening I want to be alone with you. Come here.'

Obediently she came.

Gill stroked her upturned face with both hands.

'Take your clothes off,' said Gill.

'What about yours?'

'Then you can take mine off.'

Charmian unbuttoned her jacket and let it fall to the floor. This was followed by skirt, bra, tights and, stepping out of her high-heeled shoes, finally knickers. Naked, except for her jewellery, Charmian raised her arms to dismantle the hatpinned toque.

'No, leave the hat, I like it,' ordered Gill. 'And put your shoes back on. That's it. Now it's my turn.'

Two days later, sitting in the country, Hugo Rattray-Smythe, who was reading his morning paper, came to the Cazalet gossip column. Most of it was devoted to the wedding of Charmian Sinclair and Sir Toby Gill. Pictures proliferated and there was a list of the most important guests. On her husband's arm, wearing a very fetching hat and holding one single long-stemmed

rose, Charmian smiled into the camera. She looked…
here Hugo searched for the right word and came up
with *triumphant!* Or maybe she just looked like that
because he, Hugo, felt vanquished. No, if he was honest with himself, an uncomfortable pastime, he *was*
vanquished. He still found her behaviour that weekend
incomprehensible. He wasn't now, of course, but then
he had been Chairman of Circumference, Man of Influence, entertaining her right royally in his own house
and she simply hadn't wanted to know.

Puzzled, Hugo shook his head.

He scanned the photographs. Normally at this sort
of event some of the participants were on the Rattray-
Smythe social circuit.

Good heavens! He peered at one of the shots. Wasn't
that that gardener chappy, who, come to think of it,
had been a friend of Charmian Sinclair's. The one who
hadn't been about to marry one of the Norfolk Wyndhams but another obscure one. Wearing a shirt and
neckerchief, he was standing beside a woman whose
good looks immediately caught Hugo's eye. He looked
at the caption which said 'Mr and Mrs Giles Hayward'.
Not so obscure now.

He went on through the gallery until, 'Fuck me!'
said Hugo. For there were Oliver and Alexandra Curtis.
Alexandra, always very dashing, although not always
very easy, was wearing a slim long-skirted suit which
might have been Armani or, on the other hand, might
not have been, and a cartwheel hat of epic proportions.
It was the opposite end of the spectrum to the toque
worn by the bride, but just as effective. Of course,

thought Hugo, casting his mind back, Alexandra Curtis never did dress like the other executive wives. Out of habit, really just to find out the connection, he looked at the caption and was staggered to read: 'Mr and Mrs Oliver Curtis, brother-in-law and sister of the bride.'

What?

Hugo laid down his toast and marmalade, put on his half-moons and read it again, just to make sure that he had not made a mistake.

His eyes went back to the photograph of Lady Gill. In the inconsequential way in which the mind throws up certain things in certain situations, Hugo's mind threw up Corinthians now: 'For now we see through a glass, darkly; but then face-to-face...' For the first time since he met Charmian Sinclair, or Lady Gill as she now was, he saw Face-to-Face. He remembered saying to her that day in the country, 'What is it that you have against Reg?' 'Let's just call it a personal vendetta,' she had said. Hugo had been puzzled by this reply at the time but too hellbent on seduction to waste precious time analysing it. Now he saw exactly what had been going on. Revenge. Revenge of an Italianate and subtle nature, for Spivey's disappointment and rage at being passed over for an honour had been curdling. It had quite clearly been the one thing in the world he wanted most of all. And the revenge hadn't stopped there either. He, Hugo, had not got off scot-free, either, for what about his unintended £500 donation to the Cat Protection League? Still unaware, though not destined to remain so for very much longer, that the doubtful provenance of both his private picture collection and the Circumference works was the biggest open secret in the City, courtesy of Austin Sinclair, Hugo hoped that, given the dire financial mess the rest of Circumference was in, they would all be too busy mounting a rescue to notice Charlie's scam. And then at least, thought Hugo, for whom the outlook was bleak without his Chairman's salary, nobody will call in the loan secured by using the paintings as collateral and I'll still have something to live off. Failing that, bankruptcy beckoned.

Hugo resumed eating his toast, which suddenly tasted like sawdust.

27

Charmian had conceived the idea of an Indian honeymoon partly because neither she nor Toby had been there before and also because, according to Alexandra, the Maitlands, friends of the Curtises, had recently been there on holiday and had enjoyed it. It's completely different from anywhere else, thought Charmian, and, hopefully will take his mind off business for the duration.

This proved to be over-optimistic. At the beginning Toby let himself relax into the change and enjoying Charmian. India moved slowly and trying to hurry anything up got him nowhere. In that way it was alien to his temperament but at the same time it was seductive. They were driven everywhere and as small town succeeded small town, the initial overriding impression was one of tropical heat and colour. Under brilliant skies dark-skinned beautiful women of enviable carriage billowed along the roads in saris of red, purple, hot yellow and cerise, often with earthenware pots on their heads. One of Gill's abiding memories would be of his own vivid wife wearing a garland of roses and jasmine, bargaining for saffron in the flower market in Bangalore. All the same, in spite of diversions such as this, his austere, work-orientated side found it hard to come to terms with the slow pace of life and what he regarded as Indian inefficiency, a combination of which caused achieving anything to take twice as long as it should have done. Even the Oberoi had a magnificent disregard for time. It did, however, as befitted a first-class hotel, have a business centre. For Gill, whose absence from the London business action was just beginning to cause him to chafe, this was like finding an oasis in a desert.

'I must make some telephone calls and send some faxes,' said Gill, bent on contacting at the very least Mildred, his broker and his merchant bank in that order. In the event, when he did so, it transpired that very little had happened since they left. The lull was almost unnatural and indicated to him that a lot was probably waiting to happen very fast.

'Try not to think about it so much, darling,' advised Charmian. 'Why don't you just live for the moment which is *here,* and not in London?'

'Because I'm simply not programmed to operate like that,' said Toby.

'Well, in that case I should get all your business sorted out while you're here because tomorrow we're going to be out in the sticks.' The sticks was in fact destined to be the high point of their trip. It was the ruined city of Vijayanagar, deserted capital of an empire which had ruled most of South India in the sixteenth century.

'Good God, Charmian! You're not telling me we've

been booked into a hotel without a fax?' Gill was
aghast.

'I'm sure they'll have a telephone and a fax even,'
said Charmian, who was not sure of any such thing.
'And even if they don't we're only there for two
nights.'

Two nights and two days. *Anything* could happen in
that time.

Their next hotel, which was in Hospet and had the
air of not being in the twentieth century at all, confirmed all Gill's worst forebodings. It was not even
called Hotel, but Tourist Home.

'What you have to understand,' pointed out Charmian reasonably, 'is that here this is the equivalent of
the Bangalore Oberoi, the Hospet Grand, if you like.'

Toby was not amused. 'Let's hope the sights are
worth it.'

They were.

Their driver took them to Vijayanagar via Hampi
village where, to Charmian's astonishment, she found
the Aspiration Bookshop. 'Books! Postcards! Writing
Paper! Pimples removed!' enterprisingly announced a
notice outside it. Inside she found a book about Vijayanagar and bought it.

The city itself, which covered miles, stood in the
midst of an extraordinary landscape. Surveying this,
Toby decided that maybe it was worth putting up with
the deficiencies of the Hospet Grand after all. Massive
red boulders studded the landscape, quite often one
balanced upon another as though a pensive god put
them there. Touched by the early morning light they

appeared to glow, rosily threatening as though illuminated from within. Their gargantuan size and haphazard distribution around the ruins put both Toby and Charmian in mind of the beginning of the world, of primeval times when the earth was in eruption and whole continents were being forged. Or maybe comparatively recently but still hundreds of years ago, a massive earthquake had realigned the scenery. Whatever it was, the effect was savagely dramatic and at the same time eerie with the unnerving intimations of morality which underlie the ruins of all once-great cities. There was nobody else there at all.

'*Sic transit gloria mundi!*' said Gill.

They went first to the Royal Elephant House where a flock of bright green parakeets, startled by their arrival, shot shrieking into the blue air.

'The elephants had a grander house than mine,' observed Charmian, marvelling.

'I hope you're not complaining,' said Gill.

'Not at all, merely comparing! And very glad I'm not an elephant too. But let's go to the House of Victory, where,' announced Charmian, 'I'm going to read to you aloud!'

'Really?' Toby was amused.

The House of Victory was an impressive, ornately carved edifice. Stairs led up the front of it to a high platform. Toby and Charmian climbed these and perched on the top, looking out over the remains of a once-great civilization.

'These,' said Charmian, 'are extracts from the sixteenth-century chronicle of a Portuguese called Paes.'

'You must know that when it is morning the king comes to this House of Victory, and betakes himself to that room where the idol is with its Brahmans, and he performs his prayers and ceremonies...after the king has entered inside he comes out, and with him a Brahman who takes in his hand a basket full of white roses...and the king, taking three handfuls of these roses, throws them to the horses, and after he has thrown them he takes a basket of perfumes and acts towards them as though he would cense them; and when he has finished doing this he reaches towards the elephants and does the same to them...the king sits, dressed in white clothes, all covered with embroidery of golden roses and wearing his jewels... Many Brahmans stand round the throne on which rests the idol, fanning it with horsetail plumes, coloured, the handles of which are all overlaid with gold; these plumes are tokens of the highest dignity; they also fan the king with them'

'That,' observed Gill, 'is the way I should like to live!'

'I thought it was the way you *did* live,' said Charmian.

'What does he have to say about the women?' asked Gill, deciding to ignore the last. 'Describe the women.'

'They have very rich and fine silk cloths; on the head they wear high caps which they call collaes, on these caps they wear flowers made of large

*pearls; collars on the neck with jewels of gold
very richly set with many emeralds and diamonds
and rubies and pearls; and besides this many
strings of pearls... So great is the weight of the
bracelets and gold and jewels carried by them
that many of them cannot support them, and
women accompany them assisting them by sup-
porting their arms.'*

'Sounds all right to me,' was Charmian's verdict on
this, 'although not *all* the time. It would get in the
way!'

'Would depend what you were doing,' Toby said
drily.

Charmian continued.

*'...with these maidens, they say that there are
twelve thousand women; for you must know that
there are women who handle sword and shield
and wrestle—'*

'Reminds me of you, darling!' said Toby.

'I shall rise above that,' replied Charmian. 'But here
comes the climax. Sit and imagine!'

*'There went in front of the king many elephants
with their coverings and ornaments, as I have
said; the king had before him some twenty horses
fully caparisoned and saddled, with embroideries
of gold and precious stones, that showed off well
the grandeur and state of their lord... Thus ac-*

*companied the king passed along gazing at his
soldiers who gave great shouts and cries and
struck their shields; the horses neighed, the elephants screamed, so that it seemed as though the
city would be overturned, the hills and valleys and
all the ground trembled with the discharges of
arms and musquets; and to see the bombs and fire
missiles over the plains, this was indeed wonderful. Truly it seemed as if the whole world were
collected there.'*

Enjoying the cadences of her voice evoking past tri-
umphs, Gill murmured aloud, 'But where is *my* victory?'

'In a manner of speaking,' reminded Charmian,
'you've had it. Rattray-Smythe's gone, Spivey's gone,
Circumference is on its uppers. What more do you
want?'

'Not generalized revenge,' said Gill. 'I want to have
my own personalized parade, just as the kings of Vijayanagar did. I want to be *seen* to be the winner.'

Charmian closed the book.

'Before you put it away, let's hear what they did to
their enemies.'

'Here's one traitor's comeuppance, but I warn you,
it's horrendous!'

'Never mind, read on,' said Gill.

*'Then (the Sultan) ordered (the prisoner) to be
skinned alive, and as his skin was torn off his flesh
was cooked with rice. Some was sent to his chil-*

*dren and his wife, and the remainder was put into
a great dish and given to the elephants to eat, but
they would not touch it. The Sultan ordered his
skin to be stuffed with straw…and to be exhibited
throughout the country.'*

'See what I mean? If they were feeling less compli-
cated they simply had transgressors trampled to death
by the elephants.'

'Strikes me they had it pitched about right, whatever,' said Gill.

Charmian shivered. Maybe reading aloud into the
still warm air had caused a violent past to move un-
comfortably closer to their own present. She was conscious that as with the kings of Vijayanagar, in Toby's
eyes treachery and retribution were indivisible.

They sat on for some minutes in silence, separately
locked in thought before rising and descending the uneven granite steps of the House of Victory.

Back at the hotel, Gill discovered that there was a
fax machine and that, moreover, the intrepid Mildred,
armed only with the address of the Tourist Home and
a great deal of perseverance, had not only discovered
this fact but had actually succeeded in sending one. Or
rather, as it tantalizingly turned out when Toby sat
down to read it, half a one. It claimed to be four pages
yet here were only two. The second page ended with
words, *I thought you would be interested to know that
Mr Curtis…* Mr Curtis what? He looked at his watch.
Four o'clock Indian time meant eleven o'clock Green-

wich Mean Time. There was no phone in the room, it was not that sort of hotel, which meant trying to phone London amid the scrum which was the Tourist Home reception desk. He decided first to check if the last two pages were in fact still with the desk. The answer to this was yes, which in India, Gill was learning, actually meant no. By the time they had got this sorted out the fellow who manned the fax machine announced his own imminent departure.

'No more calls, sir. The lines are down. We do it tomorrow.'

Embarrassingly, at the end of this definite statement the telephone rang and a fax began to arrive, though not for him. When the inconvenient caller had finally been dealt with, Gill closed the door of the fax room and stood with his back against it.

'We don't do it tomorrow,' said Gill, 'we do it to-day! Nobody goes home until I achieve either a fax or a telephone call! Start dialling!'

At the fifteenth attempt they got through to Mildred, who was not there. Mildred's minion answered who, it gradually became apparent, knew nothing about any-thing and was further flustered to find herself talking to an irascible Sir Toby Gill all the way from India. The unsurprising upshot was that, trying to search through the papers on Mildred's desk and field the im-patient voice of her boss on the other end of the line she dropped the telephone receiver and cut him off.

'Jesus Christ!' exclaimed Gill.

'I think it is better we do it in the morning.'

'Better for whom? Not for me. Here's the number!'

They were just limbering up for the fifth attempt when the phone rang again and a fax began to arrive. Question was, was it his fax? It was. Mildred must have arrived back in her office. Thank God for Mildred. The fax ground on very slowly. Page one, page two. And stopped.

'Useless bloody machine,' fumed Gill, tempted to aim a kick at it. He decided to give up the unequal struggle. Hopefully their next hotel would be of a less primitive variety.

It was, and Gill was at last able to achieve contact with Mildred and the second half of his fax and therefore the second half of the mysterious sentence beginning: *I thought you would be interested to know that Mr Curtis...*

Reading on, Gill said, 'Well, I'm damned!'

'What is it?' asked Charmian, looking up from her book. They were sitting in the lush hotel garden.

He did not immediately answer but stared into the middle distance for a while, before bafflingly saying, 'This puts a new slant on everything!'

'What does? Toby, would you mind telling me exactly what you're on about?'

With an effort he brought his mind back to India.

'My turn to read aloud,' said Gill. 'Pay attention. It says here, courtesy of the inestimable Mildred. "I thought you would be interested to know that Mr Curtis has been asked by the Banks to step in with a view to sorting out the Circumference mess and turning the company around. It is not yet known whether he will accept."'

'YES!' shouted Charmian, jumping to her feet in excitement. 'Of course he'll accept! What brilliant news! Oh, I'm so happy for them!'

Gill was judicious rather than ecstatic.

'It certainly opens up all sorts of interesting possibilities, and, equally, for all sorts of reasons there's no doubt that he's the man for the job. All the same, it won't be easy.'

'It doesn't matter. If anybody can do it, he can! Oliver *thrives* on challenge. It's *so* satisfying, Toby. No need for you to do anything else. Oliver hasn't just got his own job back, he's got Spivey and Rattray-Smythe's jobs rolled into one.'

Mindful of the considerable amount of money he had tied up in currently rock-bottom Circumference stock, Gill said, 'From everyone's point of view let's hope he succeeds.'

By now they were about to travel to Goa and three days away from going home. Gill decided for once to forget about business and concentrate on his wife and the remainder of the holiday and was surprised at how much pleasure this gave him. I'd forgotten what it's like totally to relax, he thought. It's bloody marvellous.

In London the news of the Curtis appointment caused the sagging Circumference share price to revive a little. Oliver and Alexandra celebrated his re-establishment over a quiet dinner at Tante Claire.

'We aren't home and dry yet,' warned Oliver and then, echoing the Gill verdict, 'It won't be easy.'

Alexandra remembered Mareka Hemingway's words

but decided not to irritate her sceptical husband by repeating them. In the light of recent dramatic events she had replayed the tape to herself only that morning.

However good he thought things were before he's now going into a very good situation.

'I think all will be well,' said Alexandra, capitalizing on secret knowledge. 'Don't worry about it, just get on and do it.'

On the other hand hadn't Mareka also said: *Before it happens your husband is offered a job with another company and this company actually benefits from the upset?* Alexandra was at a loss to explain this particular cryptic prophesy. The only job offer relevant to the situation had been the one from Stellar, but, as things stood, Toby Gill had burnt his fingers as a result of the crisis at Circumference. He might be about to benefit but, if so, Alexandra was unable to see how this could be.

Aware that he only had half her attention but unaware of the pertinent inner debate going on, Oliver said, 'What do you think I should do about the paintings?'

'You'll have to grasp the nettle. What else *can* you do? After all, because Father can't keep his mouth shut about anything, half London probably knows about it by now. Rattray-Smythe's private collection is another matter. That's his problem. If Hugo has any sense at all his defence will be that it was all Charlie and that he's as staggered as everyone else by the revelation that they're all, or nearly all, forgeries. Because you can bet your bottom dollar that when the question mark

over the clutch of Circumference paintings becomes
official, his bank is going to want to cast a cursory
glance over Hugo's private hoard as well. However, I
daresay when set beside all the other problems you've
got, that's small beer,' concluded Alexandra.

'Yes, it is.'

'The other thing you probably feel like addressing
is telling Gill.'

'You'll find he knows already. Your delectable sister
notwithstanding, that's not the man even to go on honeymoon and take his finger off the business pulse.'

'No,' responded Alexandra, conscious of sounding
sour and then, cheering up, 'though, if what the Maitlands told me is accurate, conducting a business the
size of Stellar from a country like India could prove
something of a hurdle even for Gill with all his
backup.'

'That's *his* problem!'

A day later, chauffeured by Denis, Oliver sat in the
back of the company Mercedes.

'Good to have you back, sir,' said Denis, deftly piloting the car past the place where Mr Spivey had had
his nasty accident and deciding not to mention that.

'Good to *be* back!'

On this, his first morning, Oliver was due to address
the staff, all of whom were demoralized by the company's sudden unnerving reversal of fortune. Among
other draconian measures there would have to be re-
dundancies. Quite a few of them. This was not his fault
but all the same in the light of his own recent experi-

ence Oliver regretted the fact. Some of the subsidiaries would probably have to be sold off as well. Flicking open a notebook he began to draft the bare bones of what he intended to say. After that it would be one meeting after another until the end of the day.

'What's happened to Reg Spivey?' asked Oliver aloud, remembering that Denis had always had his ear close to the ground where company gossip was concerned.

'Still not very well at all,' said Denis. 'If it goes to court rumour has it the doctors are saying that he won't be well enough to stand trial.'

'It *will* go to court,' said Oliver, 'no question about it! What about Mr Rattray-Smythe?'

'As far as I'm aware he hasn't been back to the building since the shareholders' meeting. Very angry they were!' Speaking the words Denis was aware that this was something of an understatement. There had been an uproar in fact. Mr Rattray-Smythe had nearly been lynched and he, Denis, had been ordered to wait outside the hall where the meeting was being held with the passenger door open and the engine running so that, in the best Hollywood movie tradition, his boss could make a quick getaway. Even so, it had been touch and go. True to form Mr Rattray-Smythe had left the rest of the beleaguered board to fight their own way out.

'And what's happened to Neville Cruickshank?'

'According to his wife, who keeps giving interviews to the newspapers, he's volunteered to come home and co-operate with the SFO.'

By now they were approaching the front door of Circumference. Oliver tried to imagine Molly Cruickshank as a media personality and couldn't. On the other hand the idea of Neville as a fugitive from justice in Rio de Janeiro was equally hard to assimilate. The car drew to a halt and Oliver got out.

'I'll need you again at one, Denis. I have a lunch appointment in the City.'

Standing on the pavement under a taupe-coloured sky, Oliver savoured the moment. The morning was misty and, like a blurred fingerprint, the sun was a diffuse golden smudge. He felt exhilarated as he made his way up the steps.

I'm really on my way again, thought Oliver.

He took the lift up to the tenth floor and walked along the thickly carpeted corridor which was lined with paintings, though whether these were originals or copies was still to be decided. Arriving at Hugo's office, Oliver opened the door.

In the outer office sat Joan Pickard, a career secretary in the Mildred mould who had been with Rattray-Smythe for years and had spent a fair proportion of that time keeping him out of hot water.

Oliver shook her hand.

'Joan. I very much hope you'll be staying with us.'

Joan, who had been worried about the future and what it might hold, was visibly relieved.

'Oh, I rather thought you might want to promote your old secretary. The one you had when you...' She hesitated.

'When I was fired. On the contrary, I wouldn't

dream of it. You're the Chairman's secretary. None of what's happened is any of your fault. I want you! Now the next thing is to decide which office I use. Let's look at Reg Spivey's old stamping ground first, shall we?'

This was more or less as Oliver remembered it. It was furnished with modern teak and a scattering of garish abstract paintings and had in one corner, incomprehensibly, a trouser press.

'Hmm! No, I don't think so,' said Oliver.

They retraced their steps down the corridor. Hugo's own office was locked.

Letting him in, Joan said apologetically, 'I'm afraid it's exactly the way he left it. Mr Rattray-Smythe didn't like anybody else disturbing his desk, not even me.'

Oliver looked around. There was a Marie Celeste quality about Hugo's office. It appeared that not even he had disturbed his desk. A half-full glass of some amber liquid (whisky?) stood on the leather top. Beside it was a folded copy of *The Times,* which lay on the blotter with a gold pen beside it. There was no evidence of any other paperwork. Interested by the fact that anybody, apart from possibly public school headmasters, still had a blotter these days, Oliver stared down at the newspaper. It appeared that when he was interrupted Hugo had been halfway through the crossword. Framed photographs of Rattray-Smythes, including one of his dog, stood on the shelves and a golf umbrella was propped up by the door. His bookcase revealed Hugo to be a possible devotee of political biographies, most of which looked as if they had never been opened, and a definite devotee of the novels of Jeffrey Archer, every one of which was well thumbed. All in all though, it was a pleasant room furnished with antiques, including an impressive partner's desk. It was hard to escape the impression that Hugo might walk back in at any moment.

'This is the one,' announced Oliver. 'I think we should parcel up the personal effects and have them sent on to Mr. Rattray-Smythe and I'd like to change the paintings but otherwise that's it. I'll operate from here.'

In the same hall in which the rumbustious shareholders' meeting had been held, Oliver mounted the steps to the platform. Every seat was taken and, at the back, quite a few people were standing.

At his appearance silence fell. A sea of anxious Circumference faces looked towards him.

Oliver took a sip from the glass of water somebody (Joan?) had thoughtfully placed in front of him, cleared his throat and began to speak.

28

The day after the Gills got back from their honeymoon, Toby rang Oliver up.

'You're a dark horse,' said Gill.

Thinking: not half such a dark horse as you! Oliver replied, 'It wasn't all finalized by the time you and Charmian left and you've been incommunicado ever since then.'

They both knew this was not the real reason.

'You could always have contacted me through my office,' observed Gill mildly. 'Anyway, never mind about that. In the light of what has happened, I think we should have a meeting.'

'That's fine by me. When did you have in mind?'

'What about tomorrow afternoon? Let's say six o'clock. Your office or mine?'

Oliver looked in his diary.

'Since I've got another appointment beforehand in your neck of the woods, why don't we say yours? See you then. Give my love to Charmian, by the way.'

Sitting once again in Gill's office the following day, Oliver was reminded of their previous meetings when he had been desperate for a job. He noticed that the silver-framed photograph of Gill's first wife had been replaced by one of Charmian. The frenetic activity of the early days of the Circumference bid had gone for the moment. All three telephones were silent. Gill himself showed no sign of the adrenalin-induced dynamism in evidence then and looked almost bored.

They shook hands.

'Congratulations!' said Gill. He rose to his feet, went to his small office fridge and extracted a bottle. 'I seem to remember offering to stand you a glass of champagne when you re-established and now is as good a time as any.' He eased the cork and then poured out two glasses.

'Circumference! May it rise, Phoenix-like from the ashes!'

They both drank.

'Thank you,' said Oliver responding. 'If I've got anything to do with it, it will. How was the honeymoon? India, wasn't it? I keep meaning to take Alexandra.'

Gill's face briefly lit up 'It was wonderful,' he said simply. 'Absolutely wonderful!'

There was a silence, then he said, 'Has anybody got to the bottom of what the two conspirators were actually doing?'

'Not totally, but it's beginning to look as though certain significant losses had been carried over from the early days of Spivey's stewardship. They were concealed by means of back-to-back accounting with banks as pigs in the middle.'

'Ah,' said Gill. 'So, inspired false accounting. You're about to tell me that they fabricated profits and temporarily moved the losses to a subsidiary company. Such as the one you used to run!'

'Something like that. What made it so effective is that nothing appeared on the balance sheet. But for the fact that Spivey was the victim of that car crash it could just have gone on and on. Remember that Italian financial scandal? Aspects of this are reminiscent of what happened there. The irony of it is that whereas Cruickshank was receiving payment in kind for his co-operation, Spivey doesn't appear to have been on the make for himself. He simply wanted to appear the great business genius.'

'Don't we all! Anyway, given the fact that you've taken the top slot, I assume the black hole at the heart of the Circumference financial crisis is not as bad as we've all been led to believe.'

Oliver was cagey. 'You'll understand if I prefer not to go into detail. It's pretty bad but, in my view, can be turned around. It will take a long time but with a modicum of luck I think I can do it.'

'Luck's very important,' said Gill. 'Far too many people underestimate the importance of luck. Yes, I'm sure you can do it. And when you're well on the way to sorting the whole mess out, although not too well on the way, I intend to bid for Circumference again.'

He leant back in his chair and sipped his drink.

Oliver, who thought he had Gill and where he was at summed up, was astonished. 'But you've already withdrawn one bid. Rattray-Smythe and Spivey have both gone, the company's in disarray so you've had your revenge, as have I. What more do you want?'

'I want Circumference. I want it because it's *there!*' Gill shrugged. 'It will be the jewel in my crown and that won't make any difference to you, Oliver. I'm not about to remove a good manager, so whatever happens you'll remain in situ.'

Oliver drained his glass and put it down.

'Toby, I have to tell you that Circumference asked me in to troubleshoot. They have virtually allowed me to write my own ticket. It is now *my* show and, regardless of your benevolent intention vis-à-vis myself, and much as I admire you as a businessman, I don't want to be taken over. I'll go further and say that if you try to do that, I'll fight you tooth and nail!'

Gill appeared neither surprised nor offended by this vehement speech. Rather it seemed to invigorate him. He glittered with energy. Not for the first time it occurred to Oliver that there was something Mephistophelian about Gill.

Filling up the glasses he said, 'Of course you will, my dear Oliver, of course you will! And that, as far as I am concerned, is where the fun *really* begins!'

New York Times bestselling author

JAYNE ANN KRENTZ

BETWEEN THE LINES

Amber Langley married for all the right reasons. There was no passion to break her heart, no love to risk losing—just a sensible agreement with her boss, prominent businessman Cormick Grayson. But Amber's plan was not working out quite as neatly as she had intended. Because the heat in Gray's eyes made her suspect that there was more to this relationship than a polite living arrangement. Can Amber risk falling in love with her own husband?

ELIZABETH PALMER

66547	OLD MONEY	___ $5.99 U.S.	___ $6.99 CAN.
66493	PLUCKING THE APPLE	___ $5.99 U.S.	___ $6.99 CAN.
66456	SCARLET ANGEL	___ $5.99 U.S.	___ $6.99 CAN.

(limited quantities available)

TOTAL AMOUNT	$_____
POSTAGE & HANDLING	$_____
($1.00 for one book; 50¢ for each additional)	
APPLICABLE TAXES*	$_____
TOTAL PAYABLE	$_____

(check or money order—please do not send cash)

To order, complete this form and send it, along with a check or money order for the total above, payable to MIRA Books®, to: **In the U.S.:** 3010 Walden Avenue, P.O. Box 9077, Buffalo, NY 14269-9077; **In Canada:** P.O. Box 636, Fort Erie, Ontario, L2A 5X3.

Name:_____
Address:_____ City:_____
State/Prov.:_____ Zip/Postal Code:_____
Account Number (if applicable):_____
075 CSAS

*New York residents remit applicable sales taxes.
 Canadian residents remit applicable GST and provincial taxes.

MIRA

Visit us at www.mirabooks.com   MEP0800BL